12/80

"TRUE COMIC BRILLIANCE—A VICIOUS SWIFTIAN SATIRE THAT, LIKE ALL SATIRE, CONTAINS A STRONG MORAL VOICE." —*New York Magazine*

"The gay underbelly of New York . . . has the air of Restoration comedy in its mix of Baroque style and bawdy, scathing humor." —*Women's Wear Daily*

"I hope the gay community won't lose its sense of humor about this book. FAGGOTS, for all its excesses, is frequently right on target and, when it is on target, is appallingly funny." —Edward Albee

"Larry Kramer has more than come out of the closet, he's housecleaned the neighborhood. . . . A novel of courage . . . a journey worth the chronicle. A noble gesture."—*Baltimore Sun*

"RICH, RAUNCHY, ENLIGHTENING . . . A VESUVIAN EXPLOSION ABOUT GAY LIFE." —*Chicago Tribune*

LARRY KRAMER is the author of the play *The Normal Heart* (also available in a Plume edition), which deals with the AIDS epidemic, and of the screenplay for the film of D. H. Lawrence's *Women In Love,* which he also produced. He is a co-founder of New York's Gay Men's Health Crisis, the first and biggest community AIDS organization. A graduate of Yale, he was born in Connecticut, grew up in Washington, D.C., lived in London for ten years, and now lives in New York City.

Faggots

<u>Faggots</u>

LARRY KRAMER

A PLUME BOOK

BOOKS ARE AVAILABLE AT QUANTITY DISCOUNTS WHEN USED TO PROMOTE PRODUCTS OR SERVICES. FOR INFORMATION PLEASE WRITE TO PREMIUM MARKETING DIVISION, PENGUIN BOOKS USA INC., 375 HUDSON STREET, NEW YORK, NEW YORK 10014.

A hardcover edition of *Faggots* was originally published by Random House, Inc.

 REGISTERED TRADEMARK—MARCA REGISTRADA

Library of Congress Cataloging-in-Publication Data

Kramer, Larry
  Faggots.
  I. Title.
PS 3561.R252F3   1987   813'.54   87-15243
ISBN 0-452-26396-4

First Plume Printing, September, 1987

    4   5   6   7   8   9   10   11

This book is for:
Arthur and Alice Kramer;
William H. Gillespie;
and Sam Klagsbrun.

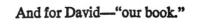
And for David—"our book."

... the ancients located the deeper emotions in the bowels.
—EVELYN WAUGH, *Put Out More Flags*

Faggots

There are 2,556,596 faggots in the New York City area.

The largest number, 983,919, live in Manhattan. 186,991 live in Queens, or just across the river. 181,236 live in Brooklyn and 180,009 live in the Bronx. 2,469 live on Staten Island, substantiating that old theory that faggots don't like to travel or don't like to live on small islands, depending on which old theory you've heard and/or want substantiated.

Westchester and Dutchess Counties, together with that part of New Jersey which is really suburban New York, hold approximately 297,852, though this figure may be a bit low.

Long Island, or that which is beyond Queens, at last count numbered 211,910. (This goes all the way to Montauk, remember.)

Suburban Connecticut (not primarily of concern here, nor for that matter are suburban New Jersey or suburban New York—but you might as well have the advantage of all the statistics, since they were exhaustively collected), which includes the heavily infested Danbury triangle area, has 211,910 also, which makes it a sister statistic to Long Island, which is as it should be since the two share a common Sound.

• • •

15

There are now more faggots in the New York City area than Jews. There are now more faggots in the entire United States than all the yids and kikes put together. (This is subsidiary data, not overtly relevant, but ipso facto nevertheless.)

The straight and narrow, so beloved of our founding fathers and all fathers thereafter, is now obviously and irrevocably bent. What is God trying to tell us . . . ?

There will be seven disco openings this holiday weekend. Though the premier palais de dance, Billy Boner's Capriccio, is closing tonight for the season so that Billy can open The Ice Palace at Cherry Grove, its closest competitor, Balalaika, run by the inseparable Patty, Maxine, and Laverne, will remain open, to cater to the hot-weather crowd on those weekends they don't make it to Fire Island.

Everyone wonders which of the newcomers will be the first to go under, because, ignorant of the above vital statistics, the fear is there's not enough business to go round.

On Saturday evening opens The Toilet Bowl. But that's meant to be more than a disco.

Later, it would be recollected as the False Summer. Everything had bloomed too quickly. Fire Island, this Memorial Day, would be like the Fourth of July. Too much too soon. Everyone was caught in the never-never land of City? Capriccio? The Tubs? Balalaika? The Pits? The Toilet Bowl? Fire Island? All cups runneth over. The weather was no help either—the glorious summer sun

16

now obviously out to stay—and thus useless in defining and dictating destinations and activities, as it usually did when cold meant dancing and very cold meant television, joints, and bed.

And here it was only May.

. . . Is there indeed a God who would understand such as:

"Baby, I want you to piss all over me!"

Fred Lemish had never urinated on anything before, except perhaps some country grass late at night when he was drunk and no one was looking.

"Or let me piss on you!"

This Fred Lemish had never allowed.

Fred stood there helplessly. Why was he inert in a moment requiring action? The guy wasn't bad-looking. Should Fred enter, or walk away?

"Or fuck my friend and I'll suck your come out of his asshole."

This suggestion Fred recognized as "felching." Was he interested in joining a felcher?

"Or I could tie you up. Or you could tie us up. Or either one of us. Or anything else your cock desires!"

The man certainly offered a range of choices. Should Fred? Shouldn't Fred?

"Are you into shit?"

Fred shouldn't.

Why was he even hesitating, Fred asked himself, instead of just walking on? Because he was horny, that's why, and this guy looked better than anybody else, there not being many here this afternoon anyway, and he wanted to get it over with and leave. That's why. And he had not seen Dinky Adams in three weeks, six days, and, checking his Rolex Submariner, which he never took off, sixteen hours. That's why, too. OK, he thought, what does

17

this man want of me? Or since the man had offered the plethora of suggestions, what would Fred be capable of doing with this man? Piss and shit he wasn't up to, though the former intrigued him, God strike him dead. It would, however, not be difficult, Fred decided, stepping in ever so casually, no commitment, only a look, to fuck the friend, who had an attractive and perfectly rounded set of white buttocks, lying just right down there, staring up at him, saying Hello.

But then Fred became unsettled—for he now looked closer at the first chap, the chunky one who had propositioned him into the cubbyhole of a space, and noted that chunky was more akin to fat and that what had at three feet appeared to be well-formed pecs (so important), at two feet were revealed as sagging tits, a definite turnoff, mini-udders, no doubt from years of being chewed and tugged. This man was also now mumbling, almost as a litany, ". . . my friend's a good slave, he's a good slave . . . ," an additional turnoff, Fred not, at this moment, drawn toward bondage either, and our Hero, rendered further into indecision by third thoughts, and fourth and fifth ones too, began to wonder if he might be sick if Master did as advertised, polished everything off by protruding his tongue into Slave's rectum to felch.

Yet here Fred was, viewing the Slave on the bed. He wondered, too, what it was like to be a Slave.

The Slave remained prone and silent, up-ended, as any good slave must obviously remain.

"What do you usually do on a Friday?" the Master asked, massaging Fred's cock.

"Huh? Unh, go dancing later. Capriccio's closing party tonight."

"Good-looking fellow like you . . . nice-sized dick . . . bet everybody's after you. Bet you'll still be here."

"Nah."

18

"Dancing, eh? I'll bet you're a wonderful dancer. Great-looking legs you've got." The Master massaged Fred's great-looking legs. "I call dancing fairy sports. Fairy sports is our athletics."

This made Fred laugh.

"No, seriously. Dancing is sports for faggots. We're the best at it. And there's no win or lose. No competition. No being last guy chosen in gym." He began to suck Fred's cock.

Fred figured he might as well stay. As long as he was here.

The Everhard Baths on West 19th Street was owned by a syndicate of businessmen and not by the Firemen's Benevolent Athletic League, as rumored—a rumor obviously and happily encouraged by management so that the boys would feel safe. The building, not dissimilar to bath houses the world over, of whatever persuasion, was large and ugly, barrel-vaulted beneath and corridored above. It contained what no one boasted was the first heated swimming pool in New York, or anywhere else, at this moment a little too fetid for everyday use, as were the entire premises, though Murray, the night manager, in response to inquiries why the place was always dirty, claimed, with facts and figures rushing round above his head, that attendance fell off after a thorough cleaning.

Diamond Drew Everard (the "h" was added for business reasons when the place went obviously gay in the Swinging Sixties), had been a beer baron who needed a congenial place to soak out for the last half of the last century, so he bought this old church and converted. "Congenial" came to mean more than that along around 1920 (then as now a three-star, "worthy of a detour," national shrine in the faggot Michelin), though undoubtedly itineraries were a bit more covert in 1920 than they are today. The genealogy found the premises passed along

19

over the years to Tammanys, Piping Rock sportsmen taking a flyer, several members of the cloth (both ecclesiastical and judicial), even a madam and her girls, all looking for a quiet turn on their investment. Up at bat now was this syndicate, one William Boner in the saddle, which evidently kept the policemen on the beat most happy with regular contributions to the Church of the Most Precious Blood, since many plaques attested to same and no harassment, which is no small feat for a business netting six million dollars cash on the barrel for providing like with like, statutorily illegal in this city and this country ind this time—but there you have it, ipso facto again.

While he fucked the Slave, hoping all the while that Master would watch only and not give vent, Fred attempted to remember his decisions:

Had he not decided to write about a Voyage of Discovery into this World in which he lived? This Faggot World.

Had he not—just three months ago, as they both sat perched and observing from the edge of Capriccio's dance floor, watching the passing throngs—quoted to his good friend Gatsby (Tall, Blond, Handsome, Fred's Trinity, Fred's Robert Redford, intelligent, witty, and wise, another trinity, yes, everything Fred always wanted in a lover, though Gatsby was not interested) from the *Penguin Companion to Literature, European:* " 'The Stendhalian hero refuses any form of authority that would impinge on his personal liberty, and in defiance of both good sense and history, sets out to remake the universe in his own image.' "

Gatsby, who had received this name at Princeton because he was from St. Paul, Minnesota, and wanted to be a writer, and who was now, at thirty-three, at last beginning his novel, which he described as "an exercise in self-loathing," and whose proposed theme was "how can

20

two guys who don't like themselves ever let anyone else like themselves and hence be available for love?" (though he agreed with Fred that one must not abandon hope, which, with intelligence, just might work), had pooh-poohed: "There you go again, Lemish. You govern your emotions to fit the scene just like everyone else. You want to be a part of things and go to all the parties and disco openings and Fire Island and have a lover more than anyone I know. Don't give me that Artist/Hero-as-Out-sider shit."

"Not true. 'Alienation, however, does not lead our hero out of society, but deeper into it, for he is impelled by a curiosity to know, down to the smallest detail, the corrupt world that he wishes to escape. Concealing his opposition, he takes part in the intrigue of his day with the secret aim of proving to himself, by the very false-ness of his conduct, the distance that separates him from his contemporaries.' Story of my current life."

"Smoke screens, Lemish! More of vour smoke screens. All you want is Love. And if you've wanted love so badly, why haven't you had it? Does not that say some-thing about The Wanter, not his World?"

And Fred Lemish, courtesy of twenty-one years of assorted forms of therapy, recently terminated, store open for business, proudly answered: "We'll see. World watch out! The Wanter is Ready!"

Had he not decided, Yes!, that as a writer and citizen/ person/liver-in-the-here-and-now he must experience, or at least witness, Everything to the fullest? (go ahead, Master, piss on me!), if he was to be the Christopher Columbus, or was it the Amerigo Vespucci, certainly the James Boswell of his faggot world, if he wanted Abe Bron-stein to produce his eventual script about this world, for all the rest of the world to see, the first respectable faggot movie, perhaps they could get Brando (though lately he was too fat) to play a role, with Paul Newman, together again, pretending it was real, perhaps, come to think of it, they were both too old, better use Redford and Mc-Queen, oh, weren't they all too old . . . where were the Newies? . . . ; and while he was so investigating, witnessing, experiencing, could he not also be proving how he and Dinky were Making It, were falling in love, also for all the world to see, two intelligent homosexuals, not running, like every other faggot, when appeared the first bump in the road, proving that It Could Be Done?!

"What you want, Tante, doesn't exist," his best friend, Anthony Montano, who was married to his position as Vice-President and Creative Director, in charge of the Winston Man, at Heiserdiener-Thalberg-Slough, had said to Fred just last week as they were leaving the Probe Cinema on Times Square after viewing *Twenty Cocks Over Tokyo*. "Buy a dog. Dogs are faggot children."

"Nonsense. It is possible for two intelligent men to be turned on to each other in totality: emotionally, physically, and intellectually. Though I am about to become middle-aged, I shall not become a bitchy, middle-aged queen. I shall not turn sour."

"I tell you, buy a dog." Anthony did not like to explore subterranean problems.

Fred persisted: "All I want is someone who reads books, loves his work, and me, too, of course, and who doesn't take drugs, and isn't on unemployment."

"And who reads and appreciates, preferably in the original Dostoevski and Proust, plus is a good cook and a faithful lover and kisses you a lot and is terrific in bed. Plus being Hot and gorgeous."

"What's wrong with that? It seems a perfectly acceptable and desirable fantasy."

"You're in the wrong country. Go around the world. Take the Geography Cure."

22

"Sprinkle isn't much of a kisser," Fred said, referring to Anthony's lover, whom Fred, naturally, didn't like or think good enough for his best friend. "Where is he, by the way?"

"Visiting his mother. He's trying the Mother Cure. Where's Dinky?"

"Dodger, his lodger, says any day now."

"Fred, they don't want us. We just don't know how to play. How to pretend. They're all out there playing. Sometimes they're Cliffs and sometimes they're Cecilias, but they're playing, and all we are is Fred and Anthony. Who would want me? I want to play house, too. I'm hungry, possessive, insecure, successful, a dissatisfied bubby. I'd run from me. Become a martyr to your work. Work is the only thing that matters."

"You *are* a martyr to your work. You work twenty-five hours a day at a job you don't even like. What has it got you? You don't even have time to get laid. Anyway, faggots don't want to know about success. It reminds them of what they're evading. I spent years becoming a success; when I tell a trick I wrote *Sleep,* it freaks them out. They either run away or start treating me like an old man."

"No, no, *we're* the evaders. Nothing's good enough for us. Work is the only thing that matters. Life is a compromise. I'm going to become straight. It's not possible for two men to get it together." Anthony pulled his raincoat on and tugged the belt tightly.

And Fred, who would not accept these opinions of his friends, and who, with Anthony, never wished to delve into why they weren't lovers—Fred told himself Anthony's hairy body bothered him, and Anthony told himself Fred was too much like Anthony—and who, now, would shortly have his Dinky Adams back and in his arms, said: "No, Tante, it's definitely time for love!"

23

Fred was close to coming when he felt the trickle of warm piss. It splashed upon his back. "I'd hoped you wouldn't do that," he muttered, now trying to come quickly.

"You like it! You like it!" the Master yelled, his stream now waterfalling.

"I'm coming! I'm coming!" Fred felt called on to announce.

"Yes, sir! Yes, sir!" The Slave now uttered at last. "I'm coming . . . !"

"Give me all your gism, baby! Pile drive that ramrod cock right through my brain!"

Fred, closer, tried his damnedest to comply.

"I feel that come inside me, baby! I feel it! I feel you! Fill 'er up! Fuck me to the moon!" The Slave had turned most verbal.

He and Fred flapped together in split-splats against the now drenched mattress. Then Fred quickly jumped up, disengaging, grabbed his towel, and tried to leave.

"I haven't sucked you out yet!" the Master/Pisser pleaded.

Fred ran out of the cubicle, not listening as Master apologized to Slave: "It's all right, honey, I'll find you another one."

Fred headed for the showers below.

Some hero, he thought.

Fred Lemish was thirty-nine years old. He was single, still, though for many years he had claimed to want a lover. He had had one or two before, perhaps nine or ten; he often had trouble defining precisely what constituted a lover and not just a trick he had turned a number of times, even allowing for a tendency toward attempted reconstructions on Just Good Fucks or root-

24

canal work on Vacation Romances Best Left Where
Found. But, by any definition, none had lasted beyond a
vague introductory offer. He usually blamed it on the
other fellow and still maintained that he was alone against
his will.

Fred had a hairy chest, wide shoulders, at last a
thirty-inch waist, after years of a slight inner tube of fat
amidships, "love handles," where new introductions so
annoyingly always placed their hands, casually, in greeting, in reality only prospecting the land beneath the shirt
to judge how hard the terrain, and hence how desirable,
before walking away, never to be heard from again, if
the merchandise was too soft, too excessive, which, in
Fred's case, it had until recently been, plus those sturdy
legs, an embarrassing liability as a child (what other kid
had fully formed calves like cantaloupes at ten?), now at
last accepted for the muscular bonus they were, along
with that hairy chest, now also useful as a marketable
difference, which the same childhood of being the only
King Kong among years of hairless Greek-statued school-
mates had not allowed, plus the requisite mustache, now,
alas, mingling black hair with strokes of gray, and, also
alas, the small but growing bald spot on the crown of his
dark head, which no amount of Head Start Vitamins with
the Mysterious Ingredients or Hair Trigger Program
Formula 6 available by mail from I. Magnin in Beverly
Hills and applied nightly with a hot towel and left steam-
ing on the scalp for twenty minutes followed by a glass of
warm milk and two additional capsules of minerals essential to the roots' natural growth had alleviated. He had
briefly attemped to camouflage the mustache and temples
with Revlon's Fabulash—recommended in California by
Frigger, he of the rock-hard barrel chest and construc-
tion-worker arms and the witty one-liners and the infallible
gift of his mouth always winning at "Come Into My Par-

25

lor," a good friend he later discovered to have tricked with Feffer on that very day Feffer had returned to Fred for their second attempt at Togetherness—the aroma from which, not to mention the resultant turgidity, he found sufficiently unpleasant to discontinue the effort.

He belonged to two gyms and attended them regularly, alternating them to avoid monotony. At Sheridan Square ("The Magnificent Obsession") Health Club, also known as "Bodyworks (but the mind doesn't)," he could muscle-build close to home with the Village faggots, a serious lot much concerned with hyperbolic results to parade on Christopher Street, though they and their conversations (everyone was "she" or "Mary" and various were the opinions on opera, recipes, and yard goods) were a bit too bitchy-queeny for Fred's taste; to him they all connoted creeping, crepuscular middle-aged dissatisfaction, on the road to leather and other arcane sexual deviances sacrosanct to the unloved, and he still had hope, if not their over-muscled definition. Most of the time he used the 63rd Street West Side Y, jauntily known as the biggest gay bar in town (and much kickier than the Y's at 23rd or 47th Streets), and here he joined fellow quipsters, a jolly, congenial lot, many of them now good friends: Frigger, when he was in from L.A.; Gatsby; energetic Tarsh; the Divine Bella; the city's famous lovers, Josie and Dom Dom; Fallow the dapper; Mikie, the thirty-four-year-old flower child; sweet Bo Peep—for his three-mile jog and his hour of serious weight-lifting.

And how his muscles had appeared! His body reacted, his pecs and lats and delts took form, his love handles diminished (Frigger's suggestion of the Waist Sweat-er had worked!), his stomach tightened, he even had obliques! He'd now entered that fatless state of being in Great Shape, certainly better shape than any of his straight friends (how many of them worked out seven

26

days a week?), and all was now obviously ready at last to lead on to consummation with Mr. Right. All those years of chunkery—was it to keep love away? For, if a faggot bartered with his body, hadn't he best get his wampum in order?

Feffer had told him four years ago to make his body over. If he had, would he still have Feffer? He didn't want him now. But he sure as shit had then. And now here was Dinky, arousing within him the exact pain, anguish, hope, love, and terror he'd not felt since Feffer. Ah, romance!

Yes, the way he'd looked at it, this was the last chance. Harden up now, slim down now, grab your man now—because, over forty, it wasn't going to be easy to accomplish any of these things. And, if he had wasted the years leading up to this moment in sloth and avarice and self-pity and chocolate and rejection and schlumpery and Algonqua and Lester and Harvard and bachelorhood and being the cruiser more than the cruised, the left-dangling more than the dangler, it was still not too late to yield and desist. And if the rest of his country desired to be thin and gorgeous and remained pretty much as they were, then he would not be like the rest of his country. And what better motivation for becoming a thing of beauty than being in love?

Fred was also rather concerned with the specific. When he was feeling poorly, if a malaise should suddenly sweep over him, he wanted to know why, what to attribute it to: had he moved his bowels sufficiently, did he have to do so again, had he eaten properly, was his protein intake for the day large enough, had he slept enough last night, or too much, did his body require some food with sugar, was he finally becoming hypoglycemic? —all of these possibilities had to be adjudged and discounted. Ordinary, plain, everyday, nonspecific anxiety could not be tolerated. If checking all of the above produced no answer, and anxiety was all that remained, then Fred had recourse to thoughts of knives and wrist slashings ("Application of the knife blade to the wrist," he would try to cheer himself with some snappy recollections from the seminal volume of Menchitt & Swinger, "indicates a perverse determination to sever the umbilical cord of some earlier trauma") and pill overdoses and jumping from heights. He was afraid of heights. He did tend to overreact. He didn't, naturally, do any of these awful things; they were just torture thoughts to ruin a nice day.

Fred was—in short—your average, standard, New York faggot obsessive kvetch. Nice though. And with smiling, dark-brown eyes. But perhaps a bit too therapeutically prepared. And trying not to ponder if what he has spent all those years and dollars and pounds (sterling, not avoirdupois, though certainly that as well) to reach is quite possibly not there to be reached, but that the True End of not only therapy but Maturity is to learn to live with the inescapable fact that 97% of all human beings are getting fucked and 97% of all faggots are, too.

He had recently studied his last year's Seven Star Mini Diary, and this had revealed:

Dates leading to orgasm: 87 (not counting street tricks, the tubs, or Fire Island; definitely not counting The Meat Rack).

Dates interesting enough to want to see again: 2.

Dates seen again: 23.

Refusals: 23.

Tubs attended how many times: 34.

Discos danced at how many nights: 47 (not counting Fire Island).

He had been dismayed at how many of the names he no longer remembered. Who were Bat, Ivan, Tommy, Sam Jellu, Beautiful Henry, Kelly Hurt (or Kelly hurt?), Joe

28

Johns, François, Watson Datson, too many of the 23, not to mention the 87, were now unrecognizable and obviously equally as unmemorable as the how many—? 100? 200? 50? 23? orgasms he had probably forgotten to tally. He had had sex, with somebody or other, one or two, maybe three times a week for an entire year, including religious holidays, but not counting, hopefully, illnesses. He had spent a whole year (not to mention all the preceding ones!) with a faceless group of sex objects. Talk about sexist! Talk about using the body as a thing! And who the hell was Tiddy Squire? Or was it Ditty Squirt? Even his handwriting was not helpful. He recalled no Tiddy Ditty, nor what they did, nor how it felt, nor where they did it, though his notation exclaimed: "really Hot, must do it again!" Checking his address book, on those rear pages reserved for faggots, because he was certain never to recognize their names if filed alphabetically, there it was: Derry Spire, March 14th—only several months ago. How could he not remember? How could he have made love with another human being and not remember? The face? The body? Something? Anything? A wart? A smell? B.O.?

Fred then thought of the long line of architects, gardeners, art directors, copywriters, dilettantes, drop-outs, unemployeds, unemployables, would-be's, waiters, actors, students, dancers, which had graced his life, wondering why he fell for some of the Great Non-Givers of the World. the Invulnerables, the Defensives, the Ones in Need ot Help, whom he, great Red Crosser, was there to ferry through sleet and shit like the schleppy Saint Bernard. And did. He had carted the body-builder/sociologist to Paris to seduce him, only to discover he was a lousy lay. (Anthony had to summon him home with an urgent telegram signed "Barbra Streisand" to get him out of that one.) He had ported the weaver/macraméist to Marrakech to hear his vow of love, only to have anxiety attacks in the Casbah. (Said attacks obviously necessitating an urgent recall to then Dr. Cult.) They had both been called Mikie. Mikies I and II were both, somewhere, wearing Rolex Submariners, which Fred had bought them at the ending. Mikie III, the thirty-four-year-old flower child, half-architect, now truck driver, still good friend, also wore his Rolex, after their affair-let on a Caribbean Firefly Cruise.

There had also been Feffer. Great Love Number One.

And now there was Dinky Adams. Great Love Number Two.

Fred had been amazed as well to discover in his address book's rear that he and Dinky had met and tricked seven years ago, a one-nighter; Fred vaguely remembered fucking him, when Fred was visiting from London and they'd cruised each other in front of a Goya Duchess on loan to the Metropolitan Museum. Dinky was then in architecture school, too, and was filled with plans for building a more beautiful world. He'd only finished a year and a half. He'd never made it. Ah, the potential! Is this what made him so very dear?

Feffer had been tall, blond, incredibly bright, gorgeous, his own age, a Wisconsin Phi Bete, who'd been wonderful until Fred unfortunately discovered he wanted to tie Fred up and beat him.

Dinky was tall, dark, bright, gorgeous, with honors from Georgetown, and Fred could hardly wait for his return. He was wonderful. Again and at last.

Fred had, at thirty-nine, hoped love would come by forty.

He had only four days to go.

Forty years old!

And beloved Dinky would soon be coming back!

And beloved Abe would produce Fred's screenplay!

And Life would at last be in order! Love and work co-joined!

He soaped his tarnished, yellowed, peed-upon body in the showers. Ah, did he not hate that word "gay"? He thought it a strange categorizer of a life style with many elements far from zippy. No, he would de-kike the word "faggot," which had punch, bite, a no-nonsense, chin-out assertiveness, and which, at present, was no more self-deprecatory than, say, "American."

Dinky Adams's ass was the first ass Fred had ever rimmed.

He had, of course, heard about rimming. It was quite popular with some of the boys. But Fred had never wanted to so taste anyone before.

It happened almost eight weeks ago, at the end of Week 4 of their "relationship," after Dinky had given Fred his first douche, really a harmless affair (and not nearly so frightening as Tarsh and Mikie, both clinical experts, had always made it sound), ("You mean you've never douched?," "You mean you've never rimmed?" Dinky had asked later, incredulous over what he considered Fred's naïve sex life. "What have you been doing all these years?"): a bulbous squeezing of a couple of cups of warm water up Fred's rectum, into which Dinky would shortly stick his nice-sized, not-too-big, not-too-small cock, while they were standing in Fred's kitchen on Washington Square, Dinky having just sterilized the douche's doucher in hot water on the stove. As Dinky had squeezed it in, Fred realized, horror of horrors, that he was getting turned on. He liked this Dinky! He liked that he was having his first douche with someone he liked. He liked that he was evidently likeable enough for Dinky to get such a nice big hard-on over him. He liked it all. Yes, he did.

And suddenly he found himself falling to the floor, Fred did, being careful to hold his water in, and getting underneath Dinky, and looking up at him, at that thirty-year-old beauty, towering above him, handsome like the devil, with black hair rakishly widow's-peaked in the center of his forehead, darting black eyes that sometimes looked at you, a round cherubic face protected by a full, short, neat, black beard, biceps the wonderful size of smooth, firm, elongated honeydews, under which resided Fred's favorite spot, those beautiful armpits, soft, wispily fluffy, nice-smelling of Dial soap, and that rest of his body, a personal triumph over childhood skinniness and a touch of bad feet, now perfected into faggot desirability: muscular, tough, smooth skin, not an inch of fat, to which he dashingly added a small gold earring to his pierced left lobe. Oh, it was gorgeous, this view from neath Mount Rushmore. It was so gorgeous that Fred's own cock became gigantic. Could it be that for all these years he was unknowingly harboring a very big cock and not only not knowing it, but not using it as well? Oh, gorgeous Dinky, up there, you who like me and have come after me, wooed me these weeks of my trying to play hard to get, not be anxious, not be hungry, not fuck this one up; you who read books and design gardens and plan interiors and love to travel and dance and cook so well; you who swung me in a hammock in your sweet little Southampton house beside a canal, our Venice, as I read to you about our shared love for England; you who smiled at me as we awoke in each other's arms after a wonderful night of love; you who have said: "I really like your profile," "You have such nice feet," "You're very important to me," "On paper we make so much sense—we have mutual interests and the sex is good," "I believe in old-fashioned marriage,

32

where people make commitments and out of respect the love just grew and grew," our first month of truly filling simple things, being alone together, you are giving me this hugeness!

Then, just as suddenly, still on his knees, he crawled around in front of Dinky's perfect ass. He took both cheeks in his hands and he buried his face in it like an elegant pillow in a perfect Italian palazzo overlooking the blue Mediterranean where they could be when they were living happily ever after. If they hadn't moved to England. Then he moved his face down and under, and inspected, like a mechanic beneath a Porsche on the overhead rack. The cock was perfect, the balls were perfect, the conjunction of all parts was perfect. Fred was glorying in the knowledge of true ownership: this Perfection is Mine! I love it!

And in he stuck his tongue into Dinky's asshole.

He just did it. It tasted good. It tasted very good. It was smooth and clean, rather like a good quality moist satin. Dinky's asshole was lined with a lovely ribbon!

And Dinky was obviously enjoying it, because he was growing an even larger hard-on than any Fred had seen him grow during their times together, which had not always been the case, Dinky's hard-ons, which was something Fred didn't like to think about or look at, as he now was looking at Dinky's own present giganticism.

Then they went into Fred's bedroom, which was a perfect room of plants and indirect lighting and soft music and a wide mattress upon a gray platform with a hanging black-and-brown curtain of duck canvas to wrap around it all as they had their secret picnic with each other. After a slight detour to the john, Fred then allowed himself once again to be fucked.

It hadn't always been such. Before Dinky, Fred had not liked to get fucked, even though he had noted over the years that those he was fucking always seemed to be enjoying it more than he was in doing it to them. No, it took Dinky to show him the way, in a manner that no number of years of advice and pamphlets and manuals on "Painless Rectal Intercourse"—replete with their diagrams of all canals and passageways and orifices and advice to "relax," so that these could bend and sway—had been able to do.

No, Dinky had showed him how. With tenderness. Dinky was the most tender lover Fred had ever known. He was soft and, while not actually giving—Dinky was not a kisser or a toucher, unless stoned, when he did both beautifully—he managed to convey in lying there, with Fred sitting on his cock above him, that the gentle movements back and forth—making them one, oh happiest moment of moments! Making Them One! Dinky and Fred! get the embroidered towels ready! order them now! find that spot in the country! sign the lease! Dinky will remodel! happily ever after is beginning right this very Now—were the most pleasing Fred could ever recollect receiving. From anyone. Did not such tenderness mean his heart beat for Fred!

Indeed, to be fucked pleasurably is a gift.

And then Fred said it:

"I love you, Dinky."

Richard "Boo Boo" Bronstein stood at the dark end of an abandoned pier by the mighty Hudson and, while he was having his cock sucked by a balding, bobbing head belonging to an older gentleman, further fantasized that with which his life was now obsessed. His own self-inflicted kidnapping.

The papers would be full of it. Richard Bronstein, the twenty-four-year-old son of the multimillionaire cake-

34

mix manufacturer turned movie producer who had divorced the sporting-goods heiress after the bar mitzvah of their second son, Richard, in order to marry the former teen-aged cover girl from New Zealand, who was then replaced by Miss Australian Butter, and then Miss South African Gold, had disappeared. Through her tears, Mrs. Ephra Lopp Bronstein, the first, rich, and American one, would announce on Walter Cronkite that it was all her husband's fault.

Boo Boo knew he would cry when he saw his mother on the news. But the experience will be very good for her, he thought. She is entirely too selfish. Besides, she should hate Pop as much as I do.

And, just thinking about it, he came in the older gentleman's mouth.

The father, Abraham Bronstein, he who was the son of immigrant German peasants, escaped from the pogroms of their native Dienstag to peddle rolls and nuts and eventually parlay cakes and cookies, pies and pizzas, into a fortune in the New World (reported in last Sunday's Financial Section of *The New York Times* as producing a record fiscal profit from all divisions, 29% over last year, $2.03 dividend per share, $146,000,000, Abraham Bronstein, Chairman of the Board), would undoubtedly suspect foul play of the most heinous sort.

"God is finally getting his revenge," Richie would hear Abe sadly confide to Walter. "For my success. For my hubris. For my not loving my Richie."

Even at this moment of climactic triumph, Boo Boo wouldn't cry.

"Unh, thanks," he said to his kneeling benefactor, who had actually swallowed the stuff, a feat which always amazed Boo Boo, who wouldn't stoop so low.

"What's your name," the balded one asked, creaking to an upright position and liking even more what he saw.

"You have a phone number so we can do it again? Indoors."

"My name is Tex. No phone."

And Boo Boo walked away.

Patty, Maxine, and Laverne were the best of friends and had been ever since they met dancing years ago at the old Tenth Floor. Each danced in a similar style, two legs implanted solidly on the ground, movement only from the knees and hips, the former back and forth, the latter side to side, hands discreetly undulating in and out and only within a modest circumference from the upper torso, eyes always straight ahead or closed. It was either a lazy man's dance or a wise one's, since its lack of caloric intensity allowed, with the aid of a few chemicals, for nonstop participation midnight till dawn and was, for all its rootedness to earth, still quite graceful.

Jack Humpstone was called Laverne because he was, with Manny and Moe, partners in the flourishing discotheque, Balalaika, and because there were three thirty-year-old friends and partners named Manny, Moe and Jack, they were christened, faggot-style, Patty, Maxine, and Laverne.

Patty, who was tall, thin, balding, hyperactive, and completely unable to delegate authority ("Listen! it's easier to do it myself than to trust just any slag"), was definitely in charge, to the relief of the other two, who still pursued independent careers. Maxine, who was Patty's lover, and who was addicted, in moments of stress, to dressing up as Elizabeth Taylor, was hefty, bouncy, and sharp ("Closets, schmosets, everyone's out of the closet. Now where the fuck are the *men*!"), and currently sold women's shoes at Lord and Taylor, where the ladies always asked for "that young man who knows my feet so

36

well." He and Patty had been together for seven years, and Maxine was not aware that an itch had now descended on his lover and it wasn't coming from crabs.

Laverne, who looked like John-Boy Walton with his neat and trim body, his youthful face and demeanor, and his slightly off-kilter hillbilly smile perking under his close-cropped steel-blond hair, was a schoolteacher in White Plains ("They are as retarded in Westchester as they are everywhere else"), where he tried to instill a love of English literature in heathen, suburban minds. He was a Southern Baptist boy from Birmingham, Alabama, and he was as together as anyone could be with an itinerant preacher for a father and a mother who was Betty Crocker All-State Finalist twelve years running, and who had discovered his own sexuality while a scholarship student at Washington and Lee, not with one of his classmates or instructors but with his Uncle Jeeter back on the farm—and who had just extricated himself forcefully from a six-year affair with Dinky Adams, to whom he had given himself in innocence and expectation, and by whom he'd been intimidated out of both.

But Jack was now going to a dyke shrink who had offered the hopeful, positive suggestion: "Mr. Humpstone, I think you may be a heterosexual *manqué*," and so perhaps not distant would be the day when his current inferiority (an impotency brought on by the fact that his cock had a head like a mushroom, which Dinky, claiming it hurt him when Jack fucked him, had utilized as an excuse to have sex elsewhere, which destroyed poor Laverne and his fantasy of love and sex melding into one by a hearthside yet unbuilt) would vanish, freeing himself up for sparking, roaring fires with the wooing Robbie Swindon, so patiently waiting in the wings.

It was Patty who had decided, when the old Tenth Floor was forcibly closed by the Fire Department—that

37

most homophobic of all city agencies—to open his own place. He'd started saving and he'd looked and looked, with Maxine as a willing, if astringently mouthed companion, for possible premises. After work (Patty had been an accountant in the cookie division of Bronstein Bakeries), Saturdays, Sundays, uptown, downtown, Brooklyn Heights ("Patty, no tripping queen is going to take a subway to Brooklyn to go dancing") until, on a very cold Election Day Tuesday four years ago, they were shown a parcel of properties on West Street, near Little Eleventh, across from the Hudson, by Alvin Sorokin (whose Immigrant Savings represented them), who told them: "A lease on this piece of shit is yours for any price." It was a piece of shit, an assortment of ill-matching adjoining sags and warps that would have done Dickens justice; the second floor of one did not greet the second floor of its brother, but Robbie, a Mormon architect who had been expelled from Brigham Young for being caught jerking off in the middle of the night and refusing to name names of any fellow Unnatural Behavers (not that he then knew any), forcing him to receive his degree in the East, showed them in sketches (Dinky had wanted the job but Patty had told him he wasn't qualified) how neat it would all be when a little money was spread around and how, after knocking out a few of the ground-floor walls, the street level would be dynamite. It would be, as it now was, a huge dancing womb of a place, suitable for thousands, with angled bleachers up to the d.j.'s nest, and, since one whole side had outlets to the street, there would be no Tenth-Floor-exit problem to disturb the awful Fire Department, still carrying on their tradition of unleashed homophobia. Alvin helped arrange a tight lease for ninety-nine years with the owners of the property, the Dippsy Doodle Cake Company, Limited, as Beneficial Nominee for the Lopp Trust. Patty paid $10,000 down, which was all the money he had saved from his cookies, plus $10,000 he'd begged from his aging parents in Brooklyn, plus $2,500 from Maxine and $1,000 from Laverne. It was theirs.

Robbie, always the nice smile, the black turtleneck, the handsome silver bracelet, the muscled gymnast's body, drew up plans as best he could under the grief of some difficulties pertaining to his current lover's penchant for fucking around elsewhere. To effect the extensive renovations and purchase the best of sound equipment, additional monies were secured by renting out part of the excess basement space to what Patty at first thought was Tiny Tots, Inc., a job lotter of kiddies' clothes, preschool to preteen, but which, after opening, turned out to be The Pits, a rather special gay bar. The upstairs partners were naturally upset to find competition quite so close at foot, but after Patty, unknown to Maxine, had paid a few visits to the place—as an exploratory observer, of course—and obtained true satisfaction from one blow job given and two anal intercourses, one given and one received, on his recommendation they decided not to press charges. "Listen!" he'd said, "a little competition can only help."

The strange bedfellows were to get along just fine, even after The Pits became a wee bit too notorious for the quality of its stage show, all those outré extensions of the anatomy's natural abilities, all played in various forms of repertoire, thus causing overflow crowds of uptown slummers, visiting firemen, and other assorted pleasure seekers, including New York's leading fag hag, Adriana la Chaise, disguised as a man, who, while a faggot to the extent that she evades the responsibilities that her brains, her abilities, and her energies, in a more enlightened age, would have channeled, via adult commitments, via more positive injections, into a needful society, was, nevertheless, by clitoral choice, straight, though it was her habit to enjoy slouching in dark corners, wearing military attire, sailor's suits or soldier's, and watch the boys do things to each other, and enjoy fainting when the beauties on the stage wilted to the floor, only to be watered by huge blacks wearing hip-length Goodyear waders and furry guardsman's toppers and tipping wax from large Rigaud candles that sizzled neath their stream, her distinguished presence, albeit in mufti, being naturally noteworthy enough to enter the Divine Bella's twice-weekly column in *Women's Wear,* so that Billy Boner, who owned The Pits, then imposed strict membership and attire and inspection requirements, which only made business even better, both downstairs and up.

Yes, both Balalaika and The Pits were now like old standards that keep playing and playing.

In Balalaika's office this Friday afternoon, before such a very big weekend, Patty, Maxine, and Laverne were talking, while Patty opened their weekly shipment of cookies and noted that neither Fig Newtons nor Oreos had been sent, but Pecan Sandies.

Patty, while wondering what the hell they would do with seventy pounds of greasy Pecan Sandies, thought he would try to edge into the problem gracefully. "Listen," he said, "I'm beginning to think that I don't know what sex is all about."

"That's the first I've heard about it," Maxine said, sampling several of the wrong order and beginning to study his heavy dark brows in the small mirror he'd pulled out of his Gap shirt of black-and-blue plaid.

"He told me, Leather Louie did, that it was his own special world, he'd made it just for himself, and he showed me where he strings up a number, on his gallows, erected right there, in his own apartment . . ."

"In the Dakota?" Maxine was commencing to notice several stubby black hairs bristling out of alignment.

". . . in the Dakota. Listen, he beats the shit out of

40

them with the kind of whip I haven't seen since *Mutiny on the Bounty*."

"He showed you the whip?" Laverne sensed the conversation drifting into tributaries he'd been trying so hard to leave unrafted.

"And the gallows. And the secret, hidden room, formerly I guess a maid's room. But big enough. Blood on the wall. Which he giggled as he pointed out. Giggled."

"*Nancy Drew and the Secret of the Hidden Room*," Maxine said, extricating his Avon tweezers from the back pocket of his jeans.

"He tortures himself with his sexual fantasies," Laverne ventured.

"But he's a very sympathetic person," Patty said. "And I truly feel that underneath his appetite for extreme sadism—which he talks about very precisely, very movingly, admitting that most sadists think they're ugly men, physically, and incapable of relating or feeling—there's a loving human being. Hidden. Fighting to get out."

"Certainly fighting," Maxine said, the tweezers now poised and ready to pluck.

"Did he elucidate upon his . . . encounters?" Laverne's toe was now succumbing, dipping into recollection.

"Scenes. They're called scenes. He says he prefers an evening with three scenes. The first two are pretend and the third is for real."

"How does he personally differentiate?" Laverne was sinking deeper.

"He says during the third he will push the masochist further than he's ever been pushed before. It's in accomplishing this that the true climax for both of them occurs. I hope I'm quoting him correctly."

Laverne nodded to himself. Yes, it sounded familiar, only too correctly reported. "He does it to avoid love," he mumbled.

41

"Love? What love?" Maxine plucked once, twice. "Where has love been displayed? I have heard nothing about love." Then, holding up the offending black mothers to the light, captured successfully between the grip of his forged pinchers, he added: "I'd never let anyone do that to me. There's a growing interest in this subject I find revolting. Our sexual fantasies are ruining us. Torture. Sheer torture. We torture ourselves with our sexual fantasies. What, may I ask, were you doing in the Dakota taking this guided tour with Leather Louie?"

"Listen, I was just curious. So many new things to check out. New kinds of love. Must keep up-to-date."

"I repeat: what love? Are you not confusing sex and love?" Maxine asked. What was Patty trying to tell him? Was Patty unhappy in their happy home?

"Yes, yes, who among us does not at some time confuse sex and love?" Laverne's thoughts had now slipped fully back to Dinky. Yes, yes, it was sexual fantasies that had done the evil deed.

Maxine released the hairs like so much scum and, pleased with his excisions, the even furrow of his handiwork, replaced the instrument in his right cheek pocket. "Leather Louie is a sick queen and love and sex are different items, Patty."

"Leather Louie isn't a sick queen. He's a composer who's been nominated for the Pulitzer Prize three times and has a lovely smile. I'd take him anywhere, providing he wasn't wearing his ritualistic gear." Patty now slapped Maxine's hand from a repeat sampling of the Pecan Sandies and wondered when he'd have the courage to come right out with it, communicate the news that their happy home was about to become not so happy.

Laverne hauled himself back to his schoolteacher role. "We . . . we should be smarter."

"Listen, I only said that I don't know what sex is

42

all about!" Patty slammed the carton of cookies closed. He only knew that he wanted to leave Maxine and move in with Juanito, Capriccio's Puerto Rican d.j. with the skin of velvet, tasting of honey and maple sugar.

Laverne stood up and looked out the tiny window, across the highway, over the river and far away, at least to New Jersey, so ugly, as were his thoughts of earlier eras. When would insight, knowledge, hope, and beauty meld? "No," he uttered to the far horizons, not looking to see if his best friends were ready for another of his major statements, not realizing that they no longer received them as major, just as part of his much too long ordeal of rejecting Dinky Adams. "No!" he said again. "We don't have anything together. And, as an elite, a minority privileged to count among its large, if indistinct membership, many of the world's greatest minds and talents and potentialities —though in undershirts and jeans on the dance floors of Balalaika and Capriccio at five in the morning very few of us are exactly capable of thought—as this true elite we should have more of our collective acts, and scenes, together. We have the ultimate in freedom—we have absolutely no responsibilities!—and we're abusing it. My sister-in-law does not speak to me, not because I'm a faggot, to which news she is now adjusted, as am I, but because she says I'm a coward, I'm not in there pitching to make this world a better place, I'm running away, I'm not relating to anyone successfully, I'm not proving to the world or to myself that I know what to do with this freedom, and Leather Louie isn't helping me, while she is chained to a mobile home in Mobile, Alabama. If I could do that, then I'd be listened to, respected, not scorned, mocked, feared as something unfit to teach children. But when I look around me, all I see is fucking. All we do is fuck. With dildoes and gallows and in the bushes and on the streets. My sister-in-law doesn't fuck on the streets."

43

Maxine decided enough was enough. "Laverne, please stop being so heavy." He patted Patty's tush. "When there is love, everything can be worked out. Patty, how can they not have sent Oreos?"

"No one will notice the difference," Patty answered. "And they might make a nice change." He sighed to himself. He couldn't do it.

Laverne was not finished. "What did Leather Louie give as the reason for the sadist pushing the masochist further than he's ever been pushed before?"

Now it was Patty's turn to look across the river. "Pushed to a greater connection to the ultimate, and a search for identity on the part of both of them to find out who and what they truly are. Which brings them pleasure."

"Crazy. That's what and who they truly are!" Maxine pulled out the tweezers again and studied his face in the mirror again and found out he had nothing else to pluck, causing him nervous frustration. "You're right," he said to Laverne. "We don't have our acts together."

Laverne nodded and sighed. Yes, sex and love were different items when he wanted them in one, and yes, having so much sex made having love impossible, and yes, sadism was only a way to keep people away from us and masochism only a way to clutch them close, and yes, we are sadists with some guys and masochists with other guys and sometimes both with both, and yes, we're all out of the closet but we're still in the ghetto and all I see is guys hurting each other and themselves. But how to get out! And yes, the world is giving us a bad name and we're giving us a bad name and one of us has got to stop and it's not going to be the world. But even knowing all of this . . . where am *I*? And how to say all this to anyone, when no one is listening, no one wants to hear, not even his two best friends, whom he sensed weren't listening to each other, oh what good were words, words didn't help

44

me and Dinky, what good were words when acts were all that counted?

He reached out and took Maxine's hand and he reached out and took Patty's hand and he hoped and prayed they were all trying to feel as one.

How do I feel about being pissed on?

Fred mulled this thought as he walked uptown to make final weekend plans with Abe. His body wore its marine fatigues, its sturdy work boots from L. L. Bean of Freeport, Maine, its plaid shirt of flannel, already too hot and ready to give way to summer Lacostes or gray Healthknit T's; his hand carried, how unpredictable the temperature, the Navy aviator's flight jacket by the Brothers Schott; and his heart, head, face, smile, crotch, and all interior regions wore the warm, anticipating mittens of Dinky's forthcoming return.

These articles of clothing, or permutations of same (khakis, Levis, with button flies only, and not preshrunk, painter's pants, Adidas, items of butch-ery) were the uniform. He felt safest wearing them, though he knew not why. Was it hiding? Or homogenizing? A way of staying anonymous to the outside world but recognizable to the inmates? If clothes make the man, what were they making? A way of insisting they were men, more men than men? And why was the same guy Hot and fuckable in a Pendleton and not in a Polo? And why did black boots on Christopher Street lure more fellows than brown? And were leather and jockstraps and football jerseys and satin boxing shorts all a send-up *and* a turn-on, and was this a clue to the faggot sensibility? He paused to juggle jacket and insight and to jot a note in his faithful Wire-In-Dex for future filing.

He did not, as many others did, wear-and-tell all. He

45

scorned the ass kerchiefs and keys, posted and peeking for all the boys to see: navy for fuck and yellow for piss and mustard for big cock and red for fist fucking and robin's egg for 69 and lighter blue for cock sucker and olive for military and green for hustler and brown for shit and orange for Anything and this kerchief or keys on the Left Side means I Do It To You and on the Right Side means You Do It To Me and on certain streets on certain days at certain times the code might be slightly altered if you knew certain people, and though all of this told all, what did any of it *mean*?

Yes, he thought, to Stendhal and Columbus and Vespucci and Boswell, I must now add Lévi-Strauss.

Then, striding forth with renewed gusto, pocketing his note pad, momentarily free of any unsettling thoughts, he once again renewed his pledge:

Yes! I must go forward, continue to go forth and forward, to encounter all and to forge in my smithy the uncreated conscience of my sex!

Ever since Miss Australian Butter had been replaced by Peetra Kant, a leggy model he'd discovered while viewing a South African documentary on Gold, Abe had seen little of Mrs. Bronstein Number Four. Peetra loved to shop and, since she was an organized young woman with a tendency toward great methodology, she had shopped her way from London, where Abe had viewed her, through New York, where Abe had married her, and was currently applying her vim to Paris, where rumor had it she might be about to deliver forth the third Bronstein heir, before motoring south to St. Paul de Vence for an indefinite purchase.

So Abe, while instructing his older son and lawyer, Stephen, to prepare papers for divorce and possible custo-

46

dy proceedings, and before setting forth to seek another poopsie to brighten his declining years, moved back in with Ephra.

It was not that Ephra either wanted him or was forgiving. She would answer "Who wants him?" or "Forgive him?" to a discussion of either topic. But the large Park Avenue apartment she preferred to "that wilderness he gives to me on Lake Candlewood which is not even a natural lake but a man-made lake where once, years ago, we had a happy summer," was in his name and he still liked to live in it, even though Peetra had insisted they buy the Soho loft, now Richard's, where Abe had sprained an ankle, perhaps on the night young junior was conceived, disembarking from the circuitous metal staircase from their aerial nuptial bower to make himself a hot Ovaltine to regain his strength.

Abe, home again on Park and 58th, looked down ten floors and across to where there was once a fine Mayflower donut shop and where there was now only yet another store pushing chotchkies, the chotchkification of America, and spoke to young Fred Lemish.

"Fred-chen, I worry, I worry. Is the world really ready for a faggot-sexual movie? Are the mommies of this world really ready to learn about the sodomitic activities of their bubbalahs?"

"Abe, it's time. I know it. And I must write about what I know. All these years of masquerade, writing Rebecca, thinking Rupert. There's millions of me now, Abe. The closets are empty. New York has no more full closets. Please, let's be brave, bold pioneers!"

"Freddie, New York is not the world. We are more sophisticated. The rest of the world is not sophisticated. The rest of the world is Main Street, the story of a doctor and his young wife. Please, have you given any thought to writing the story of a doctor and his young wife?"

47

"Abe, neither of us is interested in medicine. The great innovators, the landmark men, are the ones who went against the current of the main street. Besides, the first respectable faggot *Love Story* will clean up. Ryan O'Neal and Robert DeNiro together will bring them out of every household, tent, and igloo in the world."

"Fred, I am a heterosexual. Everyone I know is a heterosexual. My two sons are heterosexual. What do I know from gay?"

"Abe, you don't have to know anything. Leave the driving to me. You would be doing the world a public service. You would be helping to bring knowledge and enlightenment on a much misunderstood and maligned subject to the heathen. You would be rewarded, both on earth and in heaven."

"All of these reasons are good ones. Leave me with your thoughts. I am having a dinner appointment with Mr. Randy Dildough from Marathon. He has wooed me before."

"Abe! Why didn't you tell me? That's very exciting! I knew I could count on you. He's the most important man in movies. But maybe it's not such a good idea. I hear he's a faggot."

"This then must help us. He will help his own kind. Go, and I will meet you tomorrow as per our explorer's itinerary. Now I am tired and must go to Bloomingdale's."

"Abe, use your own toilet."

"It's just around the corner."

"Abe ..."

"Ephra keeps a clean house. I don't mind. It is part of our rules. I can use the walk."

"Abe, you never even noticed that the Bloomingdale's john is full of humpy faggots, in denim and boots, carrying their shopping bags filled with doilies and candles

48

and towels from the White Sale. Does Ephra know that you pee in such company?"

"Take your feet from the furniture. Ephra cherishes her chairs and her sofa."

Fred, so good at instant proclamation, removed his feet from their position of comfort, stood up, walked straight to Abe, and launched: "You think I joke, Abe, but today it's no longer necessary to go out of your own home to pee! Abe, today it's even considered healthy to wank off. Yes, Abe, healthy! Did you know that your thing will no longer fall off, even if you do it every day, even if you shoot your gism into a sanitized toilet? I know you don't believe me, but soon the Magazine Section of *The New York Times* will write about it, and these things will be sanctioned once and for all as healthy indoor sports, practiced by Hank Aaron and Dave DeBusschere."

"My little grandson loves Dave DeBusschere," Abe said, thinking of Wyatt (where did they find these names?), Stephen's boy. "This news would destroy him."

"Abe, I love you very much, but what makes you think he isn't wanking off right this minute? Along with his classmates. In unison. A cappella."

"Fred, bite your tongue!"

"No, Abe. I want somebody else to bite it. Somebody gorgeous, successful, brilliant, and male. And that's what our movie must be all about. The Quest for Love. A thirty-eight-year-old faggot decides he must find a lover before he's thirty-nine. He's lonely—and isn't this the human condition, so timely, so touching?, we must remember that all great stories reflect the human condition—and he wants a mate. This is the story of his Quest. The inborn, natural, lusting Quest of Man for His Mate."

"But why must they both be fegalim?"

"I could hardly make one of them a dyke. Abe, it's

49

time to write with the pen of truth. I am a thirty-nine-year-old faggot who must find true love by forty. Abe, beloved, this is my life! I've got to go."

"Don't use the toilet! Ephra has blue poison in the bowl."

"I know Ephra has blue poison in the bowl! What have we been talking about all afternoon? I meant out. Abe, don't you hear the call of freedom?"

"No. In all of this, where? I have certainly been looking!"

"You can't even piss in your own toilet! What are you going to do?"

"I told you. Go to Bloomingdale's."

"Abe . . . Abe . . ."

"Don't say my name like that! Abe is a happy name. It is Hebrew for 'exalted father.' My namesake was the father of many nations and the founder of my people and the friend of God."

"All the more reason to be a modern trailblazer."

"He was also the model of perfect submission to God's will, even in the severest trials, including to the sacrifice of his own son."

"That one I could never understand. I'll see you tomorrow. We'll commence our tour."

"The alphabet begins with Abe. And Abe Bronstein is a maker of happy cakes and cookies—though personally I would not touch them, such an aftertaste, my brother now uses cheap quality lard—and of happy motion pictures. Go. Go. I shall meet you per our plans. Seventy-two places you told me you can go to have sex?"

"Abe, New York is becoming Boys' Town. You don't know how many faggots parade up and down the streets, inhabit the clubs and bars and baths and discos and shop the stores and cruise the men's rooms of hotels and universities and bookstores and subways and how many tens of thousands go to Fire Island and the Hamptons and Jones Beach and Riis Park and, yes, there exist approximately seventy-two places where I can go on any evening, or afternoon for that matter, where I can engage in physical activity leading to orgasm, to actually touch and be touched. Yes, seventy-two places I personally know about, which means there are many more that others know about but I yet don't. And I also know that I am not seeing the same faces over and over again, that I am seeing strangers, and that they are increasing into armylike proportions. And this information, which put to proper use could probably elect a President, means only two things: one, that for the life of me I can't understand why it's taken me so long to find the right one among this horde for me; and two, we've got to make the movie! Abe, until domani."

Abe Bronstein, bored with his business, bored with the fights with his brother, Maury, who preferred breads and biscuits when Abe, quite accurately, had predicted the surge in America's sweet teeth, bored with his bimbies, and bored with his two sons who never called to chat or visit, had turned to movies as a means for other, more creative, outlets for his energies.

At first it was just a chance to get out of the loft on Saturdays, when Peetra was apt to require more money for shopping. Then he would go up to Third Avenue and take in a movie, see perhaps something intelligent from England or a nice color film from California with such pretty photography, though maybe that tootsie is a better looker than she is an actress. Then he noticed in his *Wall Street Journal* that certain movies made a great deal of money, many millions if they hit just right, and he be-

51

gan to take a closer look. Soon he was reading his *Variety* each week, and then he was going to Brentano's to buy screenplays published in paperback form. From there, he started attending the Museum of Modern Art in the afternoon, to sitting with the old ladies and gentlemen with nothing better to do than cluck over young Conrad Veidt or miss the point of Griffith and Pudovkin and Eisenstein, and if they didn't like the movie, they would kibbitz in the darkness, driving Abe crazy. He decided the Museum of Modern Art was the noisiest movie theater in town and he took to attending the Carnegie Hall and the Bleecker Street and the tiny old house on St. Mark's Place where the audiences were all more serious and the seats were all falling apart.

And then one day, feeling excited, courageous, Abe decided he would make his own first film. A lesser man would have sought affiliation within the established industry; a man of Abe's standing in the financial community did not lack for contacts. But he'd been in business long enough to know that every business was more or less alike, filled with hanky-panky, mumbo jumbo, and lawyers, lawyers, lawyers, all dished up by the residents to hand to the immigrants. So he went about it quietly, in his own way. First he found a book he not only thought would make a good movie but also reflected something he felt worth saying. It was a novel about connections among big business, organized crime, and the United States government, and how they all helped each other. He purchased the rights to film it and, having enjoyed an English import called *Lest We Sleep Alone* (written by one Fred Lemish), which he also understood from Richie had become a cult favorite at college campuses everywhere, he looked for and hired Fred to write him a script. *U.S. Mobsters, Inc.,* made unpretentiously and out of the country for a budget of nine hundred and fifty thousand dollars of Abe's own money, went on to earn him a profit of four and one half million, which represented an awful lot of cookies. So he was encouraged to proceed apace.

He was now searching for his second property, as he had learned to call ideas for movies (yes, all businesses were alike), and it was for this project that Fred was trying to convince Abe to go gay.

Abe was also searching for something else. Like Fred, he was troubled with certain metaphysical problems in his life. I am searching for something, I have taken so much, what can I give back, were thoughts that daily crossed his brow. I have made so many people fat and they have made me fatter. Do Mr. Bronfman and Mr. Schenley worry in their nighttimes about how many drunks they have sent into the world? Or Mr. Winston and Mr. Marlboro about how many cancers? Mr. Bronfman has built a great building. What am I building? Perhaps Fred is right. Perhaps it is important for me to be his conduit of enlightenment in order to receive my own expiation. But is he not dealing in such schmutz! Fegalim! Please God to tell me if my sainthood comes from cock suckers! Perhaps it is better to wait. The Jew has always waited. For the homeland, for the Messiah, for the acceptance. We are still waiting. Perhaps it is time to stop waiting for the Leader and the Savior and to lead and save ourselves. But are these boys my Mission?

Abe, the philosopher. He stood peeing in Bloomingdale's, oblivious to Fred's shoppers, and pondered the unending powerlessness in Jewish history and realized the commonality with Fred's fegalim. And then he thought, profoundly, how there was something grand about living in hope, but also something terribly unreal and incomplete about it, because when you were hoping, you were not doing or living or experiencing the Now, but deferring and not fulfilling, and that those concepts of Judaism, on

53

which he had been weaned, compelled a life lived in deferment, nothing could be irrevocably accomplished, it was like an orgasm with never an ejaculation, and if it was great to be a Waiter, wasn't it also weak? Was it now and at last and forever time to stop waiting? But for what?!

Feeling more like Spinoza or Maimonides than Abe, he too zipped up and flushed, and headed back to Ephra's command post. He does not know it, but the horrors he is to confront in this latest chapter of his search for Meaning, Enlightenment, Where Is the Rational?, on which the emancipated Jew so prides himself, will be such as to make him . . . what? A Job? A Hitler? An Abe?

There is talk on the Village streets of a fifteen-year-old high-school student from suburban New Jersey who stands at the corner of Christopher and Hudson, outside of a particularly unsavory male boutique, and waits for assignations to suck his cock in the dark.

His cock is ten inches long. Flaccid.

He doesn't have to wait very long.

He now charges money for his endowment.

Have you any idea how long a ten-inch cock is? Measure it out on a ruler or tape. You will be amazed. Although there is some medical evidence that the male musculature is not able to constantly erect so much, this drawback perhaps does not occur in one so young. At least not for a while.

The lad is very much in demand. He loves it.

His name is Wyatt Bronstein.

Enter Ephra, Abe's first wife.

"Abe, you flushed my toilet."

"I'm sorry."

"You want to flush, you go home to what your bimby's left you."

"Ephra, something happened. I had to go again. Bloomingdale's is closed."

"After all these years, you couldn't keep your tinkle in?"

"No! And what's so terrible about that? Do you know what Fred told me?"

"I don't want to hear." Ephra covered her ears.

"Some fegalim tinkle on each other!"

"I worry for him. He's all alone. What will he do when he's old like us? If there are so many fine fegalim in this city like he says, what's his trouble?"

"His horoscope predicts great things for this year. Previously, I gather, his planets would not allow him to fall in love before he was thirty-five."

"Is he not now thirty-nine?"

"It will now be easier for him."

"Do they get married like people? What shall I get them for their house? Abe, it's such a sordid life. I must confess something to you."

"Confess."

"I must confess to you that I've read they go and do it in the bushes and on islands and, would you believe, inside of trucks."

"Where do you read this?"

"In the illustrated guidebook Fred gave to you and which you hide from me in your bottom drawer."

"Ephra, please. Don't burden your big heart."

"Why would anyone want to make love in a truck?"

"Love is many things to many people. Love is very complicated. Love is a many-splendored thing."

"Stop with the movies. Abe, I can't believe what you're telling me."

"What am I telling you?"

"Somebody even, I can't bring myself to say the word, tinkles on his beloved? Then . . . then what?"

"Then what *what*?"

"After they . . . tinkle?"

"How should I know?"

"Do they wash off?"

"I'm some sort of expert in this matter?"

"You're his producer."

"Ephra, you are too much concerned with the cleanliness. I do not know the aftermath."

"Abe, please . . . this is not easy for me."

"So, who's forcing you to talk?"

"Fred wouldn't do such things."

"Maybe. Maybe not. Ephra, don't you, in your wildest imagination, have strange thoughts?"

"Never!"

"Of course you do."

"I swear, *nimmer*."

"I tell you, you do. Ephra, it's healthy that you do. Even the Magazine Section of *The New York Times* says so. Think of the last time we made love. I know it was a long time ago, but try to remember what you were thinking . . ."

"Roosevelt was President . . ."

". . . what you maybe wanted me to do to you or somebody else to do to you . . ."

"Somebody *else*!"

"It's all right, Ephra. I'm told that women in particular have very strong sexual fantasies, maybe like a tall man on a white horse should come along and carry you away, after maybe the horse is seen doing exciting things to another horse."

"Who is telling you these things about horses!? Never, never in a thousand years would I want to see horses, any kind of horses! Abe, I don't know anymore the man I once was married to. All your Misses Non-Kosher have made you into a tinkler! Abe, Jewish people do not tinkle on horses! Abe . . . Abe . . . where are you going?"

"I have an appointment."

"Always the appointments! Do not forget that tomorrow you and Fred are taking me to the grand opening. I have read about it in *Women's Wear Dailying* by the Divine Bella. I want to see it with my own two eyes..."

And he was gone.

After his departure, feeling sorry for herself, then and now, for her abandonment, then and now, and trying to drown her sorrows in her favorite banana yogurt from Dannon's, she finally wailed out to nobody in particular and the walls (hung with two Picassos and fifteen of that nice Jewish painter, Chagall, all of which she had received in the settlement, settling what, she wanted to know) in general: "Men! I am hating you all. And my mother, who was not a woman with a smile, had good reason to warn me from all of you. You think of no one, Abe, and you never have, not me or not even your own two sons and heirs, Richard and Stephen, to whom I have given so much love and sacrifice and pain and anguish and hope and tenderness and who, both of them, are not even calling to say thank you."

The thankless younger son and heir was now back in his Soho loft and deep into bodily communication. Boo Boo Bronstein was performing, along with most of our other leading faggots, that necessary ritual preparatory to every weekend's outings known as the "pump-up," as he did his daily two hundred push-ups and five hundred sit-ups and four sets of twenty-five each of his bench presses, tricep presses, chin-ups, seated curls, and shrugs on the extensive set of home weights he'd purchased at Herman's against that fast-approaching day when he just knew he'd put his plan in operation. He was going to kidnap himself, but he certainly wasn't going to break his routine. It would be bad enough not being able to go out and parade around the Village streets for hours and hours, showing off his nicely proportioned body, six feet, narrow waist, bulging biceps, well-defined pecs, lats like wings, all calculated, or so he hoped, to take the eye of the beholder off his dark, swarthy, unhappy-looking, and rather Jewish face.

I'm going to be a faggot! I'm going to be a faggot! Boo Boo had first realized with terror two years ago during his junior year at Yale when the distinguished grayhaired portly, gentile professor of his History of Art: Greek Sarcophagi class suggested they have a tête-à-tête in his book-walled house on Chapel Street "to discuss the argument put forth in your paper on the marble frieze of Noxos." After six-and-one-half glasses of some fancy vintage wine, Boo from an early age not being a cheap date, he was laid back, as he somehow knew he would be, and, shivering with the apprehensions and expectations of the guilty, cursed, and damned, which he also knew he would be, he allowed his already erected cock, for the first time, to be sucked.

How did it do that? How did it turn into such a straight and hard flagpole without my even knowing it?, Boo queried his inner self, trying his best not to enjoy it, nor to enjoy the professor's hands and palms and fingers, rubbing and massaging, much as they must have done to countless other priceless treasures, his nicely developing upper torso, which Boo had acquired courtesy of 1) covertly perusing, like something dirty, in a side aisle of the Yale Co-op, a picture of Arnold Schwartzenegger in a book called *Pumping Iron*; 2) commencing the loss of fifty pounds of rather recalcitrant baby fat; and 3) two hours a day of working out at the Payne Whitney Gymnasium. Yes, up and down and over and across went the professor's mitts, and up and down and over and across went the professor's tongue and mouth, and out of that flagpole flew the nice-flowing, good-feeling release.

To be followed by the guilt.

"It's not very large," the professor later said, which also didn't help.

This was the first verbalized confirmation of Richie's suspicions. Not only was he a faggot, but his flagpole was not quite the standard-bearer a Bronstein boy was meant to hoist in battle.

"But," the professor continued, bending down to lead the troops to action once again, "it certainly tastes splendid and your pectorals are perfect. You have the body of an ancient Greek. I believe you're what's called a Number."

I want to be a Number! I want to be a Number!, Boo Boo realized over the succeeding weeks as he moped still lost on campus, his eyes to sidewalk or well-trod grasses, acknowledging no one, or as he sat alone in his Silliman single (who would want to room with him?, a feeling no doubt emanating from those earlier formative years when he shared a john with his older brother, Stephen, who had nicknamed him Boo Boo for his petulance and his whining insecurity: "It's either 'Boo Boo' or 'Lemon,' take your choice, I suggest the former, at least it's euphonious"), staring at the pea-green soupy shade with which Yale walls are nourished, and thinking of his teacher's mouth and trying very, very hard not to seek it out again. I mustn't do it, I mustn't do it, it is Wrong! Even though for those three seconds prior to ejaculation and two seconds post, on each of the many succeeding encounters during the semester (he received a final A), Boo had dim thoughts of what he'd been missing all his years.

The guilt, however, ah yes, The Guilt!, was such as to eventually extrude into a courageous confession to his Pop that he was suffering mightily, "Pop, I got these female problems," so that Abe, himself in guilt that, like father: like son, financed what amounted to two years of intensive psychoanalysis at Yale's famed Child Study Center (Richard was never to know that his case had entered the international journals as "A Famous Son: The Transmission of Psychoneurotic Mishegas from Old World to New") with a Dr. Rivtov. For four hours a week, through his junior and senior years, Richie, as the dour doctor waved his club foot by the reclining patient's right eye, was shrunk, wherein they both discovered how terrified were his kishkas of: a) his poppa; b) his momma; c) himself.

Armed with this useful knowledge, he graduated. And disarmed by the additional enlightenment that his cock still saluted his fellow men only, a reflexive action not dissimilar to the knee that jumps when struck by the hammer, of which both he and Dr. Rivtov naturally disapproved, though neither carpenter had come up with anything remotely resembling a new set of drawers, he tried to make the best of it. And not to be terrified that his Pop would find out. And not to be terrified that his Pop would find out. And not to be . . .

This had amounted, up till now, to allowing his flagpole to be saluted and nothing more.

But he knew there was more. He saw it with his eyes and he dreamed it in his dreams and he fantasized it in his daytimes and he knew he was in trouble.

For he knew there was a pit of sexuality out there and that he longed to throw himself into it.

I have to! I have to! he would torture himself before several hours napping in his lofted bed. Because it's part of the faggot life style—to find abandonment and freedom through ecstasy—fucking and being fucked and light s & m and shitting and pissing and Oh I want to be abandoned! and where's my copy of the *Avocado* . . ., which he would then reach for and wonder when he could courageously answer those ads placed by seekers of "willing victims" and "hot humpy young dudes to do things to."

Then his torture thoughts stretched out to Fire Island. This weekend I promise I'm going to try! He'd never been there before, not because of its physical inaccessibility but because of his physical fear. How to parade around, half-naked, along those fabled boardwalks and strands, in front of all those staring eyes, eyes belonging to humpies far humpier than he? Could he do it? And into that fabled Meat Rack! The sexual pits incarnate! Could he do that, too? Throw himself down there? And could he do it with class, so that they'd look at him and point him out enviously, and say: "There goes that rangy cowboy, Rich Bronstein! You know who he is!"

Yes, how to throw himself into those pits? How?!

One million smackolas. Wouldn't they help?

And then my Pop could find out. And then my Pop could find out.

But by then I'd be free!

And Rich!

Yes, one million smackolas. They would surely help.

And if I don't do something quickly, they'll make me marry that spaghetti heiress, Marci Tisch!

While Fred walked across town to the Y, now thinking of his mother, and Abe left Ephra for an early dinner

61

with Randy Dildough, Anthony Montano left his Beekman Place penthouse and headed south. Fred's best friend—tall, dark-haired, dapper, Omar Sharif as an Italian diplomat—was heading, oh wondrous joyful shining late afternoon in May, for the Village streets.

There he would get his cock sucked, his cock that had not come in twenty-three days, his wonderful uncut wop cock that deserved better things, as did its owner, slaving for Irving Slough was not an easy life, the Winston Man was not an easy account to square with one's conscience, Winnie might be cute but people are dying, as am I, as is my cock, both of us feeling overwhelmingly the need for relief and release, I am working too hard, it's not working hard enough, it's sometimes, too often, soft and wavy, and that's for hair sprays not for cocks, and what is happening now that I am getting older and there's no kisser in my life?

Fred thought of Algonqua. One year ago he had told her!

Algonqua Lemish!

She who was the middle daughter of five achieving siblings of Russian peasants also making the long schlepp to the New World, from there to here, from rags, if not to riches, at least to groceries, they always ate, her poppa, Herschel the Unsmiling, and her momma, Lena the Undaunted, ran a grocery store in Hartford, where Algonqua grew up, graduated from Normal School, taught first grade in the morning, sold shoes in the afternoon, and coached foreigners in English at night. Then she met Lester Lemish, potentially so fine, and they settled down, outside of Washington, D.C., he to not realizing that potential, and she to serving humanity, the American Red Cross, twenty-four hours a day of looking after The World—Home

62

Servicing, Bloodmobiles, floods, fevers, epidemics, fires, Water Safety, tardy alimonies, bandaged wounded, wheelchaired to ball games, garden partied prisoners, indigent Army wives, paraplegic veterans, missing children, wayward husbands, AWOLs, yes, Handicappeds Anonymous —thus becoming a determined breadwinner, a courageous lifesaver, a tenacious turner of losers into winners, *the* Director of Disasters, yes, a wonderful humanitarian and *A Gigantic Ma*!

ALGONQUA LEMISH!

Algonqua had had her left tit lopped off a year ago. She held court from her eighth-floor bed in the Georgetown University Hospital as if deprived of her best and most useful feature, rather a startling reaction from a widow of seventy and one for whom Fred and Ben automatically assumed sex came not easily if at all. While it is generally construed by all children that their parents never fucked, Fred was reasonably certain that his rarely had, or why else would he have always had such problems with kiss and cuddle and body and closeness and semen and cock and rectum and that interco-mingling of the physical, bodily, and sexual attributes with which all man is blessed?

In that hospital room, there and then, one year ago, the commencement of the New Era, Fred Lemish had, finally, at just thirty-nine years of age, informed his mommy he was a faggot. He had not planned to do so. Had not all friends advised: Why tell? They cannot understand. It will make them unhappy. Why upset apple carts? But Fred would respond with: Why must I go on leading a secret life in the back streets? This only means I am ashamed of myself and this life and I would like to stop being ashamed of this life and me and who and what I am.

He had spent the afternoon on a visit to the shrine.

63

He had gone, after twenty years of various journeyings in the Outside World, to the homesite of his pubescent days. He had knocked on the Hyattsville garden-apartment door with his best successful movie-writer smile, clutching an old clipping from the Washington *Post* with his picture (taken upon the occasion of *Lest We Sleep Alone* opening to the only grotesquely bad reviews it received anywhere in the world; you can't hit a homer in your own hometown), thrusting it to the shabby young housewife and present tenant: "My name is Fred Lemish, I grew up in this apartment, this is my movie for which I was nominated for an Academy Award for Best Adaptation of a Work from Another Medium, which I first thought meant something from the supernatural, would you mind if I came in and looked around?" The helpless woman, rendered speechless by such fame, allowed Fred in, in, in and back to the teeniest of rooms (they had seemed so big growing up!), look Fred, look at the corner where you first jerked off, sure still looks dirty enough, some of that schmutz is *me,* look, there's where your bed was, next to Ben's, that bed in which you had your first wet dream after reading Havelock Ellis under the covers and on which you played, though obviously not nearly enough, "doctor" with the little girl from downstairs, and look, there's the closet you hid in to watch older brother Ben, the jock, take off same, and you later bent to smell, no one was looking, you can smell, take a heady sniff of brother Ben, and there's the corner where, under the rug, you hid a forbidden treasure, a picture of an erect penis, bartered for three packs of Luckies and ten pink diet pills, yes, a diet even then, and there's the same Venetian blind you pulled down and closed tightly so you could have your first experiences with another boy's body, his name was Fred, too, your fellow eighth-grader, once a month or so, allowing sufficient time for guilt to subside and hunger to return, always during the day, when no one was at home, ah, memories are made of this.

In the hospital room, he re-arranged into their nighttime array, at Algonqua's request, the twenty-three vases of flowers. Ben's office had certainly sent flowers. They didn't know her but they sent flowers. Ben was important to them, senior partner in Washington's top firm of accountants. Where were the flowers to her from his friends in New York, who didn't know her either but to whom he was important?

There was a strange closeness coming upon them, something Fred had not allowed for on this visit, nor allowed, indeed, since he'd gone into that Outside World, nor allowed, come to think of it, since those couplings with his fellow eighth-grader, Fred. If he'd inherited her determination that "my boy can do anything!" ("as long as she's Jewish"), he had also inherited Lester's fears and tremblings. Drs. Isaiah Cult, Clive Nerdley, Tracy Fallinger, M. R. Dridge—these had been his substitute nutrition, the Metrecal of his life. He'd told *them* everything, his system, he hoped, now purged, the colonic irrigations of his mind, psyche, brain, id, ego, superego, unconscious, subconscious kishkas (where did one become another, or were they each the same, and how connected were they with the heart, and how did any of them become the Staff of Life, that crooked crutch with which to creak along?). No, he had not planned to tell her this evening. After such radical surgery.

He was helping her to walk, up and down long corridors, past other wards and wings and basket cases, her arm through his, leaning on him, getting her exercise. Yes, he felt close to her for a change, and she felt it, and it was this closeness, for the nonce overcoming his temerity in the presence of her usual Tower-of-Power routine, which encouraged his voiding of the beans, true confessional, tonight the night, Susan Hayward letting it all hang out, radical surgery indeed.

How to phrase it? *Ma, I want to fall in love with a fella.* Beat step step kick kick over out jump fall down dead. *Please tell me it's all right to fall in love. With a fellow fellow.* whyamisoafraid? Ah, yes, Lester had been right. Lester had always called him a sissy.

"Ma, there's something I've been wanting to tell you. Did you know that I'm a homosexual?"

Thirty-ninth floor, Fred! JUMP!

She did not take it well. Was he expecting a trumpet voluntary, a huge welcoming round of applause, kisses to the balcony, and grateful recognition from the star? Well, the old lady looked sad. Yes, she did.

And this made Fred, growing so fast his pants were getting shorter by the second, miffed. He wanted more courage and support from this woman of gargantuan strength. Madam, if you thus elect to choose weakness, hurt, injury, frosted with self-pity, then I, at this belated bar mitzvah of growth, do not approve, he thought, being careful not to consider that he'd been choosing similar weak-necked stratagems for years, like some overgrown pansy in the garden that can't quite keep its head from bending low. No, he did not think this. But he did think: You can't make the rules forever.

Finally the sibyl spoke. "I always knew there was something."

"What do you mean, you always knew?"

"That professor of yours at Harvard, I always suspected there was something. He invited you to Europe and you wouldn't go. You paced all night in your room . . ." She was referring to a night over twenty years ago.

"You remember?"

"A mother remembers."

66

"He was in love with me and I was frightened."
Brave as a Green Beret today, are you, Fred?

St. Joan on the Cross looked around for some words.
"I only want you to be happy," she finally said.

"I'm happy! I'm happy! I want you to know I'm
happy. I wouldn't have it any other way. If I had a choice
today, I would choose to stay the way I am." Good for
you, Fred! Good courage! Stout lad! (Stop calling yourself stout! You're thin, now. You're thin!) What did it
take for you to get all this out to her? Twenty-one years
of Shrinkery for you to get it up guiltlessly?

"You promise me you're happy?"

"Yes. I'm happy. I'm happy."

"You promise me?"

He took her hand, which was through his arm anyway, and held it. "Yes."

"Well, anything that makes you happy makes me
happy."

Lies on both sides were gratefully accepted. He
walked her back to her room and helped her into her bed.

Six months later, same hospital, after her other tit
had been biopsied and reprieved, she lowered her voice
to ask him: "What do you want me to do with that book?"

"What book?"

"You know the book," she lowered even lower.

"The one about homosexuality you asked me to get
you so you could read and learn and try to understand?"

She nervously looked to see if her roommate was
listening and had heard. "Yes," she said, clearing her
throat.

"What do you mean, do with it?"

"I'm finished reading it." Her voice still remained
much too confidential.

"It's yours to keep," Fred chirpily answered, full-
throated, fortissimo, *molto voce,* bravo. "It's not some-

67

thing you have to tuck away in a bottom drawer. Where is it?"

A reply was not forthcoming.

"You haven't? In the bottom drawer?"

She busied herself with smoothing blanket and cover-let and quilt.

"I'm ashamed of you," he said. "What did you think of it?"

"It made me sick," escaped her lips.

Well, that's just wonderful. Thanks a heap. That really makes me feel just swell. Thirty-nine floors up and Fred once more wanted to jump.

"What do you write about, young man? Your mother tells me you're a writer."

Algonqua's eyes blinked rapidly, avoided Fred's, ran around the room and walls and ceiling.

"My life," Fred said to the neighboring bed, a gall bladder tomorrow morning, "Jewish," Algonqua had iden-tified her, "despite her name," which was Lincoln.

"How interesting," Mrs. Lincoln said. "What about your life?"

Algonqua coughed and looked toward heaven. Per-haps, like Clare Boothe Luce in the Holy City, some plaster would fall and change the subject.

"And what has been so awful in your life that you have to write about it?" Mrs. Lincoln, a definite gall bladder, persevered.

A crossroads. He was torn. Should he be strong and honest, what care?, the bold, brave pioneer? Was this not what he was trying to stand for, The Hero in Action, since he had, a lifetime ago, dealt with his now ex-Mother?

Or was it Mature to Avoid the Issue, hiding under that rug any iota of opportunity for either Mrs. Lincoln to sympathize with Algonqua or Algonqua to feel sorry for herself?

68

Or should he give the old Ma one more stab of the scalpel? Take that! you old switchboard operator with your connections still plugged in! Take that! Take that! you Gobbling Turkey who's not giving me Thanksgiving! Take that . . . It was quite obvious that Algonqua the Altruistic was shitting in her hospital gown that this son she no longer recognized might peel off (for the camouflage it was) her prideful labeling of "My son, the successful writer."

Yes, Fred, anxiously desiring either a jump or a number of Greenberg's brownies, had to decide at this moment whether to add another helpful label to her list.

Finally he answered Mrs. Lincoln: "You'll read the reviews."

While we're at it, and with so many of our leading faggots yet to introduce, dare we pause a moment to tarry over the likes of kvetchy, schleppy, nasty Lester Lemish? Yes, he passed through his lifetime a sissy and a coward, a doormat with nary a star of love to guide him, though he would have named himself a true man through and through. Dare we offer a requiem moment to the ghost of Lester Lemish?

He certainly was a screamer. *Go out and play with the boys! Stop playing with the girls!* he'd helpfully bombard the younger son who wouldn't listen to the Yankees or the Redskins, little knowing that such an impressionable lad would choose to obey both dicta to the lifetime letter. "You sissy!" he'd then helpfully append, chomping on his fat cigar, and adding further traumatic damage, as such a word delivered from father unto son and indicating a tidge of lovelessness could possibly so intidge.

But wasn't it Lester who backed away from challenge

and risks? Wasn't it Lester who was terrified of life and sex and life and family and life and Algonqua? Lester, downed by the Depression, defeated into second-rate accountancy positions, never paying much, thus freeing up Algonqua to ply her oh so many active employments and deployments, more lucrative, and in so doing taking his ball games and his balls away. Oh, Lester Lemish, with a degree from Harvard and one from Harvard Law School, Phi Beta Kappa from the first, *Law Review* from the second, why did you lie down and die, in so doing, almost, *almost*, bringing down your younger son, you idolized your elder, he played ball.

Yes, Lester Lemish, your totally poor record in Fatherhood included an inability to kiss and hug, keep bargains and promises, call and say Hello, inquire after studies and well-being, offer love, do anything but pull the Disappearing Act, with its constant curtain line: You Are Unwanted! I Reject You Through and Through!, delivered unto Fred, and truly bringing down the house. Yes, Lester Lemish, you were the first in the long line of danglers who held out the lollipop but who wouldn't let Fred lick.

So, Lester Lemish, ye who hated your son and whom your son hated right back, ye whom he blamed for making him go out and suck cock to find one of his own—and if we are going to get pyrotechnical on the matter, and evidently we are, let it be said that Fred had strong feelings on The Subject: It was men and their insecurities that made him queer and bent and faggot (were women the worse of the two evils?, and hence by the bye, with more demanding strings attached for payments on demand?, Algonqua would eat him alive!) (and he did not know that Dinky's situation was just the reverse: it was his Poppa who sang to him "How Are Things in Glocca Morra?" and his Momma who was the weak and rejecting, and needful, one), and he'd found nothing in

70

all his comings and goings to make him feel otherwise, nothing but gropings for cocks to make his own seem real (is this any different, Fred, from the millions of straight men looking for the tit their mamas once gave them, or didn't?) and while there's a current trend afoot attempting to indicate that homosexuality might be caused by genetic intrusions or embryonic hormonal imbalances, and there may be truth or succor found in this, or anything else the genes boys might come up with, and wouldn't it be nicer, easier, neater, cleaner, certainly more convenient, if homosexuals were born just like everybody else?, there is also that other school of thought, established by S. Freud and his dishy disciples (including the Messrs. Cult, Nerdley, Fallinger & Dridge), which posits that a dumb dodo of a daddy and a whiz bang whammerino of a Ma (who made Algonqua be so fucking strong, Lester, who?) can turn the trick as well (though what about Lester's own eviscerated childhood, his own tyrant of a Mamma, she who single-handedly ran her own grocery store in a neighborhood of polacks and schvartzas and put two sons through Harvard without aid from any husband in sight, he having been evacuated when she sensed aroma of pussy not her own?)—yes, Lester Lemish, Fred thinks IT WAS YOU who drove him thusly, thus wishing your ending in hell, not for making him a cock sucker, because Fred has come, finally, to quite like that, but for thinking him a coward when in fact it was you who did not give him the image of a Man who could kiss and love and hold someone close, someone to look up to and emulate and be.

Lester Lemish died a couple of years ago today. Algonqua, in a sadness for his memory, had called both of her sons this morning. She spoke to Ben's secretary and Fred's answering machine.

The funeral had been held at the Washington He-

71

brew Congregation. The rabbi, Earl Chesterfield, Oxford-educated, plummy-toned, and a nose job, had not known Lester, and since the Lemish name was not a graven image on the donors' tablets, the services were short.

Ben and Fred had escorted Algonqua down the center aisle. She was in her moment of some sort of triumph, bawling enormous heaving Whats and Whys, wearing the black-and-violet Garfinkel shantung and tulle she'd bought years ago for Fred's Harvard graduation, since altered, who would notice?, as she passed the many friends she'd spent a lifetime being nice to, hoping they would be nice back to her.

Fred, not an easy loser, was enormously, tenaciously gratified that he was not allowing a tidge of remorse to graph his heart. The day was sunny and so evidently was his interior. Thank you, Messrs. Cult, Nerdley, Fallinger & Dridge. The bastard, the prick, the old fat fart has finally fled this earth. Had not Fred waited a good many years for this, his own moment of some sort of peculiar vengeful triumph? Hadn't he wanted it, dreamed of it, fantasized it, since he was three? And could he now not find love at last? For had not one of his new clairvoyants prophesied that love would come "with the death of a white-haired man?"

Lester had requested burial among the war dead at Arlington, not because of any patriotic gesture, or comradeship for any remembered brothers-in-arms, but because, as a veteran of the First World War—the Great War as the English know it—he was entitled to free interment. So in he went, for nothing. Fred, ever ready for a dramatic moment with a dramatic moment, had even fantasized a funeral oration, should anyone ask him to speak, which they did not, that would begin: "I shall now speak ill of the dead."

One of these days he will finally realize: What a wasted life! What fine potential down the tubes!

● ● ●

Dr. Irving Slough had placed the following ad in the *Avocado,* which had been answered by Dinky Adams:

SEARCHING

Lover wanted. White youth under 35, masculine-looking appearance actions tall slim dark hair good body with definition, all wanted by very affluent New York doctor/executive white 50's with houses Fire Island Sutton Place and Greenwich. No strings attached. Your own bank account. Am keenly interested in life and all repeat all its many splendors, including traveling, sports cars, expensive restaurants, fine living, additional items. Young man must be sincere, able to relate to older man, desire Greek home several times a day. If interested, please re-read. Take particular note that youth must be masculine both in looks and behavior and not involved in anything like hairdressing. Answer in detail, with photo essential, to Box 11991 Madison Square Station.

Dr. Irving Slough (pronounced, not as by the British, "sluff") had come to his oldest and dearest friend, Hans Zoroaster, to exchange some niceties for tomorrow's opening of The Toilet Bowl.

Irving, who was from Baltimore, had been born Schlepp, a perfectly good German noun meaning the train of a dress. He was fifty-five, though not feeling it, with the very handsome face and smile and teeth of the young Cary Grant, unfortunately recently co-joined with the expanding body of W. C. Fields, and many promiscuous years of wonderful memories when the Fields part of him had been more Randolph Scott.

Irving enjoyed thinking of himself as a modern Renaissance Man. That he was a doctor his many patients would agree; Irving was expert in attending to many a present-day malaise, from smoking to homosexuality, quite often by hypnosis, though lately he'd heard of effective results from brief periods of incarceration, which he thought he might soon be testing; that his credentials came from rather foreign universities bothered them not. But shrinking was only part of his fame and had come after his initial success as a silent backer of heterosexual fuck films. *Up Your Lazy River* and *My Bare Lady* had subsidized his medical studies; the firm and forceful personality had forged the psychiatric success. And then had come the logical next step: since so many of his satisfied patients were high on corporate ladders, what more sensible act than to form an advertising agency to promote them and their concerns? Hence, Heiserdiener-Thalberg-Slough, now number seven in international billings, and an even richer, fuller life for Irving.

"It's so difficult to know what to wear, Irving," Hans said. They were in the photo-lined ground floor of Han's handsome East 68th Street town house, photos of all the glossily gleaming smiling faces of fifty, count fifty, of America's most handsome young men. And Hans Zoroaster loved all his famous models as if they were his sons. He never ceased looking at them, as he did now, emitting one of his unconscious sighs of prideful paternal pleasure, another fifty-five year-old man, though thin, he'd always kept thin, and immaculately dressed. "The first part of the evening is devoted to the *Women's Wear* crowd and then events will obviously turn into more sturdy and nourishing fare and this, for us, requires two outfits."

"Stop it, Hans." Irving was referring to the sighing. "You have never found love from one of your boys. You only allow them to break your heart. When will you cease your foolishness?"

"Look who is talking! You who put ads in fuck papers! Where is your Dinky and where is his love? Two weeks of trial 'old-fashioned' marriage, an exclusive honeymoon, and then, poof!"

"Yes, Dinky went away," Irving courageously admitted, "but he has just sent me a postcard from Savannah saying he is returning, and he said to me before he left that he likes me and that we have many similar interests and that the sex is good and that on paper we make sense. So I have hope."

"He is twisting your heart, not calling you, disappearing, sticking his thing into you only whenever you order from him another plant or bush."

"He is redoing my terraces and he has great talent for beauty in this area." Irving was not courageously admitting that Dinky had also told him he was additionally seeing a Fred Lemish.

"Do you know that last year four hundred and nineteen of *Fortune* magazine's top five hundred corporations used my boys in their advertising? How is that for market penetration? How is that for bringing beauty to this world? I too bring beauty."

Hans said these words from a flat position, looking upward from the long white Bishop's table, his sheer batiste shirt opened for Irving, who, with a clean, sharp needle, was repiercing for the opening, Hans's pointed right tit.

"You know, I too have my chickens," Irving said, smiling. "I have my Malmouth Chickens, which I have made into the chickens one out of two chicken-eaters eat. I have the Winston Man . . . I also have Necessa Autos, which put Manila on the map as a major automotive exporter, though perhaps a bit slow in spare parts. I have the Monomain Railroad, the Ivascar Home Deodorant Plan, the Pan-Pacific Group of Companies including Marathon Leisure Time, I have Bronstein Bakeries, I have the fashion empire of Dordogna del Dongo . . . Yes, Hans,

I think this will prove a clean repiercing. I have wrought from a tiny nothingness a power which attracts greater powers that would not so many years ago so much as piss on me."

"I would piss on you," Hans said softly, knowing full well that Irving would choose not to hear. So, after a suitable pause, he continued: "Do you remember our first conversation, so many years ago in Frankfort? Krafft-Ebing. With him everything was a case history. 'Case 196: I am an official and as far as I know come from an untainted family.' Dressing up in drag was 'effemination.' When he really wanted to get juicy, he would write in Latin. Remember? I was seventeen before I realized that *immissio penis in os* meant sticking it in the mouth."

"And *immissio penis in anum,* those who practiced that, he called us moral imbeciles and moral depravities, certain barbarous races devoid of morality. I grew up in constant fear!"

"I, too! And there in Essen was my mother effeminating in tailored tweed suits and there was my father with his pet pig. How far we've come!" He had not meant to have his philosophical point end on such an upbeat, so he lowered his register and appended: "To what?"

"Yes, Hans, how far we've come," Irving agreed, once again not electing to pick up on Hans' little pudendum. Instead, he paused in mid-operation and waved his needle in the air. "You must listen to my latest realization. I am writing it up for the *International Journal of Psycho-Sexual Hysteria,* of which, as you know, I am on the Board of Advisors. I shall say that it is my considered heterosexual opinion that every faggot, though I shall not use this word, considers his homosexuality as very special to him, in the sense of sacrosanct, like a pain which he has lived with a very long time. Thus it becomes a sacred pain, and one which is difficult to challenge on the one hand, or

76

to share with another faggot on the other, whose comprehension of exactly the same pain would seem to make him the obvious choice of sharer, helpmate, lover, but which, in fact, makes him just the opposite: makes him a combatant in the same arena, fighting to see who is the victor over the same spoils—these spoils being the same Pandora's Box of pain."

He finished with a flourish, a descending splurge with his needle, a bravura sweeping gesture not dissimilar to the final sew-up on one of his eviscerated Malmouth Chickens before a pop into the oven, and indicated to Hans that he could now button up his shirt and rise. He knew, too, that Hans would look up at him now with gratitude, with worshipful eyes, admiring not only his skill, but also his knowledge and perception. How important it was to have a good audience!

Hans, as he had been doing uninterruptedly for thirty-five years, ever since their meeting in that German gay bar, both young soldiers, Hans not knowing Irving to be an American spy, so long ago, what difference had any of that warfare meant for today?, tried again: "If you were to allow me, I would give you a little pain." But then, as he sat up, and dangled his feet to the floor, and stood, and as if, at last, the show might soon be over, he looked at his cherished friend and asked: "Please to tell me truly about your two-week marriage." He was almost sad that it had not worked out for Irving, just as it had not worked out for Hans.

Irving answered, looking into space, as if Hans were not present, which in fact, for Irving, he was not. "It was, for me, wonderful. Even though it was most unsatisfying. Dinky is frightened, with which he refuses to agree with me. If you arouse him slowly, he will fuck, though not the three times a day I advertised for. It is no doubt much

77

easier for him to have sex with strangers. But I find I am in love with him. He is very dear and touching."

"Wonderful! Dear and touching! You are not getting even a little heinie!"

"I know. I know."

"You are a psychiatrist! You should know better!"

"You are right. You are right. I ought to know better. He is driving me crazy. But he is the first person to come along in many moons to press my buttons. My youth, which was also so wonderful, so promiscuous, so 57 varieties of fun, was also . . . a few years ago. It will be me! Dinky exudes this to me! I believe this!"

Hans said softly: "Irving, our time is running out." Each time he heard of another Dinky, Hans felt himself slipping further and further away from a co-starring role, even a supporting player's, in Irving's, and his own, aging saga.

Irving, thinking of Dinky, thinking of no Dinky, thinking suddenly of two old men in a limed-oak paneled library, surrounded by a wall of beauties, both with much money in the bank, and little else, for once admitted agreement. "Yes, Hans, it is," he quietly answered.

"Perhaps this is a start," Hans said, kissing his dear friend on the cheek; he would have made the mouth but Irving parried. "Perhaps just this admission is a start. Come, we shall go upstairs and I will show you some new items."

As they climbed the stairs of the town house, up to the top of the aerie, Hans, trying to lighten the atmosphere, waved ephemerally toward the skylight and asked one of his rhetorical questions: "Do you think that boys all over the world are wondering if somewhere out there there is a group of intelligent, like-minded individuals, devoting ourselves to stimulating pursuits, and if they could only find us, we would be the perfect future . . . ?"

Irving, not in as good shape as Hans, heaving himself upward as best his bulk would allow, schlepping, no, mustn't use that word, dragging, no, that is not the right word either, huffing himself up the four flights, and a non-smoker, too, replied: "They do. And they, too, will use hope to blanket disappointment. I have told you many times that we are no different from other people, who are base and self-centered and greedy. And hopeful." Yes. And hopeful.

"The voice of the true psychiatrist!"

"No, the voice of the successful advertising man."

They reached the top where Hans opened his private preserve, a double-doored closet that housed his leather and accoutrements and sex toys and incunabula.

"Irving, please to take some of these new chains. I bought them thinking of you."

"No, Hans, only the leather executioner's mask." He pulled it down from its shelf, from among the full battalion of items for all extreme occasions. He was now feeling better. Those recollections of earlier days of triumph had perked him up. Why should it be any different now? He was still the same Irving. His mind, which had always been his strong point, was still the same Irving's. And one of these days he would introduce Dinky to leather, and take him to the Marquis de Suede and let him choose anything he desired, and they would then go to his secret hideaway fuck-nest in Tudor City with the terra-cotta floors and have a wonderful night of scenes. Just the thought and anticipation made him throw off another realization. Perhaps he would use this, too, for the *Hysteria*. 'What we have invented, Hans, is a new religion. Oh, not the moralistic and old-fashioned theological kind with that God who does not want us, but one with brutal splendors, magnificent contemporary rites and rituals, scenes, gestures, sacrifices, humiliations, terrors, tremblings, mortifications, degradations, phantasmagoric transfigurations into other realms of feeling, new realizations that will come from this cleansing purge, and then transcendencies unto a New World of our own making, with our own new rules and rewards and justifications." No, perhaps this was not for the *Hysteria*.

Hans listened. He had heard it before. He had once believed it. Now, again, he did not respond with adulation. "This is only because we wait too long. This is only because we become too old. So we make up some new religion to excite us and get up our things. We should have been lovers years ago, my friend. We could have worked it out."

Irving coldly returned from his fantasies to reply: "I am not too old. I do not feel old."

Since there was a sinister finality to his icy tone, Hans only shrugged and pressed no further.

And Irving decided that now was the moment: "Hans, I must tell you, and I am sorry to bring to you, my old friend, such news, but we must now commence a search for a new Winston Man. Winnie Heinz, he is too old."

"What! My biggest star! My reigning beauty! What are you doing to him? He is not even forty!"

"You must realize it is not me. It is the client."

"Ah, yes, it is always the client."

"A younger image is desired. We must find a new model."

So Hans packaged Irving's leather borrowing in a Bergdorf's box, lest a doorman be suspicious, and he handed it over silently, and silently as well they descended, down the many stairs, no ephemeral questions going down, until, at the bottom, at the front door, out of old habit, they kissed each other, as do the Europeans, on both cheeks.

"Good-bye, Hans, I shall pick you up tomorrow for The Toilet Bowl."

Anthony Montano stepped out of his cab at Sheridan Square and faced the gauntlet of Christopher Street, over-run this late afternoon with thousands, bodies on the prowl, pieces of meat, exhibitionists all, things, faceless faces, all in uniform, what am I doing here?, Gatsby was right: "Nothing has changed since the Tenth Floor, the music hasn't changed, the look hasn't changed, drugs haven't changed, and bodies haven't changed." Everyone's been to the gym. Even the uglies have muscles. If I wanted to be rich, I'd be in the gym business. I can't compete with this. My forty-three-year-old body won't muscle up like that. I'm out of it. I worked four hundred hours last week, in fucking bondage to cigarettes and Irving Slough. Poor gorgeous Winnie. I hope I don't have to break the news. One hundred and fifty thousand dollars a year, Poppa. Are you proud of your Anthony yet? "Hello, there!" Haven't seen that one in years. He got fat. Now who is that one? And over there? Jesus, the Sisterhood walks the streets. World hates faggots. *Want my cock sucked.* Frigger said to hit the docks. I must be out of my mind. Häagen Dazs up to a buck a cone at the pot-bellied gouger's. Milk the faggots dry. Must write to Mimi Shera-ton. Only one protecting us from what we're putting in our mouths. I'm in love with Mimi Sheraton. Would she marry me? Oi. What have I done with my life? Who wants to be in this? Boring me. Boring Sprinkle. I am going to die. Without ever having lived in Hollywood. I should have been the reigning wit of Hollywood. I'm funny. I would have brought back madcap comedy. Great career wasted. Thrown away. Mary Tyler Moore needed me.

She's gone now, too. I'll compose an Ode to These Streets...

Ah, the streets, the Streets, *the streets*, let us pause for an Ode to The Streets, Gay Ghetto, homo away from home, the hierarchy and ritual of The Streets, incessant, insinuating, impossible *Streets*, addictive, the herb superb, can't keep away from you, always drawn to you, STREETS, speak of them singularly in the plural, like Sheep, Kleenex, Jell-o, blending, coalescing, oozing, all into one, all for us, how dramatic, how important, how depressing, fucking loneliness of walking alone and looking, displaying, on the streets—where so much time is spent, summer and winter, cold and HOT, You Can't Go Home Again, anyway you can't go home, who wants to go home, no cock suckers at home, dreary home, how many nights, hours, days, weeks, months, years, who's counting, do these fellows, not me!, walk The Streets: Christopher Washington Greenwich Hudson West and Sheridan Square, such a parade, *everyone dressed alike!*, Hitler could recruit right here, the Gay White Way, Black, too, and Spanish, French, German, Italian, for Christ's sake, Icelandic, those firemen really visit, every guidebook advises Hit Those Streets!, Mary, Show Them Pecs, Strut Them Buns, Pad That Crotch, Visit Them Bars: Keller's, Ty's, Cell Block, Ramrod, Stud, International, Peter Rabbit, Bunkhouse, Rawhide, Badlands, Tulip's, Boots and Saddle, Cynthia's, Tubie's, Mine Shaft, Glory Hole, Pits, Anvil, Cock Ring, tomorrow night the new one: THE TOILET BOWL, *oi!* ...

Anthony then hitched up his Levi's, which carried the wonderful nine inches of his cock, coiled and ready, recollected that the Pope, God bless Her, had just come out, yet again, against the faggots, "indecorous and sacrilegious," who could blame Him, Toilet Bowl indeed!, wished his best friend, Fred, were with him to throw down these gauntlets together, pocketed the small Oxford volume of *Classic British Short Stories* he had thought might be useful in luring a fellow of like-minded intelligence, wondered, again, why he was having so much difficulty getting it up of late, was this his Change of Life?, must come from working too hard, don't like doing this trip, but have to do it, got to get it off, medical emergency, psychiatric one, too, and plunged across the highway toward the River. Somewhere, over there, in that big former shipping palace, must be a savior to put a poor man out of his misery and in some nook or cranny suck my cock.

In a handsome apartment of English and French antiques, deftly combined with American Ward Bennett, on East 66th Street, between Madison and Park, lives the Winston Man. Yes, Virginia, there is a Winston Man.

It is unfortunate that his personality is so submerged in this nefarious product, but the fact remains that to his friends and to his fellow models at the Hans Zoroaster Agency he is known, not by his given name, which is Duncan Heinz (his father is a very distant and almost as rich cousin to the pickle-soup-ketchup family, though devoted not to foodstuffs in his own financial empire but to the manufacture of rubber goods for home and farm, more specifically, though naturally the family does not spread this about, the production of items of "prophylaxis" for the conduct of sexual intercourse, their Model B-12 widely used in animal husbandry, particularly suited for well-endowed bulls), but as Winnie.

Winnie's is the true beauty of our moment in time, the face that, years from now, when we remember, and we shall remember, will be looked back upon as representing our era. His glacially green eyes, his perfect classical nose, his hay hair, his skin of an overall perfection that could sell cream to cows or butter to Danes, all represent today's desirability and have served to make him not only America's highest-paid male model but also the ideal god every faggot looks up to as what he'd choose to look like if he could choose to look like anyone.

Winnie's Philadelphia Main Line background was evident in the tweed and flannel, button-downed and Shetlanded aura he had maintained ever since being expelled from the University of Virginia for a disinclination to read. He still looked thirty, claimed to forty, and still didn't have to work, his father's "health products" fortune more than ample to provide for him. But a Master of Winnie's at the Hill School in Pottstown had encouraged in him a lifelong desire to go his own way, be his own man, when he had taken the then thirteen-year-old lad aside after a particularly clumsy dropping of a right-field fly and told him point-blank that he was going to be a fairy when he grew up.

Winnie, or more correctly, Dunnie, as he was then called, didn't know what a fairy was, such being the insularity of Main Line education even then. So calmly, that same night, with that quest for curiosity, that vigor for knowledge which deserted him at some point between Hill and U. Va., he asked one of his classmates, a cute Jewish scholarship student from Shreveport named Sammy Rosen, whom Dunnie had been spending a lot of time with because Sammy was well-versed and hence helpful in time of test and trial, and as luck would have it, Sammy knew, as Dunnie knew he would. Sammy also shivered as he dispensed the knowledge, so both of them realized, at precisely this moment in time, that they were about to learn even more comprehensively what a fairy was.

"Want to come to my room and have some of my Mama's brownies?" Sammy began haltingly.

It was as simple as that.

"What will you do when you finish college?" Sammy asked, trying to keep the conversation light, even though he'd been wet dreaming for several months about such an opportunity as was obviously now creeping up on both of them, as they sat on his bed munching away at Mrs. Rosen's brown squares and waiting for whatever was going to happen to happen.

"I think I'm very handsome," Dunnie said quite matter-of-factly, in response to the question. Was this not a Future Great Model in embryo even then? "Don't you?"

". . . Yes . . .," Sammy replied, wondering what one thing had to do with another.

"I wish to do something that will allow the world to appreciate my handsomeness."

"Oh. Like be a movie star?"

"Heavens, no. I don't want to have to talk. I just want to be seen." And to illustrate his point, he cast a long look at himself in Sammy's bureau mirror, which was tilted just his way. "And, of course, to be talked about. And worshipped and adored."

"Oh."

"I guess that means I have to be a famous model, though even that's less than perfect. I really don't want to be associated with any product. But I guess that can't be helped. But I'll see to it that my picture is large and no one will pay any attention to whatever it is I'm selling."

This news hung in the air for moments as the two boys—like cute animals in Walt Disney cartoons, which, when confronted with anything intractable, simply engorge it whole—stuffed huge brownies into their mouths. Dunnie was pleased that his future was clear and Sammy was impressed with such direction.

Then Dunnie prophesied again: "I'll tell you something else. I don't want to get married. Ever."

"How do you know that?"

"I know it. My parents are married, so I just know it."

"I . . . I know it, too." Sammy continued to marvel at such common sense. Then he recollected the fairy business and asked: "Do you . . . do you look at me in the showers as much as I look at you?"

"Yes. I do." And Dunnie, again giving himself the look of the loved in that tilted mirror, further said: "I think sometimes we're lucky to know certain things early, like being shown what's in the crystal ball at the beginning of your life instead of at the end. I know I want to be looked at by everybody and to pass around my beauty . . .," at this point he took Sammy's damp hand and used it to make his further illustrative point, ". . . and have everybody touching me all over and letting me do the same to them and . . . maybe we better not tell anybody about this . . ."

Poor Sammy. He was not only on scholarship but was also getting very excited. His schoolmate, between reaching for the maternal brownies, was massaging his penis, now bulging mightily within Sammy's only pair of gray-flannel trousers, which he had begged his mother and father to buy for him on the trip to Philadelphia at the start of term and he had summoned up all his courage to ask for them and to say that every boy in class had at least one pair except him and his dad had mumbled something about how the fucking scholarship Sammy had should include a gray-flannel-pants allowance but had bought them for the boy anyway and Sammy had never been able to wear them without a slight tinge of guilt and if Dunnie rubbed him anymore he might explode white stuff all over the gray and then he'd have to throw the pants away.

"Please, Dunnie, could I . . . please . . . take off my gray flannels?"

And that of course had been the beginning of the end, or of the beginning. It was only seconds before both boys were completely naked and opening themselves to the joys and conflicts redolent in this early tender moment of exploring themselves in the boay of another, holding on to each other's dickies as if they were holding on to their own. It was as if each were rather hungry from some already precocious deprivation now being at last fulfilled, their little hands grabbing their little things, Dunnie even returning kisses and not worrying that the lips, too, were Jewish. Unfortunately, Sammy could not contain his involuntary reflexes for too long and his little load of white stuff melded not with the gray flannels from the Brothers Brooks but with the brownies from the Mother Rosen. It came so suddenly, the spurt of liquid, that he looked down upon himself as it quivered out, then just sat there studying the improbable combination of semen and chocolate.

Dunnie was also looking at the brownies rather strangely. Suddenly he smiled, and finished himself off with his own hand, directing his own whipped cream to make the dessert before them even classier. Sammy then watched him pick up a creamed-upon square and eat it. But Dunnie, as he ate, did not look at what he was eating. He looked at Sammy. And without saying a word, he held another brownie a la mode in front of Sammy's mouth and Sammy opened his mouth and ate it, too.

With such sweetness did both lads gain their practical introduction into what a fairy was.

It was at this moment, too, that Duncan Heinz IV learned that he could use his body to get anybody to do anything for him that he wanted. To please him. To test

87

his new insight he reached down and pulled up Sammy's dirty white sneakers. "Put these on," he said.

Sammy, as if hypnotized, did so.

"Walk all over me." Dunnie said the first thing that came into his head.

Sammy got up on the sagging mattress and walked all over Dunnie as best he could, finally falling helplessly into his classmate's arms. Then they held each other close, felt each other's soft (both mothers had raised Ivory babies), teen-aged skin, and fell asleep.

This shoe experience stimulated in Dunnie a life-long fascination with items for the feet. Winnie now has a full wardrobe of shoes and boots and loafers and rubbers and galoshes and waders and sneakers, high-top and low, for police and army and infantry and paratroopers and navy and fishermen and cowboys and chefs and stevedores and linemen, garbage collectors, Indians, postmen, wardens, tractor operators, loggers, engineers, so many refinements within a major category! He also has them in assorted sizes. One never knew. And not only did he seek for sex with young boys, but he also much preferred young Jewish boys. If he couldn't get a former, he'd settle for a latter, even an older Jew. For, after all, wasn't his father one of America's leading anti-Semites?

He is now, as we have discovered, the Winston Man. The true symbol of America's masculinity, at two hundred thousand dollars per symbolic year. There he poses, Winnie does, in front of all America, nay, the World, on billboards and in magazines and newspapers, from Albuquerque to Auckland, and from Zanzibar to Zaire, which come to think of it is not all that far, in his washed-out denim shirt, daringly opened one button too many, staring straight out at you, honest, direct, green-eyed, wonderfully virile, in that confrontation which Hans and Irving, Anthony, Troy Mommser, all such good and supportive

88

friends and helpmates, fellow toilers in the tobacco fields, have helped him to refine and make profitable, and which has made him into the man whom millions of women consciously and as many men unconsciously inhale as they inhale.

He is, of course, worshipped and adored by his brothers. He is looked at, pointed to, touched, walked near, on streets, in bars and baths and discos, in stores, in crowds, at the Gay Synagogue, wherever our crowd gathers, by his brother faggots. "He is the most beautiful man we have ever given birth to," Blaze Sorority wrote in his *Avocado* column. "He is divine, divine, devoon!," the Divine Bella wrote in *Women's Wear*, continuing with: "Long Reign King Winnie!"

King Winnie, twenty-five odd years later, still looking in the mirror, albeit now one of Regency ormolu, studied his lines and thought perhaps he needed a nap before tonight's orgy at Garfield's.

Dare I enter this building? Anthony stopped to light his first joint. Do I really want to get laid in an abandoned warehouse? What will they think of me at the office? The Great Creative Leader in this kind of a scene? I disapprove of this place. I disapprove! It is mindless and destructive and ugly and I have always tried to live my life in a special and discreet way. And what about the danger! The rip-off while being sucked by the ambidexterously adept. And the Ultimate Danger! De-cockization! *Oi*. Go home, Anthony. Read an important book on the British Empire. *I want to get laid. Get it off. I need to come.* ok, ok, NONONO, go home, kill yourself, get out of the Ghetto, My Life in the Warsaw Ghetto starring Sister Mary Montano in Carcere, why doesn't Sprinkle come back?, why am I, a forty-three-year-old grown man, involved with a twenty-three-year-old who loves not only me but twenty other guys as well? Plus a few girls. He does it with ladies. I can't do it with ladies. Are they learning something in school today that I didn't learn? Fred hates him. Fred wrote me: "I note that Sprinkle's thinking has recently been guided by the mystic calculations of a former used-car salesman and convicted thief whose philosophy is propagated via a nationwide chain of assemblages, much like Dunkin' Donuts." Gain a lover, lose a friend. And what has Fred got that's any better? A lover who's disappeared!

Frigger crawled out through the small doorway and stretched his rocky body in pleasure. He was wearing his cruising outfit, clipped-off T-shirt and one half inch of visible Jockey short revealed above his jeans. While he made his living decorating the homes of movie stars in California, he came East occasionally to do the odd p.r. job, thus allowing himself to claim Bi-Coastialty, AC-PC, and to stay at the 63rd Street Y where there were so many cocks to suck.

"Would you believe ten inches and he's still in high school?" Frigger said, wiping his mouth, his cruising wardrobe evidently having proven most alluring.

"What's the rest of him look like?" Anthony asked.

"Nice. He'll go to the gym soon. He wants to be a trampolinist. He's going to go places."

"Yeah. Down the sewers."

"Want me to come in there and hold your hand?"

"Sure."

"Want me to come in there and suck your cock?"

"Of course not. You're a friend. You're family."

"So what. You've got a big cock."

"How do you know?"

"Important news travels."

"You're insatiable. How many times have you done it today?"

"Six. Seven. Ten. Who knows. It's still early. I do it till my mouth feels like putty I've still got some feeling left. Where's Fred? Still waiting for Dinky?"

"Yeah. He won't listen to me. Not even a call or a postcard."

"I fixed them up. I thought their neuroses would mesh. They both talk about love. Dinky was after me and when I rejected him he went off with Laverne. Though we continued to fuck secretly, of course. I think I'll hit The Pits and grab a beer. See you."

Anthony watched as Frigger crossed the highway. Then he turned toward the building. Why am I still hesitating? He lit his second joint.

Randy Dildough stood in his thirtieth-floor suite in the Pierre Tower and looked downtown toward his thirtieth-floor office in the Pan-Pacific Tower and thought that it would be wonderful and fitting if he could walk from there to here. If a Jesus walked on the water, couldn't a Dildough fly through the air?

Randy did not think his last name an unsatisfactory one—combining as it did allusions to the American Big Three: sex, money, and food—because Randy tried not to think that anything about his fine self was less than perfection. And with such positive thinking, Randy has risen to the top, president of Marathon Leisure Time, part of the Pan-Pacific family of companies, headed by Myron Musselman, and at only thirty years old!, a true feat, to achieve control of a major American supplier of entertainment at such a young age, no doubt reflected in his constant yclepture by the nation's press as the Kennedy of Leisure Time.

He is attractive, his trim, compact, streamlined strawberry-blond-headed body sporting the snappiest of custom suits, shirts, ties, shoes, manicures, to which totality is added an exuding of strong sexuality, as so many men of power so exude, together with his dandified love for the dazzling, insolently manifested in his rabid acquisition of the latest in chauffeurs, Malibu houses, electronic wizardies, posturings, rare flowers, the company of only the greatest stars, the biggest deals, and his secret cavortings in the dens and vicepots and cesspools of the underground faggot world.

Pause to reflect on this. The head of one of America's major Stock Exchanged companies is a faggot. No mean feat, again, this.

He loves living on that dangerous razor's edge. On the one side, he satisfies his need to constantly glitter, dazzle all of his audience, baffle all of his victims, and look down from Up There on everything down here, as he continues building his empire by destruction of the enemy, humiliation of his rivals, in so doing becoming, in the grand tradition of his country, The Big Man, The Hero, silhouetted against the landscape as etched by Forbes.

And, on the other, stands the Dreaded Secret, which he knows could fell his growing redwood.

Such conflict, particularly in anyone who's horny, would, needless to say, streak a blow dry with a certain frost of confusion. Who could ask for anything more?

So, while it will not be the custom to present case histories for all of our faggots, let's tarry a moment on this particularly unusual one.

Cunard Rancé Evin Dildough was born thirty years ago in Stockton, California, of two fine Americans, Yvonne and Ralph Dildough. The name was Dutch-German-French-English and, as the family had distinguished branches in each of these fine countries, Ralph's father had been reluctant to change it when he emigrated to America and discovered shortly thereafter that an instrument of the same pronunciation, if different usage, was making the rounds. Ralph owned extensive and fertile farm acreage that prospered with grapes and asparagus, and he had loved his only child very much. Yvonne, too, was a diligent teacher and a watchful and loving mother to her growing boy. Both parents were deeply religious, well-read, well-educated, well-versed in Gesell, Ilg, and Spock, and were most supportive and constructively critical throughout all of Randy's formative years. He had, in fact, the perfect American upbringing.

Stander F. Lure, in his classic study of homosexuality, *The Perversion of Mount Ararat* (which takes as its text the Biblical maxim: ". . . and the sons of Sennacherib shall rise up and smoot the father of his own thing . . ."), has this to say: "There are certain instances when perversion develops from no known cause—where parental figures have been accepted and where roles have not been confused, where, in fact, there is no reason at all obvious why the offspring should have emerged warped and abnormal. When this occurs, one must look for other, perhaps deeper and less obvious causes: incredible boredom in the home, for instance, or the desire of the child to be different if only because his parents appear so perfect, or, as a possibility, and please bear in mind that I offer this only as a possibility, where the child is just plainly a wayward, restless wind."

Randy lay dormant and did nothing abnormal until the age of fifteen, at which time he had his first experience with sadism. Like so many things in life, it was unexpected and unplanned. It happened like this:

The ninth-grade class, of which Randy was a member, was preparing a play of its own devising about the discovery of gold at Sutter's Mill. The woodworking class had dismantled part of the stage floor, in order to facilitate the building of a mock river bed, in which Nancellen Richtofen, portraying Mrs. Betsy Ross, the first woman to discover sparkling sands in the river's stream (the children were allowed to mold history as they saw fit in this early landmark attempt at psychodrama) would wade, only half of her pencil-thin body visible to the audience, the other half standing on a newly constructed platform built several feet below the level of the stage floor. Nancellen, being a tall girl, already six feet at fifteen years (useful for a Bendel's model later but a pain in the heart now), it was decided by Mr. Petronius of Woodworking II to make the lower portion about seven feet long, the length of a good coffin, he mused to himself, half in jest and half in wish fulfillment, because, if you asked him, the whole play was a fucking waste of time, tearing up a stage just so a string-bean girl could proclaim: "Oh, sparkling sands, what doth I witness neath your trickle?," and dangerous, too, in case she, or anyone else for that matter, should fall forward, either by tripping or being pushed by one of the many playful lads who might be overdoing the admonitions of Mr. Proctor, the director and history teacher, to "Be boisterous, boys, remember you are rough and tough, the sort who made this country Great!"

Randy's role in this pageant was to wear an enormous black cape and, in the person of Lord Baltimore, come from England to survey "the scene" in California before going off to Maryland to stake his claim, wave it about with furious rippling sounds and sinister motions, rather like Dracula, so that Nancellen and three boys several feet her juniors, each equipped with a mock rifle, would be mightily frightened and one of the boys would yell "Fire at the Stranger," and the three boys would fire at Lord

Baltimore, killing him, thus causing America's entry into the Boer War.

Worried that he might fall into the pit if he did not rehearse his cape maneuvers, Randy decided to go to the auditorium after school to do just that. Approaching the stage, he heard gurgling sounds from the mock river bed, and stealing up behind the small-scale version of Sutter's Mill itself, complete with posters proclaiming "Wonder Bread is made here from our fine flour," he peered down on the fucking figures of Nancellen Richtofen and fat Hattie Illcit. Joining them together was the first two-headed dildo that Randy had ever seen, perhaps one of the first to reach Stockton, certainly the first to be used by two fifteen-year-old girls on the premises of its junior-senior high school auditorium. Back and forth the two girls slid, up and down, top to bottom, tipsy ho and a bottle of rum, slithering with mounting enthusiasm and completely unaware that Randy gazed down upon them and his namesake with a growing interest and finger-pinched nose, perhaps because Hattie was a girl known around town for not being big on Johnson's Baby Powder. As the dildoettes came closer and closer to fruition, Randy, in one of those first seizures the inspiration for which he was never able to pinpoint, grabbed hammer, nails, several boards of original stage planking, all courteously left available in a sloppy pile by Mr. Petronius' boys from Woodworking II, and set to work sledging in time to the grunts and growls from below. By the time orgasm was reached—the young ladies miraculously attaining it simultaneously—darkness had overcome them, along with a drop in oxygen.

"Was it that dark in here the last time we done it," Hattie inquired, "or is it just because I might of landed my face in your cooze?"

95

Both girls then reached up and found the truth: not only were they boarded in but someone had obviously been witness to their actions.

Randy, standing on top of them, felt a surge of power zitz through him. In the dark protection of the auditorium and his Baltimore cape, with two coiled females only inches beneath his feet, completely in his power and ignorant of the invisible force that held them captive, only this shadow knew, the True Dildough, with great pleasure and tremendous gutsy motions, yanked his full-grown penis to a gigantically pleasurable orgasm. The spurts of his semen, like some fire hose uncoiled into action, lobbed into the air and scored a direct hit on the Wonder Bread sign. He stood there for a moment, afterward, feeling wonder-ful himself, feeling completely his own man; he then replaced his penis neatly inside his Montgomery Ward corduroys and went home, stopping, courteously, on the way, to place an anonymous call to the police, informing them that two girls were caught fucking with each other under the school stage and an old man had sealed them in. The girls were duly rescued but, unable to dispose of the enormous dildo, they were both expelled. (Hattie married the town plumber and Nancellen, her six-foot form soon filled out in more pleasing proportions, went East to Miss Porter's, Vassar, New York, our story, and full-time devotion to the Sapphic code.)

Innately, at this juncture, Randy sensed that he was on the royal road to self-knowledge. Little did he know that the pattern, like a quivering Royal-pudding-mold left longer in the icebox, was now being set. The reflexes were being conditioned. World beware! He had enjoyed himself, God knows; but once you've enjoyed the thrill of jerking off over two bodies you've buried alive at fifteen, what can you do for kicks at sixteen? And wouldn't you be completely worn out, exhausted, bereft of both ideas and energy by the time you were fifty? To hell with fifty; what about thirty?

Well, our lad was now only sixteen and one day he decided to crucify a saint. There was a saint in his high-school class, recently moved here from Salt Lake City, one Robbie Swindon, who never had a bad word to say about anyone and who always had a smile and a word of positive thinking for each (we all know the type), in addition to which he was not only good-looking, the president of his class, and liked by all the girls, and boys, too (we all know the type), but his private parts, which Randy had witnessed in the ever-popular gym period, brought out a strange sensation in Randy's mouth which made him want to know that type, too. He could not put his finger on it exactly, but he instinctively knew that he wanted to take that saintly penis in his mouth and suck it. He had never done such a thing before and he had not had it done to him, nor had he read about it or heard about it in the casual banterings pubescents so often enjoy during their periods of Open Play. All he knew was that he was going to somehow capture young Robbie and suck that thing.

As fate would have it, events played into young Randy's hands or, if you will, mouth. Once again the auditorium and a pageant would prove useful. This time, Easter, with its ever-stirring panoply, its mythology made tangible, its "Christ the Lord is Risen Today, Allelujah," would turn the trick. When it came to playing Jesus, there of course was no one in the entire school to hold a votive candle to young Robbie. There he stood, or rather, hung, that beautiful lithe body, clad only in cut-down Fruit of the Looms, leaning against the old rugged cross, reincarnated from Sutter's Mill leftovers, his palms

97

and shoulders and feet rubbed black and red with burnt cork and Tangee lipstick, his still hairless armpits circled to the wood with thick white rope, his eyes thrown agonizingly heavenward. Yes, he was nigh unto perfectly cast, and watching him, Randy almost came in his own pants. How to get that dick in his mouth? How to do it?

He elected outrageous tactics. When the stage lights dimmed, then expired completely on the tableau of lone figure up on Old Rugged, Randy disconnected and pocketed several prime fuses from the backstage main electrical complex, then stealthily made his way on padded feet (in this pageant he was more happily cast as a Roman centurion, his body only lightly encumbered with his briefs and crosshatched strappings, his already erect penis easily available for exit through a distinctly non-Roman conjunction of royal purple sash and Y-front Jockey's) to the center of the stage where Robbie hung crucified.

"Who's that?" Robbie whispered, hearing footsteps nearing him and wondering why the stage lights had not retwinkled in the East when the curtain had closed, as they'd rehearsed it.

He received no reply. He did however feel a heavenly wet sensation in his genital area and, being a good Mormon, wondered if perhaps something in the nature of a quasi-religious experience might be transpiring, much akin to a Catholic's stigmata of the hands. He did not know whether to cry out in puzzlement or prayer. If God were in fact rewarding him in some way for being such a good Jesus, as his Mommy had indicated He might, he decided he'd better recite some passages from a particularly latter-day prayer of Joseph Smith's.

As he mumbled and recited, Randy sucked and slobbered, and Robbie's penis shortly heeded its call to glory. The bigger it got, the more fervent the liturgical incantations, and, at the moment of orgasm, Robbie, for one brief moment, thought he was entering the Kingdom of Heaven. He almost passed out. It was his very first coming. Randy had bagged his first virgin. Swallowing every drop that the young Jesus had given him, Randy then climbed down from Mr. Petronius' three-stepped stairway to paradise and withdrew into the wings. And not a moment too soon!

The auditorium lights went on, the curtain swung open, and there, before a simply riveted audience of nine hundred boys and girls, swung a wan and exhausted Jesus, his panties down around his lipsticked ankles and his dangling (unfortunately uncircumcised and therefore historically miscast) penis dribbling the last few drops of distinctly mortal fluid. Neither Robbie nor his audience knew exactly what was up, or down, though all were beginning to consider that whatever had happened had nothing to do with Easter.

Randy, beside himself with the joy of completion, a task well mastered, stood now in a cubicle in the empty boys' room, wiping his own wet member off with toilet paper. Yes, he'd brought it off. What next?

Let us not toil with his continued exploits in secondary school. Since he began more frequently tarrying with the fellows who hung out at the notorious Casa de Blanca, it was not long before he learned that the male body appeared to be limited in what it could give and receive from another male body. A fuck here and there, a blow job, a jerk-off—: once you've been to the White House, where's left to visit?

With the solution of this problem he was fortunate, as have been so many successful men, in acquiring the services of a mentor. Lance Heather was a true teacher. Randy met the handsome young blond Alan Ladd while they were both on a college student tour of Universal Studios. Despite the effeminacy of his patronymic, Lance was the leader of the Los Angeles organization known as the Defenders of Zeus. This group met twice a week, more often if their bodies recovered, in an abandoned ranch house in Nichols Canyon. There they played not only with ropes and thongs and whips but also with chains and buzzsaws and live snakes. Lance had not been kidding when, on that guided tour, he had promised Randy "many a new kick and thrill."

And so it was while watching one of the members fucking himself by sitting on a stationary twelve-inch rubber dildo while being bound hand and foot, the dildo impaled to a cross, the cross mounted on a stage, and the fellow also sucking the cock of a gentleman clad entirely in chain mail, except of course for his genitals, which were exposed, and enormous, and holding in his hand while mouth-fucking the impaled acolyte, not one but two hissing rattlesnakes, reputed to have been defanged but dripping something from their mouths nevertheless, all of this witnessed by forty-nine other members, each donged with grease, each jerking off either himself or a fellow clubber, in some sort of cockamamie version of the daisy chain, don't Southern Californians have wonderful imaginations, whatever happened to King of the Mountain?, well, perhaps this was King of the Mountain—it was while watching all of this, and of course participating, he couldn't be a spoilsport, that Randy had an epiphany. He began to realize to what lengths it would soon be necessary to travel to receive kicks sufficient to cause erection, and while he was finding these ceremonies reasonably exciting (and certainly a nice time-out from his studies), in that he had a good stiff one on while those two snakes were up there hissing away, he knew he had neither the time nor the abundant imagination to play "Can You Top This?" every time he wanted to get his rocks off.

So and thus, while he was dimly aware that his rejection of Lance Heather, who was mightily enamored of him, was not taken graciously (and might prove bothersome in the chapters of his life to come), Randy knew it was time to reroute his direction, to quit both the Defenders of Zeus and Pepperdine University (a rather rightwing, religious place, on the way to Malibu) and, with an appetite whetted by so much experience in theatricals, to enter show business at last.

His lengendary rise has been amply documented in the annals of business and finance, not to mention the tabloid press. He went from mail room to board room in lickety-split time by a combination of charm, insolence, innuendo, instinct, chutzpa, brains, various chicaneries and good lucks—in other words, your typical American rise to the top, stopping along the way to mingle among these woofs and warps those other typically American threads that have so helped to weave his legend. From the mail room of a major network he sighted and rescued the skids-ing career of a once-famous chanteuse, restoring her quite miraculously to international chirpdom while zinging from her new revenues an over-generous portion of her notes; through this song he met and thoughtfully escorted to premieres a famous actress, only to be shot, in a parking lot, in his groin, by her jealous husband, a major studio's Head; he displaced said Head in said studio's affections, elbowing out as well his own sagging Uncle Darrel; he conveniently married a convenient Lesbian, only to be shot at once again when she turned and took up with a jealous Mafia chieftain; he forged some checks and launched his first successful Number One Nielsen series, *Men At War!*—yes, he'd made it to the top, and the annals of business and finance, not to mention the tabloid press, noted all with grateful thanks. Such good copy! Such a captain of industry! And such a cocksman! (And still a virgin!)

He is of course now friendless. Such power does not allow for true friends. He has smiled rarely, offended many, and wound up King of the Pile. He has made Marathon Leisure Time Number One. He is now the leading purveyor of America's film and television entertainment.

He sits, so high up there, sipping a Kir from a glass of Baccarat, waiting for Abe Bronstein, sooner or later they all come to Dildough, minioning to his feet, taking another sip, musing on his favorite pet project: he would find a new James Dean; another sip, pausing to reflect that his own personally supervised potential blockbuster of *Bronty, The Last Survivor*, the story of a dinosaur from another world who gets into a bit of trouble in this one, was premiering just this very day from coast to coast; another sip, and then an unsettling thought: What do I really want?, followed by: I could be President . . . of Pan-Pacific, certainly . . . but why not my country? . . . I obviously possess qualities others do not, and then the crepuscular realization, mustn't let it in, oh, here it comes!: Why is there such contrast between what I might be and what I continue to be? . . . Why am I not utilizing to the fullest my abilities? . . . Why allow I my inner fantasies to propel me . . . the other way? . . . Why am I not becoming a part of a plot that would change my life, instead of plots about . . . dinosaurs . . . and cocks? . . . Yes, what do I really want? I have everything already, how can I surmount the fates, take bigger and bigger risks, the ones that could set the world and not my rocks atingle and aglow, bigger and bigger crap games, propelling me further and further . . . to . . . where? . . . and what? . . . and . . . whom?

And then . . . the final thought . . . : Do I want . . . can I have . . . am I capable of . . . a friend?

● ● ●

No, I must not do this again either.

On his way to the locker room upstairs, Fred had stopped and had his cock sucked in the basement toilet of his beloved West Side Y.

He had had to pee, and had headed directly for the open urinals, looking straight ahead (always looks straight ahead at open urinals, because they are undoubtedly fronted by disreputable sorts), and he had noticed, by chance only of course, and only out of the corner of his eye, a handsome young man, in tight jeans and body-hugging T-shirt, with welcoming brown eyes under dashing, waving locks of black, fronting the next stall, standing right beside him, this creature for a fantasy, looking with those eyes from under those locks over the partition down upon Fred's cock. Fred could hardly pee.

But could Fred not succumb to The Romantic Spirit?! The boyish open-eye-edness of young Coleridge, the noble nose of thoughtful Wordsworth, the brisk and winning way of wiry Keats, "I have been half in love with easeful Death," no, that's not apt, the innocence and charm of slender, shambling Shelley, "Love, love, infinite in extent, eternal in duration," that's more like it!, the zenithic swagger of dark and moody, Lord-ly Byron, (who hated his mother and whose daddy died most young), (and who felt himself an old man at only twenty-eight!)—all this and these were standing beside him, with a pinch of the Paul Newman's thrown in. Lord Newman was looking at his cock!

And now he was stepping back and waiting for Fred to do the same, waving his thing with his hand and reaching down to take Fred's, then leaning his head close to Fred's so that they could kiss, then reaching round him and holding Fred in a hard, tough, he-man's embrace. Ah, yes, the Romantic Age and Spirit!

Suddenly a third man jumped out from one of the

toilet stalls behind them. Fred jumped, too, but Byron-Wordsworth-Shelley-Coleridge-Keats obviously knew that the newcomer was an old-timer, not much to look at anyway, certainly no threat, with the messy look of a perpetual student, no front runner, who, in any event, sat down at B-W-S-C-K's booted feet, by the urinal's Ubangi lip, and proceeded, from the floor, to suck that bardic cock, Lord Newman now bending over to suck Fred's, at the same time—all at the same time—breaking open a popper and ramming it into Fred's nose so that his orgasm, summoned hastily by the excitement of this Forbidden Moment, now flushing through him (along with further fantasies that it was Dinky's mouth down there around him), all of this and these and them sending him through the roof in a way that no ordinary licit sexual encounter had in recent memory, what a way to begin a workout at the gym!, here it comes, Dinky baby, I'm whooshing a large load right out of me and into you and . . .

Fred stuck his thing back in and rebuttoned his fatigued marines. What had he done? He could have been caught. And arrested. Intelligent human beings do not go around doing it in public johns. With or without a muse. Or do they? Anyway, this one just had. Come on, Fred, admit it felt good. He recollected, from that seminal volume by Trudge & Naster: "The warring conflict in man between the intellect and the libido shall never be twinned." From this he now took comfort.

"Thanks," he mumbled to the kneeling poetaster, who now looked less like a Paul and more like a Herbert or a Harvey, a middle-aged derrick in a young man's rig, who waved So Long, Honey, as he continued to be ministered to by Young Messy Student, who was now the popper's recipient, and walked out, thinking to himself, OK, there's nothing in the world like a good blow job, nothing in the world, particularly a covert one, yes, it felt good, and upstairs he went, to his locker and the early-evening crowd of worker-outers, joggers, lifters, gymnasts, squashers (with naked humpy bodies in the steam room later for dessert), in profusion, goodie, yummy, to smoothly jog his daily three. He'd had the pause that refreshes. Yes, today he'd tried two new things. A golden shower and a tea-room. His investigations were proceeding nicely apace. Progress was being made.

The jogging was followed by the pumping of iron, unh, phew, fush, straining, another rippling muscle for Dinky, my definition increaseth every day, two hours a day's more than I ever spent with any shrink, uhn, umk, add another bench press, pucker out those tits for him to pinch and suck, leg raise for the stomach's smile of beauty, arm curl, want my arms as big as his, unhh, yunk, rretch, no gain without pain, fewh, plutz, nunh, Dinky where the fuck are you? I'm waiting impatiently. Uhnh. Phew. Zlink. I'm ready for love.

At precisely this moment when Boo Boo Bronstein is considering being kidnapped, a handsome young stranger arrives on our scene. The good Lord giveth one just when He considereth a taking away. Ecology liveth.

At 7:03 P.M. of this Friday Memorial Day weekend, Timmy Purvis arrived at Port Authority Bus Terminal on Continental Trailways 101 from Mt. Rainier, Maryland. He walked in, looking at the signs: Authority, Asbury Park, Adirondack, Amber Lantern—everything began with A. A new beginning.

Timmy had come to New York to have fun. He was sixteen years old and he knew that what he had been having in Mt. Rainier, Maryland, had not been fun. Though it was considered to be a suburb of Washington,

D.C., it was as far away from that metropolis as the poor are from the rich. Timmy's folks were poor, but of course noble and upright, and for Timmy—a perceptive one for sixteen, but then so many things are starting younger these days—dowdy, dull, and just not on the same vibrating wavelength. He knew this when he would look at his Ma's big cow brown eyes or his Dad's lined and honest face and he would say to himself: Who are these people, I don't want to be like these people, I don't want to be like anybody in Mt. Rainier, Maryland, ever, ever, ever. Imagine complaining about the price of food and getting up at 6:30 every morning to go to work.

Thus, a departure was in order and the sooner the better. He just up and did it, with a sense of direction, spirit, and commitment that would do any organism proud. He left them a note: "Dear Mr. and Mrs. Purvis, I am now sixteen years old and desire to be my own man. I shall continue my education in the World. Please don't hurt and please don't look for me. I don't want to come back. Good-bye and fond remembrances, Timothy Peter Purvis."

And to New York he came, without giving his past, his Ma, his Pa, a second thought. He briefly considered changing his last name, to make the break more irrevocable, the return impossible, but he decided not to for the moment. Later perhaps. Or perhaps he might want to change his first name instead. Major alterations could wait. And whatever happened, it could only be an improvement on Mt. Rainier.

Timmy arrived in New York a virgin, again not such an unusual statistic these days, though from television and movies he knew all about sex and all the possibilities available to him, divisions and subdivisions, paragraphs and headings and fine print. At this moment he was unconcerned about the totality, or which clause he might elect. He did know one thing: he knew he was exceptionally attractive. People would look at him on the street and continue looking, even when bumping into someone. Sometimes these lookers were women, but he noticed that he liked it more when they were men. He hadn't learned yet to use this to his advantage, though he had premonitions he was walking around with a useful tool.

He was five feet ten inches tall, with dark-brown hair and that open handsomeness which formerly was called "Arrow Shirt" but is now called, for some reason, "all-American," and then only by the halt or lame. His skin was that deep white which tans nicely and is associated with health, vigor, keeping regular, drinking milk, chewing Wrigley's, using Colgate, and walking in Keds. At this point he had been trained for little but bodily functions. What will he learn in this biggest of our big cities? Will such beauty as walks by the name of Timothy Peter Purvis grow up to be as profitably adept with his physicality as the Winston Man, and as internationally sexually desirable as Winnie, the young Paul McCartney, or the late James Dean?

He walked through the terminal, through the arcade, through the waiting room, and toward the john, for he, too, had to pee.

"Jesus," Durwood said to Paulie. "Look at that number."

"He's going to the john."

"We better follow him."

The Port Authority was being tended to this evening by Durwood and Paulie, talent scouts for R. Allan Pooker, pornography man and head of Stud Studios.

Yootha Truth and Miss Rollarette were there as well, Yootha clutching his ratty fur coat to his thin black body as if it were December, which, for Yootha, who has not eaten in several days, it was. Miss Rollarette, in tatty white organdy dress, a flat-topped granny hat with waving poppy, and his Tinkertoy magic wand, was resting his roller-skate-clad feet from the long run uptown from Pier 48, on the Hudson at Christopher Street, where he had been visiting with the boys, waving wisdom, and watching a few blow jobs in the late afternoon waterfront's light.

"Miss Fairy Godmother," Yootha looked over to Rolla, "I would do anything for one dollar ninety-eight."

"You're too skinny, dear. Blacks are now acceptable as sex partners but your competition grows fiercer as your people push themselves into uppity mobility. You must get your act together."

"Honey, fuck off. To get my act together, I need bread. Both kinds. I need clothes and I need exercising at the gymnasium of my choice. Also, I can no longer steal foodstuffs from the A & P. They know my ravaged face."

"Your problem is one which faces many of our boys. Would that the social-service organization I plan to establish when my fairy comes in were already a reality. I would dispense funds immediately to aid you. How's Forty-second Street?"

"No longer rewarding. I believe a civic clean-up has been undertaken."

"Bloomingdale's?"

"I can't go in Bloomingdale's looking like this!"

"True. Have you tried the public lavatories? I understand the Black Duchess has been doing acceptably at Thirty-third Street on the IRT."

"I get sick of loitering at the loos. The smell am so rancid, Rolla. I am not a tea-room queen. Besides, I am looking for a more lasting relationship. And I don't want no man who looks around toilets."

"Poor baby, poor baby. Miss Rolla understands." He touched Yootha's sunken shoulders with his wand.

"Won't do no good, won't do no good," Yootha mumbled.

In the toilet, Durwood was peeing to the right and Paulie was peeing to the left of the urinal that was receiving Timmy. Timmy knew that something was up. He'd noticed the two young faces noticing him. They looked kindly enough, a year or two older than he was and plain, if neat and confident. Though why they were descending upon him in a toilet when they could just as easily have spoken to him either before or after was something he did not understand. Until he noticed they were looking diagonally down as he shook his penis of its last remaining drops.

"Not bad," Durwood said. "A winner." And then, looking at the winner's face: "About sixteen, I'd say."

"Not bad at all," Paulie agreed, zipping up his pants, not having peed at all, and walking with Timmy to the sinks. "My name's Paulie, this here is Durwood, and we think you are one hunky number. Wanna go and get a drink?" Paulie had recently moved here from Florida and had met Durwood in just this very way.

Timmy stopped to wet his fingers under the faucet. He looked at both of their faces in the mirror, a trick he remembered from not a few Movies of the Week, and tried to study them as he considered.

"I didn't expect anything to happen so quickly," he finally said. "I'm not even out of the bus station. I don't even have a place to stay. You guys queers?"

"Yeah," Durwood said. "We are also faggot talent scouts. We sit here in this bus terminal looking for interesting new faces fresh from the outside world. You play your cards right in this city and you will be rich and famous in a way that neither one of us will ever be. You're, like we say, a winner."

"My name is Timmy."

109

"Tim. Tim sounds better. Shorter. Butcher and to the point."

"I don't know," Paulie said. "Sometimes people want Timmies instead of Tims."

"Paulie, you're starving to death as a Paulie. It's a ninny name. I told you time and again since you hit this town to change it to something smart like Brad."

"Brad." Paulie wrinkled his nose. "I'm no Brad."

"Come on, Tim. Let's go across the street to the A & O and have us a talk. They have a great sound system."

"Maybe a Tyrone. Maybe a Humphrey. Maybe even a Dinky," Paulie added, thinking of the handsome bearded guy he'd fucked with every night for an entire week just last month in Miami, before Paulie got fired from his job as attendant at the Club Baths, where the fucking had transpired, when he should have been changing used sheets, and thus not being on the premises the eighth night when the stranger said he'd come again. But he had waited outside and he hadn't shown, so that, he'd guessed, was that.

Durwood shook his head. "Paulie, wise up."

Timmy smiled at Paulie. Paulie blushed.

"You are gorgeous," Paulie said. "You really wipe me out. I've never seen anything like you. Stuff a towel in my mouth and shut me up."

Now Timmy blushed.

Paulie shook his head. "Oh, babe." He let the words slip out, a little cry of sadness and happiness, both at the same time, that someone he was meeting, someone so beautiful, could also be so innocent and shy and inexperienced and was this what he himself had been like how many weeks ago?

And Durwood said: "You are lucky in your first new friends. Boy, are you lucky."

In the main waiting room Miss Rollarette and

Yootha followed, with their eyes, the progress of the trio of young men crossing the floor and toward the 41st Street exit.

"They went in there two and they come out of there three," Yootha observed.

"Miss Three is a confection. They're going to the A & O. Come, Yootha, I shall buy you a glass of milk."

It was early for the Alpha and Omega. By eleven it would be packed with young dancers, the ones without the money or the connections to enter Balalaika or Capriccio, and certainly persona non for Fire Island Pines. But all of those places were like Paris; they represented nice spots to visit . . . someday. Here, in this unrejuvenated ballroom left over from some earlier dreams, everything was a bit more basic. It was cheap, in the way cheap was understood: no admission charge, and the waiters, who hustled you like crazy to drink, didn't throw you out if you didn't. Here the clothes were a little flashier than downtown, the heels a little higher, the hues a little more pronounced. Spanish, Cuban, Puerto Rican chic is defined a little more specifically on their own turf. And who knew but that there might be the odd old sugar daddy who arrived at midnight and noticed in the dark the sweater's sequins or the eyelid's glint.

Right now there were only about fifty guys in the place. The music was loud and ample, a wholesome job of it; the bass and treble were not as ideally separated as Balalaika's important system, where Patty had spent heavily to approximate sonic boom, nor as insidiously addictive as Capriccio's even more lavish set-up, where Billy Boner, who also owned this place, had dictated speakers simply everywhere for raising consciousness higher and higher and higher. No, here there was only

111

music, undoctored, dished up loud. But since it was certainly an improvement on the Maryland Teen Scene and Youth Club, Timmy was impressed.

He and Durwood and Paulie were already seated with Cokes when Miss Rollarette skated across the dance floor to their ringside table.

"Permit me to introduce myself, young fellow," Miss Rolla said to Timmy, touching both his shoulders with his wand in the act of knighthood. "I am Miss Rollarette and I can be seen all over town. I skate back and forth in this my kingdom and it gives me pleasure to welcome a new citizen."

"Hello, Rolla," Durwood said.

"What is your name, child?" Rolla asked, ignoring Durwood.

"Timothy," said Timmy, trying on the longer, more formal version for size.

"Timothy. A good name. Rolla approves. Will you be an uptown child or a downtown child? The Village or the West Side, or, good fortune smiling upon you, the East Side below Ninety-sixth? You certainly evince enough potential to escape the suburbs."

"I don't know yet."

"If these gentlemen are counseling you, you will no doubt shortly be actively employed. A word of warning . . ."

"Shut up, Rolla," Durwood said.

". . . about our fair city. We have good faggot folk and we have bad faggot folk. Just like everyone else. I myself, being well-heeled and in constant communication with my mother in Ho-Ho-Kus, New Jersey, whose sensibilities I would in no way injure, am able to see all sides from on high. I hope you will feel free to seek my advice, should your own judgment require counsel."

"Thank you very much."

112

"I am impressed you have accepted me for what I am. You have not seen fit, as so many new arrivals or fresh-mouthed kids, to giggle at my appearance and make jest. Yes, I find you impressive."

"I used to dress up in my mother's dresses," Timmy shyly confessed.

"Ah, did we not all do that! The difference is that I have perpetuated the fantasy. I am a living dream." And, in so saying, he turned on point, and rolled his way back across the floor to Yootha and his glass of milk.

Paulie shivered. "She still gives me the creeps. I think she's a witch."

"She . . . he . . . certainly is unusual," Timmy said. "How does . . . it . . . make a living?"

"I believe he works for the Army recruiting office. Isn't that a hoot? Now, can we get down to business?" Durwood pulled his chair closer to Timmy.

"Who is that with . . . him?"

Paulie squinted his eyes to look across the floor; he was tired and, though he had youth on his side, certain of his newly assumed activities were wrecking his health and stamina. "That looks like Miss Yootha Truth . . ."

". . . who is a starving nigger and a lesson to us all," Durwood finished. "Now, can we get down to business?"

"Go ahead."

"You need a place to stay? You need a job? You need instant pocket money for the hundred-and-one things a fella longs for? You need a base of operations from which to get your feet on the ground and launch your successful moon shot into this our Biggest Apple? I know the man who can provide each and every one of these here items for the one and only you. His name is R. Allan Pooker. He is not what you would call a swell fella, but he pays on time and the sheets are clean and he doesn't hit you or anything like that."

"Is it like that movie musical, *Oliver*?" Timmy asked.

"No, it's not that bad."

"Oliver." Paulie tried on the name.

"What do I have to do?" Timmy inquired, his eyes again on the poor shivering young black thing across the room, lapping up the inside of his empty glass like the hungriest of scraggy cats. "And how much will he give me for doing it? And is it any fun?"

"I guess the best thing for us to do is go down and let you ask him yourself. Come on."

The three of them started across the dance floor, toward the entrance. The music was playing Direne Jones' "Doin' It Twenty-Four Hours a Day Don't Make It Love," and Paulie stopped in the middle to join a small group of daytime strays swaying to the beat, then peeled off by himself, softly establishing his own back-and-forth motion, with an animation and an interest he had not been seen to hitherto possess. He then pulled Durwood to him with one hand, and then with his other he pulled the watching Timmy as well, so that the three of them were in a circle with Paulie's arms around them both.

Timmy paused a moment to reflect upon his reactions. Events were happening quickly and he was not unaware that he was dancing with two youngsters of his own age and sex and in rather sleazy surroundings with an assortment of fellow chorines the likes of which Mt. Rainier had never seen. He did not, he decided, find it unenjoyable. Besides, he had always liked music and he thought that Paulie was cute, in a way that reminded him of Elaine Loomis, who had a round face and safe smile and sat across from him in Home Room for years. So shortly after Paulie had put his hand around his waist, he put his own arm around Paulie's, causing the lad to give an involun-

tary shiver, which brought a look ceilingward of mock
disapproval from Durwood, which made Timmy smile and
put his other arm around *him*. Now they danced like a
tight little unit, their insularity a protection from the outside freaks, why were there always outside freaks?,
looking in, here no exception, two transvestites and a
Cuba Libra, and the more sinuous Direne's voice became,
followed by Rose Tundra's insistent, commanding version
of that classic, "Dance! Dance! Dance!," the closer the
three came together, so that Paulie's lips were brushing
Timmy's and Durwood's both and they were all holding
each other tightly like girls in the locker room before the
first mixer of the season. When the beat thumped into
crescendo and glissandoed into an open plateau, Timmy,
vaguely aware that his crotch was fuller than uusal, he'd
never got a hard-on while dancing in his bedroom, thought
to himself: I might as well show them what I really can
do, and spun away and performed a few graceful and
intricate steps and turns which he had perfected in that
bedroom, never imagining he'd be showing them off quite
like this, including the mock hesitation both arms right left
right right that he'd noted some kids using on a Don
Kirshner TV. Rock Special, and this caused Paulie to
duplicate the movements, and now they were dancing together—Durwood tried but couldn't get the tricky hesitation right—Paulie and Timmy, looking like, though they
would never have heard of them, young Tony and Sally
de Marco, which one Tony?, which one Sally?, in and
out, arms over and down, touch hip, touch hip, down
down over and back. Paulie's eyes closed, his own crotch
running over, and Timmy's eyes closed, and they instinctively touched chests and bumped groins and whirled
about to collide asses and then knock hips, right and left,
and as Rose Tundra droned on and upward, their own
movements became slower and their gestures tiny and

115

delicate, weaving a spell for the coming moment of climax and ending, neither one realizing that their sweat was co-mingling, just that it had been a good brotherly get-together and workout that would remain as a nice memento of Timmy's first High in the big city, which would soon evaporate and coalesce into the rest of the night, which was now about to commence, as the song was over, or rather whipped into a third one, a foot-stopping clinker of completely non-urgent intensity, designed to clear the floor and aid the waiters, which also cleared the air of mood and closeness and opened the eyes of our two dancers, who looked at each other, wrinkled their noses in distaste, hitched up their startled trousers to their former height, and instantly marched off the dance floor, smiling, friends, grabbing the less terpsichoreanly gifted Durwood, and headed, all three joined in arms and new fellowship, toward the door, waving to Rolla, waving to Yootha, Timmy feeling more a part of *something* here than he ever was back home, and out toward R. Allan's and that new beginning.

Blaze Sorority was a pen name. His real name was Alvin Sorokin and by day as he was an assistant vice-president at the Immigrant Savings, specializing in trusts for the elderly. However, as B.S., the eternal Blaze, he moonlighted, writing twice-monthly features, sort of historical overviews, for the *Avocado*. There has been much talk of late that the *Avocado*, as the faggot world's very own and special paper, has been less than courageous, more puerile than pertinent. Not true. With columns as perceptive as those Blaze was turning out, the faggot community has no basis for complaint. Blaze told it all. Witness this piece, written earlier this month:

116

. . . let us try to summon up inspiration from our illustrious ancestors, those forefathers who, had they opened their mouths, would have made our cause great a few years earlier, had they had the guts to cry out "here I come, ready or not" to all and sundry, the world at large, and stood there long enough to have their toesies counted, would not have placed us in the mess we're in today. I am of course talking about Leonardo and Michelangelo and Napoleon (who had a small one) and Socrates and Aristotle and Alexander the Great (the Great "what?") and James Dean and Richard the Lion-Hearted and Richard II and Walt Whitman and Lord Byron and Tchaikovsky and Dag Hammarskjöld and Brendan Behan and Marcel Proust and E. M. Forster and Cole Porter and Lorenz Hart and Hart Crane and Emily Dickinson and J. Edgar Hoover (who wants her?), Noel Coward, Somerset Maugham, Henry James, Montgomery Clift, Caravaggio, Willa Cather, Velásquez, Virginia Woolf, Gertrude Stein, Queen Christina, Milton, Cellini, Marlowe, Hans Christian Andersen, Verlaine, Rimbaud, Lawrence of Arabia, Sir Francis Bacon, Sir James Barrie, Benjamin Britten, Stephen Foster, Brahms, Visconti, Verrocchio, George Gershwin, Senator Joseph McCarthy (don't want her either), Ravel, Rodin, Swinburne, Virgil, Strindberg, Joan of Arc, Edna St. Vincent Millay, Erasmus, Pasolini, Christian Dior, St. Augustine, Horace, Samuel Butler, Flaubert, Amy Lowell, Sir Arthur S. Sullivan, President James Buchanan who was in love with his vice-president William King, William Inge, Lord Kitchener, Charles Laughton, Hadrian, Claudius, Thomas Gray, Julius Caesar, Pompey, Colette, Cocteau, André Gide, Trajan, Lorca, Goethe, Auden, Sir Isaac Newton, Cardinals Spellman and Newman, Suleiman the Magnificent, Horace-Walpole, Louis XIII & XVIII, Herman Melville, Carson McCullers, Lord Tennyson, Bill Tilden, Williams II & III, John Maynard Keynes, Edwards II & VIII, James I, George III, (Oh, to be in England), David and Jonathan (yes, Leviticus!), Ramon Navarro, Tyrone Power, Clifton Webb, Alexander Woolcott, Nijinsky, Baudelaire, Frederick and Peter the Greats, and the Popes: Julius II, Paul VI, Benedict IX, Sixtus IV, John XXII, Alexander VI, Julius III (how dare that Catholic Church be so nasty to us!), and on and on and on and you will notice that I am not mentioning the living cowards because of legal advice, but haven't we got a lot to thank all these fellows and gals for? Thanks a lot, gang. We didn't know about you till you were dead. You've made it so much easier for us to tell the world we're here, WE'RE HERE, *damn damn damn* your hide, and we shall make our presence *known!, felt!, seen!, respected!, admired!, loved!*

And now for the news. The season's opening Fire Island dog show, toy groupings only, will begin at one A.M., not P.M., as previously announced by your reporter. (Maxine gave me the wrong slip of paper.) And, shooting forward a bit, the High Holiday services for those of you of the Jewish persuasion will be held, as in seasons past, at the beautiful bayside home of Alan ("Nana") Herskowitz, which was also the setting for the wonderful hat party, at last summer's end, which brought a little sunshine into *that* rainy day.

I'll bet you can hardly wait to start it all again! Neither can I! Another summer! I'll see you on the Island!

And now, brothers, sisters, let me be sad. Let me be. Oh, my little babies, where is he? Where oh where oh where?

And when he appears, will we know him? Will we follow him? Will we love, respect, admire, emulate, follow him?

Oh Miss God: Give us a leader to follow. A Hero! Pretty please.

● ● ●

"Leaders!? Heroes!? Whatever is that ditz Blaze Sorority going on about?" the Divine Bella, Bertram Bellberg, big and burly and with a lovely, constant smile, said aloud in his one-room apartment on Weehawken Street, his own pen awaiting inspiration for his twice-weekly *Women's Wear* column on happenings in fashionable New York.

"We have so many wonderful models and leaders! Winnie Heinz and divine Lork, whose English improves with every collection, and Horst Esterhazy, the stomach of death, muscles up to here, and Ronnie Gartenhoffer, our best dancer, and the perfect Adriana, though she's straight, and the distinguished Dr. Irving Slough, he's very leader-y, and I have heard tell about that top movieman, Randy Dildough, and Hans Z. and all his other models, and that writer, Fred Lemish, and Billy Boner, our very own empire builder, and Patty, Maxine, and Laverne, and that most gorgeous, though very wicked, Dinky Adams, whom simply everybody falls in love with, though he's not someone I'd like my brother to marry, if I had a brother ...

"Oh, goodness, dearie me, whatever is Blaze foaming on at the mouth about so!"

We now come to matters of a rather delicate nature. These would seemingly pertain to Fred Lemish's problems with his bowels and his regularity, or booms, as Algonqua was wont to euphemize them when he was a lad. Whatever had gone wrong with his early training, toilet or otherwise, he could for years not consider being out of range of a john; when he had not daily voided, he would be reluctant to leave his current home base unless he could pinpoint a clean extra-home toilet somewhere along the way.

119

While this way, as noted, had led him into the various inner sanctums provided by the distinguished Messrs. Cult, Nerdley, Fallinger & Dridge, and while their joint investigations into these sanctum sanctorums had provided him with various intellectual hypotheses as to why he might be who he was and is (including the current favorite Reasons for The Problem: 1: Algonqua smothered me to death with her "Love"; 2: Lester hated me; 3: I want to be Hurt; 4: I don't want to be Hurt; 5: I want to Hurt somebody else; 6: I seek the tensions of my shitty childhood; 7: I seek as lovers only those who embody the identical responses that Algonqua and Lester, those cocked-up fonts from whence all patterns flow, programmed into me; 8: I refuse to compete in any way with ultra-straight brother Ben; 9: I'm still trying to be accepted as "one of the boys" I never was in youth; 10: I have a bad relationship with my body and need constant re-affirmations by a bevy of parading beauties that I Am Hot; 11: The World, and God, say I must not be; 12: I'm afraid of the Outside World and its Responsibilities, plus 97 others, ((. . . but what if I was just born responding to cock and ass, like Ben was born responding to tit and cunt? . . . what if all those neurotic Reasons were just post-natal . . . re-adjustments? . . .)), plus other questions, or rather, the same question asked a number of different ways: why can't I get out of this life style that is going crazier and more out of control and more mad, and legitimized!, by the minute?, is it just a reluctance to leave the familiar and fear of exploring the new and different?), this way had also not yet revealed to his satisfaction why it continued to localize its revenge on his stomach and its adjoining tributaries.

Yes, why was everything so complex and difficult to comprehend?

And when would he get some pleasure from his ability to feel?

And when would he be able to swerve his restless passions toward shaping his deeds, perhaps toward altering the world a little?

Was he naïve?

God damn it, it's hard.

These perplexing conundrums, perhaps not yet to be answered, were ones that daily made their unsolved presence known. Perhaps the sufferer had to live a bit first —the Reasons and intellectual Hypotheses, indeed the Questions, nought until one Lived! Experienced! The Liver could be in analysis for those 12 or 97 years, but until that inner sanctum was vacated, until ONE WENT OUT INTO THE WORLD—to quest, to explore, to EXAMINE, to do!—does anything become clear . . . ?

Was Dinky, and Love, his ticket to ride?

He had made a certain amount of progress. He could actually highlight when the courageous change came about, permitting him his breakthrough, or breakout, into the utilization of nonresidential conveniences. It was when he was twenty-seven, and on a pleasure trip from his then London film-executive duties, to Dublin, to visit a married writer classmate and his very dissatisfied wife. Fred simply could not shit in their tiny room with no heat and freezing seat, and if an instrument for pure torture had been created just for him, he was sitting on it. Later, when he and the bickering couple (shades of Lester and Algonqua and their snappy banter: "It's your fault!" "He's your son, too!") were on a tour of the lyrical Irish countryside, all pale mists and the sun trying to break through to greet at least the afternoon, he was of course woefully in need of evacuation. When finally death seemed preferable, he modestly requested that the Mini Minor be stopped, he bolted behind a wen or shillalah or whatever the fuck they call a hill-cum-tree in Ireland, he dropped his drawers, gave three solid days of solid Irish fare an exit visa, and then utilized one pair of Harrod's boxer shorts and strips from the tail of his favorite black-and-white checked Turnbull & Asser shirt to wipe his blushing ass. Then he returned to his host and hostess, and their journey, feeling better in one way, not in another, when oh when would these traumas pass, such an appalling inability to control myself!, when will I be able to shit where and when I want to?, what terrors am I so internalizing?, and directing toward myself and not courageously out against the world?, the heritage traced back, its ancient lineage, always to that memory of his third grade in Hyattsville, when he had to Go, and ran, not down to the little boys' room, but thunderously, would he make it!?, all the way home, a half-hour's jog before jogging was fashionable, or necessary, hopefully scrunching in his cheeks, not quite making it, shitting in his Woodward & Lothrop Kiddie Shop (Size: Husky) underpants two blocks from Target Zero, then waddling the remaining distance, sheepishly making entrance to the garden-apartment building through its rear, furtively checking into its garbage room, removing first the corduroy long pants, and then the sack of offending offal, disposing of the latter in the covered metal can, stooping then to utilize some Washington *Star* to wipe as best he could his browned-off bottom, reuniting with the corduroys, walking pensively upstairs to the empty-as-usual Lemish residence, crying one of the last cries he can remember crying, taking a bath, disinfecting his tush and his long pants with some of Lester's Lilac Vegetal, and finally heading back to third grade, wondering what reason he could give to Mrs. Hand for his absence that would not be construed a lie.

Who knows what early traumas gave birth to such as this?

On Washington Square, in his handsome apartment of stark white walls and carpeted gray platforms, pillows and hammock, stainless steel, and floor-to-ceiling books, where he sometimes (though not of late; why aren't I reading them? or writing one of my own? what am I refusing to look at?) pretended he was Henry James, Fred was now deep into rehearsal.

"OK, kid, I've been thinking about this for a long time. I really love you, Dinky. I've missed you a lot. Your being away has made that abundantly clear. I can't live without you." No, that might scare him. Dopple & Diddy say "You must not need another person to complete your life," even if I am spending every minute thinking about him. "I think we're terrific together. Your fine mind. Our great times together. I know I'm a lot more successful than you are but we mustn't let that get in our way. I know you want to make it on your own. Not be known as Mrs. Fred Lemish. But what else does a guy make money for but to help his loved one? A down payment toward building and sharing a life together. I'll pay for you to go back to architecture school and you can pay me back when your success comes in. Which we both know it will. And I want you to come and live with me. That's what I'm really proposing . . ." I wonder if it would be cute to get down on my knees here? I wonder if he really loves me? What if he says No? So he says No. I can understand that. He wants to keep it going slowly. He's wisely said he distrusts overnight romances. Can I keep it going slowly? It couldn't be going any slower and I'm going swiftly crazy. At least I just got a postcard. From Savannah. Wonder what's in Savannah beside the old synagogue on the postcard? "To Humanism," he wrote. That's a good omen. Now let's see, what else can I throw into my sales pitch? The hotel? I think I'll hold off on that one till I need it. Always be prepared. Hope for the best and expect the worst, Algonqua's creed. No risk no gain, ditto. He really is terrific . . . "You really are terrific. We can really go places together, places that two people can't go on their own. I really believe that. You don't have to answer me right away. Take some time to think it over. Just know that I love you and want to spend the rest of my life with you and I hope you feel both of these things for me. Yep, take your time to think it over. Let me know tomorrow." If I were a man courting a woman, would I be so nervous? How would Cary Grant woo, say, a reluctant Irene Dunne?"

Then he went into his toilet to shit. He noted that the shit was falling in squiggles and this caused him, naturally, to be fearful. Had he once again come down with a case of last year's fashionable disease, the galloping trots, known medically as amebiasis, an amebic dysentery, also known in the gay world as the P.R. disease, there being a good deal of it around ("of epidemic proportions," Fred finally discovered from a Dr. Kelvin Knell)? Fred had caught it, not from foreign travel, but, so far as Mini Diary calculations could reveal, at the Everhard ("it is transmitted through feces and its fastest incubation, within eighteen hours, can only be accomplished by directly eating shit. Did you directly eat shit? Otherwise it takes three days.").

Prior to that wretched experience, which took three months and a lot of potassium-replenishing bananas to sort out, his first encounter with the squiggles was four years ago when he and Feffer (Feffer the bright, Feffer the beautiful, Feffer forever!) were traveling across the U.S. in the Ford Mustang Fred had bought for the occasion, the occasion being not the trip but the wooing and winning of Feffer, with whom Fred was convinced he was in love. The cross-country captivity, during which their love was meant to be nurtured and grow, produced, yes, a certain affection on Feffer's part for Fred ("I am helplessly and hopelessly in like with you"), and a very bad case of the squiggly shits from Fred's end over Feffer. This was diagnosed by a hippy doctor in Taos as colitis, a nervous occurrence, God knows Fred had been nervous, as mile lapped mile and he was scared shitless, or perhaps this is better phrased as scared into shitlessness, was this actually happening to him: *Love?!*

And so now Fred sat peeping down on squiggles again, and he began to sweat, wondering what anxiety-producing iota is lurking in his subconscious to effect a return of the squigglies or which of his many triumphant conquests in or near a boudoir has returned the dread ameba.

Stop it, Fred! In your shit or out of it!

Was the God of Shits passing around a message?

Jesus, Fred, are you a case!

So 'twould appear that if Fred Lemish spent half as much time writing as he did hoping Dinky Adams would say "I love you," he'd have a ten-foot shelf.

And if Dinky Adams spent half as much time legitimately planting and fertilizing as he did scattering his seeds to the winds, he'd be New York's leading gardener.

Though, of course, as we shall continue to see, he already is.

... I want my cock sucked, I want my cock sucked ... , Anthony finally, courageously, finishing his third joint, made entrance into the E & L.

The Hudson River Docks, the Erie and Lackawanna dockage area, Ellie to her friends, a huge black hole of Calcutta: interlardings of communal pierage, fingers jutting out to the water, pilings sinking, a wrought-iron inspiration with sagging seams, a mammoth cavern now useless to the outside world, a hoary gianticism—into this darkness, Anthony entered.

Lobster, brioche, asparagus hollandaise, champagne, baked Alaska, Abe's stomach, perhaps even his heart, was not accustomed to such fancy fare. Later he would take a Gelusil, but for now, in such lavish surroundings, high up in the Pierre Tower, though a bit impersonal, no touch of home, he had enjoyed. Randy Dildough had been charming. A deal was certainly in the making. Abe felt wanted.

After cigars and coffee (Abe would be up all night), Randy got down to business.

"Tell me, Mr. Bronstein, about your property."

Abe was ready. "Mr. Dildough, I must call you Randy, you are too young I should call you Mister, you have been so kind as to woo me after my big success with *U.S. Mobsters, Inc.,* that I come to you first with my second motion picture, to which end I have engaged the same writer, also the writer of that fine film you no doubt know, *Lest We Sleep Alone . . ."*

"A fine film, a fine writer, though I do not know him personally," Randy noticed that his words were peculiarly beginning to come out like Abe's.

"You would like each other. Two fine boys. Fred Lemish is his name and he is currently writing for me an original screenplay property entitled *Fathers and Sons and Brothers and Lovers,* which is an excellent title and, with the addition of 'Brothers and Lovers,' one which the masses will not confuse with the fine novel by Turgenev."

"It's an excellent title. What's it about?"

Abe sat silently on the uncomfortable gilt chair, now

126

his back was hurting, so many men his age had conditions of deteriorating discs, looking out at the clouds drifting by, the stars appearing, the city lights twinkling, all so close from here, before deciding to plunge right in.

"It is about how some sons become gayish and some do not. You are understanding me?" And he brought his gaze back into the suite.

Though in his crotch he was beginning to sweat, always the true precursor of his nervousness, Randy answered snappily: "I understand."

"I think it is time, don't you?, for a movie about gay homosexuality. Not exploitation, mind you, I am not this kind of film maker. I want an honest exploration of this new kind of love which so many of us have not understood and which I am understanding is now all over the place. What do you think?"

"I will have to think about it."

"As you know, my first film I financed myself. This second film is to be more expensively mounted and therefore I come first to you since your reputation in this field is preeminent."

Randy coughed slightly, an unexpected frog in his throat. "What field?"

"The motion-picture field."

"Ah, yes." He frogged his throat again. "Well, I am very flattered that you came first to me." He now ran his finger around the inside of his collar at the back of his neck.

"This makes you nervous," Abe asked, suddenly recalling Fred's warning on Randy's secret gaydom. "It is making me nervous, too, I must tell you. But I am also thinking that important things, the big things, are never easy and full of nervous. I have said something to offend you?"

"No, no . . . why are you even thinking this? . . . It's

127

just that the subject matter . . . stockholders . . ." Randy was trying to get a grip on himself, returning, after just a moment of uncharacteristic lapse, to his former self, which was, he realized, just what they were talking about ". . . it's not what I expected, after *Mobsters,* so nice and safe, crime, you are outlining something very controversial, and as such requires thought and reflection and of course a look at your script by Mr. Blemish, and budget and actors, and, if I am not mistaken, this is still some time in the future, you are now only commencing activity, and hence is nevertheless a bit premature, the times not ripe, in terms of actualities actually arrived at, please come to me when . . ." why was he rambling on so, both speaker and listener wondered to himself?

"But you too are a fegala," Abe said, so simply.

"No no no no no," said Randy, rising from across the tiny table room service had wheeled in, "no no no no No . . .," . . . when would they wheel big tables in?, ". . . it has been a pleasure to meet you, Mr. Bronstein, and I hope you will bring your fascinating project back to us when it nears orgasm . . ."

"How can you live such subterfuge?" Abe asked, declining the implication to stand up. "When I am wanting a young and tasty poopsie, I am marrying her."

"No, no, Mr. Bronstein, you are sailing on the wrong boat, it has indeed been a pleasure, please call again, do . . ." and Randy was now standing in front of Abe, hoping that by this closer gesture he would get the message and leave, wondering why he was not handling this episode with more cool, where was his legendary spine of iron, nerve of steel, mouth of tungsten, why was this man, who did not, simply did not, remind him of his father, the stalwart Ralph, affecting him so?

"Randy, please to sit down, I am sorry I am touching home base and I am not meaning to insult you, but do you not now even further see why such a film as this must now be made, to deal with this head on, confront it, take bull by your horns, and say: this is me, I am it, and no hanky panky, you only live life once, and we must try to understand, no more masquerade, to be a landmark man ...."

"Mr. Dildough ... aaaah Bronstein, please to leave my office, I am having other appointments, many minions waiting, backed up for days, I am not a faggot, never never never, please to leave and my best wishes to you and your fine wife ...."

"You know Ephra?"

"No, I do not know Ephra!, now please get the fuck out of my office, ah, room, ah suite! I have tried to be polite and now I am going to be not so polite. Scram!"

Abe finally stood up, shook his head unhappily, looked at the young man. "How sad," he said. "I think out loud, how sad! Now I see what problems I and you must now go through. The world must know!"

"Get out!"

"No prophet ever found it easy."

"Immediately!"

"From Abraham, Isaiah, Moses even."

"Out!"

"I get the picture."

"You do not get the picture!"

"I go. With sorrow and sadness that you deny your heritage. You do not like yourself very much."

"I do not like you."

"You are a sad person, and miss the great chance to be a great leader." Abe did not offer to shake his hand. He took his topcoat and left. I will be the leader. My Mission now comes clearer. I will help these boys!

129

And Randy? In his Tower pad, behind his closed cell door, leaning against it just like they do at the end of melodramatic scenes in his bad movies, clenched fist stuck to damp brow, chest heaving, all-over trembles turning into jerks, oh why am I punishing myself for handling this one so badly!

What to do what to do? If there were a hooker on his fluffed-up sofa at this moment, he might be fucked to death. Obviously better, if his new James Dean had only been discovered, they'd be flying down to Rio. He rushed into his towel-filled bathroom and tried to jerk off. But he caught his short hairs in his zipper and his Sulka underpants got in the way. Should he call R. Allan for a hustler? No, tonight's the night he'd promised to meet Slim. Can I come twice? I'll be lucky if I can come once. It was still too early to head for their rendezvous. He popped three Valiums and tried to take a rest.

And Abe descended, wondering why he was thinking of his Richie and where he was on the long lone road of life.

The aforementioned Boo Boo was at this moment walking the long lone road of his favorite fantasy, having awakened from the nap in his high bed, smelled the sheets, pretending someone else's nice smell was in there, too, then journeying, courtesy of his legacy from Dr. Rivtov, into his free associations, running start to finish, something like this:

No, I will not go and work in the Bakery's executive training program. No, I will not marry Marci Tisch. No, I will not do anything my Pop wants me to do. No, I will not do anything at all as long as I continue to receive my five hundred dollars a week allowance. Which will not be nearly enough to last me until I am thirty-five.

At which time my first trust fund, left me by my bubba Nellie, and netting me sixty-five thousand dollars per year for life, falls due. Until I reach forty-five, when my second trust fund, left me by my Grandma Lopp, and netting me an additional one hundred thousand dollars per year for life, falls due. Until I reach fifty, when 'that prick, my Pop, slices me my first million. Fifty! I won't be a Catch until I'm fifty! I'll be an old man! I want it now! Now! NOW! While I'm still young and wreckless, devil-may-care! . . .

. . . these thoughts then metamorphosing easily (with diplomas from Choate and Yale, where he'd been Phi Beta Kappa and had done his honors thesis on Horror Films, Richard was no slouch) into thoughts of older gentlemen tying him up and restraining him from action, thus forcing up his flagpole, not letting him fight back, the flag now flying, as he, imprisoned in his own room, is not allowed the free expression to even piss and shit, Old Glory now furling in the breeze . . . such thoughts now splintering like those early devices in German Expressionist films—shadows, masks, wipes, bleeds, superimpositions—into even more vivid fantasies of said older gentlemen holding him and embracing him and kissing him all over . . . and still not letting him arise to piss and shit . . . *No, no! My God what am I thinking!* . . . I won't let myself go any further, I won't, *I won't* . . . and by now he was deep in sweats, reaching for his first identity support of the weekend, a tab of Dringe, lying on his high balcony bed still, he hadn't rolled off and fallen six feet into the orchestra, but almost, oh God almost, he'd almost fallen off and down into those pits!

Then, the Dringe now perking, he continued jerking off, with eyes closed, and summoned presences of his favorites: Wallace Beery, Charles Laughton, Eugene Pallette, Sidney Greenstreet, Charles Coburn, all heavy

older men rolling on top of him, their pressures all too
pleasurable to bear, squeezing the life and breath and
air out of him, until, until . . . he would come, his
tentative little spurtlets causing him additional angst,
why spurted he not in huge white fountains like geysered
from all the dudes in all the fuck films he snuck in to
watch, should he be taking more vitamin E?, he'd read
in the *Avocado* that vitamin E made more spurt, and
whiter, too, as against his own rather clear viscosity,
but if he took any more vitamin E than he was already
taking, he worried his insides might slip to his outsides.
Mustn't over do the lube job. All would turn white and
plentiful in time.

But when!?

Soon . . .

After going through all of this, the now exhausted
son and heir took a capsule of Certyn to meld with his
tab of Dringe and climbed down from the balcony,
down the spiral staircase, and into the pristine and expensively appointed lower spaciousness, done in the current black-and-white fashion that had so appealed to
Mrs. Bronstein Number Four, upon whose embarkation
the premises had been bequeathed by Abe to his second
son "as a retarded graduation present," and plopped
his young and firm but pliant tush into the soft coffee-
brown leather of the Giorgio Dong chair and pulled
out from the left-hand drawer of the Arbeit & Minus-
culie stainless-steel-and-rosewood desk the folders and
scrapbooks that contained all of his dreams.

Clippings and clippings and clippings. Scrapbooks
of his childhood hobby, now his grown-up fantasy. Peer's
heir snatched. Notes under stones. Messages delivered
by strangers. Midnight meetings under moonlight. Secret
pick-ups in the woods. Ransom notes in test tubes. Grave-
yard assignations in the gloom. Lost ears of grandsons.

Brooklyn man chained in closet; wrists and ankles bound with rope; three-quarter million demanded for release. Baker's, no, banker's son kidnapped by fake electrician. Nun used in whisking of Cadillac distributor's son. Mobile Home Heiress buried alive in coffin with straw to Outside World. Hearst kidnappers demand two million dollars for free food. The Masticator kidnapping in distant Baghdad, wherein five bearded, burly men held the rich young scion for five million. The De Grungie (Swiss chocolate and ball bearings) child . . . seven burlies . . . hefty . . . swarthy . . . ooh the flagpole . . . four million and one half . . . the Lindbergh job, no, that had been a fuck-up . . . so many kidnappings all over the world . . . 57 jobs in Italy last week alone . . . why kidnapping was positively fashionable . . . the obviously In Thing to do . . . Momma can read about me in *Women's Wear* . . . play your thing out, Richie, play it out! . . . and then his favorite, the recent Bronfman job, right here in his hometown.

Then Richie would lean back even further into the Dong's glove leather, still playing out his thing, and look at all the Bronfman clippings, that face not unlike his own, that father not unlike his own, and wonder how he, Boo Boo Bronstein, could use the same floor plans and bring about a better built house?!

To calm his overactive imaginings now getting so rapidly into hand, you can't jerk off all the time, Richie, save something for the streets, the Outside World, for Fire Island!, he turned on the television, conveniently tabled on a plinth of white beside his arm. His drugs were perking, his mind was running free. He'd let his eyes stare upon the pictures, enjoy their patterns, as his new self and image and strength of mind began to tingle and to grow. Certyn and Dringe, and shortly, Festinate and a snort of Orange Fluff. And Millions! Such a lovely potion.

But there was a disturbing announcement from the Outside World to penetrate his pleasure. In Paris, the announcer of the news reported, Mrs. Bronstein Number Four had gone and done it. She had popped another son and heir! Another Bronstein boy to share the booty!

So, filled with courage and revenge, that old pal, Pop, has fucked me once again!, Boo Boo pulled out paper and picked up pen and pique and pitiless passion, and began to write.

The day of reckoning had come!

Timmy knew right away that he would not be satisfied for long with the likes of R. Allan Pooker.

"Room and board and twenty-five dollars a week. I get to photograph you for five hours each day without your clothes on."

R. Allan ran both Stud Studios and One Touch of Penis Modeling Agency. He looked as expected for this dual role: fifty, seedy, nicotined, with sparse hair, bushy eyebrows, and a drool that increased in lubricity when it liked what it saw. Which it now did. He had never, in his entire lifetime, by any stretch of anyone's imagination, been attractive, handsome, even personable, and hence his mission to bring beauty to the world was set young. He drooled early.

Timmy was standing naked, calmer than he thought he'd be with so many witnessing eyes—R. Allan, Durwood, Paulie, a few slags who appeared from the studio's salacious shadows, the hustlers on call tonight: Vladek, Cully, Midnight Cowboy—looking at him. Timmy sensed that they would not be looking at him in the way they were if he were just some average-looking kid. Too, he had looked at R. Allan's portfolio before disrobing

134

and considered himself to be of a higher caliber. When R. Allan had said: "All right, son, let's have a look at *you,*" Timmy had dropped his fears and dropped his drawers and yanked off his "Washington D.C. is for Lovers" T-shirt and kicked off his Keds and socks and stood there, proudly, knowing that he was better than everybody around him. And the others just stood there, gaping and letting him so be.

Durwood proudly bobbed his head paternally and sent additional nodding looks in the direction of R. Allan, who nodded back and at one point, when Timmy successfully complied with a request to strike a particularly seductive pose, R. Allan even blew Durwood a kiss along with mumblings of: "Good job, good job." Durwood used this moment to sidle over and request a bonus.

It was at this moment that Timmy made his demand: "I won't allow my face to be seen. The back of my head is OK."

There was silence. Durwood kissed the bonus goodbye. Stud Studios was not known for backs of heads.

But R. Allan, his eyes never leaving the sight of young Timmy's young crotch, replied: "OK. No recognizable face. I understand, son. But you'll have to trust me when I shoot you in front. You will trust me, won't you?"

"Until I learn otherwise."

Durwood couldn't believe it. He also couldn't believe it, later, when R. Allan slipped him fifty dollars extra.

"What's this? A fifty? Jesus, Mr. Pooker. Jesus, holy hell."

"You've done very good, Durwood. He's the most beautiful young man I have ever seen. His beauty is

135

such that I shall be inspired to do great work. Michelangelo, you know, was also concerned with beauty. I consider my mission similar to his."

"Right! Great work! I just know you can do it, sir. I think I'll go out and buy a few things. Maybe show Timmy the town. You don't mind that, do you?"

R. Allan nodded his permission, lost in thoughts of Timmy's perfectly clean planes and lines. He felt inferior in the presence of even just the thought of such sculpture. He knew that few had ever been so beautiful in youth as Timmy Purvis. Therefore his new star would make him a great deal of money and bring pleasure and not a few jerks off to clamoring customers around this huge and hungry world. He would feed this world. He would launch this rocket. He would be as Stiller to Garbo, Milton Greene to Monroe, Ron Gallela to Jackie Kennedy. He would write him a grand scene for tomorrow's shooting with Paulie.

In the dormitory-style bedroom, two double-deckers, a window overlooking Bedford Street, the noise from the Christopher Street spillover traffic filtering up, the bedspreads brown-and-white checkered and not unlike the one he'd left behind, Timmy watched Durwood stare at the fifty-dollar bill as he held it in front of him and marched around the room quietly following it. Then he silently took Timmy in his arms and kissed him gently. Timmy allowed it, almost languidly. He knew it meant nothing to either of them.

Paulie looked troubled. "Durwood, you always told me we would never be bringing anyone out. People got to come out of their own free will. I ain't having any of that on my conscience."

"That's what I'm attempting to ascertain, dummy. I am attempting to ascertain if we would be bringing him out or if he is already out or if maybe we would be, like, doing him a favor by showing him how."

Timmy spoke: "Please don't worry. I feel like stars are watching over me. I don't think they'll let me do what I don't want to do. Now Durwood, now Paulie, what's in this town for me to see?"

Durwood was suddenly intimidated and, without his lead, so was Paulie. And at this moment R. Allan summoned them to the phone.

Anthony Montano lay flat on his back in the darkness of the Erie and Lackawanna terminal and wondered why. He then recollected that those three joints had been of Mantanuska Thunderfuck and had been ingested to courageously propel him inwards and had done just that. So, while he might in a few moments just be able to pull himself up and climb those stairs and begin his search, he would, for the nonce, and to better ward off thoughts of imminent, surrounding dangers, or wretched concern over how to break the news to Winnie Heinz, compose an Ode again until strength, health, and muscular agility returned.

Ah, home away from home, ah black hole of Calcutta, ah windswept, storm toss'd, fire-ravaged skeleton of former grandeurs! That you are still standing!, with your three stories gutted yet still here. Holes in you for entrance, holes within your stockings, fetid waters underneath, your bottom twisted and rippling like wooden waves, *You Are a Woman!* Our Ellie, Barbra, Kate, Bette, Diana, Marlene, Tallulah, *Judy*! Survivor, standing after all these ravages upon your face and body, from users and abusers of your finery, but still submitting, still bearing outrage, how many pints, quarts, gallons of semen spilled into your pock-marked skin? . . . now, now . . . into your tent creep this warm night, creep any night, crawling in and into this biggest womb and void of spacious blackness, total darkness, tread carefully, don't trip, holes are many, beams are loose, floorboards missing, and oh the river is wide, and cold, and schmutzig, and beneath me, oi, also this building has no back, this lady wears a strapless, feel movement around me, who knows how many?, two thousand?, two hundred?, two?, me and my murderer?, me and my next beloved?, what a fantasy trip, I don't have to see you and you don't have to see me, you are John Wayne with real hair, and so up up up, I am now getting up, ignore handpainted fluorescent warning: LAST JULY A GUY WAS MURDERED HERE AND ROBBED OF HIS CARTIER WATCH AND STABBED IN THE GUTS with under-scrawling: "Glad to hear someone's got guts," up up up and . . . as I grow more bold, does not a proud woman inspire a return of strength, she's made it, I Can, Too, sing it, Barbra: "He's my man and I love him, no matter that he's left me," sing it, Greta: *"Mein Mann ist mein Herz und meine Liebe und mein Leben,"* sing it Vera: "There'll be birds of love and laughter, when you come back after," sing it, Edith: *"Mon homme, mon homme, mon homme, mon hoooommmmmeee,"* and Barbara, fat Barbara, our new cookie, sing the anthem: "Who's going to make me gay now?," yeah, girls, you made it, so can I, my heart's still beating, my tits aren't sagging, my pecker's hopefully still pecking, I've made it through another winter, now I deserve a break today, go out, go up, go show them that I'm still Alive! Show them that I'm still gorgeous and still gutsy and desirable, and while I may be going down the tubes, I'll go down getting my cock sucked as I start another year of life!

This place is a fucking football field!

Play Guts Ball!

● ● ●

138

The last city orgy of the spring season was held at the home of Garfield Toye, a gay activist and member of the law firm of Harbinger, Kildare, Bronstein & Sport, who was not expecting to hold it. He had saved this night for his friend, Nancellen Richtofen, with whom he had planned to attend the New York debut of the Russian basso, Nicolo Loosh, in a performance of *The Daughter of the Regiment*. But Nancellen had called this afternoon and said, and only a bitch dyke could pull a trick like this and get away with it, that she had come up with a hot date for the night so could she please use the two tickets herself, thank you very much, I'll see you Sunday at the Island, good-bye, and that was that. Garfield had a free evening on his hands. He considered going to the baths, Friday being two-for-the-price-of-one night at the Club, which meant a preponderance of younger fellows taking advantage of the economy and—and this is what decided Garfield on staying home—a larger number of older timers trying to take advantage of them. Besides, what was the point of having a Central Park West penthouse in the sky if not to stay at home, make a few phone calls, and ask some friends to drop in for a quiet evening *chez moi*. Word would be passed around with speed, and by nine, or ten at the latest, he would have an apartment full of humpy numbers. Garfield just loved being a faggot in New York. One got things done so quickly here.

Winnie Heinz came bringing a Gentree shopping bag, which he said contained only a few old sneakers, and Troy Mommser, who was Winnie's creative director at Heiserdiener-Thalberg-Slough, came with several other models from the Hans Zoroaster Agency: Lork and Yo-Yo and Carlty, 1) sandy, 2) dark, 3) blond, tall, and handsome, the very best, no doubt about it, Hans certainly had the eye, and Maxine came alone: "Laverne's with Robbie Swindon, who's now courting him, now that

139

they are both divorced from former entanglements; I don't know where Patty is; he said he'd meet me here," and Blaze Sorority came, too, though Garfield wondered who had called that cunt, who could never keep his mouth shut, in print or out of it. Garfield fully expected to open the *Avocado* next week and see his entire life and guest list exposed. Oh, well, might as well relax and enjoy it.

A call to One Touch of Penis had brought Vladek, Cully, and Midnight Cowboy, Penis's top three in billings, all for free, they must be horny now that summer's coming, Long Island's beckoning, and business is falling off. They brought three youngsters, including that Paulie whom Garfield had paid fifty to only just last week, he sure is looking pale and run-down, and also including one of the most beautiful morsels Garfield had ever seen, he thought he heard his name as Timmy, and one look at that Junior Adonis and Garfield knew he'd never afford the likes of that forbidden fruit. The three kids went off into a corner with Troy Mommser, who always was a quick worker, and who seemed to be passing the early grass this evening, plus a little angel dust, judging from the smell of things. Garfield watched as Timmy Gorgeous inhaled on, could it be his first encounter with the weed This was hard to believe, but the lad was obviously receiving instructions and doing as was told. So we have a new girl in town, thought Garfield, his mind then automatically reminding him: corruption of the morals of a minor—ten to twenty . . . , then eyeing Maxine and hoping that tonight he wouldn't change to drag.

The black contingent arrived, headed by Morrison van Gelding and Hubie Snint. They both were hulking figures you'd cross the street to avoid if you didn't know them but Garfield did and knew they both were pussy

140

cats. Blaze, New York's reigning schwartza queen, at the sight of so much black flesh, practically expired in the excitement of his anticipation; Garfield knew where that one's mouth and/or asshole was going to be after lights out. Morrison and Hubie each had a cute little white boy in tow, like their prize pugs on leashes: Morry's was called Wilder and Hubie's was called Slim. Slim was evidently just in from the Coast where he was a math teacher and he'd met Hubie and Hubie's eleven-inch wonderful instrument while cruising Central Park. Morry said he had informed a few of his black friends at Legal Aid about the event and that Garfield might have some additional dark meat soon.

So, all in all, what with the ones he'd called and the ones they'd called and the ones who had been called by them, Garfield knew his doorman would clock about eighty single gentlemen in before (a new record) nine-thirty. Through the portals came, among others, five attorneys, three art directors, seven models, ten would-be models, twelve said-they-were-models, one journalist, three hairdressers (one specializing in color), two antique dealers, one typewriter repairman, one manager of a Holiday Inn, one garbage collector, two construction workers, one toll collector from the Verrazano-Narrows Bridge, three policemen, two firemen (one from out of state), seven hustlers (three full-time), one elevator operator (Garfield's landlord's son), one bass player, five doctors, twelve students, one ethnic dancer, two restaurateurs (one fancy, one shit food), one judge (rather old, but Garfield had to remember business), one newscaster, one weather man, one football player, one folk singer, four truck drivers, twenty-nine on unemployment, eleven unidentifieds, and the new assistant Orthodox rabbi for a congregation in Seattle. And these were just the starters. The evening had all the earmarks of an eventful one, and

141

Garfield, already busy in the maid's room with a Puerto Rican efficiency expert, was thus occupied when Winnie Heinz, from across a crowded room, fell in love with Timmy Purvis.

Timmy did not know that anyone was looking at him. He did know that everyone was looking at everyone else, as he was, too, much like you rummaged through the loose tomatoes at the Safeway to locate the one you liked the best. There was so much to look at, his mind was such a jumble of impressions, that he knew he might as well just relax and go with the evening, because it was already too exciting to make much sense of. His head was beginning to have the light buzz he was told to expect by Troy, who kept injecting the thin cigarette into Timmy's mouth and telling him to "suck, suck, you gorgeous number, and hold it in like this," and then expanding like a peacock to illustrate, and Timmy, since he was feeling so wonderfully good, figured that he was now experiencing his first "high," which he had heard about in Mt. Rainier, but only heard about. Troy seemed to be paying that little bit of extra attention to him and he sort of liked the way the big man—not fat, mind you, just large and hefty, in his handsome business suit and aviator glasses—did so. He was old enough to be his father, if only his father had had the sense to be as attractive and worldly and well-dressed and to smell of nice cologne and just-brushed teeth, and Timmy was a bit surprised to discover that a tingly feeling was appearing not only in his head and arms but in his crotch as well. He found himself relaxing into Troy Mommser's warm, enveloping arms.

"Oh, you little darling," Troy sighed as he nibbled at Timmy's ear and then kissed him warmly on the lips. It was Timmy's first true kiss from another man on a non-familial level. It wasn't bad. And in such a nice, comfortable, homelike apartment, too.

142

"Come on, you beautiful thing," Troy said, practically picking up the young package and carting him into one of Garfield's homelike bedrooms.

Winnie watched all of this and his heart sank. Why was he not in the right place at the right time when it mattered? Why had he not brought his own dope this evening? Where was his own angel dust? He could have turned the little kid on. Oh, he was beautiful, and his heart wanted to hold him, no, he wouldn't walk over this one in boots or have him walk on him, he just wanted to hold him and kiss and cuddle and go for weekends in the country and swims in St. Thomas and make a life together, my goodness the entire gamut of a fantasy future was jelling before him. What is happening to me?, Winnie worried. I'm not like this. And I don't even know his name. And he doesn't look Jewish. And I thought I was pegged into yids. And he's off with Mommser. Oh, well, Troy is a nice man, my friend. If anything, the kid will be bored to death with such a nice guy before long. So, swallowing his impatience, he joined a little cozy corner foursome that included a black kid wearing a Star of David round his neck, to kill the time until the moment when his cutie would be free.

In the dim-lit bedroom, king-sized walnut, pulleyed drapes to match the walls, and four inches of Bigelow underfoot, Timmy was naked in Troy's arms. On the king-sized walnut. Troy's big strong barrel chest, warm with soft hair, was something he wanted to curl up against forever. It was safe, he just knew it—was this what it was all about?—and he wanted it to go on and on and on and on. They both tried to pretend there was no one else in the room, not too easy a task when there were twenty or so, each busy in his own way. But if one could ignore the grunts, the smells, the sounds of suckings, the patches of wet sheet, the three hustlers, Vladek, Cully, and Mid-

143

night Cowboy, practicing a muscle-flexing gymnastic triangle by the headboard, the three models, Carlty, Lork, Yo-Yo, forming an observing triptych at the foot, yes, models all, and paid for the same thing, plus a busy Paulie, who should be home resting for his big scene due tomorrow, darting about looking for his own future, plus Maxine sticking his head into groupings, searching for Patty and wondering if it might not soon be time to change, then one could more or less imagine that one was more or less alone.

"You sweet little thing," Troy mumbled once again in Timmy's ear. Timmy was aware that the range of descriptive appellations being piled upon him was beginning to grate, but he said nothing in reply. At this point Troy heaved his big self and reversed positions so that he could suck young Timmy's young cock, while placing his own huge thing close enough to the lad's mouth so that it might get the same idea. Troy was certainly enjoying himself—young flesh was always a treat—but he did wish that the handsome thing were just a wee bit more experienced and didn't just lie there so passively and would The Gnome be here tonight because his supplies of dust and dope were running low. The pretty ones are always bores in bed, Troy thought to himself, realizing that he was in a position, as Heiserdiener-Thalberg-Slough's creative director, to know, choosing as he did all the male anatomy for their masculine accounts, of which there were many, H-D-S being New York's butch agency, not only Winston, but all of those other rugged ads where half-naked guys cavort in the surf with either menthol sticks or underarm deodorants, or else the more clothed lumberjack approach where humpy numbers run through pine trees with axes to proclaim their regularity due to some natural ingredient, or else some incredibly butch Hotness who could never, never, be a hairdresser stands there with comb and scissors and slyly intimates that only her hairdresser knows for sure—Troy had created these all and had had not a few of the models before, during, and after conception—wasn't God good to him, then and at this moment, what was it with him that he so attracted youth?—was it just that he looked like what everyone wanted for a father, without the threat or the control?, he kept his mouth shut, he liked to laugh, he didn't get possessive, and being dressed by Paul Stewart when everyone else was dressed by Army surplus made just that extra bit of difference.

So Troy sucked on, vaguely aware that Timmy was having trouble encompassing as much food as Troy was offering. But the lad was trying, bless his heart, and that was something. Then suddenly, before Troy could wedge his nourishment a little bit further into Timmy's perfect if still impractical mouth, Timmy's perfectly inexperienced cock began to emit his little load and Troy, the perfect gentleman, concentrated less on himself and more on keeping up the excitement to the last second for the young boy who was obviously having one of his First Experiences. Ah, well, Troy thought, I'm the daddy once again.

"How was that, you little pumpkin?" Troy asked Timmy after a suitable pause, as the lad lay against his chest again and they both, also again, were trying to be oblivious to the hovering presence of the thirty others who had watched with relish, all instinctively ceasing their own activities to rush to bed center when the main act peaked.

"Mmmm," Timmy mumbled. It had been nice. Should he admit that it was his first time? "It . . . you were my first."

"Holy shit," somebody muttered in the dark.

"A virgin," sputtered another.

"I didn't know they still made them."

"He just did."

145

"Fucking Troy, he's done it again."

"Don't pay any attention," Troy whispered to Timmy. And then, patting the lad's head: "I loved every minute of it. How do you feel?"

"Fine."

"No guilt."

"Unh unh."

"That's a relief," Troy said, feeling a bit of it himself, one certainly didn't need an upset violated virgin on one's hands. Then, patting the firm white tush, he said: "You know, you're good-looking enough to be a model."

"There she goes again . . ." Words from the ᴄarkness.

"Honest to God, Mommser. You had him. You don't have to make him a star."

"Make me a star," came the unmistakable cleft palate of Midnight Cowboy.

"Honey, all that mouth is good for is sucking cock. And be grateful it's good for that."

"I think I already am a model," Timmy said, a bit confused by all of the smart chat, which, to him, bordered on a foreign tongue.

"There, you see, Troy. Somebody beat you to it."

Timmy continued: "Only I do it with my clothes off but they don't photograph my face."

"Well, you can't be too careful," Troy said, then deciding that he might be a pretty one but let some other agent usher him to the big time, and deciding at the same moment that he couldn't stay in this position another minute without breaking his back. "I'm flying to Tokyo in the morning, but perhaps I'll see you when I get back."

"What's in Tokyo, Troy?" someone asked.

"Will you shut up and finish sucking me off," someone else ordered. "I've almost come twice and you stop to hold a geography lesson."

Winnie, who had just concluded a deal with The

Gnome for a gram and a half of Best Angel Dust, sampled, purchased, delivered on the spot, was doubly pleased when he saw Troy come back into the living room, fully clothed and alone.

"Where's the beauty?" Winnie asked him.

"I think he fell asleep."

"How was he?"

"I was his first. I feel one hundred and five. I didn't even come."

"You were his first?" Winnie felt hugely despondent. How could he have missed out so outrageously?

"He's beautiful. So are you. Go take a look." Troy caressed Winnie's cheek as he thought to himself: Poor baby; about to be unemployed; I'm glad I arranged a shoot in Tokyo so I don't have to tell you, and said: "See you in the factory."

Winnie watched Troy leave. They'd been friends for years. Then he went into the bedroom to look for the kid.

Timmy was definitely not asleep. He was being devoured by ten men. Two held his hands and played with his fingers, while another sucked his toes. One, of course, was sucking his front thing while another, of course, had a finger up his back thing. Another naturally played with his young marbles and one more sucked each of his titlets, one after the other, then back again, and the soft adolescent nipples for their first time puckered slightly into older ways. Another man had his fingers in both of Timmy's ears. Another, soon several others, massaged his stomach, touched his teen-aged skin, touched him all over, wherever prior prospectors had not staked their claims. Timmy was being worshipped like a god. If this was New York, then he wished to live enthroned here forever.

"Suck it, man, suck that chicken cock," someone exhorted.

Timmy wished they wouldn't talk so much.

"Suck it, suckerooooo . . ."

Timmy winced. "Be quiet, please," he requested.

And they were quiet. But active. In a few moments he felt the returning tinglings in his solar plexus, the beginnings of his river's rush upstream from its source to its dispatch. He felt it moving, slowly, warmly, exceedingly pleasurably, and he lay back, back into all the flesh and arms and sheet and warmth and desire and strength he could feel support him, as this pleasure took over and left him to visit another receptacle, a licking tongue in a warm mouth, which was slurping away like a kid in an ice-cream parlor.

Timmy wished the slurper wouldn't slurp so much. The orgasm was over, he realized, when the slurping began to bother him. Then he opened his eyes and looked up at someone standing over him.

It was the Winston Man. He knew he was the Winston Man. The whole world knew the Winston Man. He had masturbated over the Winston Man, taking his father's American Legionnaire magazine into the bathroom and jerking off with the faucet running, wondering how one ever became as handsome as the Winston Man, wondering down deep if it would ever be possible to meet someone so perfectly handsome, so perfectly perfect, and perfectly the perfection of one's dreams. Yes, seeing him there, Timmy winced. He winced at first because he thought he might be hallucinating from the drugs. He winced at second because he was suddenly frightened to have yet another dream metamorphose into reality—too many dreams were coming true too quickly today in New York, things he hadn't even known he was dreaming about. And he winced at third because he didn't know what to say. Whatever he said to such Perfected Beauty he felt would be insufficient.

148

The Winston Man spoke first: "Hi. My name is Winnie."

"I . . . I know."

"Now how do you know. We're just meeting for the first time."

"You . . . you're the Winston Man."

"That's right. That's why I'm called Winnie. And who are you?"

"Tim. Tim Purvis."

"Hello, Tim Purvis. Would you like to come home with me?"

Winnie helped Timmy find his clothes, scattered to the four corners of the room, and helped him dress, pushing away other hands which, Laocoön-like, wished to impede. All was silence. Even slurpings had stopped. Winnie felt the silence and felt the eyes upon him and young Tim. Something in the room was ending, phase one of the evening perhaps, and with the departure of Adonis, Junior and Senior, something would be drained away, some of the energy, some of that ideal physical fuel necessary to heat the rest of the night. Winnie felt this tangible atmosphere and knew that he and Timmy were responsible for it. Still no one spoke.

Instead, two arms reached up and pulled Winnie down, backward, and pinned him to the bed. Since these arms belonged to Vladek, the Hungarian hustler, thick, hairy, and overbeefed in bicep and wrist, Winnie could not resist. Another two arms began to unbutton his shirt, another set to extricate him from his trousers. Others attended to Timmy, like handmaidens to the Princess in some movie about ancient Egypt, pulling him down and back, removing his raiment. Soon the two naked beauties were side by side on center stage, the edges of the wide expanse of king-sized bed now packed with spectators, each watching the animal of his choice, as if two cocks were pitted in the arena, which, in truth, they were. Winnie and Timmy, mesmerized by the moment, by their naked exposure, by the sheer exultant glory and joy of being so visibly, forcefully worshipped by forty pairs of eyes, now growing to fifty, sixty, seventy, as the word spread round the apartment: "the hot stuff's in the master bedroom," "which one's the Master's bedroom?," and other rooms evacuated swiftly, as naked bodies, eighty flavors of manpower, fought to witness beauty meet perfection meet beauty, these naked witnesses now coalesced into one huge grabbing organism, with undulations of its own, as a group and not as individuals, all swaying, holding, watching, breathing, wishing, empathizing, true Stanislavskians all, as Winnie held Timmy close to him, and Timmy surrendered to the cherished bondage, and they kissed as two long planes of flesh layered together like some delectable French pastry, then began to twine and intertwine, into cruller or Danish, receiving pleasure from each other's movements, from the touchings each to each, each growing hard, Timmy still too young to know that this, his third time coming within one hour, would be a record many of them, try as they might, could not emulate, Timmy learning how to experiment with his tongue and fingers, learning how to duplicate the movements perpetrated upon him by Winnie's tongue and fingers, Timmy, being Crisco-ed anally by a strange hand reaching from ringside, Timmy, on his back, receiving, from Winnie, for the first time a man's cock up his ass, so this is how they do it!, his own legs grabbing round that famous narrow waist, wanting to cry out in pain, the virgin on her wedding night, her hymen pierced, he thought of that, of reading *23 Ways to a Sexually Fulfilling Marriage* in a plain brown wrapper, hidden in an old suitcase under his parent's bed, expecting pain, trying to ward it off by thinking of the widest hole he could think of, like the La Brea

150

Tar Pits, and emulate that, but no, there is no pain, for Winnie's deep inside of him, up, he thinks, to just beneath his heart, he feels his heart massaged, he feels the love within it, imprisoned within it all his lifetime up till now, begin to explode out, start to ooze toward Winnie, like a life handed over, take my life, Winston Man, take all of me because you are the most beautiful human being I have ever known and felt and I want to spend the rest of my life with you, just like this—"Fuck him, fuck him . . .," there they go again, soft chantings from the witnesses, "Fuck his tight young pussy . . ." Shut up, Timmy tries to call out, if he could only speak, don't ruin it all with those ugly words . . . "Fuck him, fuck him . . ." and Winnie fucks this virgin chicken, excited in a way that he has not been since little Sammy Rosen at Hill School in Pottstown, Pennsylvania, and getting pleasure from a fuck, no boots, not even a Jewish boy, no extra paraphernalia necessary, though he wished the lad were circumcised, well, perhaps this was nice for a change, the beginning of a new era, feeling his own love grow as he comes closer and closer, no, hold it back, make this time last, uncircumcised only requires extra cleanliness, extra attention to smegma, hold it back, hold it back, make it last, wanting to cry out: I love you, you little fucker, but not doing so, never say "love"—what is happening to me?, it must be the audience, it must be the angel dust, why am I turned on so?, Jesus God it never has felt like this, his little ass is squirming for more, wriggling about wanting me to fuck it, look, no don't look, at the drops of blood on Garfield's Bill Blass sheets, Christ he really is a virgin, "oh my Christ I'm going to come!" and damn it, come he does, and, would you believe it, at precisely this same moment, always a good omen, Tim shoots his own small load, up and into the air to stick to Winnie's stomach like squirt against the ceiling, and Winnie falls on

151

top of Tim and the two adhere together, clutching to each other, holding tight to prolong the moment, unconscious, oblivious to the fact that around them eighty, no maybe only sixty-five, other orgasms have been reached with such intensity that this night, Garfield will be proud to remember, will go down in history, and he will go down as the Perle Mesta of the Orgy Belt, where is that fucking Blaze!, he hopes that ditz has seen it all, there he is, pierced against the wall by a gigantic black cock like some invoice impaled on a white man's desk, yes, Blaze is here, Garfield's future is assured.

Winnie's eyes opened and looked down at Timmy's, looking up at him.

The Winston Man spoke first: "I think I'm falling in love with you."

And Timmy answered: "I love you, too."

And they held each other tightly, and each began, unseen by other, to cry. If this was love, this was wonderful, and the moment must last forever, and each tried to memorize the feeling and what their senses were doing, so that, forever, they would be able to remember, to summon up at will. They held on to each other, neither knowing how to get the hell out of here before it's too late, not knowing that it is now about to be too late.

Against the wall, Blaze Sorority is being fucked in a standing position by nine and a half inches long and two and a half inches wide. Gone are thoughts of mortgages and loans and trusts and immigrants' savings, even *Avocados* and role models. All he knows is that heaven is near, with the thump thump thump of two hundred and fifty pounds of solid black flesh against his own frail back as that elephantiasis of a cock goes in and out of him doing untold pleasurable damage to his intestines and rectal area but caring not one whit. Blaze is about to enter the Kingdom of Heaven. "Shit, shit, *Sheeetttt*

. . . jam that nigger stick into my pussy muff here I cooooommmmmeeeeee!!!!" and, at the same time, the nigger stick's owner, one Jefferson Monroe, an assistant dean of urban affairs at State University at New Paltz and just down in the city for the evening, starts ramming his nigh-unto-dangerous instrument up, up, awkwardly up, so that Blaze's feet are off the ground, and not only is Jefferson shooting into Blaze at the rate of 2000 cc's per minisecond, but Blaze is depositing come all over Garfield's maroon-and-green, sheep-patterned, raised flock wallpaper, forty-seven dollars a roll at Schumacher's and through decorators only, and not washable, and, while Jefferson is yelling ". . . you done take our cotton fields *away!*," and pushing Blaze even further off the floor and into the air, so that now he is screaming "Put me down before you split my asshole, you asshole!," Garfield Toye, the genial host, the calm Gwen Cafritz, is running naked into the room with his roll of Charmin towels, hoping to rub Blaze off the flock wallpaper before it's too late, before several thousand dollars in now dipped sheep can be kissed good-bye, Garfield whimpering loudly, forget fame, legend, and history: "You fucking mess, you dribbling cock-fucking idiot, you have destroyed my home!" and Blaze yelling back, still up in the air, when *will* Jefferson's thing detumesce?: "Don't be such a prissy housewife, you Central Park queen!," and someone is yelling: "Cool it, Garfield, you can't have an orgy without some muss . . ." and Garfield is scrubbing and rubbing and the flock is now flecked with loosened dots of green and maroon and bits of Blaze and no longer are sheep safely grazing in this particular area, and Blaze, now being gently lowered to the ground as Jefferson's fork-lift finally descends to the main floor, purrs "easy does it, baby, that feels niiiiiceee" and he turns around and he and Jefferson embrace, and, for an instant, Jefferson's fire hose of a penis flops in the

153

air, scattering various droplets of their mutual efforts, and at this second, Timothy Peter Purvis, late of Mt. Rainier, Maryland, bolts up from the bed and rushes to the nearest bathroom to be sick. He jumps up from the bed so quickly that Winnie can't catch him or realize what's up, and he rushes into the bathroom and shuts the door behind him and vomits as if his life depended on voiding everything within him at this particular accumulation of his life.

What he does not notice is that in the king-sized American Standard bathtub, installed by Garfield at great expense and for just such use as this, four figures are intertwined, two black, two white, arms and legs and erect cocks all jutting at differing angles like some corporate symbol for IT&T or the medical profession, black flesh swirling with white and blended into something Duncan Hines might call Marble Bundt.

Morry van Gelding, only three years ago all-American linebacker for Baylor, stepped out of this emanation, his enormous black being all concerned for the young boy retching out his guts. "Here, let me hold you, baby. What have you gone and ingested that makes you spit up so?" And he held Timmy from behind, his arms around the boy's stomach so that he could lean forward and spit up more directly. Soon nothing more came out and Timmy collapsed into Morry's arms, just allowing himself to be held and trying hard not to think of anything, particularly not to think of Morry's semihard cock, so awfully big. Timmy just closed his eyes.

"Hubie," Morry said to his buddy in the bathtub, "we've got to do something for this lad."

Hubie Snint, chief gardener for the Spuyten Duyvil Parks Association, where he was known for the quality of his lilies, heaved himself out of the porcelain, pulling up from under his huge triceps, like some mother hen,

154

young Wilder and Slim, one under each wing. The white boys looked exhausted, perhaps used would be a better word, though Slim would not take his eyes off Hubie, who at eleven inches was one and one half inches Morry's senior and as such abnormal.

Hubie patted Slim's head. "You still want more?"

Slim nodded calmly, but said nothing.

Hubie unwinged and bent over and reached into the pocket of his trousers, which were crumpled on the tile floor in a pile of four sets of Levis, flicking away a speck or two of Timmy's insides, and extracted a light-blue tablet, which he then took and, looking ever so kindly into Tim's young bloodshot eyes, placed on the lad's tongue, after opening his mouth with his huge soft paws and admonishing: "Here, boy, take this and you'll be fine." Timmy swallowed it.

"Yes," Hubie said to Morry. "We've got to do something with these lads."

Wilder, practically doubled over from being over-fucked, took this moment to announce: "I've had enough. So long, Morry. See you soon." And he grabbed his stuff and hobbled out. Hubie closed and locked the door behind him. Then he and Morry took Slim and Tim in their all-encompassing arms, rocked and held them within, and softly sang and chanted in their best Third World style: "We've got to do something with these lads, Ibi Dibbi, we've got to do something with these lads . . .," and Timmy, having no idea that the blue tablet just ingested was mescalin and that he was about to continue his wonderful adventures, began to perk up a bit and even managed to mumble, along with Slim, who Timmy noticed was not bad-looking at all, along with these two black giants, each waving a talisman of mythic proportions, ". . . we've got to, Ibbi Dibbi, we've got to, Doobie Doobie

155

. . ." The chant grew louder and louder, when a pounding was heard but ignored. On the other side, Winnie Heinz was clamoring for his lover.

"Open up! How's Tim? Where's Tim?" cried Winnie, to no response.

"Your name Tim?" asked Hubie of Timmy, who nodded back. "Who's after you?"

"That's Winnie," Tim smiled, "the Winston Man."

"Winnie the Winston Man . . . ," Hubie and Morry and Slim started chanting, ". . . Winnie the Winston Man, Ibbi Doobie . . ."

Outside, Winnie thought he heard strange tribal rumblings and pounded even harder on the threshold.

"Let's let him in," said Slim. "Let's look at Winnie the Winston Man."

So Hubie flung wide the gate and in fell Winnie, now no longer restrained by Jefferson Monroe who, having sensed that his brothers within were busy and wished to brook no interference, on their behalf had interfered and crooked an arm round Winnie, just in case, and Winnie saw a smiling Tim, a naked Tim, a drugged Tim, a Tim whose cock was hard and being sucked by Morry and whose smooth skin was being Intensive Cared by Slim and who was this other black man giving him the evil eye?

"What you want, Winston Man?" asked Hubie.

"I . . . I want my Tim."

"*Your* Tim?" and looking at young Tim at this moment seemed to indicate that this particular possessive pronoun was not quite applicable. He was bathing in a sea of sensations, unaware of the treacherous undertow.

Winnie was hurt. He was hurt and jealous and offended in a way that he had never been before. He had sworn love for this cute little twit from nowhere and now here he was giving all his all to all. Winnie, never one

156

known for prissinesses or jealous tantrums, just looked at the lad, turned on his unshod heels, and left the john, closing the jungled groyne behind him ever so quietly to make his subtle point. He then retrieved and re-entered his clothing as fast as he could, hoping no one had noticed his Waterloo, they were all too busy reslurping anyway, and quietly, proudly, grandly, sadly, maturely exited through the hall and living room and foyer, a lover in pain, past the islands and inlets and peninsulas of fuckers and suckers and kissers and talkers, huge dabs of bodies still in there pitching, dueling each other as in some Shakespearean production upon stages of thrust, no one noticing Winnie, past those too zonked out or too zonked up, The Gnome now vending Escatrol for the long evening still to go, how could they not sense Winnie's pain?, he'd go home and smoke more dust, past the kitchen where the first wave of munchies had struck and mouths voracious for something else now dug deeply into Entenmann's, Keebler's, Nabisco's, Bronstein's, Garfield (searching for mop and bottle of Mr. Clean) always had a fine supply of shit food, no one waving So Long, Winnie, Have a Nice Day, past familiar Jews and familiar faces, fellow Zoroastrians: Lork and Carlty and Yo-Yo, at present too busy to be concerned by Timmy's competitive beauty, now past young Paulie Polaroiding Maxine at last rigged up as Elizabeth Taylor, yes, past all the yearning breathing masses huddled on the floor and holding on to something, where was his?, as softly co-mingled tapes played Nisha Noosha's "Fug, Fug, Fug," and Reventa Marlow's now sadly apt "Getting Sentimental Over You Now That I've Left You," then stopping to pick up his bag of unused sneakers, and hustling his pretty ass out through that portal as he said to no one in particular: "Winnie Heinz is leaving; thank you very much."

● ● ●

157

"Hello?"

"Well, hello. This is a secret admirer. How are you?"

"You're back!" At the sound of Dinky on his bathroom phone, Fred jumped up from his toilet and stood at attention.

"I'm back," Dinky's voice said. "And I want to see you."

"I want to see you, too. I sure missed you."

"That's nice to hear."

"Where the fuck have you been?" Fred tried to keep it light.

"I'll explain everything. I'll see you later at Capriccio?"

"Absolutely."

"Save me a dance."

As best he could, Fred jumped for joy.

Anthony had plunged in.

. . . Jesus that feels good, make it last whoever you are, whose is this tongue and lips and mouth oh christ it's good it's good it's good it's good to be sucked off, this is the first time in months, sex for the blind, do it in braille, who needs a name, just a hand, a mouth, a cock of course, a working waist that bends, make it last, *must not come*, think boring thoughts, New York is a filthy place, that's a boring thought, fire down below, must be someone trying to get rid of us, always someone trying to get rid of us, got to find a bigger apartment for me and Sprinkle and Sprinkle's piano and kayak, *Aaaaah!*, whew, almost came, mustn't come, must make it last, must make something that feels so good last and last, wonder when Sprinkle's coming back, why do I always have to be the breadwinner, tired of being the daddy, wonder where that ten-inch-cock kid is, "Buddy, you've got some dong!," oh, fuck off mister, now you've talked and blown it, no you've stopped blowing it, who uses words like "dong" anymore, sounds of shufflings away, must have been some old man, what am I complaining about, he did it fabulously, the old farts suck best, years of practice, damn it shouldn't have lost him, someone groping again, never even had time to stick it back in my pants, what kind of well-brought-up wop am I, walking around in the dark with my dong hanging out, the Good Sisters should see me now, From Port Chester to Pier in Forty-three Years, I went to Brown to learn this?, this one's a good sucker too, get 'er up, fellow, that's a boy, glad the damn thing still works, the way it's been in purdah for so long, I was beginning to worry, oh that feels good . . .

Fred danced and danced, like the crazy happy man he was. Dinky was back, had called, they'd dance together, these past Methuselah weeks of Dodger the Lodger always answering the phone: "He's still away on business," what business?, I said I loved him, and he's called!

"He called me!"

Fred tried to yell his good news to his Fire Island housemates, with whom he danced at Capriccio's closing party.

Their very own club was mobbed, had not every one of New York's Hottest Men looked forward to this night!, as many beauties as balloons, two thousand, three thousand, let not the Fire Marshal show this eve, a fine tribute to a fine season, Billy Boner and his flagship bringing down the curtain on the year's official end. Now came Fire Island, when all would start again, until the fall, when all would start again, too.

On Lower West Broadway near Canal, on a second floor, above a Chase, in a hangar as large and twisted as

Saarinen's at Kennedy, the cavernous white Versailles that
was Capriccio, all high cream walls and gray-flannelled
floors, and the widest field of shining waxed wood on
which to move and glide and shake and boogie and turn
and hug and hold and sweat and show the muscles,
wiggle the ass, bump your crotch, clutch you tight, spin,
spin, wave and shout, look and smile, say good-bye to all
our cares, with all our brothers, a lifetime of friends,
beside, around, above, bleachers stringing round all sides,
everything bathed in light and sound, that legendary
sound!, which Juanito, Patty's Juanito, secret Juanito,
Puerto-Rican-handsome, English not so good, in his control room, assisted by Jacente, turned into greatness, as
he placed, song after song, with that pride, dignity, love
for his work, that distinguishes the best d.j.'s and makes
them heroes of our moment in time, his Vlandor Arm with
its Nefisto cartridge on its Zee-able turntable, thus activa-
ting speakers of base horn, woofers of mid-base, lenses of
mid-range, horns of reinforcement, arrays of super
tweeters, each emitting .9034 psu's of decibelacular sound,
all engorging all of the above, Hot Men!, Dancing!, Love!,
Friendship!, this legendary spot of Heaven on Earth, our
very own beloved exclusive club, Capriccio!

And the Lights! A cacophony of multicolors, flashing
waves and arcs, cross-faded by cross-faders, series of
sequences on vertical rainbows, transformed by trans-
formers, electronics of incredible wizardry, channels for
Spin and Normal, Invert and Pause, Advance and Throb,
button after button touched to program mood after mood,
synergistically Siamese-twinned to songs and shoutings and
mind-expanding Joy.

And the Clothes! Tight T's and tight jeans and old
boots and bare chests. Or the finery of show-off: costumes
of delicate frippery or outlandish look-at-me-ism. For
tonight's party had a theme. Everyone tonight wore black

160

or white. And on parapets built especially for this closing, black-leather-thonged men in masks, above the bleachers, bumped and ground. And over the dance floor, beside the spinning mirrored globe, in a huge bird cage, white angels did the same. Billy Boner certainly knew how to spare no expense and set the scene so his members could party!

And the Men! Have you never seen so many Hot Men! Gloried, storied, muscled, fatless, mustached, youthful, smiling, sexy MEN!

"How are you!" "Haven't seen you since last weekend!" "See you tomorrow at The Toilet Bowl!" "See you Sunday on the Island!" Yes, our very own Country Club, everyone chatting, passing through crowds, such nice vibrations, all our passing Friends!

And the Drugs!

"I'm trying something new!" Tarsh yelled, his mind a buzz of wonderful feelings, his body, too, in each of its many small parts, rippling with tinglings and happinesses and electricities and energies enough to make him more than fine and best and perfect. He would tell them later all about it: It's called Super K, it's from England, it's a pre-op sedative used for children, it's a powder to snort, a cross between coke and Valium, and it's fabulous! Tarsh was proud to be the first to always try new things.

Among them all threaded The Gnome, small and runty, thick glasses, and hairy spidery legs in lederhosen, selling his Magic, introducing his Magic. TT1, three years ago, was Yellow Fever; TT2 was called Pink Rain; last year's TT3 was Gondolier, and this year's debut of TT4 was Magic, their very own exclusive drug. Tonight everyone was high on a snort of Magic by midnight, trying it out, to be followed by a tab of Glycn at 2, a half of Nyll at 3, and a hit of Blotter by 4, acid not usually ingested so late, but a long night was wanted, tomorrow was a long way off, with so many events to follow after that.

161

Sleep was for lazies, drop-outs, unconcerneds, incompetents, misser-outers, and the plainly slags and drags.

"He called me! I'm meeting him here tonight!"

Fred took no drugs. He'd tried them all, found no answers, and he was on a pilgrimage for answers. "They are identity-supporting, not identity-giving," he would try to say. "And I want to prove to you what a good time can be had by simply staying straight."

"Dinky's called me!"

Fred tried to yell his news to Tarsh and Gatsby and Mikie and Josie and Dom Dom and Fallow and Bo Peep and Bilbo, with all of whom he shared the house at Fire Island Pines.

Tarsh, an NBC newsman out of Brandeis, was their leader. He was red-bearded and short, with a perfectly muscled body, and he was their first attender of events, all happenings: books and movies and plays and museums and current trends and thoughts ("Something new is coming! We've got to go out and look!"), Tarsh filled them in and hoped they'd follow, concerned, as were they all, to find the best of times.

Bo Peep, from Vanderbilt and Kentucky, a management personnel trainer for an insurance company, was also short, with blond hair fluffy and ringing his sweet, angelic face. He wished to be Mrs. Tarsh, but wasn't.

Josie and Dom Dom played the city's famous lovers. The McShays. Josie McDonald and Dom Dom O'Shay. Josie was a Fordham banker, currently on a leave of absence, which was probably just as well, for how would a bank view his currently shaved head, which made him a bald Charles Bronson. Dom Dom, a Cornell city planner for the state, was tall and gangling, but just as handsome. They were a matched pair of beauties, tonight in twinned sets of white ducks and sailor's middies. No one knew they never fucked. Though Josie longed to. But Dom Dom was

162

also busy seeking everything "that synthesizes the essence of today."

Fallow, from Notre Dame to Seventh Avenue, was their stylist. Fallow the Dapper. Fallow tonight in Korean army bermudas, old Best and Company Teen Shop shirt with frayed collar and cuffs, black knee socks, and parachute-jumping boots from the Khmer Rouge. Fallow was the one they looked to for the latest trends in dress.

Bilbo was their yardstick. Bilbo the Drugged. This little cuteness from William and Mary, a concert pianist of astounding gifts who never practiced, unemployed, thirty-five, as were they all, round and about, if Bilbo was still standing, there was hope yet for them all.

And Mikie, dear Mikie, sandy, perky, bubbling, questing, never finding, Fred's Rolexed Mikie III, their flower child, their twinky, their Berkeley half-architect drop-out now driving trucks, fearful, but of exceptionally good heart and soul, now banging his tambourine, the mastery of which was to be his project for the summer.

Tarsh, never missing a beat of music, filled a balloon with a hiss from a cartridge of laughing gas, just like the dentists used, and sucked it all into his lungs.

No support from the brotherhood, Fred thought. Well, I'm happy. I'm trying. You can all stay single if you want to. But not me.

Then Gatsby, his friend, his fellow writer, his fellow waiter for his own true love, opened his eyes and smiled at Fred and said to him: "I'm glad."

Back down on those docks, also on a scouting expedition, were Leather Louie and Lance Heather. You will recall Lance as the rejected suitor of Randy Dildough, back in those hissing-snake days. He is still looking particularly good, a taller Alan Ladd, and he has just been accepted as a part-time instructor at Columbia in its Linguistics Department, where he will also work on his doctorate, hence requiring a change from West Coast to East. He's also hoping to pick up where he left off with his old partner in reptiles. But Randy had not returned the several phone calls to his New York Marathon office.

Leather Louie, dark, twinklingly sinister, hooded-eyed as ever, was, as always, a vision in shiny black and studded hides. He and Lance had recently met at the Eagle's Nest and recognized in each other the signs of the true cultist. They had of course not made love, since both desired to crack the whip, but they'd exchanged tales of scenes rampant, scenes triumphant, scenes wide-screened, Technicolored, multidenominational, and had decided to throw in their motorcycle gloves together. This evening was such a togetherness.

They were jointly seeking a special victim to audition at Louie's Dakota-eaves apartment, wherein, in the extra bedroom reserved for torture, now resided a brand-new stock-cum-gallows, recently arrived along with its attachments allowing for electrically, battery, or manually operated peccadilloes to please most occasions, all purchased at moderate cost, and via the *Avocado*'s helpful "New and Useful Products for the Home" column, from San Francisco's Abused Furniture Boutique.

This special victim, lucky fellow, would be auditioned for a special performance at tomorrow's special opening of The Toilet Bowl.

They were about to meet such a victim.

Back at Capriccio, Boo Boo Bronstein danced alone. Since he didn't know anybody, dancing partners were no problem. He could stand in the middle of the whirling pack, glue his feet firmly to the wood, then sway and gyrate, later even Rockette kick and double turn, in his drug-high way, eyes closed of course, and pretend they were all, every one of them, his dancing partners!

Following the momentous announcement on the evening news, Boo Boo had written his note in rough draft. "Two beefy swarthy burly fat and dangerous men want one million dollars through my mail slit or else they'll communicate all to Walter Cronkite." Only a first draft, of course. Perhaps I'll improve later on my prose.

Then he'd figured out his plan: I'll lock myself in my loft. And Abe will stick the millions through the mail slot. And when he and the police finally break down the door, the beefy swarthy burly fat and dangerous men, and the million, will be gone. Then they'll untie me. I'll be safe. With my one million!

Is it too naïve to think that such a simple plan could work?

Then he'd augmented his Certyn and Dringe with his Festinate, stared for a long while at the wondrous patterns in a crystal door-knob, then gone to the Grand Union and purchased four hundred dollars' worth of stock-up goods to last through a long siege.

The only question that remained was when to purvey the hot potato now residing in his back left Levi pocket to his Pop.

Dance on, oh Richie, till your fortune comes!, he thought, ungluing his feet and executing his first triple turn of the night, I am the most handsome Number, my workout has worked out!, squinting his eyes open just a crack to see if his gifted choreography might just have drawn an admiring glance or two.

And so they dance, our friends, in various circlets of together or alone.

Patty arrived, in white tie and tails, to join Laverne dancing with Maxine, now Elizabeth Taylored from head to toe, batting his eyebrows neath turban, testing: one-two-three-four, wanting to talk but impossible to manage words and maraschino-ed lipstick synch, but watching Patty's glances dart around and come to rest upon Juanito's booth. So the rumors Maxine had tried not to hear were true! And yes the moment of doom was near! And here, in our competitor's space. And can I pull myself up to Catty Tin Roof Heights!

Laverne looked at his two best friends. Again he suspected there was trouble and he wondered why he couldn't reach out and offer succor. But to which one? And where was Robbie Swindon who said he'd meet him here? And where was Dinky, whose postcard from Savannah just received this afternoon had said the same? And how would he, Jack Humpstone, handle said convergence? And when would calm come after storm instead of thunder?

Fred never stopped looking for Dinky to appear, from out of the shadows, across a crowded room, back into his arms, and away we go: into the moonlight, into Life! Around him danced so many chapters of his past. Early tricks, late tricks, so many tricks, No More Tricks!, faces from the streets and tubs and dancings, Mikie III, do three Rolexes make a tradition?, the Coty Hall of Fame, the only major star who's missing is Feffer, and Dinky, too, of course, hurry up, Dinky!, what's that crazy song they're playing?, something about . . . no!? shit in Alabama? . . ., have I committed the Cardinal Fairy Sin with Dinky: said I'm hungry, said I love you?, no, he's too together, why on our first date he said about his parents, "They did the best they could with what they had and at that time," no, he's too together, he'll explain everything, I feel good!

• • •

Fred and his housemates stood by the punch bowl. Frigger, on leave of absence from the streets, but still competitive in such matters indoors, and checking to see that his rock-hard midriff was showing, watched as Fallow, adjusting Korean shorts, walked over to a cutie and began to Make An Impression.

"My, Fallow certainly moves quickly," Frigger said.

Dom Dom agreed. "With a speed approaching Concorde's boom."

"Can true love bloom in the Ghetto?" Josie sighed, wiping his bald head in annoyance that sweat could sweat even here.

Bilbo lurched and contributed: "My new definition of jaded is when you find a cock that's too big."

"No," said Frigger. "It's when conquest is our own reward."

"But," Tarsh, their bellwether reminded them, "conquest *is* our own reward."

The crazy song grew louder as Jacente took over the co-pilot's seat. Yes, it was about shit in Alabama! "The Alabama Aw Shits—trouble and strife, you got 'em, all of your life, and you pass 'em on to me . . ."

The singer was none other than Miss Yootha Truth.

Fred spied Dinky, sneaked up behind him, put his arms around him from the back, turned him around as romantically as he could, and kissed him on the lips.

"It's so good seeing you again!" Cary at last with Irene, or better, Katharine Hepburn!

"Unh," said Dinky, disengaging, his eyes upon a coupling just adjacent. "Yes, well, how you been . . . ?"

Dinky was wearing nice gray flannels and an Italian print shirt plus leather-tasseled moccasins and he looked

167

most handsome and distinctly dressed unlike anyone else. Even his golden earring seemed to twinkle and his black beard seemed more neat.

"Fine, just fine. And better for seeing you."

"Well, that's good, that's good. Will you excuse me for a moment?"

I forgot he doesn't like displays of affection in public, Fred reminded himself as he watched Dinky walk over to where two men were themselves kissing hello. Fred wondered who they were. Fred also felt a sudden little tidge of hunger.

"You guys didn't waste much time," Fred thought he heard Dinky say.

"I got your postcard from Savannah," the one who was Laverne replied. "Who's the lucky lady in Savannah?"

"Hi, Dinky," the other kisser, Robbie Swindon, cheerfully added, his arm still around his Jack.

"Robbie's love is just the kind I always wanted," Laverne said. "The kind you never obliged me with. He's most devoted."

Fred looked behind him on the buffet table to see if the donuts were out yet. When in doubt, eat donuts. Don't look. Don't listen. Eat donuts.

And Laverne's lips reached over and Robbie's lips obliged them.

Dinky grabbed them, two bodies, lips and all, and pulled them apart, the lover-who-had-left-him and the Other Woman, and then the three of them became entangled in arms and punches and grunts, bodies and arms and pressures exerted ineffectually in wrong directions, so that Laverne fell to the floor and Robbie bent to pull him up and Fred sighted and reached for and ate in one gulp one glazed-with-honey donut, not his favorite, but no chocolate ones in sight, and Dinky tried to slug, was it

168

Robbie or Laverne or two for the price of one?, and at this perfect moment Patty, black tails flapping in his wake, rushed up, sighted, at last, Laverne, down on the floor, fell to kneel beside him and, oblivious to what he might be interrupting, hissingly whispered: "Listen! I'm sick of it all, so here!" And he pressed some keys into Laverne's hardly waiting hand.

"I'm doing it! I'm doing it right now!" Patty continued hissing. "I've had enough of Maxine and his Elizabeth Taylor. I want a man! Juanito is waiting for me, we're going away for a few days, here's the keys to Balalaika, please mind the store till I get back!"

And he then jumped up and ran away.

Dinky had also retreated. Fred pushed through some fellow punch-y donut eaters and caught up with him. "Hey. Er . . . I guess this isn't the moment for a romantic reunion."

Dinky stopped, looked around at the huge crowds milling all about, many of whom had no doubt witnessed his embarrassing fightlet, then hitched up his Italian print shoulders and faced Fred. "I've got this terrible sinus headache. I better go home and inhale some steam."

"How about some champagne and your favorite ladyfingers from France? A welcome-home present for you waiting to be claimed on Washington Square."

"That's nice. That's nice. You going to The Toilet Bowl tomorrow night?"

"Yes."

"I'll see you there. We'll talk there. We'll have our reunion tomorrow night."

"Want to give me a clue what's bothering you? Ann Landers has a great shoulder."

"Tomorrow. We'll talk tomorrow. Got to go. You're looking good." And Dinky pecked Fred's cheek and would have walked away.

169

But Cary had his arms around Kate's waist again. "Hey, remember . . . , I wrote you a letter . . . , and, er, the last thing that I said to you . . . ?"

"What was that?"

Fred approached the subject gingerly. "I said, most poetically, after a wonderful night of . . . I said I'm in love with you."

The music seemed momentarily to have stopped its tune. Instead came slowly dragging chugging chordal "jungle music," Fred liked to call it, impossible to dance to and beloved by those on Downs, Neldies, Paradexes, Ovlomoves, Frankensteinian plodders with heavy-soled feet as sole anchors to earth, "A Down is an Up when you're dancing," was Bilbo's explanation, its insistent whining one-note pounding, as if to say to all: I am alone, I am alone, I am all alone.

"No, you're not," Dinky said, pecking Fred's cheek a second kiss and smiling merrily and successfully walking away.

Bo Peep had seen it all. The little blond-haired angel, fully understanding, for hadn't he had it all so many times with Tarsh?, rushed up and embraced his housemate, Fred.

"Oh, Fred, I understand! It's the oldest story in the world."

"What story is that?" Fred tried to play it cool.

"Dinky knife you?" Frigger said arriving. "I heard he was here. Well, don't start playing Philip in *Of Human Bondage*."

"He's not feeling well . . ." Fred tried to make excuses.

"Ah, what happened to courtship?" Josie asked, arriving, too, with Dom Dom, word certainly had spread fast. "You didn't want to give yourself to just anyone who'd walk out the very next morning."

"Who wants to stay past the next morning?" Bilbo asked, arriving next.

"I'm still here, darling," Dom Dom said to Josie. "We've weathered the worst."

"When does the best begin?"

Fred looked again for donuts, where were the chocolate donuts?, he felt the approaching of an Attack.

"Anyone got an Up?" asked Bilbo.

Dom Dom said to Josie: "Excuse me, but I want to check out a number." He patted Josie's head. Then Fred's.

"You see?" said Josie, gazing after him. "True love can bloom in the Ghetto."

A new voice was heard: "How are you all, my dearies! Are we having a good time?"

It was the Divine Bella, Bertram Bellberg, tall and stocky, grinning face and expectant eyes, his enormous chest and back Brillo-ed with hair curlicuing out of his workman's overalls and with a huge felt sunflower smiling from his cleavage. "Fred Lemish, are you having a good time?"

"I don't think so, Bella."

"Well, you simply must, you absolutely must. Life is passing us by. Don't go and fall in love. Bella warned you. Everyone warned you. You just won't listen. Bella believes that what we most want out of life is our good times. As Richard Burton said to Deborah Kerr in *Night of the Iguana,* there are two levels where we can lead our lives. The real and the fantastic. We have to disco and drug and fuck if we want to live fantastic! Come, my dearies, let's dance!"

And Mikie rushed up to join them, banging his tambourine, feeling ever so good, and embraced Fred: "Oh, Fred, is this not a night of nights! It's the beginning of the summer of our lives!"

● ● ●

171

... yes, that feels good, oh good, oh god, oh good ...
Anthony was still in the darkness of Ellie.

Fred Lemish, deciding he was entitled to a bummer,
and determined to get the most out of it, walked all the
way from Capriccio to the Everhard, hitting on the way
four donuterias, two delicatessens, four grocery stores,
one late-night A & P, one ice creamery, interlarding these
with curses upon his head that he was not getting a good
night's sleep to face a morrow fleshing out some scenes for
Abe, you'll never become a great writer this way, and a
few flagellating inquiries into just what Dinky's words and
behavior had meant and could he wait till The Toilet Bowl
to find out and was there some sort of game going on here,
the rules of which he'd not yet been informed?, no! no
games with this one! I am not going to play any more
games! and ... stop it, Lemish!, the guy was confronting
a personal problem of which you were not aware and he
said he'd explain everything, he kissed you, twice!, made
another date with you, just you soft-peddle that talk about
love till ... and where are your guts and patience and
determination and you've waited this long, another twenty-
four hours, during which you'll gain five pounds, can only
... make you go crazier!, how can he say I don't love
him?, is that telling me anything?, it ain't tellin' you he's got
his finger sticking out ready for the ring, Charlie, did I
misread?, I'm such a big reader, all those lovely nights of
love, were they a fantasy?, nah, he's too together, he'll explain it all to his formerly once-thin Fred ...
As he fumed and sent up black smoke, he consumed
one package of Wise Ridgies Wavy Potato Chips, still
made the original way by Borden, Pareve for Passover;
one package of Funyuns Onion Flavored Snack, crispy
crunchy, good eating anytime, from Frito-Lay; one package

172

of Old London Cheez Doodles fried for double crunch by Borden, with ferric ortho phosphate, vitamin A palmitate, and mononitrate; one package of Doritos Nacho Cheese Flavor Tortilla Chips, Frito-Lay, with diosodium inosinate, diosodium guanylate, and keep America beautiful, don't be a litter bug; one package, ubiquitous Frito-Lay, should he write them a letter?, they were drowning the market, also about their spelling: Bakon Snack (he *had* written to First National City Bank when they mutated to Citibank; the stomach and the language were obviously in for hard times) Imitation Bacon Flavored Wheat Chips, with hydrolyzed vegetable protein, destrins, and carboxymethylcellulose; and several assorted donuts and several assorted ice creams and several assorted diet sodas to wash it all down and on he marched, deep in quandary and deep in burps, feeling rather nasty, rather fat, rather unloved, rather sick of it all, and hoping that this last donut would do the trick and accomplish the deed of rendering him rather fed up.

Several additional chemistry-set derivatives from General Foods and ITT Continental brought him to the tubs. Tonight was obviously going to be, in all ways, a night for shit food.

Rancid and ratty would best describe the atmosphere of the Everhard Baths at this prime hour. In this outpost of civilized behavior and democracy in action, the redolent smell combined the distinct odors of popper, dope, spit, shit, piss, and a bevy of lubricants. Hundreds of assorted bodies paraded through refuse and puddle-spotted floors, barefoot, bare-chested, protected only by sarongs of towel from complete usurpation by passing eyes. Earlier arrivals, the younger ones at any rate, in good physical shape and desirable, would by now have ejaculated in some manner

173

or other, approximately three to six times, while older soldiers, passing thin-walled moans and groans, would by now have received approximately forty-nine rejections as they heaved pasty white frames from cubicle to cubicle, reached out exploratory fingers of hope to inhospitable cocks, listened for anticipated "I don't think so"s, "Get out"s, or more polite "I'm resting"s, and, eventually, exhaustion being the better part of their valor, settling for one of their own kind, taking ten minutes to get an erection and two seconds to come, then grabbing their clothes and heading for home.

As a shuffling mulatto attendant showed him to his room for the second time this date (Murray recognized the good customers; they never had to wait in line), Fred's spirits were still low. Here he was in the home of basics. Perhaps the place was a world in microcosm, human life reduced to its most simplistic, that awful moment when a name and an identity were no longer essential. If somebody didn't want you, forget it, and find somebody who would take the merchandise as is. He could now feel like a Frito-Lay, laid or unlaid, depending on his shelf age, freshness, spoilage retardation, and understand where chemicals might help.

Since it is late, let us tarry no longer with descriptions of this temple of sex. Suffice it to say that Fred:

a) walked around for twenty minutes getting the lay of the land and deciding that there might be a few possibilities he would return to check out;

b) rejected the advances of a midget in a jockstrap, as well as several Orientals, to whom—he could never figure out why, was it his hairy chest?—he was always so attractive;

c) ran into, then beat a hasty path away from, his suck-Master/fuck-Slave felching acquaintances of . . . was it only this afternoon?;

174

d) grimly shat again, the Everhard toilets enough to keep one constipated for days, as his eyes focused on the graffitied door before him, with its prize-winning: "Fernando sucks Clive Barnes";

e) returned to his cell, sat on the bed leaning against the wall, trying to look casual, seductive to strangers, and not consider this whole ambient scene as true inspiration for a Kafka (who would certainly be at home in Prague writing about it) and, from this uncomfortable position, rejected the advances of three men who courageously entered, each long past thirty-nine, one drunk, one rotunda, and the third with a limp; tried to encourage, sort of, but not overdoing it, that scares them away, seven faces who appeared in the dim light worth encouraging to enter for a closer-see, but who evidently declined the honor because they passed on. How could that fucker say that I don't love him!

The closest he came to, is the word contact?, was a pleasant-enough-looking young man, by name Harold, who jumped up on Fred's cot with one of Fred's leather-thonged work shoes, which he then proceeded to tie around his balls, creating a somewhat pendulum effect.

"Does this turn you on?" Harold asked.

Fred looked up and tried to think. Does that turn me on? He came to no ready answer.

"Do you think I'm kinky?" Harold persevered.

"Nah," Fred replied, knowing this to be not the desired response, though it certainly was for him.

"I do."

Fred nodded the nod of the acquiescent. He was tired. He didn't need the paraphernalia. The guy had a nice body. Why couldn't they just kiss and fuck?

"Couldn't we just kiss and fuck?" Fred looked up at the boy and his boot.

"Don't you know anything kinky?" Harold, the clock

having stopped, started the shoe up again. Fred wondered if it hurt. He thought that the old adage "if the shoe fits" now took on new subtleties.

"Tell me what you want," Fred said, wearily making an effort.

"You tell me. I'm shy."

"So am I."

Harold allowed a long pause. Obviously lack of the necessary tension and excitement was deflating his game. But he tried: "Last week a guy twisted his balls so they stood straight up. That drove me crazy." He looked down on Fred. Obviously it did not drive Fred crazy. Fred recalled the piss-and-suck twins. Harold needed lessons. Harold seemed disappointed and untied Fred's shoe from his pouch, now, Fred noticed, somewhat lengthened, were longer scrotums coming into fashion, the next kick . . . ?

"What's the matter?" Harold asked, annoyed, jumping down to the floor and opening the door. "You got a lover?" With a note of petulance and wonder he made his curtain speech: "There's a whole world going crazy out there and you won't do anything your mother wouldn't do." He threw in the boot and left. Exit childe Harold.

Fred tried to jerk off so he could leave. His heart and his hand weren't in it. He then endeavored to make one final round of the wards, giving himself the old American locker-room pep talk: yeah, Coach, I'll go out there and fight and rush rush rush and look look look for any, *any*, half-way decent asshole or mouth to take me before jerking myself off in the old locker room before finally, sorry Coach, guess it wasn't my game, my day, my year, my lifetime, hitting the showers.

He hit the showers. He washed his body for the second time this date beneath this stream, wondering how the two pieces of shit lying on the shower-room floor had appeared, plus the adjoining cockroach, up-ended, prob-

176

ably fucked to death, glad somebody got something, he thought, looking down at it, then drying off and heading back upstairs toward his room. Some days you just can't get arrested.

And then he saw one! A perfect specimen of what he'd best start looking for again if Dinky was going to play Nervous: early thirties, blond and handsome, an obviously intelligent face, yes, a definite possibility to take his mind off his present Dinkylessness.

He jumped into action, feeling a sudden surge of love for the old tubs, the whole scene, this is what it's all about, the chance of life!, a fondness for storms weathered together and a harbor in view, for happy moments after miserable ones, for HOPE.

He hastened after Mr. Perfect. Where was he? Where the fuck had he disappeared to among these crowded corridors of towel-clad parading flesh?

There he was! Fred gulped. Not bad, though perhaps a bit too stern. And, as occasionally happened when Possibility reared its impossible head, Fred became a slightly helpless, slightly speechless, bordering on the ditzy, futile wreck.

Randy Dildough, for it was he whom Fred was approaching, saw that he was being cruised by a nervous man who was definitely not his type, this immediately conveyed to the suitor by an avoided eye contact and an ongoing journey. Randy, not a top executive for nothing, recognized the nevertheless note of persistence and hoped he would not have trouble ditching this one.

Why did I let Slim talk me into it? What the fuck am I doing here? And without even a pair of dark glasses. What if I run into somebody I know? Or there might be a fire! Or a raid!

Randy shivered as these dark thoughts and questions tingled his handsome sturdy body, fully knowing the answers: the joy of playing with fire! and terror!, a drug habit that couldn't be licked. Well, it's better than shoplifting, he thought, recalling an earlier turn-on he'd reluctantly put back on the shelf when executive duties increased.

Walking around and viewing all the potential, Randy wished that Slim would not be here. It had all seemed a cute, if conciliatory, idea, when, after a particularly annoying disagreement over the WATS line to Los Angeles concerning his lack of return for Slim's birthday, Randy had accepted the compromise of Slim's: "I'll come to New York for the holiday weekend and meet you at the Everhard at four in the morning, so you have plenty of time for dinner with some big shot . . . and anything else, and then we'll find a big black stud and have a threesome. You always enjoy seeing me get fucked by a big black horse and you asked me what I want for a present, that's what I want."

So Randy continued to poke along the hallways and into the cubbyholes, wishing he'd convinced the kid to take a Cartier tank watch instead.

Timmy and Slim sat in a cubicle waiting for Randy to show himself.

They had left Garfield's with Hubie and Morry, all flying high on whatever pink-and-white pills Hubie was popping generously in all directions when a decline in spirit warranted and, at Slim's request, had headed for the tubs.

"He's medium height, reddish-blond, very handsome, and I wish to fuck he would hurry up," Slim said to Timmy, wondering if he should go out himself and look for his lover, if lover he was, always in New York when home was in Los Angeles, if lover he was, when all Slim seemed to do was cook and clean and be there on the several nights a month Randy wasn't out dining with the stars, if lover he was, who had sex with him rarely and much preferred getting off on watching Slim get fucked by someone else. It's too bad Hubie and Morry had left in self-disgust —the drugs too much to allow their black Colossi to colossize—, and shame for letting down their brothers everywhere.

At this point, a familiar face stuck in his head.

"Hey, there, gorgeous, remember Yootha?"

Yootha Truth plopped down on the bed with the two of them, causing Slim, as yet unintroduced to this foreign element, to move away a bit. Yootha wore, in addition to his towel, a smart little sleeveless jacket of sequins appliquéd on see-through net. "I am exhausted. I have been humped by twelve different white gentlemen. I have, however, not found love."

"Where did you get the money?" asked Timmy, recalling Yootha's condition earlier this evening.

"Honey, Dame Fortune has finally smiled on this swishy schvartza. I was cruising the Doubleday Book Store at Fifty-seventh and Fifth when I am seeing a portly gentleman of approximately sixty-three years of age and impeccably dressed in gabardine military twill and broadcloth shirt give me the eye in Non-Fiction. I immediately walked past him with a smile and toward the staff men's room, which only I know is rarely used save by our loitering sisters, to whom I am saying 'shoo shoo,' and in moments in walks my prince who looks side to side and, seeing a clear coast, enters my stall. He immediately inquires 'how much?' I, not expecting such bountiful tidings, because I would have done him for free, I mean who wears broadcloth shirts anymore, also undershorts made from pongee silk, a forgotten quantity, silk, also undershorts . . . I am saying 'My pleasure,' and he is saying 'No, no, you must be

179

paid,' so I am saying 'No, no, my pleasure,' and he is saying, 'No, no,' so I am letting this problem hang in the air while I am doing on him an extra special good and fine and satisfying job, hoping all the time he will whisk me off forever to his triplex overlooking Central Park from the Fifth Avenue side, though his thing was not so large as I would have liked or expected from such an imposing gentleman . . ."

"Then he spirited you away in his Rolls-Royce," Slim said, recalling his own earlier experiences.

"No, he then asked if there was anything in the world he could do for me, and I, in return, replied that I had ambitions to become a famous rock-star singer, and happened by chance to have in my pocketbook a demo record of a song I and some of my uptown slag sisters put together one rainy day, and he took same, jotting down my name and mailing address and giving to me fifty dollars."

"You stoned?" Slim asked.

"Yes, I am stoned. I am stoned and I am happy and I leave you now to pursue more of same." He tried to stand up, but fell back down, then upped himself again by using Timmy's shoulder as a ledge. "Come, young beauty, give Yootha a shove back into the world."

Timmy helped the happy, former scraggy, black cat out into the corridor where they strolled along taking the night air.

"You take that job with R. Allan?" Yootha inquired.

"Yes."

"Well, then, you be careful. R. Allan is not to be trusted."

"Maybe I shouldn't take the job."

"Honey, it's a home and we all got to live somewhere. It's more than I got. Just be careful. We have to look out for ourselves in our little apple jungle." He then touched Timmy's face with his thin, dusty hand. "You're knockout handsome gorgeous. But I hope you got brains. Or can get them fast. Or else you'll wind up doing stage shows at The Pits, having twenty pounds of chain pumped up your keester."

And off he waltzed, his sequins twinkling down the corridor like the tacky stars they were, leaving Timmy to stand there at an intersection, holding up traffic, as at least twenty men of differing colors, creeds, ages, and desires, all hoped this beauty might flash a green-light look at him.

One of these twenty was Randy Dildough. He looked at Timmy Purvis and thought that Timmy Purvis was the most perfect speciman of the male sex he had ever seen. His search was ended. There, in one body, was compounded every dream, fantasy of youth, adulthood, too, the ideal speciman he must have for life. Not only would he get this paragon, even, if necessary, and it would be necessary, Slim-ming down his life, but he would turn him into a bigger star than James Dean ever was, thus making it possible to spend every moment with him, taking him out in public, perhaps even acknowledging that male love did exist.

He beckoned to the lad with a crooked finger.

"Come here," Randy said, never pausing to think if such movie-studio tactics worked in a bathhouse.

Something about the man's look made Timmy feel cold and frightened and helplessly responsive. He found himself walking over to him and saying as coolly as he could: "What do you want?"

"Do you have a room?"

"Yes. I mean, I'm sharing it with a friend."

"Could we get rid of him?"

". . . yes."

Such tactics worked in a bathhouse.

Timmy led Randy back to home base and in they went and Randy saw his lover, Slim, and the two of them looked at each other suspiciously, wondering what the other had been up to, and Slim decided to give him the benefit of the doubt, because seeing him, just seeing him, the selfish executive prick, made him realize how much he'd missed him.

"You found him," Slim said to Timmy.

Timmy, knowing as sure as he knew anything that trouble might have been avoided for the moment but not for very long, said "Yep."

Randy took his lover in his arms. "Happy birthday, baby."

Fred prowled the corridors looking for the vision who was Randy Dildough. Keep active, keep busy, idle hands are the devil's workshop, don't think of Dinky and your current case of The Why Didn't I Do Such and So's and The What Might Have Been's. I shall corral this new one, somehow summon up witty repartee and dazzling displays of intellect and interject casually that I am responsible for the movie that nine out of ten faggots simply adore and then another dollop of wit and razzle-dazzle and he will point his finger saying "I want You!" and I will come and all my future lifetime problems will be solved. Yeah. Just like Dinky.

He looked into an open door. Inside, the man of his fantasies was sitting talking to two beautiful young boys. Oops, he likes chicken. Forget it, Fred. Forget it! He's not even a real blond. He's a reddish. You don't like reddishes.

But Fred stood there mesmerized. So much beauty, particularly in the Junior Department, in one cubicle. Perhaps the three of them would start doing it together and desire an audience. I shall be an audience.

Instead, the just-deposed prince of his dreams looked up at him, grimaced and uttered in distinct tones of unmistakable discouragement: "Get lost, you crud!," thus causing "one of America's finest, most talented screen-writers, why doesn't he work more often?" (Albert Surge, San Antonio *Alamo Torch*) to once again, would his losing streak never end?!, fall into disrepute.

But if he was hurt, wounded, now that the blow had fallen, had he not almost expected it, and what was the pain of being called a crud by a stranger compared to the stomach ache of Dinky preferring an evening sucking steam?

So on he marched, attempting to pick himself up, dust himself off, and, as the song goes, start all over again.

"I guess I'll take another walk," Timmy said.

"Hey, what's your name?" Randy asked, reaching into Slim's jeans and pulling out a cigarette, which Slim knew Randy only did when he was working something out.

"Timothy Purvis."

"Well, Timothy, I'm Randy Dildough. Where are you going?"

"I'll let you guys fuck."

"Want to watch?"

"I don't want anyone to watch," Slim answered, looking at Timmy with not the friendliest of eyes.

"Come back later," Randy said. "We'll all go out for breakfast together." And then, noting that Timmy's clothes were hooked up there as well, so that he'd have to come back sooner or later, he threw his cigarette on the floor and began to wish his lover additional birthday greetings.

Timmy walked the corridors. Life was becoming compli-cated. Something in that Randy's eyes had bored inside of him and touched something. But what? And wasn't he still in love with the Winston Man? Yes, I am. Honestly and truly.

So in his red- white- and blue-pilled way, he prowled back and forth, slowly, methodically, one floor after the other, looking for the Winston Man. Everyone else seemed to be here tonight; perhaps Winnie would be, too. Passing doors and throngs and orgies and twosomes, threesomes, solos, barging into rooms to study faces, hoping, behaving like an old-timer, fearless, drug-courageous, he was in love with Winnie and Winnie he would find. He pushed away all grabbers, ignored smiles and hellos, thinking only of that moment earlier this evening when perfect bliss and harmony were experienced and exchanged like vows. He, Timothy Peter Purvis, would be faithful to those vows. Wasn't that what love was all about?, this fine thought now guiding his feet faster and faster, now through the first-floor maze of lockers, past the long line of impatients waiting to get in, down to the showers, by that first heated swimming pool in New York, into the sauna, now into the steam room, wading through the mist and fog and impenetrable atmosphere, bumping into bodies doing things with bodies, in corners, on slabs of concrete, neath jets of drizzly steam, all rained upon by drops of scalding trickle from the ceiling, baptizing all, and on the very stone-hard floor itself.

And there, as luck would have it, was Winnie. With the guy Randy had called a crud.

Winnie was down on his famous knees, sucking off the Jewish cock of Fred Lemish, a little older then he liked them, but young Jews tonight seemed hard to find. Fred, of course, could not believe his good fortune, this, again, was why he loved the baths, for the jackpot nights, like riding the subway and knowing you're better than somebody, this gorgeous beauty certainly thought so, where had he seen that face?

Timmy watched Winnie and Winnie looked up and

saw Timmy watching and this apparently made Winnie go crazy, now demanding something of his partner, Fred could not quite understand what.

"What?"

"Walk on me! Walk on me! Walk all over me!"

Well, it was an unusual request, and while he preferred to have a continuation of the cock suck, still it was a day of new attempts, breaking the sex barrier, so Fred found himself looking down upon the now supine body of this beauty, it certainly was a gorgeous face and body, now, gingerly at first, be careful not to slip, I wonder just what kind of kick can come from this, for either of us, what the hell . . . New Thing Number III!

Timmy didn't know what to make of it. But if what he was witnessing was all new to him, he responded to it nevertheless in time-honored fashion by becoming jealous and furious and pushing the Crud Person off of his Winnie, and he bent down to kiss his man all over, his man who evidently didn't want to be kissed, this kid was beginning to be a pain, he's not even put off by my most perverse acts, Timmy not believing it as his Winnie threw him off and back against that concrete wall, hurting his head against its curve, not believing that his Winnie could have done that, thrown him such a curve, not believing that his Winnie is now walking away from him, leaving him!, and all alone in this steamy circle of hell.

Furthermore, Winnie was walking away from him with his arm around the Crud Man's waist, they're going off together, oh who will I hold on to for dear life?, in this, his moment of his second greatest abandonment, not noticing that his earlier worshipper, the man who is now about to become so very important in his young, impressionable, malleable life under the Big Top, the specter lurking in said steamy shadows who is Cunard Rancé Evin Dildough, is now watching him, still wanting him.

Timmy looked up and saw Randy and immediately felt relief. I want, I need, somebody's arms around me right this very minute, and to these waiting arms he goes. Disbelief on both sets of arms is rampant, on the part of young Timmy's that they feel so good, and on the part of our Randy's that at last they hold his sought-for conquest, something so perfect that nought else compares, do I really, actually, maybe, have a heart in working order that can make me feel so warm and good?

Whatever hidden fantasies are coming true, the two of them stand there tied up in minglings of passion, need, affection, desperation, sweat, hard-ons, or is it hards-on?, neither could, in a steam room, distinguish which from which. But holding each other they definitely are.

And watching this, was it not ever thus?, and hurt in a way that the biggest prick in the world could always do, about-to-be-ex-lover Slim, now tapping hand to forehead to signal "So long, Randy," then walking off into the mist of morn, and from our story, going . . . going . . . quick, Randy, lest it be too late . . . Gone, unnoticed by the loser, from his Randy's life . . . so ends one near climax to our evening? morning? who can be quite certain which?

"Come along, young Timothy. Do you know who I am?"

"No. Who?"

"I'm your new lover. I'm going to make you a star."

And Anthony? Anthony was preparing to come.

. . . oh that feels good, this one's even better, this one's a real find, make it last, don't come, Anthony, don't come, make it last. . . .

Well, perhaps not. Perhaps he's not ready.

• • •

Fred is now with Winnie, Winnie is now with **Fred,** Randy is with Timmy and Timmy with Randy, Boo still twists and kicks alone on the thronged Capriccio dance floor. Laverne is asleep with Robbie after having successfully used his mushroom, Patty and Juanito are honeymooning, Irving slumbers, dreaming about "Dinky, my Dinky, wherever you are . . . .," and isn't it wonderful that at last it looks like a few of our boys might be bedding down for a rest?

However, while getting dressed in his room, Fred panicked. Who was this strange man with the perverted tastes he was going home with? Recalling a night in London when a handsome Frenchman he'd picked up in Piccadilly Circus had threatened him with knives, recalling how First Love Feffer had one mysterious evening in New Orleans tried to tie him up and whip him with a belt, recalling how Feffer ever thereafter claimed Fred to be a true masochist, sending vibrations out to all the world's true sadists that he was just begging to be punished—all of these nocturnal emissions prompted Fred to immediately jump into his clothes, leave this one at the tubs, you've been laid enough for one day, go home, get some sleep, you've got a date with Dinky to rest up for, run into the hall, and go check out before Mr. Strangeness can get dressed.

He ran right into the arms of Dinky Adams.

"Unh, hi," Fred said, not knowing what to say.

"I was just thinking about you," Dinky said, knotting his towel more tightly round his waist. "I was hoping you might be here."

"We do have this telepathic relationship," Fred answered, opting to play this unscheduled reunion with Calm.

Sucking steam, eh? Well, there is that steam room down-stairs.

"I have something to show you. Come on."

Dinky led Fred down the third-floor corridor and up a back and cordoned-off stairway to a fourth-floor addition, as yet unopened to the public. Here, Dinky had been contracted to decorate all the cubicles into smart designer rooms, like Bloomingdale's. He led Fred on a decorator's tour from one to another, each different, brown for those who thought in tones of brown, yellow for the yellow, lion stripes, army barrack, Joan-Crawford-hatbox black and white, even one papered in Piranesi prints.

"You did all of this?" Fred asked, attempting to be suitably impressed.

"Yes."

"Terrific. Most imaginative."

Taking Fred's hand again, Dinky then led him beyond the special suites and to a huge black open void and there, miraculously, mysteriously lit, appeared a gigantic, bigger and longer and chrome-ier than any Mack, truck stretching the width of the building, a fantasy tunnel the guys would go crazy screwing in, built with his very own hands, certainly a wizard bit of carpentry.

"You made this, too?"

"Yes."

"Yes. Most terrific."

"Want to get fucked?" Dinky asked him.

Fred nodded Yes. Dinky then indicated that he should wait in the back of his handiwork while he went to the end suite, where Billy Boner lived and slept, and, its occupant not home, borrowed some Crisco and some poppers.

While Fred undressed and awaited his long impending ascension unto heaven, inside a truck, the happy face of

188

Winnie Heinz descended and waited, then became the sad and dour face of Winnie Heinz as he realized he'd been stood up, he waited for no Jew, too bad because he seemed like a good walker, your loss, Mister, I am finally going home.

He thus departed safely and only shortly before the famous Everhard fire.

Randy had gone back with Timmy to his room to find it filled with smoke. Randy stifled it as best he could with towels and mattress, it looked benign, get the hell out of here anyway, I've got my Timothy, want to enjoy him, down to my locker, collect my clothes, and get us back home to Pierre!

Dinky and Fred shared a joint, then Dinky greased up his cock and Fred's asshole, then stuffed their four nostrils full of amyl, then proceeded to make entry, whereupon they both discovered that Dinky's cock would not stay hard. A few body rubbings were then attempted by both hunters, like two woodsmen's sticks. Ignition did not spark. So much for old tricks from the forest. Finally Dinky rolled off and lay in Fred's arms, cuddling up close to him, curling up small.

"I just haven't been into sex lately," he said.

Hoping this didn't auger trouble, best skate over this one lightly, it certainly just feels good to feel him again, what a body!, Fred said: "Sinus headaches can be very troublesome. It's OK. We don't have to fuck. It's just nice being with you again. Unh, by the way, who was that fellow I saw you with tonight?"

"Oh, that was Laverne, Jack. I told you all about him. You know, I finally realized tonight I didn't love him anymore. After six years. That's what I was doing in Savannah. I went away to think. I finally rejected him. It's a good feeling. I feel . . . purged. I felt so good I cried."

Since he himself couldn't, Fred was impressed with people who could cry. He was also pleased that this cleansing news meant hope for him.

"Yeah," Dinky continued. "I'm through with Irving, too."

"Irving?"

"I told you about him. Irving Slough. I answered his ad in the *Avocado* for a lover, no strings attached."

"Why'd you go and do a crazy thing like that?" You told me?

"I told you. I was trying to think. He insisted on this two-week trial marriage. I had to promise not to see anyone else. I did it as an experiment. To see if I could get into somebody I wasn't interested in and who didn't turn me on sexually. I really missed you. He wanted to have sex three times a day."

"Three times a day!" Fred thought this not excessive. "How often did you have it?"

"Once a day."

"You did it once a day with Irving Slough!" escaped Fred's lips.

"You know, you look terrific. Your body is fabulous."

"I owe it all to you."

"You owe it to yourself. I liked you chunky. I just told you not to get any fatter."

"Unh, did saying I loved you have anything to do with your trying on Irving Slough?"

"You didn't hear me when I said you were going too fast."

"I thought we were going slow as molasses. I thought we were both big boys and ready to handle it." No, I didn't hear you when you said that.

190

Dinky ducked this one with a kiss on Fred's cheek.

"Hell, there's nothing wrong with being nervous," Fred said, after kissing him back. "Why, I'm nervous, too. Why . . . that's one of just many things we have in common. Like both of us having two eggs every morning."

"No, we're not the same. You know what you want. I don't."

"I don't know what I want," Fred found himself saying.

"Of course you do. Look at your life. You have everything you want."

Fred wanted to say "except you." Instead he said: "Everybody knows what they want. They just won't examine their behavior closely enough and see what it means. So that was Laverne? Why did you stick it out with him for six whole years if it wasn't working from the beginning? I could never figure that out."

"I wanted sex and love together."

"So why didn't you have it?"

Dinky squirmed slightly. "Jack and I never made love like you and I did."

Fred did not catch the squirm. But he did catch the past tense. And he also now caught another curling up closeness. Dinky was patting his cheek. Tenderness. Ah, tenderness. Did he have an elusive angel in his arms, frightened, needing care and nurturing and nonthreatening evidence that my love is good? You got it, kid. All of the above. Column A and Column B. He reached over and kissed Dinky's forehead and patted his cheek right back.

Very softly, Dinky said: "Sometimes I think I've never really been in love. Sometimes I think I'm not capable of it."

Ohmigod. What is he saying? What have I got here? A case of rotten apples or a case in need of help? Do I

191

love him? Yes! Is this a challenge? You bet your sweet ass. His, too.

"Maybe you'll be the first," Dinky said.

There! You see! Hope! Fred, his role as the true teacher—he would bring knowledge and insight to this pupil in need of both—now quite clearly chosen for him, happily answered in his best new pedagogic manner: "Everyone is capable of it. You're born with the need."

What Fred thought to be this shattering fact of life elicited no response. So, feeling suddenly like he might be trying on some straight jacket, in which he would not be free to say just anything, as he'd been doing in all these recent post-Cult days, he reached into his mind for a tranquilizer. Had not Tishbar & Goober written: "True love necessitates the ability to accept another person in all his moods and guises." Was here the clue to how he must proceed? Patience. Understanding. Tolerance. So he said nothing. It was very hard for Fred Lemish to say nothing. But it was not so hard to say nothing with Dinky Adams in his arms.

"You're really terrific," Dinky softly said a few moments in time later.

"So are you. You're terrific, too."

Dinky looked up at the top of his truck and its row of tiny bulbs stretching out toward some horizon. "We'll really have a nice time tomorrow night. I promise you. And we'll go back to Southampton again. And then there's Fire Island for the whole summer."

Fred had entered Meltsville. Did not this moment of tenderness and closeness mean that under this newly appearing cautious Adams exterior a heart beat for Fred!? That wonderful inner Dinky, potentially so fine, so truly truly fine, forget any disappearances and rejections, we'll both learn, we'll strip away exterior geegaws and unkind

192

fripperies, we'll peel them away and find the true, true You. And us.

Dinky bolted up suddenly. "Do you smell smoke!"

They grabbed their clothes and ran, out of the truck, past the fantasy rooms, through the door, down to the third floor, into a nightmare, joining hundreds of other running bodies, naked, Dorothy Lamour-clad, or in part attire, cocks swinging out in fear, or shriveled up in same, or still erected from interrupted orgasms and pointing the way down, joining hundreds more on the second floor, where were the fucking sprinklers?!!, the one stairway now almost impenetrable with smoke and brothers climbing over brothers, bodies that only moments before were touching in more passionate ways, trampling over older ones not able to push and shove as once they could, this place was meant to be safe!!, the stream now feeding into the vestibule, where flames could now be seen grabbing toward the stairwell and the further fuel of naked men, all tackling fate like football players in a game they'd never played, pushing and shoving and kicking and elbowing and biting from backfield positions to gain that extra yard.

Fred and Dinky, holding hands, made it to the street, then to across the street, joining the lucky ones waiting, watching, crying from the safety of the fifty-yard line, to view the blaze scimmage to the sky, carrying with it the smell of flesh, like some incredible pot of Grandma's chicken soup, a blazing cauldron of somebody's bubbalahs, a potent portion of rear ends, as was the team of jumping bodies, hurling out from windows into nets that weren't yet there, the friendly benevolent firemen still unarrived, some stalwart fellows trying to catch the falling players and breaking arms instead . . . and everyone wondering who was left inside.

193

Seven brothers perished in the famous Everhard fire. They included our Patty and his Juanito, who had elected to come here to spend their wedding night.

But it would be several days before the bodies, any bodies, could be identified.

Two other discos opened tonight. Dracula and Destiny One. The former opened to a crowd of only seventy-five, no one knew quite why, something had gone wrong, word hadn't been sufficiently passed or else mysterious leaders elected not to go, the place and all its money down the drain, no hope for saddened Mervie, Doug, and Si, two leather queens and a black, who'd begged and borrowed and fucked for every dime. So much for Dracula. "And what a terrible name!" Bella proclaimed.

The latter, owned by Italian fellows with connections in high places, opened to two thousand strong, humpies who danced till dawn amidst neon profusely used in intricate designs one watched recede into infinity, one's destiny, in the mirrored walls, and thought it only so-so and wouldn't catch fire at all. "And they have a bar!," Blaze cried; "what drug addict drinks?" And really Capriccio is still our favorite very own, so why to join another?

Anthony was still waiting to come.

He had ingested yet another joint of serious smoke and was yet again struck down. He awakened just as the sun might be coming up in the East, but Ellie is still pitch dark. He has awakened because, though he is prone, he is prone on his side and someone is sucking him off and someone is rimming his ass.

. . . here we go again. Feels like two of them down there. How jaded can I get? Do I mind that one of them

194

is licking my ass? Oi, do I have to come to this cesspool and pass out every time I want to get it up? Why have I been so impotent? I used to love to play with myself. It's been through a bad period, a period of warts and bumps and rashes and itches and various impedimenta to sexual exposure, Dr. Blue could not proscribe, nor could Drs. Portnoy, Himmel, Svell, Mnish, mumblers, fumblers all: "nervousness," "change of life," "will go away," "leave it alone," "don't think about it," "keep your hands on top of the covers," wonderful medical advice this day and age, what are we coming to?, when am I coming?, wish the guy in front would be replaced, how do you get rid of a second-rate cock sucker working in tandem with a first-rate ass licker?, oops almost tripped over my pants, "Do you want to be circumcised?," *No, I do not want* to be circumcised!," "Keep the noise down over there!," get away from this one fast!, Sprinkle you look good at moments like this, who is this?, the ass licker back again, guess he must have liked my taste, *Oi, what am I doing here doing these things?,* assholes are un-Godly, used for shit, not miraculous channels for the birthing of babies like the ladies have, hey somebody wanting to get fucked, sticking his ass on my . . . he's all greased up already, wonder how many have been up here before me, come on Anthony, *stay hard,* fuck this gorgeous number, oh shit why can't I get it over with and come!, come back good cock sucker wherever you are, at least that's safe, can't catch anything from another guy's mouth, or can you?, fuck I'm going to jerk off in a corner, how do you find a corner in the dark?, what's this?, oh my god feel the size of this one, "Hey, Mister, five bucks and I'm yours," "You the friend of Frigger's?," "Guess so, who's Frigger?," what are you holding a friendship conversation for, for christ sake?, he's put a forty-three-inch cock in your hand what are you going to do with it what do you want to do with it it's a freak!, "Hey, Mister, you've

195

got a big one too," pat him on the head, only fifteen eh?, tell him to go home, where was I when I was fifteen?, I sure wasn't in a cesspool of an abandoned dock beside a polluted river playing with yardage, "Hey, Mister, you got a hairy chest too," what am I supposed to say to this child?, he's playing with me and I'm getting hard, "My dad has a really hairy chest," "Unh, that's nice," "Wanna take me home?, I'll come for free," jesus fifteen-year-old kid is kissing me all over and he feels nice. No. No. Mustn't feel nice. No more children. Already have Sprinkle. Must have a one-to-one adult mature relationship, not being momma, not being poppa, oh he feels good I think I'm going to come I think I'm going to come I think . . .

. . . I came. Anthony Montano, his life at forty-three totally wasted, the great talent that might have been, the writer of blissful Hollywood romantic comedies who instead is pimping for cancer sticks, must now go home. Become impotent again. Forget semen. I'll never see semen again. Get out of here, Anthony, push your way through the blackness, sun coming out, Moses Heston parting the Red Sea, cockless in Gaza, Fred says I'm on the fence of life, won't fall in either direction, whatever that means . . .

"Hey, Mister. I'm coming home with you whether you want me to or not. I really like you and I don't want to lose you. My name is Wyatt and I'm going to be a famous trampolinist."

The early edition of the afternoon *Post*, on an inner page, carried the one and only mention of the news:

BIG BUST AT SWINGING GAY SOIREE

Police early today raided an unlicensed cabaret in the wholesale meat district that allegedly featured a sado-masochistic show in which a nude masked young man swung from chains while sex acts were performed on him.

The raid was supervised by 10 police infiltrators, one of whom, Plainclothesman J. J. Nopps, was dressed in leather.

The bar, situated in a damp basement beneath Balalaika, a popular homosexual discotheque at 2240 West Street, is known as The Pits, and had been operating without proper licensing.

Charged with promoting obscenity was William Boner, 57, of no discernible address, owner of the club, who was not in evidence.

Also charged was Timothy Peter Purvis, 16, no fixed address, the alleged "victim" in the sado-masochist show.

According to Nopps, Purvis, wearing nothing but a black mask, a leather belt and a leather apparatus on his genitals, was swung from the ceiling as he was whipped and penetrated anally with various objects by an older man, not apprehended.

As a sidelight, a middle-aged woman, dressed in man's clothing, managed to escape by disappearing into a throng that had gathered outside, all evidently members of the Mizrachi Women of America, Brach Joy Cohen Chapter, a religious organization that claimed to have recently taken title to the premises through a charitable contribution from one of its members.

In one of the rooms, Nopps said, homosexual films were shown, and in a darkened kitchen individuals took turns performing private homosexual acts "for no charge."

Police seized 180 cases of beer, 25 cases of liquor, 73 cases of diet soda, an assortment of drugs, two nude black dancers, $14,000 in receipts, and sado-masochistical equipment, including two black leather jackets with Police Dept. patches on them and an assortment of whips.

● ● ●

The perpetrator of these acts upon young Timothy, our Randy Dildough, was euphoric. What a charge! he'd come in his fucking pants! The hard-on had started in the Everhard itself, with the flames licking and danger lurking and Randy loving every dangerous moment of it all. They'd rushed down and out and, instead of heading home, Randy wanted more. The Pits, he'd heard about the infamous Pits, why end this evening on such a charred note, let's head for The Pits and more! Pausing only momentarily to purchase some unknown tablets from unknown pushers vending outside of the Everhard's entrance when business inside had so suddenly gone up in smoke, they'd hopped a cab to take them to the continuation of their evening's merriment.

And there, in that bowel of darkness, filled with bodies so thick you could cut them with a knife, and somebody probably was, they'd had more pills and a few beers and Timothy had told him about his love for the Winston Man and how his heart was broken and then more visits from unknown pushers and then, and then . . . pushing young Timothy into black arms and . . . watching him be strung up in punishment for telling Randy such awful news about his Other Love.

As he stood naked thirty stories up on his Pierre's carpet, looking in one of the seven full-length mirrors of his suite, his cock got hard in memoriam. The scene! the cheers and catcalls of such an admiring audience! Young Timothy so beautifully displayed! his own new love performing just for him! More pushings! And such a finale! Such a climax! Cops and cops and whistles and chargings and shouts of fear and rushes toward exits and hundreds of frightened faggots, once again, pushing and shoving and belting and screaming and Randy had come in his pants!

As he now again wanted to do, though he didn't

have his pants on, in front of that mirror, looking at himself again and thinking: You're shriveling, Dildough . . . you're shrinking back into nothingness.

For Timothy was gone, and so was Slim—no one here beside him, only himself in the mirror—yes, James Dean Purvis was gone, lost in the fracas, while Randy was having too much fun attending to his own escape.

How to get him back and up here, how to get my cock back up here, as Jimmy Dean had got it up there for me in a way no recent escalation had so pleasurably done?

No doubt he'll be at The Toilet Bowl tonight. I wasn't planning on going, of course. But now I'll have to.

What am I saying! I'm a President! I can't go on like this.

Yes, Timothy's the one for me. I'll stop all of my nonsenses and settle down with this one. Enough of snakes and fires and raids.

In this business, you're only as good as your last movie. Well, Timothy will be my last movie.

He then recalled that he had promised Adriana to have tea with Dordogna del Dongo. Three Valiums were taken to rest up for that.

Back home in Loftsville, Boo Boo Bronstein, too pilled-up to sleep, was feeling most unrefreshed and empty. He tried jerking off thinking of himself as "Rock" and then as "Tab." But his rose by any other name this early morning was not rising.

He then confronted the four weeks' supply of Drake's Ring Dings and Yankee Doodles and Grand Union Small Early June Peas, which he liked to eat straight from the can. He then confronted the reason why he'd bought them. He then decided not to confront the reason why he'd

199

bought them. He then was left to face the only thing left to face: OK, here I am, now what do I do?, time on my hands, I am bored out of my fucking tits, *Yuck!*

I'm going to go to Fire Island tomorrow. I'm going to go to Fire Island tomorrow . . .

I could go to Australia and with very little capital open up a stand on the beach and sell my special tuna-fish salad. I'll just bet they don't have tuna-fish salad like mine down there. The secret ingredient is chopped fresh string beans. And Grand Union Small Early June Peas. I'd begin a new and richer, fuller life. A new and poorer life you mean.

There's only one way you're going to get your money, Richie. If you're tired of hand jobs, you're simply going to have to blow Abe's safe!

Why am I so scared?

Tuna-fish salad in Australia! You're a Yale graduate for Christ's sake. Where's your courage, man? He owes it to you! He made you what you are today! And now he's gone and made another one!

He then went out on his fire escape to water his plants. They weren't doing very well. Neither am I. Then he realized that policemen could climb this fire escape and look in his window and see that beefy, swarthy, dangerous men were not in residence. He would be surrounded by the law and confronted with his hoax and his ineptitude. I think my plan is full of holes. I think I need an alternate plan. I think I should stop thinking.

But back he went to his scrapbook of clippings. And back he went to his flagpole. He perused them both. The former was thick and full of news. "Mobile Home Heiress Buried Alive in Coffin with Straw to Outside World." That's me. That's how I'm living now. He looked at the flagpole. Are you my straw? My Straw to the Outside World? "Many millions and she lived."

It seems a bit unusual. But it had worked.

Richie, let's think this one out.

Why are you kidnapping yourself?

So I'll get my money before he finds out I'm a faggot.

Is that the real reason?

Yes!

Then why not blackmail him? It's ever so much cleaner.

It just takes a little bit more in the way of guts.

So, feeling very sorry for himself, and for his loneliness and various abandonments, then and now, and for his lack of spunk and future, he pulled out the pen and once again put pique-full thought to prose.

"I love you, I love you," Wyatt Bronstein continually mumbled, even in his sleep, as he cuddled closer and closer into Anthony's furry being high up o'er Beekman Place.

Anthony realized it had been a long time since anyone had said that to him. He also realized that it had been a long time, if ever, since anyone had kissed him and kissed him, thus making up for so many years of lack of same. He also realized that he had committed an incomprehensible action, bringing home a fifteen year old. He also realized that he was glad he had.

It had been wonderful. Wyatt, courtesy of Anthony, had come three times, twice from having that ten-inch pipe blown, and once, God have mercy on Anthony's soul in some future heaven, from being, for the first time, yes, Anthony had been its first violator, the taker of the kid's hymen, fucked, and not only been fucked but coming simultaneously!, i.e., without any stimulation whatsoever applied to his young cock, but only from the pressure of Anthony's dong against his effervescent prostate, oh God our help in ages past have mercy on this sinning wop

Catholic pervert who in all of the above almost came once more, too.

Then Wyatt had bent down to kiss Anthony's resting organ. "It's almost as big as mine. That means we're meant for each other." And just that kiss, just those words, just that young fellow looking up at him with such uncomplicated affection, made our Anthony spurt quite unexpectedly. Such a premature ejaculation. Most embarrassing.

But the kid paid no attention to such an older man's problem. He just jumped up seventeen times into the air on Anthony's Posturepedic, then did a double-twist flip, then fell into Anthony's arms with a "I love you, I'm sorry I can't come anymore, I'll make up for it tomorrow," then fell asleep, after a few more kisses, in that sweet fetal position which so touches older men's hearts.

Fred Lemish, our hero, and his still beloved, Dinky Adams, had rushed back to Dinky's walk-up apartment in a building on West 29th Street, filled by its landlord with faggots, who fixed things up much prettier than straights. Fred loved this apartment, so much of it made by Dinky's own talented hands. There were built-in banquettes with huge patterned pillows of all colors and friendly Oriental scatter rugs and a tall armoire from Provence and bowls and vases of flowers and corn plants that reached to the ceiling and his bedroom was tiered with shelves of wicker hampers for storage and the bed was high on a pedestal of white, from which the surrounding sky and rooftops could be viewed from this sixth floor, just still within Fred's safety range.

They lay naked upon this pedestal, the sun now coming up, though not coming up was Dinky's cock, which Fred had once more rubbed against, just a little, to see if anything might happen down there. It didn't. Fred's own,

202

of course, was hard, though he was doing his damndest to will it down lest its pressure embarrass Dinky. Oh, go down, damn you, go down!, he tried to communicate to it. But Dinky now had his hand on it, checking it out, let him hold it a minute, perhaps it will inspire him. It didn't. Then Dinky took his hand away and it went down.

"Yes, you really look terrific," Dinky said. "We'll see what happens. I have a friend coming up next week from Savannah. I met him while I was away trying to sort out Jack and trying to sort out what I was going to do with you. He was very sweet. Very noninvolving and no hassles. He's an architect named George. He doesn't mean anything to me. I'm sorry now he's coming. Just a vacation romance. Nothing can come of it. He doesn't even want to live in New York."

Why am I being told all this?, Fred paused to wonder. This I didn't need. What should I say and do? What the fuck is going on here? What the no-fuck is going on here?

"He sounds nice," Fred heard himself, like some generous saint, reply. "If you had such nice feelings, then perhaps he might be something serious and you should go with it, fall in love, let it happen."

Dinky's toe gently poked over to touch Fred's toe. "But he doesn't mean a thing to me." The toe moved away. "He's an architect. He asked me to help him with a big assignment."

A hassle appeared in the Lemish interior. George was throwing Dinky big bones. Big bones that could take Dinky away for long periods of Savannah. Savannah was a long meal away. Were George's bones as big as Lemish's bones? Let's see.

"You know . . . I forgot to tell you . . . I've found some men, it all happened so suddenly, while you were away . . . who want to finance our gay hotel."

"You're kidding."

"No. They think it's a fabulous idea. I told them there are fifteen million faggots in the United States without a nice place to stay in New York, which is the gay capital of the world, plus God knows how many millions from everywhere else and all the ships at sea and . . . and . . . and they think it's a . . . terrific idea. They're straight. But they sense our time is near."

"Do you really think it could happen?"

Fred put his own foot over and back to undertoe his offer more forcefully. "It'll happen if we want it to happen."

Then our hero wished he hadn't done it.

Yet he foundered on. "We can use it as an experiment to spend time with each other, get to know each other, I've truly missed you, I wouldn't be doing this if I didn't truly think you have the talent to handle it, and see where it takes us." Why couldn't he take the risk of Dinky taking him for himself alone? That would be a better building. Without any sagging piles. Or a sinking foundation of insecure, heartful muck.

Dinky's toe and Fred's toe said hello to each other.

"It's you and me we'll work on after George leaves," Dinky said.

"Work on what?"

"Our relationship."

"Our relationship?"

"Well, our romance."

"Our romance?"

"Well, our getting to know each other."

"Well, how about that?" You see, Fred, how patience and tenderness and hope and playing footsie can all work out just fine? "He doesn't mean a thing to you, you say?"

"After he leaves, we'll see each other every night."

"Terrific!"

"Seven nights a week."

Then they cuddled into each other's arms, each somehow satisfied for the moment and rather tired from their strenuous exertions to erect such a defended splendid hotel. Dinky mumbled in Fred's ear: "My bulldog, Fred, who takes his two eggs soft while mine are in an omelet," and the sun was bright outside as they, too, fell asleep in each other's arms, warmed by the fulfillment of their mutual needs and the shining late May beauty.

In his apartment in the eaves of the Dakota, with a handsome view of Central Park, if you poked your head out of the window and looked left, Leather Louie was resting while Lance Heather continued to administer to a rather mauled, blood-patterned, lanky blond hanging happily from the gallows by his wrists. His name was Feffer.

Yes, their successful cruise on the waterfront had netted Fred Lemish's First Great Love and led to his current standing, or lack of it.

After two scenes, there was still a smile on Feffer's face. He thought it amusing, back in America only hours after four years, not even having checked in with Fred or Anthony, and already strung up. He also thought it funny that back home in the country from whence he'd fled now found him the whipped and not the whipper he'd been when he ran away from it. No doubt about it, this land of overachievers certainly did things to him. As did the thought of his forthcoming journey to Wisconsin, back to Pa, back to having to gently, cogently, successfully, extricate from Pa, nice Pa, who never told me what to do, wish you had, Pa, what can I do, Pa?, the necessary funds to live a few more years abroad. Yep, I'll punish myself in advance for all that, too.

205

So, as the tensions and the tinglings once again began to exert their pull, Feffer's truly lovely American cock began another welcome home, which made it all right for its owner, whose mind was now filling with fantasies of religious martyrs and thorn-crowned heads and heavy dragging crosses and son's sufferings beyond the ken of Pa's. Oh, Mary Baker Eddy, please forgive me for taking a few tiny pills.

Louie lipped a cigarette, the smoke curling up from his really pussycat lips in sinister fashion, and watched with admiration the neatness, the economy, the fair-haired and smooth-skinned simplicity that *was* Southern California, the surfer rampant, and Lance Heather and his tricks upon the dangling man. There were no wasted motions, no hoopla or showy overexertions; Lance was a Klemperer as against a Lenny Bernstein.

Lance administered a final tidy slash with his favorite whip, thousands of tiny strands of elephant hair, not a soft hair goodness knows, no maybe goodness doesn't know, bound in a handsome handle of South African ebony, the elephant hairs reputed to have come from land adjoining William Holden's Kenya ranch. All of them whooshed against that long and lean perfection, which Fred had for so long worshipped and for so long found so difficult to forget. Lance seemed most annoyed at that beauty, as if he could see within it Feffer's goodness and intelligence and morality (or as if he could see within it a reminder of that Dildough, still at large, vengeance unachieved), and, as he'd wanted all of this within him punished, Feffer quivered in pain and joy.

"*Ancora,*" he mumbled, uncertain where he was.

Lance and Louie nodded to each other. This one would do perfectly for tonight's big scene. Let him live this post meridiem.

● ● ●

206

Fred awakened in mid-afternoon, the sun opening his eyes, and reached over to find not Dinky but a note: He had some plantings to attend to, make himself at home, there were juice, eggs, and instant coffee in the kitchen, and he'd see him at The Toilet Bowl tonight.

So, wearing a pair of Dinky's red-satin Champion boxer shorts, and feeling young and good and butch and wanted, Fred wandered around his would-be lover's space. "We'll work on developing our relationship, our romance," wandered around with him. Yes, Fred would be patient, he must learn how to live Stages 2 through 9, when he'd always been so anxiously impatient to jump from 1 to 10. This would be his experiment.

As he ate his two eggs soft and over crumbled Triscuits, sitting at Dinky's desk, Fred noticed to coffee-cup-left ten copies of a snapshot of his inamorato all in leather. Another hassle reported in from the Lemish interior.

So, since he'd never been alone here, Fred commenced what he felt he must now commence to do. He began a thorough search of Dinky's apartment. If Dinky hadn't told him much, then he'd Sherlock Holmes out what he could, on-the-job research, the Writer/Lover-in-Action, and use whatever information he would find to subtly force-feed their true and destined if reluctantly blooming love.

In a wicker trunk under the bookcase by Dodger's alcove he found a black leather outfit, pants and epauletted shirt and officer's cap and face mask and cock sacks and a short whip and a weight to hang from the balls and long gloves and thick chains with handcuffs and feet restrainers. (Were these Dinky's?!)

In a wicker hamper on the top shelf in Dinky's bedroom, along with many assorted foreign and domestic letters filled with requests for meetings from photographs of men dressed in much of the above (the wicker hamper book-ended by those many assorted volumes of knowledge Fred had found so helpful and had then so helpfully gifted Dinky, need we list them here?), he found a thick membership directory to Inter-Chain, a world-wide organization of leather and slavery and bondage and Master-Slave with its information under Adams, D., that he was interested only in supervising bondage and light whipping and punishment and Master-only rites, together with twenty further copies of that photograph, his Dinky standing tall, cold, immobile, the whipping Master just waiting to be summoned to command, all in those leather items. (They were Dinky's.)

In a wicker hamper on the shelf below, Fred found his own earlier long letter of love and commitment, written after their douche date and Dinky's disappearance. Under this was a pledge of love from Irving Slough. In descending layers under this were similar billets-doux from a Tony, an Olive, a Piero, a Chipper in California, a very young-sounding Paulie at the Club Baths in Miami, plus a curling ancient letter to Frigger (was it ever sent?): "We have so much in common, couldn't we try and work it out?," then a photograph of someone, not particularly attractive, standing on a Hassler balcony overlooking the beautiful Borghese Gardens Fred recognized from his own Feffered fevers in that fine town, and identified on the back as "Me and Ike Bulb in Rome." And finally, at the bottom, there were pictures of Laverne, and Dinky with Laverne, when they lived in that Southampton house beside the canal and looked happy.

And then, oh was it not ever thus!, in the wicker wastebasket by the desk, Fred found a crumpled draft of a letter dated just the other day to he-doesn't-mean-anything-to-me George:

There is so much I want to say, but I'm afraid. Afraid of going too fast, pushing too much, giving too little. Afraid of tomorrow, of being hurt, of hurting someone else, oh so many things. However, your tenderness brings me back. It is something I have been without for so long that I forget what it makes me feel, or better, *that* it makes me feel. Oh, George, I feel wonderful. I only hope that I have given you at least a little of what you have given me. I hope that you are wonderful, too. On paper we make so much sense. (But words are words and to turn them into feelings is very difficult.) Maybe I should draw a tear. But a happy tear, running down a contented cheek, coming from a tender eye, my cheek, my tear. Would you understand? Do you understand? I hope so. Please hurry and come to me.

Our Hero welcomed Death.

Timmy, who was released unto the recognizance of R. Allan Pooker, obviously much experienced in handling such tricky matters, had just completed his part of the afternoon's shooting, with his co-star, Paulie, of what had appeared an innocent-enough vehicle for their bodies in the woods of Central Park.

R. Allan had video-taped him only from the front. The back part was evidently Paulie's. Timmy's own was still most sore, he couldn't remember quite how or why, he'd been so drugged, people in this city just seemed to appear from nowhere, popping them, selling them, even the cop in the jail had slipped him a nightcap for breakfast, yes, his yesterday's journeyings had been a drug sundae indeed. He wouldn't mind some more because he presently felt so down.

He ran to the nearest phone booth and directory to begin his search. In his blind hopefulness he'd expected to discover the name "Winston Man" listed there and to dial the proper numbers and rush into those safe arms and all would be heaven thereafter.

Of course it wasn't to be. No help from Ma Bell. So he ran from the Zoo and over to an elegant Fifth Avenue doorman.

"Does the Winston Man live here?"

"No, young fellow, I'm happy to say he don't."

"Where is the nicest, fanciest, neighborhood in this entire city where if you were rich and famous you would live?"

"Why, right around here," the doorman answered, further explaining that Best extended from Fifth to the East River and from 57th to 90th and that unless he had a name, it might prove rather difficult locating a cigarette model, no matter how famous the face.

Not knowing that the object of his stubborn adoration, his only salvation after his detours with that nasty Dildough—make me a Star indeed! he ran away and left me hanging!—was at present performing, as must all famous models after such a night, Sleeping Beauty, having Dedrominixed himself to bed at dawn, his skin and loveliness rejuvenating, until this very evening, when he'd put in his Toilet Bowl appearance, Timmy took a deep breath and plunged right in.

He knew he hadn't much time, he had to get to the Bowl himself, to watch his film debut and, more important, perhaps to find his Winnie there. But, just in case, for now, he started here with Fifth, headed east, hit all the buildings, looked at all the mailbox names, asked the doormen, studied all the faces in the lobbies, on the streets, hoping against hope he'd find his man, his face, his beloved, not knowing when he visited the brownstone, 66th off Madison, that up above, right up there, the name is Heinz, sleeping, so continuing, next next next, ignoring cruises

210

from many a resident, many a dog walker, 73rd Street finished, Fifth to Park only, crisscrossing the area like a darned sock, still no clues, no leads to Winnie, persevering, he'd find his man, *Yes I will!*, the little boy lost and needful, crying *I want my Winnie!*, Winnie, why can't you hear him?, why can't you hear when love is calling, screaming, yelling, bawling out for you? Turn on your antenna, fine tune the reception, picking up no static, only the clear sign of Tim Purvis, lover, looking. Not finding.

Irving Slough was not at the Sutton Place hearthside he shared with his mother. Nor was he in his various offices on the 54-55-56-57th floors of a Lexington Avenue skyscraper. He was in that small *pied-à-terre* he kept in Tudor City, the hideaway love nest he kept just like his two straight married partners, Heiserdiener and Thalberg. And here he waited all afternoon for Dinky to come and fuck him, as a call from him earlier had indicated he might do, if he had time, and had Irving remembered to send the check for the monthly terrace maintenance and new plantings?

This morning Irving had gone to the Village and to the Marquis de Suede and there he had picked up the special order he'd placed in a moment of miff after Dinky's lam out of town on the conclusion of their shotgun wedding. He didn't think he'd use it, but he thought he'd pick it up now anyway, and if Dinky was a good boy, then he'd use it on someone else instead.

Irving was not at heart a nasty man. He thought this as he strutted in his leather gear before his mirror. The boots with three-inch heels and cross-over bucklings at the ankle. The chaps tight around his thighs and hips and holding in his stomach firmly while revealing his still not too generous cheeks. The shirt with stringed crosshatchings to display his hairy chest but disguise his sagging tits. But, for all his studies at the Universities of Niesdorf, Glantcha, the Isle of Wight, he could never fully, completely, understand the subliminalities of his attraction to leather. For let his cock touch leather and it instantly staticized, erected unto magnitudes unknown in tweed or cotton, and brought to his already forceful personality a surging, throbbing stature that oozed around him like a contagion he thought could render victims to his feet in droves. Such an authoritarian fabric, leather! Perhaps this was enough to know. Not think of it as gift wrapping for the s-m package, that replacement box for the parental authority I wanted as a child, and *wo war mien* Pops? Was it not better to wear it, do it, live it, than suppress it? That only leads, on an international scale of course, to war. And he did get such wonderful sensations in his schlang when men chose to grovel neath his leathered self.

Dinky had yet to grovel. Would Dinky grovel? Or would Irving do the bending? Yes, Irving was also considering for the first time in his life that he might like to get down on his hands and knees and allow a dog's collar to be put around his neck and to be led around on all fours. This morning he'd even bought the collar. Interesting.

What was Dinky doing to him? Should he wear his gear tonight, in public, for Dinky to see him? A shining black knight, a fantasy man for Dinky's dreams, to spirit him away? Was this how he could get Dinky? Yes, time was running out. I am open to intimacy, I understand all human problems, I have a strong sense of myself. So why am I still so unsatisfied, so alone?

Why is that child so ungiving and withdrawn! True, as a youngster Dinky had said he was a "Pretty Boy," a role that he had hated. Everyone wanted to fuck him. So he grew his beard and muscles so no one would fuck him anymore. Yes, he could then humiliate everyone, as I am sure

212

his parents humiliated him. Humiliation is so essential to Catholics. And to faggots! So many of my fantasies in sex are of vengeance and retributions and humiliation and anger, against men!, and . . . why cannot I admit my hope of finding security in the warmth and love of another man is vanishing? . . .

Yes, he'd go out like this tonight and surprise his Dinky. I shall overcome all fears that my partners will find out or see me. Enough of Adriana as beard. I want to shave. Just as I encourage all in our therapeutic sessions to so do.

Then he worried that tonight might not be so good. Tonight was an opening that would be covered by *Women's Wear* and filled with slummers and celebrities and socialites, now that gaydom in this city is so chic. They will probably disappear after an initial look-see, but one never knew, one could not take chances, there might be that one person hiding in a shadow later when more heavy scenes transpired—a patient, a partner, a client, a client's perverted wife. No, best wait till Sunday, Fire Island, my party, The Meat Rack, I'll show my leather to my Dinky there.

So he plopped down on the large fuck bed with its rawhide spread to wait for Dinky's call and to contemplate a photograph in the *Times,* of a young man from Oxford in tweed hunting jacket and holding furled brolly, with that long blond hair and those high cheeks and the fine skin and patrician nose, all bespeaking Class and In-ness, neither of which Irving felt close to possessing, not even after dining with The President or making as much money as The Queen.

Yes, the strong sense of myself is built on a bed of quicksand and never never will I have what I want! Irving knew all this and still he thought of Dinky, fantasies of Dinky's dangling cock and Dinky's white tight tush, and

still he gazed at Master Oxford gazing back at me, might
you just not come across the sea and whisk me off into a
wild romance, played against the drama and background
of tropical nights and sunny sandy beaches and much
lovemaking tempestuously on floors, wickedly rampant in
bathtubs, closets, naked under moon and stars (no, maybe
not naked, a diet first, *no,* Oxford will take me as I am!,
and love me) . . . but wait, Oxford would not like me in
leather, and anyway it's time to change, so off come military hat and boots and jerkin and chaps and jockstrap and
cock ring, back into the closet they go, try not to look at
fat chubby in the mirror as it changes back into Egyptian
cotton and lisle and Countess Mara and vertical stripes and
wing tips and a more respectable form of drag, oh he was
sick of hiding, sick of Tudor City, sick of time running
through the hourglass of sadness, sick of not being able to
hold hands with someone in public, and kiss in the
presence of partners, and say: "Hi, honey," "Hi, sweet-
heart," " Hi, pumpkin," "Hi, Love," oh, where now were
Tad or Bart or Whynn or Chauncy or Gatson?, all gone,
why do I go through them all so quickly?, Whynn, the last
before Dinky, summarily dismissed along with a few thousand and a ticket to London when he threatened revela-
tions, he wished him momentarily back for old fuck's sake,
that fine body, that fine if unformed mind, why were they
always unformed?, why did he always wish to form them?,
why did his heart always go out to all the Dinkys?, let me
teach you, let me give you, let me treat you as I would
have been treated, he wondered if that Fred Lemish suf-
fered the same curse, he obviously did, for Dinky had
showed him Fred's seventeen-page letter of love, his "Ode
to Possibility and Potential," just you wait, Fred Lemish!,
when you come to this, he thought momentarily of touch-
toning One Touch of Penis, have them send that cute
Paulie over, no, Dinky still might come or call, the hours

214

of waiting for those promised: "I'll call you later"s, ah Penis, should I?, shouldn't I?, we could do it quickly, it isn't Acapulco but it is a floor, no, he'd save his all for Dinky, and continue waiting, Dinky-less, going to a Toilet Bowl, swathed in vertical navy pin stripes from Scrill, Naw & Derdip of Old Bond Street, vertical helps fatties, what is wrong with me today?, I need a new lover in my life, the old ones leave me wanting, is this what old age brings?, I need something like tutti-frutti used to taste when I was ten, where will I go on lonely nights now that the Everhard's burned?, and then, looking once again at *The New York Times* and Master Oxford, Irving Slough tried fervently to wish the image from the page and into his arms, the two of them on the Royal Road to Romance, take your choice, Master Oxford, immissio penis in anum or in os?, as he zipped open his Scrill, Naw & Derdip and jerked off.

As our Saturday-night grand opening comes closer, let us join two distaff members awaiting the arrival of Randy Dildough.

Dordogna del Dongo, a handsome woman, redolent of flaming red: her hair, her dress, her essence (her eyes are black), confides, in her living room, expensive views of Central Park, from the Fifth Avenue side, damask and toile and flimsy nettings of gentle gauze and chiffon and crepe de Chine, billowing o'er furniture gathered from the globe's four corners, elegant, unusual, original, uncomfortable: tables of tusks, sofas of puffs, side chairs of slats, floors of marble, walls of wool, an impressive decorator's dream in lemon-green-white-limestone-cement-and-Harris-tweed, to her good friend, Adriana la Chaise: "I am nervous."

Dordogna is called Dordogna. She does not have a nickname. And, while nervousness can be a touching quality in a woman, Dordogna and nervousness will never be on intimate terms.

While sounding German, her husky accent is not. But she had been educated abroad, on the island of Sylt, where she had met, fallen in love with, and married her first faggot, Helmut del Dongo (who does have a nickname—Mutty), thereby relinquishing her maiden name of Jones.

They were two innocents then, Mutty and Dordogna, she already described, he medium, wiry, pie- and pasty-faced, both only twenty-five, and they played with each other and at life as if the enchanted cottage in which they dallied would never be spooked.

But it was not to be. Dordogna soon discovered that there was more to a man than his providing her with an ancient name, a vast inheritance, a jetting into the society in which she wished to deplane, her own bank account, a skyscraper duplex, and pleasing companionship, including a shared passion for marbles—and that Mutty was simply not providing it. Along about the second year of their blissful, storybook marriage, she began to have dreams about gigantic cocks, often more than one at a time, all somehow protruding from Mutty's body, she impaling herself on one, on all, on one after the other, and being transported unto a rhapsody thus far unplayed.

Not being an hysterical young woman, she attempted with the suavest of psychological devices to lure her Mutty toward scaling more lascivious heights. At first she would merely play with him, which, since he did a great deal of this by himself, provided scant results. She then reversed her body so that they both might practice mouth-and-mouth resuscitation, also to little avail, beyond a slight proneness on his part toward gagging. Eventually, with the aid of marijuana, scented unguents imported from the East, where they were thought to know about these things, plus a great deal of time and patience and loving words and soft music and the burning of a special incense imported from the West Coast, where they were thought to know about these things, she managed to make him semi-hard.

In despair, she finally asked him directly: "Mutty, *querido,* what would make you nice and hard?"

He paused a long moment before answering. After all, his marriage was at stake, a marriage the del Dongos of Argentina not only sanctioned but thanked their lucky stars the boy has finally stopped his *Selbstbefriedigung* (jerking off) (there is much German feeling in Argentina) and taken a woman, even if she is from Flatbush and common, but who will ever know with that accent and a classy name like Dordogna?

However, Mutty knew he couldn't keep up the charade forever, that his softness was only going to make Dordogna, an insistent type, try harder, and anyway he had his own realizations (once you have tasted cock, you can never forget it) to contend with. He figured he might as well get it out and over with.

"What would I like?"

"Yes."

"Anything in the world?"

"Anything! Tell Dordogna."

"To make me nice and hard, Mutty would like that you would on the wall opposite to this bed of swan project pornographic films of men doing things to each other." He felt cleaner for his confession.

To her credit, Dordogna took it like a mensch. She lay back on their feathered bed, stuck his rich fingers into her fine Selbst, and had him befriedgte her off. Then, relieved of her tension, she relaxed and tried to think things out.

"You must have what you want, Mutty, without guilt. I could not keep you away from sucking your cocks."

"Who says you have been keeping me away?"

217

"You have been leading a double life?"

"Not so double. I thought you knew."

"I never knew."

"Now you know. And I am more in love with you than ever."

"And I with you, Mutty, more than ever."

So they cuddled together, played a good game of marbles, and then she looked at her bank balance and decided that she would become a successful designer of men's clothes. That fancy South American name should be so useful.

Two years later three million men around the globe are wearing her suits and sports coats and slacks and lounging robes and Argyle socks. Her casual style was an instant success, the satisfaction of an unfulfilled international need. She now has a bank balance to rival Mutty's father and is considering branching into Cologne.

Mutty on his part found bachelor's digs, kept in daily touch with his still wife, and spent two glorious years sucking cock from city's bottom to city's bottom. He is dimly aware that he has yet to find the companionship he enjoyed with Dordogna, she is still my best and only friend, he has thought to himself many times, but then he is now mature enough to realize that one cannot have everything and besides she is now such a success as to frighten even a del Dongo.

Dordogna continued to play nervous. "Adriana, whatever will I say or do?"

"Oh, Dordogna, stop it! You'll know precisely what to say and do. You always do."

Adriana the helpful, Adriana the romantic, Adriana the bosom buddy to the current and fair, Adriana the rich, all that English beer, Andriana still looking good for sixty, not so bad for a tired English bohemian leftover from the edge of Edna St. Vincent Millay, now hiding in a sea of faggots, for whom feminine beauty was not the keystone, outrageousness was!, making them tons more fun than straights, Adriana was placing her young pal, Dordogna, in the path of that nice young mate of hers, whom she had run into just this morning at The Pits and warned him: "Darling, if you're going to be quite so visible, we'd better find you another beard!" Yes, Randy Dildough was due shortly for tea.

"I suppose," Dordogna said, checking herself in her mirrored wall and ceiling, deciding that she was flamingly beautiful and huskily, muskily so. "I am always having faggots," she then said. "Why am I always having faggots?"

"Darling, you love faggots. They are a challenge for you. You will not rest until you turn one of them on. I know and respect your chase."

"I suppose." And then, after a wave of her long chains of real gold and a swing of her Oriental bracelets, she asked: "Why, do you suppose?"

"Do you wish my best Hampstead Heath interpretation?"

Dordogna nodded and rattled.

"Because you and I, I consider my own problems just as yours, are terrified of real men, mainly because real men are such godawful bores."

"True. So true. And no challenge whatsoever."

"And they are not interested in what we are, things which faggots know so well, things of beauty and moment, things of fashion and fun, things of this instant and long ago, they love old things." Then, pausing to consider that she was an old thing, she added: "The only trouble . . . one does so want now and then to get laid."

The meeting was not an instantaneous success. Randy was, naturally, nervous, and Dordogna could find no clue to how to play her hand.

She tried flattery, demureness, an interest in films and

219

other current events. Adriana tried a few off-color jokes and then excused herself to go home and dress.

Alone, Randy was even more nervous with the woman. But then, inadvertently, she hit upon her clue.

"You are such a powerful man," she said. "You must tell me about power."

He suddenly found this woman honest and sincere and interesting. He began to relax. He then recalled she had a husband. He relaxed even more.

Well, it's a start. And, thinks he, she does seem so terribly interested. Perhaps she is. After all, he is important. But then, thinks she, so am I. Two Important People Belong Together think both of them. Could I live with that, thinks he. Could I live with that, thinks she. She has not put a foot wrong. Nor has he. They are dancing well together. She wonders if he is possibly bi-sexual. That would make things so much easier. He wonders if she is possibly a dyke. That would make things so much easier. He wished he knew a dyke who could tell him if Dordogna was a dyke.

He said: "I am to receive the President's Medal, given semi-annually to that young businessperson who most embodies the ideals of our nation."

She said: "How wonderful! I am to receive the Man of the Year Award from the International Consortium of Masculine Accessories."

He said: "How wonderful! It's nice to know a Man of the Year."

She said: "It's nice to know someone who embodies the ideals of our nation."

Yes, it's a start indeed.

Finally, after seven cups of Formosa Oolong, he shook her hand and kissed her cheeks and promised to call her early in the week.

She asked him at the door: "Tell me, are you going to this quaint Toilet Bowl I am hearing so much about?"

"Oh no no no no never."
So she knew where to find him later on.

Did not our Fred have much to analyze! After a return to his Henry James abode for an evacuation, he paced around his premises for approximately ten minutes, querying his inner self for indications on how Cary Grant might conceivably have handled any of these new plot points, coming to no ready conclusions, either as Cary's scriptwriter or his own, before deciding his castle was more akin to a prison and heading out, for deeper concentration, to the streets. He walked down Christopher, already running over at mid-afternoon, thinking that if he had to parade through this sewer, among these slags (but they're my friends, I'm a slag, too, I'm in this zoo, too), once more in his lifetime, don't they know there's something better? (where!), he'd slit his wrists indeed, Menchitt & Swinger notwithstanding.

So I am on that fence of life I am always condemning Anthony for so straddling. My mind is saying: "Get rid of that loser! Cut your losses before you cut your throat!" And my internal organs residing slightly south of that fine thinking machine are saying: "You ain't over this one yet, Charlie."

Should I walk away? This thought came to him as he found himself at Dinky's building. My goodness, have I journeyed so uptown so quickly? How about a postcard? "Dear Dinky, I was searching in your wastebasket and I found your sweet note to George." Or a telegram? "I was ransacking your belongings and I found your leather and chains."

Or a letter of declaration posted, Martin Luther-like, upon your front door: "I love you, you want to love me, you said George doesn't mean a thing to you, we can work it out, just you wait and see, leave it up to me."

Then he walked home again to hold telephonic communications concerning Dinky's own creative letter writings with both Gatsby and Anthony.

Gatsby naturally said: "You must confront him! How can you let the prick get away with it!" He also said that he'd reached Chapter Two of his novel, was considering a move from the city, "too much fucking interference, and what's happening with your own fine script?"

"Fine, fine, just fine, everything's coming along just fine," Fred answered, throwing a guilty look at his unused IBM.

And Anthony had naturally advised: "Why confront him? Maybe he never even sent it. It was in the wastebasket! Forget it. Don't overreact. You know you tend to overreact. And if he said all those nice things to you in person, give it a try." He also said that he was personally feeling very warm toward a young trampolinist, "so who am I to give you advice? *I* should slit my wrists. But then I think that if I were my father, I'd probably be doing it with a chorus girl. What do I know, Tante? Why are we persisting with these losers? By the way, he wants to go to Fire Island. Can we come and visit?"

Gatsby had also said: "Lemish, you're in trouble. You want to love so much you can't afford not to believe. See it through, see it through. And learn from it. You're strong enough."

So, feeling strong enough, Fred walked again, this time uptown to the Y, taking with him some comfort from those important words from Flatchkind & Krasspole: "Human sex obviously reflects human experience for better or for worse. And said human's human fear is that other humans will find him wanting, thus making it difficult for him to change without patient, beneficial, therapeutic, outside aid." I shall be his outside aid. Who's had more beneficial, therapeutic, outside aid than I? I shall help him change. He wants tenderness? Tenderness he will have. I wonder what to call what I gave him before? Do I need a recall to Dr. Dridge? No! I can work this out myself. I must also, among many other items, try not to think that according to Vonce, Noodrick & Pelt there are three roles one can play as a homosexual: one involving being the daddy to someone who is the son, another, therefore, being the sonny to that pop, the third involving looking for yourself in someone approximately identical to you, and that it looks like Adams, D., is an experienced actor of all three. Along with a few others . . . Well . . . , Dinky's searching. Well . . . , so am I. I shall also try not to think that Dinky is showing distinct Fefferisms. Can I handle same four years later? God knows we all have problems. What's a little leather? It's even rather sexy. No, I shall not be self-righteous. And I must not be dismayed by a casual tidbit plucked from the garbage to a person who means absolutely nothing to him.

Feeling ever so much better now that Decision had been reached, he jogged his jog, worked out his workout, and stepped upon the scale to discover he'd made one hundred and fifty again. A good omen.

But, just in case, he also stepped into the punching-bag room and courageously approached three mean-looking blacks.

"Excuse me, but I have never hit anybody in my life and I was wondering if you could give me a few pointers on how, if I had to, I could punch a guy in the face. Without hurting him, of course."

Of the 2,639,857 faggots in the New York City area, 2,639,857 think primarily with their cocks.

223

You didn't know the cock was a thinking organ?
Well, by this time, you should know that it is.

Fred jumped off of his fence and into The Toilet Bowl.

Its street, West 14th, by that sparkling Hudson, was mobbed with many thousands strong, waving tickets in the air, pushing toward that tiny door, let me in, oh let me in, while searchlights dueled with their outstretched arms and with the sky and with the neighboring ancient warehouses used by the day for meat. Mounted policemen were trying their proudly perched best to keep the streets clear, their horses not obliging, so that arriving glitter queens, descending from rented pumpkins, flaunted hauteur that far-from-red-carpets were deposited for their welcome, they'd go home, but rushed to queue instead, joining beauties of both sexes caught in the eternal conflict of which to maintain: their finery or their place in line. "Darling, we're living *Day of the Locust,*" was the constant cry.

Fred greeted Frigger at the door. "You have obviously done your usual superb p.r. job," Fred said, waving his v.i.p. ticket as Frigger ushered him in past glaring, jealous, waiting eyes.

"Come right in, come right in," Frigger invited him, and in Fred walked and up Fred was lifted, to a tenth floor, and into the newest of New York's mammoth caverns of mirrored heavens, another city happening, vistas, roads leading this way and that, balloons and buntings and flowers and lights and trees and fountains and sparklers and music wrapping it all in a Tiffany blue box of life. Billy Boner certainly knew how to spare no expense and set the scene so his guests could party.

And were they not all here! The Beautiful People all in force. Models and beauties and heirs and heiresses,

224

from museums and magazines and foundations and organizations, charitable, tax-exempt, international, department stores, frockeries, Sotheby's, embassies, hot-dog kings and TV stars and rock faces and physical culturists, a legion of decorators, a score of Wall Streeters, designers of tablecloths and designers of lives, harlots and humpies, Godivas and Casque d'Ors, shrinks and shirkers, conversationalists and cruisers, gaggles of gossamer ladies and gents, sports heroes, pitchmen, newscasters and weathermen, real estate and art and craft and camping and display and publishing and all continents and all major cities and all leading countries, rivers, streams, creeks, crannies, a slummer or three from Washington, the Mayor, the Chief of Police, rival Families, and the press, thank God, the press. *Women's Wear* could be truly pleased!

"It's gorgeous!" The Divine Bella, their correspondent on the spot, gushed up to Fred, in hostess white, a huge orchid pinned to his neatly starched and Oxydol-clean Exxon uniform. "You must see it! You simply must see it all! Every taste has been catered to and I for one wish to live within these walls forever!" And he rushed his big self off to gather more names and items for the several pages his publication had promised him for this important, newsworthy opening night.

Fred stood by the main entrance, where the checkroom indicated that an entire wardrobe could be left for the same fee as a coat, and studied the signposts. Lusitania Lounge. Rancho Notorious. Dixie Disco Dancehall. Martha Mitchell Memorial. Jackie O. The Radziwill Annex. Crabb and Weissmuller. The Fucketeria. Where to begin? What does it all mean? I'd rather not think about what it all means. How to use it all in my script? Where's Abe? Where's Dinky?

●   ●   ●

"Ladies and Gentlemen! . . . The Toilet Bowl is proud to present its first main event of this proud evening, the one, the only, Guestess of Honor, our First and Foremost Very Own First Lady of Song, Our Very Own New Disco Queen . . . *Miss Yootha Truth!* . . ."

Miss Yootha Truth? The crowd didn't have the vaguest. Who the fuck was she? But then that song started, the song that last night, was it only last night?, everyone had been asking about, "The Alabama Aw Shits," so everyone immediately knew who was Miss Yootha Truth, and they rushed into the gargantuan Roseland that was the Dixie Disco Dancehall, all flickering light bulbs and real fake n. ons and stars, and plopped themselves down on the virgin floor and sniffed their ethyled wristbands in readiness, and Miss Rollarette skated among them with his wand, creating the proper mood and atmosphere and entrance for his star. And out he came.

"Rolla, we've started!" Yootha had said just minutes earlier, while they waited for their entr'acte backstage, where he unfortunately had to share his dressing room with the fucking and crucifixion acts. The make-up table was confused with Crisco and Muguet de Scandale, and Yootha vowed it wouldn't be long before he'd not have to be so mortified again. "We're on our way!"

"Yes, Yootha, we are. And Rolla is proud of you. You are now setting a fine example for all my boys. Rolla is additionally most honored that you have requested him to be your Maid of Honor on this, your first night of many nights of tribute. It is reassuring that some people do not forget the earlier kindnesses of strangers."

"I couldn't have done it, Rolla, without your support and belief in me and my talent."

"Now, dear, wasn't it a man in a Doubleday's men's room that got you started on your rise to fame?"

"Oh, Rolla, I long to see him again! I dream of him

226

and hope that one fine day I shall see him across a crowded room and we shall rush into each other's arms and live most happily ever after."

"Just write another song about it, dear. Out of your pain."

Now, with the crowds going wild, bobbing and swaying and sniffing to Yootha's intricate mouthing of the words, as the song boomed out over the huge sound system, Rolla's own flat-brimmed granny hat also nodding its poppy to and fro, both singer and Maid of Honor shivered for their success. Yootha thought of Billie Holiday, and the Supremes, and Diana, and Donna, and thought, too, of this floorful of faggots and foreigners, none of whom two days ago would have given him the time of night, but now were whistling and clapping and cheering one of their own. So, throwing out his long white-gloved arms in upstretched love and thanks, bending his frail body in artistic gratitude, then standing upright again to acknowledge the acclaim with thrown-back chin of pride, then up with the arms again, mustn't be quite so energetic, the net is flimsy and the seams are frail, but let them know it, let them know!, the new star cried out to his legion of new worshippers: "I forgive you!"

The Toilet Bowl was launched! In Dixie Disco Fred danced and danced with Tarsh and Gatsby and Mikie and Josie and Dom Dom and Fallow and Bo Peep and Bilbo, all of whom he'd be with tomorrow in the house they shared in Fire Island Pines.

The music was in high gear, society slummers really cutting rugs, these boys can certainly dance and show us a good time!, building to Up and Upper and Uppest with an overlay by that clever Pepino of "Now Is The Hour For Us," on top of "Old Acquaintance," with, from the seventeen left-handed speakers the additional rhythm of "Jingle Bells," and just barely audible but a clever bit of bouquet garni nevertheless, from speakers twenty to twenty-five, on the right, a low feed-in of his prized recording of the theme from "Cobra Woman," played on the lute by the composer himself, all of this beneath the overriding blanket of "Honey, Where Has Our Love Gone To," the tensions of many thousand bodies so minutely matched to the music's every whim, matching their evening's drugs, coordinated with Pepino's own, so that clashing cymbals jerked them Up like the electric shocks of Disp, then Down with marimbas and cascading xylophones to the low of Flayl, all of this codified, amplified, innuendoed, transmogrified beyond any body's pure cognition, the smashing of the brain!, all it felt was GOOD!, these boys can really show us how to play!, Fred dancing in all of this, among his friends but waiting for Dinky, "Forgiveness, Patience, Tolerance, Tenderness, are my new keystones, Rome wasn't built in a day," he even thinking that in this mélange of sound, such a nice gesture from Pepino, he'd heard the theme music tossed in from his own *Lest We Sleep Alone*.

In the Lusitania Lounge, all fitted out most smartly with the gleanings from a sunken Cunard liner, Irving Slough was holding forth. He leaned against the portholed-backed crush bar, surrounded by his friends and associates, were they not the same?, and felt proud. Here was his dear Hans Zoroaster, surrounded by seven of his beauties, including Winnie, ah yes Winnie, well . . . , and here was his old friend and beard, Adriana la Chaise, and here, too, was his fine vice-president, Anthony Montano. And do we not all represent a veritable rainbow of the panoply of today!

For Hans was all in brown leather, his freshly pierced

tit gleaming with a ring of Van Cleef gold, and Winnie was in a modest half-naked Indian costume, his body lightly burnished with Germaine de Laszlo's Get Ready for Summer Tone # 4, and the models—Lork, Carlty, Yo-Yo, Dawsy, Tom-Tom, Pusher—were all dressed alike in St. Laurent suits, and Adriana was dressed like a Marine, and carrying an enormous mailbag, "Working-class haberdashery is now so chic," and Anthony wore his conservative suit and tie, and Irving . . .

"To us and our noble profession, to which we owe so much!" Irving toasted after tipping the cute waiter in the bikini and pinching his bunny's tail.

His group toasted him back with averted eyes. For Irving had finally done it. He was appearing at last in public in full leather drag. From head to toe he was all in basic black.

Winnie was having difficulty following everyone's words. He was dusted, marvelously so, The Gnome's stuff was the best, no doubt about it, but Winnie knew when no one was looking at him and this always bothered him, dusted or not. He sensed underlying currents neath the dust, particularly since Irving, a kisser, had not kissed him as he usually did, and Anthony kept fidgeting with his fingers as he directed his look-out to exterior shores.

Irving continued his toast: "We have been taken in! Where others have not! We have risen to the top, to be in control, always providing we not be too obvious, not rub their noses. How many places allow us to be so creative? Where else could we be so much the unseen power!" He was suddenly overcome with such gratitude that he grabbed an armful of models, three or four of them, not Winnie, and cooed and cuddled them, and ruffled their finery, and then continued toasting with full hug: "Yes! We have commercialized the human body! Yes! To Advertising!"

And everyone mumbled: "Amen."

"So tell me honestly, Anthony, do you really like it?" Irving struck a peacock pose. He put one hand on the crush bar and stuck one up as if he were gazing out to sea and he smiled at the portholes as if even they were winking back their full approval.

"Stunning, Irving. You really bring it off," Anthony's eyes were still looking for young Wyatt, also out at sea, who had been dancing in his arms in the mellowness of a closed-eye moment of butterscotch, only not to be there an open-eye later.

Hans said: "Tonight, Irving becomes a man!"

Anthony shrugged, then put a sad and protective arm around Winnie, as he thought: My boss a leather queen. Oi, Irving, we are the half-people in the half-art run by the half-talented, the stunted, it ain't as good as the real thing, where is my real thing?, Fred and Ginger didn't dance in Toilet Bowls! Wyatt, wherever you are, come back! But he said: "Yes, Irving, you're a vision."

And Irving looked around him now, too. Where was his Dinky?, to see me on my blackhood night and be most approvingly surprised!

"Ladies and Gentlemen! On our Junior Stage, past Dixie Disco, to the left of Lusitania, adjoining Rancho Notorious, and outside our Fucketeria, rush rush rush and give your attention to our next scene of the evening— The Mister Thick Dick, Mister Long Dong Contest!"

That did it to Ephra Bronstein's kishkas. Dicks and Dongs! She knew what they were!

First Peetra and that newborn pisher in Paris. Then the Mizrachi mess (it simply did not pay to be so charitable). And now this place. Which made her sweat. She did not like to sweat. She did not like to sweat and she did not like to see so many fine fellows dancing with fine fellows. Why had she insisted that Abe bring her here? Particularly an Abe she was finding most difficult to communicate with in her golden years or any others. Ach, it took so much energy to be a part of toute society! Perhaps she should just retire to her Candlewood Lake and take some final vow of withdrawal like the nuns. Dicks and Dongs and Abes and Pishers and Sweat! She had rushed to powder her nose and have a quiet drink of water.

Now this.

Not that this Ladies Lounge of some place . . . she could not bring herself to say it . . . the Johnnie Bowl . . . , which was inexpensively decorated in pink paint only and concrete floor since after tonight it would probably receive little use, overwhelmed her . . .

But something which called itself a Nancellen Richtofen did.

This very tall drink of water sat opposite her, staring and smiling and staring some more, always talking, chatting inexhaustibly, then even a hand, ever so gently, on the knee . . . She was handsome, in the way that that nice Claudette Colbert had been handsome, if not so tall, and she was piercing Ephra with deep-blue eyes of intelligence and unwavering interest, all of which, or rather none of which, her current B'nai B'rith course on "Fully Utilizing the Energies of Your Golden Years," had cared to deal with.

At first, Ephra hadn't noticed her. Then she noticed her a teeny bit. Then she noticed her a great big bit. Then she thought she was appalled. Then she decided she was not appalled. Then she decided that, Mama, wherever you are with your tennis racquets and sporting goods (had not

231

Poppa parlayed a few baseball bats into the Number Three sporting-goods company in the country?, unable to become Number Two or One because golf and tennis were still then gentile games and "they" preferred to buy from their own kind, Wilson and Spaulding, so goyish), Mama, please to forgive me, but I am an old lady, also number Three, no, Number Four, no, Not Even in the Counting, yes, I am an old lady who wants some Number One Good Times before I die. And was God not giving her a last clue on what she'd been missing all these years?

For the intense interest on the part of this younger woman was giving the older one hot pants.

"You are not Jewish?" Ephra found herself meekly inquiring. Did our Ephra have an unknown thing for shiksas?

"No. A German name. An American girl." Nancellen's voice was calm and evenly pitched and direct and honest. She knew how to cruise. She also had a penchant for older women, her own mother, now boarded up under her own stage out there in California, having been a cunt. Now here was Mrs. Ephra Bronstein, a mother-type certainly, and not without resemblances to her own—handsome, trim, chic, with only a superfluity of bosom in excess, a desirable excess, yes a most classy exterior, the riches of the world on the outside of her, is what I want on the inside of her?—yes, Nancellen, as her many conquests could tell you, was not one to beat around the bush, or rather, was one to do just that. She also was, at thirty, feeling the pressures of advancing age. Most of her Lesbian friends were now settled down, as opposed to most of her faggot friends, who never seemed to roost, and she was tired of being the single woman at all those dinner parties. Her career as a Bendel's model had led her to a job at Catholic Charities, which

232

had led her into feeling much warmer toward herself. So perhaps she was ready for a relationship.

So she continued her plunge. "I am going to call you my Q.M. My Queen Mother."

"I am begging your pardon?" Ephra was not well-versed in chat. Yes, everything this evening was totally incomprehensible to her. Why, only a moment ago three little minties had rushed right into this very Ladies Room and felt her dress and its fabric's texture and begged her to tell them where she'd bought it. Boys interested in dresses! But then had come Nancellen to the rescue. With a "Knock it off, you fairies!" So effective. Nancellen. Such an American name. Had she been there waiting all along?

"Tell me, my Q.M., have you ever been to bed with a woman before?"

Ephra looked up as several further male intruders, this time naked sprites, their ding-dongs bouncing up and down, rushed in and then rushed out with happy cries of silly glee. So these are Fairies, this is Fairyland. Did just being here require a different tongue and language?

"Please," she finally said, "please don't talk such things, you are giving me excitement and now all I feel is confusion and I want my husband, Abraham, who is never with me when I need him." And up she stood.

Nancellen, sensing that such seeds planted must be harvested, or at least watered, as soon as possible, immediamente, pronto, schnell, otherwise the drought sets in, winter comes, love dies, stood up with Ephra.

"Mrs. Bronstein, my Q.M., I think we might be meant for each other. It may not be tonight, for I sense this not the best of moments to show you the tender love you are obviously missing. But I shall find you. And you will have had time to think. And yearn. And

233

to fantasize your Nancellen. And to be ready for her when she calls. And should you by any wild stretch of your journeyings be in the vicinity tomorrow of Fire Island Pines, I live on the Ocean at Sunburst."

Then Nancellen bent down to kiss the soft top of the Seligman and Latzed coiffure, and to touch the Dorothy Grayed soft cheeks, and to run her own long unpainted fingers o'er that ample B.H. Wragged bosom which had known much life. Ephra shivered. And it was not a shiver from cold.

Then the tall one left the short one, standing alone. Again alone. She went out to seek her Abraham. She could not find him. So, what else is old? So she went home. Yes, home again. Alone.

Though he was trying to feel and look chipper in his old and most favorite De Pinna seersucker, Abe was not succeeding. He felt far less jaunty than his suit. I am a new Poppa. How do I feel about that? How do I feel about a new son? She can't have him! She's a no-good! She will give him a bad name! She only blackmails me into larger alimonies! But what do I do with him? Ephra does not want him. Ephra will not even discuss. What do I do with such a mess?

He had wandered off the beaten track and into the murky, shadowy, smoke-filled darkness that was the intimate meeting room known as Rancho Notorious. Looking around him, as best his gaze could penetrate, he began to feel even less jaunty, less chipper, more seared sucker. Men dressed like cowboys or in shiny black outfits were lined up, standing immobile like cigar-store Indians, stares fixed into space, not looking at each other, not smiling, not saying Hi and Hello, What's New,

How's the Family . . . Yes, they are looking like things or pieces of meat on a rack. And none of these companions appeared to appreciate the sartorial splendor of seersucker. Abe had received many a withering eye.

Yes, the place was dark, in the way pogroms were dark, though nobody seemed to be complaining, everyone seemed to be milling about without protest, what do they see in each other?, how can they see each other?, their faces come and go as the mirrored ball up there turns around; here is a handsome young fellow in denim, right now I should be in the denim business, with on his baseball shirt "University of Miami."

"Miami? I've been there many times," Abe tried to chat. "What did you study there, if I may ask?"

Miami, big and hunky and not meant for ordinary men, looked at Abe, then quickly looked away. Then, as if some vestigial rule of politeness, to such an older, fatherly type, unaccountably reasserted itself, he mumbled: "Political Science."

"That's very important today. What sort of work do you do, if I may ask?"

Evidently I cannot ask because Miami has walked away. In political science he will go absolutely nowhere.

Have I seen enough? The dancings? The schvartza boy singing in a dress? The crowds rushing to see two fellows play with pee-pees? Now I have heard whispering of doings "Behind the Green Door." Location scouting or not, I am not up to Behind Green Doors alone. Where is Fred? Who is meant to meet me here and take me there? And where are the nice nightspots where in the old days you just sat and drank some vodka and a pretty lady lady sat on top of a piano and sang her sad songs about love?

He'd looked for Ephra, not too much, just a little,

that was like the old days, too. Why couldn't he make up his mind what to do with that woman? After all these years. Was she like some old suitcase he just couldn't throw away?

Once again he began thinking about, and wondered why he was thinking about, his Richie. His Richie who had so rarely given him anything to think about. He had said many times to Ephra: "I'm perfectly willing to pay attention to Richie if Richie would only do something worth paying attention to." That Richie had somehow managed to get into Choate and Yale, Abe attributed more to his own name than his son's abilities, and that he managed to get honor grades at both institutions Abe attributed to cheating. The last time Abe, if pressed to remember, had given the lad any true thought was when he *was* a lad, thirteen, and entering the son's bathroom by mistake (he had been away for a marriage and not known Ephra had reassigned the toilets), and perceiving a revoltingly heavy odor, and looking questioningly at his younger, and allowing his gaze to trail down the boy's naked body, he inquired why the genital area was overlaid with smelly mauve cream. The son, sheer terror rendering speech impossible, turned his face to the wall. Abe bent down to retrieve from the floor a depleted tube of depilatory and then smacked Richie as hard as he could, splat! with one hand, splat! with the other hand, until the tuchas of his younger son and heir, at that moment hairless, was truly very red.

"How will you become a man! Life does not come to the hairless! When will you learn to grow up! When will you learn to become a conniver like your Pop!" were all the words Abe could call upon to yell.

Yes, that was the last time, and why couldn't Richie have been like Stephen the football player, Stevie the Class President, Steve the champion intercollegiate boxer,

Steve-ala the successful lawyer with that nice wife and sonny in New Jersey and why am I thinking about my boys in such a place as this? *All* my boys!

It is difficult to be philosophical in such a place. That black shiny stuff is leather! So much leather. Such a goyish fabric, leather. Though certainly none of these zombies is Jewish, particularly with such a sign on the wall as: WELCOME S.S. BERLIN!, with drawings of men's goggle-hooded eyes and motorcycles, such goyish transportation, motorcycles, and an arrow pointing to something called "Cherry Grove," which sounds most American to me.

So the Nazi invasion returns! So Hitler lives! Nothing has happened in space and time. I hoped I would not live to see it again.

His son, our Richard, would not, at this current moment, be in agreement. He was beyond space and time. He was beyond three dimensions. He was beyond care and woe and fear. He was Certyned, Drayled, Festinated, Orange Fluffed, Magicked, Codinexed, Misdayted, and a few Othered. He felt wonderful. And he had made a new plan!

Everyone in this Toilet Bowl was his friend. "Hi, Tiger!" some bald pate yelled in greeting. "Hi, Tiger, yourself!" Boo Boo yelled in greeting back. Yes, tonight he even had enough courage to take a flyer up Park Avenue to growl at His Eminence himself, to leave with the doorman the note in his back tush Levi pocket, like some process server evicting, at last!, the one remaining holdout rent-controlled tenant who'd refused to move. Yes, he, Tiger, would do that. Yes, he would. Yes, he would.

Yes, tonight I'm growing stronger, Boo Boo is becoming a Man!

237

What a place this was! He left the slumming straights and was allowed by a black guard to pass Behind the Green Door. I'll just take a little look. As a sort of prelude to my pits of sexuality. As a warm-up for Fire Island tomorrow. Rumor has it it's all here. Somewhere. I'm only taking a peek. Being an explorer. Explore these inland waterways. I always wanted to travel. Jackie O they call this one, eh?

He counted fifty urinals standing up. Along with all those men in front of them. Seems innocuous enough. And he thought there were fifty, although he could be counting double. But in the adjoining sister suite, the Radziwell Annex, he was perplexed to count the fifty urinals lying down. He wasn't lying down. The urinals were. Along with all those men in front of them.

"Hello, Uncle Richie. What are you doing here?"

Uncle Richie knew the voice and knew the form and knew his fifteen-year-old nephew, Wyatt, and plotzed.

"What am I doing here?! What are *you* doing here!"

"Hiding."

"From what?"

"Er . . . I'll tell you in a minute. Do you come to places like this often?"

"Places like what? How the fuck do you know so much?"

"Er . . . I'll tell you in a minute. Uncle Richie, as long as you're here, why don't you show me your thing."

"I think I'm having an anxiety attack."

"What's an anxiety attack?" Wyatt put his Uncle's hand against his crotch. The Uncle did not take his hand away.

"Feeling your nephew's cock is an anxiety attack."

"So you have been to places like this before. I'm glad. Now we have something in common."

Boo Boo gagged.

"What's the matter, Uncle Richie?"

"Where did you get . . . *that?*"

"It is kind of big, huh?" Wyatt proudly took it out for closer admiration. "It's ten inches. I've had it about a year now and I charge ten dollars for it and I have $2,579.63 in my Morristown Friends School savings account."

The Uncle double-plotzed. "Jesus, Wyatt, how the hell do you ever expect to get into Yale doing things like that!"

There were a few groans from adjoining clumps of shadows doing things to each other. Richie protectively tried to shoo them away from his young relative. With his free hand.

"It's OK, Uncle Richie. I'm quite experienced."

"Wyatt . . . you're a fucking freak!"

Wyatt didn't want to, but he began to cry. It was beginning to close in on him that the Big Boys' World might be a lot more to handle than he'd been accustomed to having handled. It had been much easier just charging for it in the dark. But now he'd fallen in love with an older man who seemed to be in constant rather nervous states (didn't it get easier when you got older?), only to be dancing in his arms and look up to see my own grampa walking along the edge of the dance floor, causing me to burp, grab my crotch which suddenly hurt, then run and hide in this place, only to discover my very own Uncle who seems to be in worse shape than Anthony. Yes, Wyatt began to cry. "Don't you like it, Uncle Richie?"

"What the fuck are you crying for!" Boo Boo was not sympathetic. Though the two of them had never been close, Wyatt had, indeed, always looked upon his uncle as something of a necessary evil, he never remembered Wyatt's birthday, and Richie was jealous that his brother, Stephen, loved his own son more than he'd ever loved Richie, nevertheless they were still kin, so Boo Boo shook

239

Wyatt by the shoulders and berated him once again: "What the fuck are you crying for! Are you crazy! You've got something that every man in America, the world, the Entire Universe Since Time Began, would give his left, right, nut, his tits, hell, his soul for! Stop it, you silly ninny, and get down on your knees and thank God!"

Wyatt started to get down on his knees and thank Richie, but Richie pulled him back up again.

"Stop that!"

"I just wanted to see yours!"

"Why aren't you using it on a girl?! You've got to use it on a girl!"

"I showed it to one and she fainted! Have you shown yours to Marci Tisch!?"

Richie sighed. He understood. Poor little fella. Poor big fella. "Well, listen, Wyatt, I don't know what to tell you. You know any older women?"

"Uncle Richie, I don't think you're very well-adjusted."

"Listen, Wyatt . . . ," the Uncle was trying very hard not to get hard, not to get excited, not to lose his drugged-out state—which this evening he'd calculated had cost him twenty-seven dollars even, no sales tax on drugs, and would have cost him only twenty-two if he'd brought more Magic last night, but The Gnome had already upped the price after his new line's successful launch—and tried not to look at that hose pipe still dangling out below, and not add the size of it to his owner and equal that both of them were his nephew and twice as big as his and . . .

"Uncle Richie, you have a hard-on."

"You little pisser!"

"Where? . . . where? . . ." someone croaked from the darkness.

"You little son-of-a-bitch freak!"

So croaked Richie as Uncle and Nephew, now joining his elder in a state of suspended animation, rushed to join each other in family togetherness, Uncle bending low and putting into his mouth the wholesome largesse of Nephew, practically choking, forcing himself to continue, get this Bronstein jewel in, why the fuck, oh why oh why oh why the fuck couldn't I have had one this size! Was this another item to lay on stingy Abe?

He sucked and sucked, look at me sucking, I'm usually the suckee, it really is a big kick sucking on your own blood, do I go blind or grow hair upon my teeth, oh Dr. Rivtov please don't look at me now I've got a big enough load of guilt, and at this moment young Wyatt—overexcited and usually not such a premature ejaculator, but then it wasn't every day one had one's only Uncle, no I think I have a new baby Uncle, gee I wonder if he'll like to do this too?, in one's crotch—shot what tasted like a very small jet of watery semen into his older Uncle's mouth, said Uncle, was this his entry into sexual pits?, his very first fountain from his very own Ponce de Leon?, yes said Uncle now wishing he was unrelated.

"That was very nice," Wyatt politely said. "I hope we can do it again very soon."

"Don't be so fucking polite!"

"Why not? I liked it."

"You're supposed to be overcome with Jewish guilt!"

"What guilt?"

"For Christ's sake, don't they teach you anything in that school?"

"You're still hard, Uncle Richard." Wyatt was unbuttoning.

"Of course I'm still hard! I'm only human! Keep your hands to yourself!"

"It isn't very big. But Mommy says best things come in small packages."

"It's big enough and anyway I've got to learn to live with it and I told you to keep your fucking hands to yourself!" His own Nephew telling him he had a small cock!, as if I didn't know, oh as if I didn't know and had to live with . . . now this . . . ten inches of my own blood . . .

"OK." Wyatt removed his hand and stooped down to use his mouth instead.

"OooooóhhhhhaaaaaahhhhhhhiiiiiiiI!" emitted Richard, causing helpful vibrations in the dark room, the excitement of others always useful as a turn-on elsewhere, Uncle now knowing he was lost, his own Nephew sucking his cock, it was more than Ripley could print, Dr. Caligari put in his cabinet, hey Guinness Book of Records, is this a dingeroo!, oh daddy mommy brother God Rivtov forgive me all. Richard ejaculated into Wyatt's mouth.

"I never did that before. It has a very interesting flavor."

"I never did either and doesn't it just." Richie buttoned up his Levis. He then slumped down on the cold, damp floor. "Oh, Jesus H. Christ on a crutch, whatever have we done." He wanted to cry.

Wyatt sat down next to him and tried to pet him into comfort.

"Don't touch me! Clothe your nakedness! What shall we do?"

Wyatt zipped up his pants. "I really think you're making a very big to-do over this, Uncle Richard. Did I do it wrong?"

"You did it perfectly! You did it as if to the cock sucker born! You little cock sucker! Don't you know that what you've, correction, we've just done is considered by ninety-nine and ninety-nine one hundredths percent people as abnormal, immoral, illegal, dirty shameful, wretched, that's it, *wretched,* oh, oh, *Oh . . . ,*" and he

242

now held his head with both his sinner's hands, expecting, no, bringing upon himself the onslaught of doom.

"Stop it stop it *Stop It*! ! !" Wyatt's turn now came to croak, null and voiding the high-pitched excitement in the shadows that Richie's earlier emissions had so recently encouraged, now himself terrified, joining his Uncle in shaking and quivering and wondering what to do next as anxiety, fears, tremblings, weakening of the kishkas, were all passed along from generation to generation. "Uncle Richie, if you're so miserable, you really should get some help!"

Richard, at this moment, fortunately, well, let's hope fortunately, but then his record has not been so good up to this crossroads, suddenly turned mature. Something dim and distant was stirring in his brain . . . a dangerous sign? . . . "It's OK, Wyatt. It's OK. I think I overreacted. My support system momentarily let me down. It's going .o be OK!"

The two of them held on to each other.

"It's going to be all right!"

"Uncle Richard?"

"What?"

"If I come and lived with you, I wouldn't have to go home. Then we could do it again."

"We mustn't do it again *ever!*"

"Uncle Richard I like it so why can't we do it again you're the crazy one!"

"Hey, Cliff, you two must simply calm yourselves down," came from nearby.

Dead silence.

Richard was still thinking.

Penultimately, the Nephew said to the Uncle: "Uncle Richie, you are a mess."

Then, finally, the Nephew broke the news: "Uncle Richie, Grampa Abe is here."

• • •

Junior Stage was also a bit of a mess. The winners of the contest, Mister Thick Dick and Mister Long Dong, both of whom had been hired weeks ago, were having a spot of trouble with their act, which, like Arthur Godfrey's Talent Scouts, they were to be allowed to perform now that they'd been acclaimed the winners. Mister Thick Dick was meant, ever so slowly, to fuck Mister Long Dong, and then, ever so slowly, since both instruments were extremely beautiful to watch in action, vice versa. However, Mister Thick Dick was too thick to enter Mister Long Dong, no matter how much Crisco, how many poppers, how many impatient catcalls from the crowd of uptown slummers, no faintings tonight, was this the best the fellows could trot out?, perhaps it's time to pack it in and head back to Regine's, and the vice versa was not working either because Mister Thick's asshole was very tight tonight, having been over-fucked the night before and over-Sanforized with Preparation H.

Fred and his housemates now all stood by the punch bowl, which was located adjacent to the Green Door. Tarsh was reporting on his explorations.

"Martha Mitchell is all full of toilets. And Crabb and Weissmuller is full of showers! And they have those new attachments where you switch the lever and instead of water falling on your head you can douche it up inside of you. It's the very latest and a big time-saver on the old-fashioned kind."

"I must get one," Mikie said, adjusting his hooded sweat shirt and then remembering he didn't have a shower to attach it to, one of these days he'd find a home, tomorrow at the Island would certainly be a start, and wasn't he glad he didn't bring his tambourine this evening, there was so much else to do with hands.

"It sounds a bit excessive to me," said Gatsby.

"What's excessive?" asked Dom Dom.

"Somebody who does it more than you do," Josie answered.

Maxine rushed up, flying high, not only in seven-inch Ferragamo's, not only in a sequined Elizabethan turban three inches higher than any he'd floated before, not only with padding that bosomed him six inches further forward than he had previously protruded, not only in swathed and tufted and quilted taffeta thirteen dollars a yard more than he'd ever splurged, but also on a full contingent of his favorite Mandrax. He spoke to the group in general, none of whom he knew personally, just as faces from Balalaika's past: "We simply must not forget Balalaika, fellows," he said. "We're still open! Don't be monogamous. The raid only closed The Pits. You must come back and dance! And one of these days we'll finance a complete take-over of the Village from Christopher Street to the River and call it ours, just like they did in *Passport to Pimlico,* and soon we'll have our own senator and our own President and our own university and our own medical center starring Chad Everett . . ." and off he went, still looking for Patty, where was Patty? He thought he saw Patty! He hobbled faster, his lips pursed out to call: "Where have you been!" It wasn't Patty. I don't care.

"That one is going round the bend," Fallow said, looking after him. Tonight he was dressed in tight khakis, gray-flannel jacket, striped broadcloth shirt, neat rep tie, work boots, best keep it simple with so many straights in view. Then, looking around at all the beauty, in person, in the slides of last summer's glorious fun projected on the walls and ceilings, mementoes to remind them all of what commenced again tomorrow, he sighed: "I was in love three times last week. But tonight, oh Mary, do I not forget them all! Are we not constantly assaulted by so much beauty! Click! click! click! New York is a marketplace! And the next one is more gorgeous than the last. Oh, Fred, I forgot to tell you. Feffer's back in town. He called me and said he'd see you later."

The time bomb that was Fred's stomach reactivated. Evidently, after all these years, that beauty could still affect him, even though it was over, and long ago. So Feffer's back in town. And where was Dinky?

"Excuse me," Fred said to them all, almost knocking over Bilbo, who was precariously perched next to Mikie and Bo Peep, who were next to Dom Dom and Josie, who tonight wore matching Levi pants and Levi shortie jackets, and if Bilbo fell over, the whole line of dominoes might go over with him, "but I think it's time for me to go and explore."

"Good for you!" said Tarsh, brushing a red-bearded kiss across Fred's mustache. "Dig you later." Tarsh was always most supportive whenever any of his friends, particularly Fred, who could be most critical of their stylish lives, showed any inclination to be a Lewis or a Clark.

Fred caught Gatsby looking at him. "Boy, am I ever strong enough," Fred said.

The entire Dixie Disco Dancehall became slowly covered in wisps of mist. It was a magical, mystical fog, clouds gently obscuring a heaven that obviously was up there. One moment everyone was earthborn, and the next moment everyone was flying in jet planes all his own. In seconds, the enormity was layered like a Scottish low-land at dawn. Swathes and sheets and cumuli of turbulent smokes, all made from dry ice and carbo-orthodranite, which produces twice as much haze with half as much carcinogen, wrapped each and every dancer in his own world.

246

It was eerie and it was wonderful and special and personal and impossible to recognize your nearest neighbor.

And as the music got louder and the mist began to clear, gigantic columns polka-dotted with tiny, blinking, spinning lights were lowered from the sky. Slowly they came toward earth, like some ancient Baalbek revisitation. Then the columns themselves began to twist and turn and the hordes of dancers threw up their arms, awaiting them, come closer come closer, I spread my legs to embrace you, and fifty of these idols came closer and hundreds of drugged-out dancers rushed to straddle them as best they could, humping them like neutered dogs.

Winnie Heinz—in his half-naked Indian costume and further angel-dusted out of his tits, so that even his leather nappie and modest yellow feather and softest Pachogie moccasins seemed not there, he felt completely naked for this world, his own perfect body carrying his spirit and soul, like ancient braves, breaking new paths, to be followed by the rest of the tribe—weaved in and out and round and under the approaching columns, in a happiness he had not felt since . . . oh, who could remember when?, spinning, reaching, dancing, moving, the freedom of his spirit on this night was a lesson to all imprisoned souls. And as he weaved and threaded among the columns, he was followed, as he knew he would be, by scores of worshippers, fans, admirers of his self, *the* model, oh he did love moments such as these. Who needed love or lovers or cigarettes or Irving's kisses when this whole wide world is mine?

He heard whispers: "He's so gorgeous!" "One night with him is all I wish!" "Him and to have his figure!," he could never hear enough, and he pretended he was one of Mr. Ziegfeld's favorite stars, coming slowly down the highest stairway ever built, anywhere, one step at a time, magisterially, my kingdom at my feet. He reached out and softly touched faces that hovered near. Hands reached out to touch him back. To receive my blessing. My magic. My sacred beauty's spark.

Then he embraced a column, holding tightly on to it as it gently started its ascent back to that heaven. The columns were rising again! And Winnie, one arm and one foot firmly holding on, waved to his kingdom, as he slowly twisted back to heaven, too.

The crowd went wild. If this were a planned event, then it could not have been better staged. If it was spontaneous, then wasn't this what nights like this were all about, what we'll talk about in years to come? The night that Winnie Heinz ascended up to Heaven.

And watching him ascend was Timmy. He'd made entrance at last, still wearing his jeans, his T-shirt advertising his Nation's Capital, still no time to shop, after waiting hours on the ground, pushing and shoving to keep from being pushed and shoved, the outside line now stretching to the very River itself, throngs still panting to get in, dreaming of the orgiastic paradise that awaited them Up There, still out of reach. He might be one of the stars of the evening, but R. Allan hadn't given him one of the special v.i.p. tickets.

And now there was Winnie still out of reach, too. Oh, still so far from reach!

"Ladies and Gentlemen . . . boys and girls . . . men and MEN . . . our next event, our feature film of the evening, rush rush rush to our main arena, adjoining Rancho Notorious, past the Lusitania Lounge, to the left of the Green Door, yes, rush to our Fucketeria as it premieres this evening our very own triple-R-rated cinematic extravaganza . . . *Babes in the Wood!* . . ."

Randy Dildough's dark glasses made The Fucketeria appear more shadowy than it was. But he'd been in back rooms before—The Anvil, The Mine Shaft, the late Toilet, after which tonight's flushings were perhaps meant to be a commemorative stamp, and of course, just . . . whenever it was, The Pits—so he was not unfamiliar with the gladiatorial yells and screams and urgings, boys will be boys when having so much fun. And, yes, he could vaguely see the banked risers tiered from floor to ceiling and yes, he could sense these risers rising with pure male flesh. It was good to be back. Though he couldn't see his Timothy. And it was of course for Timothy that he'd come.

A slight bend in the road had occurred upon his return from Dordogna. As if she hadn't been enough, he had then been summoned by his Pan-Pacific boss, Myron Musselman. Initial audience reaction to the blanket, coast-to-coast release of *Bronty, The Last Survivor*, was slightly less than reassuring. Too early to tell, nothing definite, mind you, but best to huddle all P-P and Marathon top brass, strategize, plot new plans and ploy new possibilities. That dinosaur simply must heave itself into profit or else there's trouble. Randy had performed like a wizard, it was his dinosaur he was saving, shuffling new ad campaigns, realigning theaters, switching A plans with B plans, dealing out New Deals. Now they could only pray that nature would take its course.

So where's Timothy? Now that I'm ready!

All eyes were on the ceiling, and why not?, for projected on this ceiling was tonight's feature film. It was a co-production between Stud Studios, R. Allan Pooker Productions, One Touch of Penis, and Gemeinschaft Brüder

Grim, certainly all pantheonic names in this particular firmament, and starring that young ass of the moment— Randy had forked out one hundred bucks for that one, little Paulie's—how astounding that Paulie's looked better in the movies, ah the technological wonders of my beloved cinematic craft, what an incredible ass, rounded, upswept, globular, milk-white, so smooth, talk about wanting to eat something with a spoon, Randy's tongue and taste buds teetered momentarily in infidelity, but wait!, young Paulie is co-starring with the naked and gorgeous body of . . . no, it can't be! . . . my Timothy! My Timothy a Fuck Star! . . . R. Allan had underlooked his promise in order to show the world Timmy's . . . whose eyes, realizes Randy, on screen as off, radiate that huge gap between reality and fantasy, which all the great stars' do, my talent scout's eye is still intact, but wait!, what am I seeing?, what's happening? Full Frontal Nudity? How can I make a James Dean out of that! My Timothy is soiled! This act will go into international distribution. What a truly tawdry lad. Declining dinosaurs are bad enough. I simply won't let myself fall in love with a porno star! Dildough, get a hold on yourself, man. You'll never become Irving Thalberg this way. Get out of here. Go on! Get! Ignore the fact that your cock is getting hard just watching those two young lads performing . . .

On the screen, immortal words were being spoken.

Paulie said: "I want you to punish me harder hardest hardingest!"

To which young Timothy replied: "This is the most wicked awfulest most punishing pole stick I ever seen and I am going to punish you so good you will never forget it!"

Well, thought talent scout Dildough, perhaps his diction needs a little work.

And Paulie answered: "Now that you've a real strong weapon, you must punish me the most!"

As long as I'm here, thought Randy.

So he settled back into a lower loge, craning his head back to look up at his rising star. Hadn't Marilyn Monroe a pornographic past she had overcome? Listen to this audience reaction! Look at this audience reaction! That's the true test. The seat of the pants test. Watch young Tim push the pole in. What grace of movement.

Then the clever cutaway from the pole to Paulie's now paler ass receiving it. Receiving what appears to be a major starring portion of tree.

And so as the tree went in—or is the expression "if the tree fits?"—Randy leaned back even farther to enjoy the show. Have to keep abreast of what the competition's up to. It's the least I can do.

While we're projecting on the ceiling, and while Randy watches Timothy, and Tim watches for Winnie, and Fred is looking for Dinky, and Irving is looking for Dinky, and Abe is looking for Fred, and Boo Boo and Wyatt are hiding from Abe, the heretofore unseen Billy Boner peeks his head into The Fucketeria and looks up and catches a sight of Paulie, an even paler Paulie, the look of the now near-dead Paulie, just the way Billy Boner likes them, I must call R. Allan and get a date with that one, he looks infinitely more attractive than that dusky dinge I diddled discreetly with in Doubleday's Non-Fiction, even if the song looks to be a hit.

And Laverne, who tonight again is having troubles—where *was* Patty?, Maxine is going crazy, will Dinky appear again and slug my handsome Robbie Swindon?, in whose warm safe arms I'm now dancing in Dixie Disco's darkness —is suddenly further unsettled as his Robbie breaks the beat, and gets down on his knees in front of him, and proposes.

251

"Will you, Jack Humpstone, please take me, Robbie Swindon, and come live with me and be my love?"

Fred had not rushed to the movies when everyone else had. He was exploring Behind the Green Door.

How do I feel about the symmetry of two porcelain-filled sister suites? How do I feel about rows of johns lined up in something called the Martha Mitchell Memorial Room? Is there danger lurking? Or is it tame, like a movie set? How do I feel about the sounds of plop plop? Very humanizing. Two thousand years of progress.

Now he stood in front of a jail cell, evidently as yet unchristened.

"Come on, Lemmy, try it just for me," Feffer had begged him on that cross-country trip, in their pink-and-gray-satin room in the Pontchartrain in the Garden District of New Orleans. "What's a little long black leather belt?" "You're kidding! I love you!" "Then try it just for me." Fred had then allowed himself to be tied up. What's a little clothesline? With a little knotted sheet thrown in. And there stood above him that blond beloved Mister Right The First. Dangling his little long black leather belt. What's a little long black leather belt? At first it tickled. Then it whomped. "Yes, it hurts." And: "No, it doesn't turn me on." And then Feffer had patted his head so softly. And he'd never made the suggestion again.

Feffer had been the brightest and would recite verses by Dante in the original Italian as he and Fred cuddled in beds from coast to coast, after days with John Singer Sargent in the Indianapolis Art Gallery and hot fudge over rainbow ice-cream cake in that same Pontchartrain and holding hands on a misty London-fog-type morning under the arch in St. Louis and running barefoot through the sand dunes of Alamogordo and falling down and holding tight and rolling over and laughing and wasn't this what falling in love was all about? Verses by Dante!

They alighted eventually in Los Angeles where Fred accepted a rather unfelicitous assignment writing a movie about folks from the Outside World who find a heavenly paradise avec singing monks, a job he took to keep those verses beside him. For Feffer now wanted to return to the original Italian, "where two men simply don't live together, Lemmy, they just don't." Desperation always being the better part of screenwriting, Fred also took some of his monk money and hired Feffer to write a script about anything his heart desired. "I'm not about to do this if I didn't think you could do it. I think you're a truly gifted writer."

So they both sat writing their scripts in the yellow-and-white Loretta Young cottage Fred had rented, until came both scripts' ending, the climactic tremor, the L.A. earthquake finally arriving, the Feffer da Roma Fault: "I . . . I'm worried I'm not capable of love," and back went Feffer to Roma and there Fred followed him, what's a few thousand miles?, to woo again, to fall on bended knee *in mèzzo a* Piazza Navona, only to be rejected in mid-proposal, causing a Lemish rush into the famous Tre Scalini to consume, no doubt a record, twelve *tartufi cioccolati* and never see Feffer again.

Fred came back to Now, biting his tongue—was it in memory of the rejection or the overconsumption of *tartufi cioccolati?*—and he realized he was sitting in the jail cell, on its floor, and that several loitering gentlemen were looking in on him and waiting for his instructions concerning his wants or needs. One of them came closer, out of the darkness. 'Twas Dinky. He was wearing a nice Brooks Brothers pink button-down shirt and those black leather pants and boots.

How do I feel about those black leather pants and

boots? At least I feel OK about Brooks Brothers. "I want to talk to you," Fred said.

"Now why do you want to talk on a nice night like this?" Dinky smiled in answer and as he noted Fred was noting the pants and boots. "You always try to make me think just when I don't want to. Don't let's talk about anything. For I have here in my hand one very ripe banana. Wouldn't you like to get fucked with a banana?"

Since, with his other hand, he was poking at Fred's own banana, not so soft and just as ripe, Fred decided talk could wait. What's a little talk? Yes, talk was inopportune at moments like these. *No!* Have the confrontation! I found your Inter-Chains! I found your letter to that midnight train in Georgia! But Dinky had helped him up and they were hobbling to one of the more private rooms, evidently dotted round this part of the bowl like the Thousand Islands. And here they were disrobing and here Dinky broke off a tiny bit of squooshy banana and gently poked it up Fred's ass.

Hoping his years of atheism wouldn't be held against him, Fred prayed that bananas would do the trick and make Dinky's cock hard at last. He tried to peek. So much for God. So much for Chiquita Banana. Perhaps I'll play with it. Which he did. And it got hard. Thank you, Chiquita.

"But you're hard!" Fred inadvertently exclaimed as Dinky moved away.

"I guess I just don't feel like sex," Dinky said, lying back and putting his head on Fred's stomach and looking up from the gray-carpeted floor at the gray-carpeted walls.

"We don't have to. I'm . . . unh, just glad that me and a banana can still turn you on."

"I guess I get overwhelmed with your expectations."

"No expectations! Absolutely none! No commitments! I just want to get fucked!" Lies, Lemish! All lies! ". . . Er,"

254

he ventured, ". . . what's wrong with expectations?" Were bananas and fuckings mushing away?

Dinky shook his head. "Jack always said I intimidated him."

"I don't think Jack ever understood you at all. We're both strong. We can handle each other."

"Can we?"

"Sure. Sure."

"That's good. That's nice. Sure." Dinky pulled out two cigarettes from those pants, which he noted Fred was still noting, and lit them up and handed one to Fred and then proceeded to tell him the story of the dolls.

"I guess I was eight years old. My grandfather took me to F. A. O. Schwarz. I really loved my grandfather. He wanted me to choose trains. They had these elaborate trains. For my birthday. I looked at them for about ten minutes to please him. I wasn't very interested in trains. Then I took him by the hand into the next room. That's where they had these dolls. Really beautiful dolls. All dressed up in pretty clothes with elaborate and intricate detailings and stitchings and fine fabrics and pearl buttons. Just like real ladies. I looked at them for a long time. They were so beautiful! They were the most beautiful things I'd ever seen. And I wanted them. Two weeks later on my birthday a big load of trains arrived. I went up to my grandfather and I said 'I have to tell you something. I know you're very generous but I didn't want the trains. You want to give me what I want, don't you? You love me and want to give me what I want? Well, I don't want the trains. I want the dolls.' And the following week, I got three dolls. With a big collection of clothes. They were terrific. I dressed them up differently on different days and I sat them down at the dinner table to serve them meals and had them talk to each other and on the extra chairs I put some of my mother's clothes so they'd have grown-ups

255

to talk to. They were beautiful. That's why I liked them. And I had got what I wanted. And that's all I've ever been interested in. I mean . . . beautiful things."

"That's . . . beautiful. We're really peeling away the layers of the old onion, opening up, getting to know each other. How many people can you talk to this way?"

"No one. Don't know what made me think of it. Yes. It's nice."

Fred inhaled deeply. They were on their way back on the track. Check off Stage 1. Stage 2, here we come.

"Come on," Dinky said, patting both Fred's upper and lower cheeks. "Let's get dressed and have a dance."

"What about the banana? I'm currently very into bananas."

"Well save it for breakfast. I always like a banana before breakfast."

"We going to spend the night?"

"Sure."

Stage 2 manuevered! Stage 3, here we come!

On the parapets above Dixie Disco Dancehall, Winnie bobbed and swayed. He looked down at the tiny ants. He looked out at the twinkling columns and moons and stars. He was in heaven. He loved it. It felt wonderful.

Weeeee . . . I am in love with life and me and my angel's dust and I am the golden boy and I thank my angel's dust because it's the most wonderful wonder in the world it helps me makes me want to flyyyyyyyyyy! . . .

Boo Boo was having trouble standing up. The news that his father was on the premises had naturally been upsetting. He had not known his Pop to be such an attender of events. Good old Pop. What if he finds me here? He wouldn't come back *here!* But what if he did? Then I'd have to give him the note! Richie, Jesus Christ what have you been planning for all these years? Boo fell down again. But Wyatt helped him up again. Good old Wyatt. Good old Wyatt with the ten-inch cock who called me a mess. Yes, Wyatt's knowledgeable proficiency as a tour guide through all these inland waterways had been upsetting, too. "Why are the urinals lying down?" "So you can lie down, too." Of course. How logical. Very sensible. I've never traveled anywhere. Oh, I want to travel! Yes, this kid has been around. Good old Wyatt. When Boo stumbled and fell yet again, and Wyatt had righted him yet again, Richard Bronstein knew he'd found his help.

No, I couldn't! Why not? Who better to trust than ten inches of your own blood? Ten inches!

And what better time than now! Pop's out there just ready for the plucking! And if he can have another Bronstein, so can I!

"Now listen, Wyatt," Richie said decisively as he let his frame sink down on to the more or less dry floor in an alcove outside of Martha Mitchell. "How would you like it if I could fix it so we could be very rich and live together and you'd never have to go home again ever ever? I mean really, really rich. *Really* rich!" He laughed out loud, not because he'd had the guts to expose his gutsy plans, but because he sounded just like Ed Sullivan. Boy, am I drugged, he thought.

"Uncle Richie and Wyatt Bronstein At Home," Wyatt said, thinking of his mom's nice engraved cards from Cartier and then thinking, boy, his Uncle certainly was drugged.

Then Richie pulled out of his back pocket a rather crumpled and soggy note, which he proceeded to recite aloud. "Abraham Bronstein, come to your son's loft with one million dollars or else swarthy and dangerous faggots

257

will bury Richard with Barbara Walters. And Walter Cronkite."

Wyatt, who was having difficulty shooing off a rather strange Marine with a high-pitched voice who kept offering seven dollars and fifty cents for his legendary product and pulling coins and bills out of a big satchel bag "to show you I'm serious," answered: "That's not enough."

"Two million, do you think?"

"No, no, one million's fine. I mean . . . you planning a kidnapping?"

"Yeah, but shhhh . . ."

"In your own loft?"

"Ten dollars and I have a very nice apartment on East Seventy-second Street . . ." The Marine was back again.

Wyatt, an experienced television viewer, realized he was confronted on both sides by rather peculiar prime-time dramas. He turned to tune-in his Uncle. "That's pretty stupid."

"You're right. You're right. Son of a gun, just what I've been thinking recently. It should be some place more exotic than the loft, but not too far-fetched. Boy, it's going to be good doing it with you."

"Eleven seventy-five." The Marine seemed rather upset that Wyatt was negotiating on both sides. "But you have to do it with me."

"Where we going to do this, Wyatt?"

"I don't know. I'm going to Fire Island tomorrow anyway."

"You've been to Fire Island!"

"Tons."

"You been to The Meat Rack?"

"Tons."

Son of a bitch, fifteen years old and he's been there tons. "Gee . . . well, maybe we could do it at Fire Island."

"Twelve dollars and we have to do it right here!" the Marine insisted.

"Will you please go away!," Wyatt hissed at him. Then he turned back to Richie. "You mean you've never been there?"

"I'm going to go tomorrow, too. Unh . . . tell me about this Meat Rack place."

Wyatt didn't know which side to appease. It was just like when his Mom was on one side of him wanting something and pulling one of his arms and his Dad was on the other side pulling for another. He thought he'd be torn in two. How to keep peace in the family? "Let's see. It's a big forest at the end of the boardwalk which is very spooky and full of dramatic scenes. Go away I told you!" he hissed once again at the Marine who had evidently come up with fifteen bucks "and that's my final dramatic offer!"

"How dramatic?" Boo Boo liked the sound of this. "Do they have coffins and bury people?"

"Well, it is very dark . . ."

"You know, Wyatt, I can see you've got a true Bronstein imagination. Boy, are you really a helpmate. It's going to be great living with you."

"Isn't that incense?" Wyatt had been reconsidering all offers.

"What's a little incense after you've burned your bridges? Let's work this out. Give me a pencil and paper."

"I haven't got one. Wait a minute." He conversed with the Marine who rummaged in that satchel and came up with a Cross pencil and a piece of paper from an Hermès diary.

Boo began to write. Always a dangerous act.

"You really are on a trip, Uncle Richie."

"Why I'm having a wonderful trip. I'm in Australia."

"Uncle Richie . . . ?"

"With one million bucks."

259

The Marine, at this point, dropped out of the negotiations.

"Uncle Richie ... ?"

"Don't interrupt my creative flow."

"Uncle Richie ... ?"

"What!"

"Are you serious?!"

Timmy still waited in the thinned-down Dixie Disco, his eyes still nervously on heaven. He'd tried to get up to those flies where the columns were presumably resting. But he couldn't find the way. And no one had been able to help him.

People, now pretty much exclusively male, were still rushing back and forth, cascading from one playground to the next. He noticed the group of models from Garfield's orgy last night looking at him critically. So he stood tall and cool and proud and stared right back. He somehow thought this was how Winnie would play it.

Then he saw Randy Dildough coming toward him, hand outstretched, a beaming and welcoming smile again upon that face.

"A very fine performance, Timothy! My congratulations. I certainly know how to pick them."

Timmy looked him right in the eye and decided to play this one as Winnie would, too. "Go away, Crud Man!" he said, and walked away to further make his point. That should show him. Leave Tim Purvis hanging indeed!

Boo Boo finished writing. And then, pausing only to let his mind, or what is currently left of it, caress the loving thoughts: sexual proficiency, orgiastic participation, and money here I come! Soon they'll all be saying: "There goes

260

Richard Abraham Bronstein! You know who he is!," he grabbed his new helpmate Wyatt by the hand and confided to him: "I think this should do it. Let's go and burn our incense!"

Fred and Dinky, hand in hand as well, had exited Behind the Green Door and bumped right into Abe.

"Fred-chen, where have you been? This place is not for me. I want to go home. Tell me, how do you meet people when no one talks? Even a hooker on the street, I'd go up to her, say hello, what's your name, where are you from, how much do you charge?"

Fred and Dinky both laughed, Fred, feeling so good, kissed Abe and introduced Dinky, and then Dinky said: "You don't talk to people when you cruise. The secret is to just look mean."

"What please is a cruise?"

Fred answered, waving his hands about in his best screenwriter's descriptive way: "Think of this place as a great big store, with lots of merchandise on display. But you don't really look at it too closely, because you don't feel like shopping today. You look at it . . . obliquely. You give it a little look, pretending not to look, but being able to see, out of the corner of your eye only, if anyone else is pretending not to look back at you. If you see someone else pretending not to look, you look the other way. Only after a few moments do you look back, to see if he's still looking. And if your eyes look, at the same moment, you'll only let it happen for a second, and then you'll look away again."

"It's very complicated. You want to write a movie about this? The pace will be very deadly."

". . . hi Gramps . . ."

Abe looked, and there was his grandson.

261

"Meine kleine Wyatt!"

". . . Gramps, I got this note for you . . ."

And kleine Wyatt, pushed from out of nowhere into prominence by a helpful Uncle no longer there, plopped the piece of Hermès paper into his Grampa's hand and then tore off like hell.

"Who was that, Abe?"

"But wait! My Wyatt!"

Dinky looked and saw Irving Slough coming toward him all in black.

Abe had read the note.

"Abe! What's wrong!" Fred looked upon an Abe now all in white.

"I . . . I . . . I . . . speak to you later." And Abe rushed off and into the crowd as well.

Fred turned to Dinky beside him. Dinky wasn't beside him. Dinky was talking to a stranger.

And Irving Slough saw Dinky talking to a stranger.

"Gentlemen and Gentlemen! Men and Men!, our final attraction of this momentous evening, rush rush rush back to The Fucketeria, for our grand and climactic event!, you ain't seen nothin' till you've seen our grand and climactic event! . . ."

And the crowds began to rush rush rush!

"This is Dennis," Dinky said, introducing both Fred and Irving, not only to each other, but to a tall and blond and not very special-looking young man dressed all in leather.

Fred asked himself: Who the fuck is Dennis? And: So that's Irving Slough? Two weeks with *that*?

"I forgot to tell you both about Dennis."

And Fred watched and Irving watched as Dinky took a dog's lead and collar studded with silver knobs from a hook on Dennis's belt and put it around Dennis's neck.

And Irving's thoughts runneth over: Who the fuck is

Dennis? And: So Dinky is in leather and boots already! So Dinky is in leather and boots already!! Is there no surprise left he hasn't surprised me with? And: So that's Fred Lemish. Yes, Fred Lemish is coddling his Pandora's Box of Pain. He does not understand that Dinky is collaring this Dennis as a retreat from all our pressurings. And: This Dennis is his defense against feeling and involvement, his barricade thrown up against any commitment or anger, love or pain. And: How can I use all of this to my advantage? Particularly when this Dennis, and this Fred, are pains in my box, too. Dr. Irving Slough put his hand to his own belt and unhooked his own dog's collar.

Dinky, his eyes on no one, said: "I forgot to tell you that I had this date tonight with Dennis. We're going to do a leather scene."

Irving found himself heaving his fifty-five-year-old body in creaking basic black leather not so broken-in as he thought, down to its knees, and offering up his own canine accoutrement in homage, and then further bending into grovel as he kissed Dinky's chunky boots. "I thought we had a date. Do it with me, too," he begged.

"Get up, Irving," Dinky said. "You look very silly in leather. But we'll experiment later. I'll show you a few things later. Dennis doesn't like threesomes. Do you, Dennis?"

Dennis obligingly shook his head No.

"I thought we were spending the night," Fred said, his stomach's ballast heaving from port to starboard with nary a port to rest.

"We will. We will. Tomorrow on the Island. We'll spend the night tomorrow on the Island."

"What are you going to do?" Irving asked jealously, pulling his own port back up.

"Oh, Dennis will crawl around naked on the floor with his cock in a nice little black leather case we're fond

263

of and I'll order him about and he'll obey me. It's all kind of silly. It doesn't mean a thing to me, fellows. Believe me. I might even have to leave him for a few minutes to go out of my room and laugh. You see, I can step in and out of it and look at it from up above and outside of it and think my goodness isn't this silly and then step right back into it with him. I usually wind up fucking him. And letting him shoot all over my boots. He really likes my beautiful boots." And he tugged on Dennis's lead and Dennis obliged this time with a Yes.

OK, Lemish. Now you've heard it. Now you've seen it. Rome built and destroyed in a day. How do you feel about it? Still on your fence? How do you fence with this fence? Quick! This is a moment desirous of action. Quick! what's the Proust line?—that we're attracted to those people who have qualities we hate in ourselves? Is he attracted to me because he hates his perversions? Or am I attracted to him because I hate myself for wanting to be Dennis right this very minute? Marcel, come help me! Whose fantasy man is whose? And why is it that both of our fantasy men seem completely different from those we're choosing! Sweet & Dreckness! what did they say? Quick! In their semenal *The Abandonment to Sex* . . . ? . . . "Two lovers must feel free to explore their fantasies with each other to the utmost . . ." What two lovers? What love? Where's love? Tomorrow! Always tomorrow! What's going on here today? Why is he doing these things? To himself! To me! I'm a fucking towerful power of rage! I'm all wound up!

And wind up Fred did. Just like in his lesson at the Y. And slugged his Dinky in the puss. Take that! Dreck & Sweetness! And down went Dinky. Splat.

"Fred!" Gatsby rushed up. "I suggested a confrontation, not a main event!"

Fred fell into Gatsby's arms, his Robert Redford to

the rescue. "He's fucking himself up!" Fred tried to tell his friend. "And he doesn't know it!"

"If he's smart enough, he would know it," Gatsby sensibly answered. "And if he doesn't know it, he's not smart enough and you shouldn't want him," he just as sensibly continued.

But what had any of this to do with sense! Fred tried to find words to tell them all. "You . . . you . . . you don't know what you're involved with!"

"You're crazy, Mister," Dennis said, none too pleased his Master had been floored, but helping him up anyway.

"No, he's not," Irving said, nodding, looking at Fred. "He's in love." And he walked away. Angry. Very angry. I think our Dinky must now be punished. For the error of his ways. Tomorrow in The Meat Rack.

Bo Peep, who had seen it all, rushed up to help man the comfort station. "Oh, Fred," the sweet face said, "it's the oldest story in the world. You must say to him I'm not going to see you anymore as long as you treat me this way. I'm more special than you're treating me."

"Have you said that to Tarsh?" Gatsby's sensibility once again intruded.

"Well, not exactly. But I will."

But Fred had walked away, too. Events were now passing beyond the realm of even Cary Grant.

Fred paused outside The Fucketeria. He tried to give himself a good talking to. OK, buddy, you feel simply terrific. You're having a dexedrine high. You have just performed an act of courage best executed in our era by Nurse Nellie Forbush when she extirpated that man right out of her hair "and sent him on his way!" OK, buddy, you go on your way now, too. You look terrific. Everyone says your new body is superfine. Now . . . now . . . now

... go into this Fucketeria place and use it! Go in there and become an abandoned, passionate Thing!

"Uuchh!"
This sound escaped Fred's lips.

Yes, he had entered The Fucketeria and yes, he had become accustomed to the gloom and the sounds of slurp-ings midst the presence of brothers. Fred saw on neigh-boring risers at least seventeen faces he recognized to talk to, not here of course, but knew well enough to puzzle how one had sex in a bathtub full of friends. Perhaps to combat this, The Gnome, busy as ever in moments of need, rushed and darted about with his cigarette-girl's tray of goodies, seeing to it that a healthy round of Magic was available to all.

"Uuucchh!"
Yes, he had dropped onto one of the lower bleachers and then wished for the seventeenth time this weekend to be Dead.

"Uuuuccchhhh!"
For there before him, there on center stage, in center arena, in media res, beautifully lit with pin-pricks as in the best Broadway shows, his hands and feet bound to rough wood, upon a cross, erected for this main event, his Ameri-can debut, hung the lean and lovely body of his First Beloved, Feffer.

"UUUUUCCCCHHHHH!"
For Feffer is being whipped by the two whippers who are Lance Heather, in matching tones of brown Bavarian leathers, and Leather Louie, in matching same of black, with an armada of arcane implements culled from far and near, slash slash slash, the crowd is going wild!, this place is truly the winner!, this scene becomes a milestone!, this night goes down in history!, all further triumphs hence-

266

forth are measured!, slash slash slash, Feffer's body evidently loving every whip and fanny and slither and driblet and shameful ignominy, and Fred, Whom-Am-I-Ever-To-Fall-In-Love-With!?!-Fred, still dry-eyed in martyrdom, slowly rises from his lower riser and like some Jewish acolyte who just might be approaching insight and knowledge, walks slowly up up up up to the First Love of his life, so vividly perched up there before him.

"Hi, Lemmy." Feffer focuses his eyes, looks down, and smiles kindly. "I tried to call you but you weren't home. I didn't want to talk to your machine."

"Is this what you wanted all along?"

"Not much difference in it either way. It really depends on what you feel like on a particular night."

"Oh, Feff." What's going on here? I know what's going on here, but what's going on here?

"Now, Lemmy, don't go and get sentimental. This really doesn't mean very much."

"Your little long black leather belt has come a long way."

"Well, it has been four years."

"You want a lick?" Lance offers Fred a turn at bat.

"Go fuck yourself."

"Go fuck yourself yourself."

"Gentlemen!" Leather Louie mediates.

"So long, Feff." This time I'm leaving you. Though where I'm going I don't know. Have I been to so many places like this that I'm going blind?

" 'Bye, Lem."

And Fred walks away. And out of The Fucketeria, where the scene and scenes continue. And into Anthony, his best friend, so kind of fate to proffer his best friend, in this moment so calling for extreme unction.

"This is Wyatt," Anthony, avoiding Fred's eyes, introduces a quivering young fellow.

267

"Unh, how do you do?" Fred, now glazed beyond any donut, automatically offers a hand.

"I'm in love with Anthony and I'm going to go and live with *him!*"

Anthony shrugs. "What am I going to do, Tante?"

"You didn't tell me he was a teeny-bopper." Fred continues his exit walk. Solo.

Meanwhile, in Dixie Disco Dancehall, there is suddenly much commotion.

Winnie Heinz has fallen to earth. He had paused, up there in heaven, reached out, thinking: I'm almost there, but here, still here. He had thought momentarily that he saw the truth, right over there, through to the end, and now I must reach out farther, truth is farther away, if I'm going to reach out, reach far, Winnie, reach far and you'll be there, my angel's dust will take me there . . . And out he'd reached and fell to earth below. Ashes to ashes, dust to dust. Oh, Winnie! Good-bye. Proud beauty! Duncan Heinz IV. Looking thirty, claiming forty, actually forty-five. Now joining the sands of history on this famous night. Winnie Heinz is dead.

Timmy cradles his Winnie in his arms and softly cries. He had seen it all. That fall of grace. He looks up and addresses the few spectators left in the empty Roseland. "He was the most beautiful and sophisticated thing I'd ever seen. He taught me everything. He taught me love."

Frigger dashes in, pulls a decorative bunting from a column, and quickly wraps the beauty in crepe. He wonders does a body hex or help an opening night. He wishes everybody would go home. His mouth is hungry.

Milling bodies think passing thoughts. That one's had too much. I must watch out. How much have I had tonight? I always told you smoking kills.

Hans Zoroaster rushes up to view the body of his late great model.

"What is your name, boy?" Hans cannot take his eyes from young Purvis.

"Winnie Purvis," Timmy answers in memoriam.

"I shall make you a star!"

But Timmy hasn't heard. Or he's heard it all before. So what? He's suddenly very lonely. He needs some arms to hold and warm him. He's suddenly frightened that his bite of the Big Apple is more than he can chew. Here comes that Dildough. He really wasn't so bad.

But Dildough has returned with fire, ice, and the suitor who is the handsome gymnast-architect with the silver bracelet, Robbie Swindon. His face had been vaguely familiar to Randy from somewhere. Had he ever done a scene with him? Yes, Dildough is back to his former self. A scene we'll certainly do tonight! So good to get back into known roles. He looks down at young Timothy. "So long, Timothy." And off he and Robbie start toward an elevator down.

"I am so happy to be seeing you again so soon!" Dordogna del Dongo, her flaming-red hair swaying and her gold bangles clanking and her deep dark eyes muskying, has finally found her man.

"Next week! . . . Save me an evening! . . . save me two evenings! . . ." What am I saying? And Randy grabs that Swindon and makes it through the elevator door before it closes.

"I'll bet he'll come to Fire Island," says her friend, the everhelpful Marine, our Adriana.

"Such a coincidence that you have invited me, too," Dordogna says.

Hans says again to Timmy: "I shall make you a star!" Even his gold tit now radiates anticipation.

The Divine Bella, fresh from golden-showered triumphs in Jackie O and smelling a column item, hears these words from their most important model-maker. He immediately bends to kiss this newest beauty of our moment in time. "My precious, I am enraptured, such a world and life is now in store for you!"

"Phew," someone says. "What do you use to get rid of the smell of piss?"

"You buy it at a pet shop and it's called Fresh Pussy," someone answers.

Lork and Carlty and Yo-Yo and Tom-Tom and Dawsie and Pusher all now rush up to reluctantly get a closer look at Timmy. Now he's really competition. Hans beams that his children like each other so.

Dinky, without Dennis, whose passion for a scene had evaporated when he'd seen his Master decked, nods hello at that elevator door to Frigger.

"I wasn't late," Dinky says.

"You were four fucking hours late," says Frigger, referring to that night seven years ago when Frigger had refused to wait any longer and had left Dinky, as he now again does.

Here comes Laverne, alone. He'd been unable to respond on the spot to Robbie's proposal of marriage. He'd promised a decisive answer at the Island tomorrow, which of course now is today.

"Can I give you a lift?" Dinky asks his late lover.

Laverne sighs. He hates himself as he hears his answer: "OK."

Fred's gone home.

Such a night of nights.

Josie and Dom Dom, wearing matching hues of tired sagging grays, leave The Toilet Bowl holding tightly.

"Oh, Dom Dom, what's happened to kiss and cuddle?"

"They're coming back in the eighties."

Yes, such a Night of Nights!

• • •

And Rory Neutra, a film director's son and in charge of cleaning up with his staff of twelve, made the following census of trashy items after all had gone: one coffin, two sets of portable gallows, seven hoods, two executioner's masks, one artificial arm, ten high heels, four net stockings, twenty gross of used poppers, eighty-three empty bottles of liquid same, fourteen rubbers, seven diaphragms, one damaged dildo, ten pairs of ladies' underpants, ten sets of Chafeze, forty-seven jockstraps, twelve basketball player's shorts, fourteen numbered jerseys, seven cock sacks, twenty-one falsies, five cock-and-balls harnesses, six ankle shackles, seven bras, two corsets, eighteen whips, one pair of Gloves of Silence, two force-feeders, one mace, forty clothespins, one cattle prod, three boweling balls, one surgical ass-spreader, several odd lengths of rope, several unmatched links of chain, one Ping Pong paddle, five empty containers of Joy Jell (one each of raspberry, orange, grape, licorice, and Persian Rose), two depleted tubes of Sta-Hard, seven dual inhalers, one universal harness, three Crisco-ed pool cues, one pair of thumb cuffs, one pulsating vagina, four vibrators with worn-out batteries, one copy of *The Complete Enema Guide,* a couple of dog collars, one meat tenderizer, five blindfolds, three unmatched spiked gauntlets, one pair of slave hobbles, 1,453 roach ends, 17,543 cigarette butts, seventy asshorted cans of Crisco, two hundred Vaseline empties, one hundred and twelve depleted Intensive Cares, ten knives, forty-two cock rings in various sizes, seven tit rings, one black leather jerkin, one empty pill case, twenty-seven kilos of dried semen scraped from simply everywhere, seventeen pounds of shit, one hand-lettered sign: DANNY'S PISS CLUB MEETS EVERY SUNDAY E & L—B.Y.O.P., one lavender letter: "I love you so fucking much I can hardly shit," twenty pale faces popping out from the interior for air and light and wanting to

271

go back for more, and an exhausted Blaze, fast asleep in Jackie O and dreaming of models, models, models.

Two other discos opened tonight. Mission Accomplished, owned by fellows in Las Vegas, kept five thousand overexcited and eager customers waiting on the streets till three, but once inside, free strawberries, top-drawer sound, and the legendary Tino D. J., plus a balcony (the place had been a former opera house, which stretched up to heaven, from which one could look down on all the dancing fleas) made it a Possible, only time would tell, the efficient Alfestra bei Icker, press agent to the bisexually affluent, was being summoned and Alfestra had worked wonders in the past. Fury's Place, named after a former body builder turned drag queen out of Atlantic City who thought he had a lot of friends but didn't, closed on opening night.

Fred went home to void and purge his system. A douche, an enema, to love that wasn't love. So long, Feffer, so long, Dinky, hello . . . what?

He wrote to Dinky on a sweet note card with a bowl of cherries on a background the color of sand:

Well, kid, I have seen the future and it shits. Georges and Dennises, Irvings and Lavernes, dog collars and cock cases, all, alas, are love gone wrong. Like when you squeeze the tube with the cap still on and the toothpaste squirts out the wrong end.

So your Fred must reluctantly tip his non-leather cap and bid you a fond, but sad, adieu.

Keep right on with your plantings, though! Engorge all those empty terraces! Watch everything

272

grow! Now that the sun is shining, your many indentured customers will no doubt find their needs expanding and their Dinky will be there with annuals and perennials, heavy vines and nipped-in buds.

Me, I'm tired of being potted by your many promises, dripped down intravenously into one of New York's 100 Most Neediest Cases, frugally, lest the weeping willow live.

As an old cake-eater, I can tell you you're strictly hung up on crumbs.

When will you stop being: 1) A Loser. 2) Dumb. 3) Blind. 4) Frightened. 5) Afraid of Trying? With this communication I cease being 1-3.

I hope before your roots rot and your willow drips too low, you'll harvest a soupçon of Romance and Moonlight, you'll reap a scintilla of Responsibility and Love, and you'll taste a few good licks of . . . Expectation.

Good-bye from your late bulldog, Fred.

He considered the prose. Did it scan? Was it sufficiently metaphoric? Was it light, fluffy, but with an undercurrent of heartrending hurt and meaning? Ah, how little experience he'd had in dealing with problems of the heart! But then, who had?

So, trying to perform like a Great Person who has just discovered the cure for a heretofore incurable disease —Greer Garson as Madame Curie, Joan Fontaine in *Letter from An Unknown Woman,* Roddy McDowell in *Lassie, Come Home* . . . Fred Lemish as Mother Courage—he marched up to West 29th Street, taking with him a roll of Scotch tape, another note card, and a pen, in case he wished to revise or rewrite along the way.

At the shrine, he waited until an early worker left the

273

building so he could gain entrance. Then he took off his shoes and walked up the six flights stealthily and he taped his note, as was, to Dinky's door—at last Martin Luther and his Ninety-Five Theses on the church in Wittenberg, not a Jewish town—trying not to imagine what Dinky was doing to Dennis on the other side of it. Ah, was there any pain as agonizing as that caused by the knowledge that your beloved, correction!, ex-beloved, was doing it with someone else? He has rejected your body, he has said he prefers to do it with another body, come on Lemish!, cut the crap!, how much shit are you willing to take just for the memory of a little intimacy, how crazy and hungry can you be? With this Bowl of Cherries, your *Ladies' Home Jour-nal* days must now be over.

So up went the note and down went its author, still stealthily, Butch Jenkins departing *Scene of the Crime,* back down six flights, re-entering his Weejuns at the bottom, walking tall out of the building, his hair now dry but his brow making up for it, giving the finger to Dinky's sea-green Dodge pick-up, and heading home. Ever so much stronger. Out of my hair. Yes sir, yes sir. And back to behind his picnic curtains on Washington Square. Alone. To try and sleep alone.

Dinky was of course behind that lettered door with Laverne. Yes, Laverne was back in his old stamping grounds, his very own apartment, which he had vacated six months ago, causing Frigger, always ready with a one-liner, to quip to Dinky: "Darling, you've done what every queen dreams of doing! You've wound up with the real estate."

Yes, Jack and Dinky, the two lean, handsome, youthful beauties of thirty, they'd been an admirable pair, the going-to-be-an-architect who quit school to live with the teacher of English when they thought they were in love and bought the house by the canal in Southampton and opened a store where they sold beautiful things, and failed, were side by side once more, naked upon that pedestal bed Dinky'd made with his own hands.

Both found the conjunction strange. Dinky was trying to embrace Laverne. Laverne did not wish to be embraced.

So Dinky pulled out a bedside volume and thumbed to a page. "I found this quote in Trollope. I've been reading this new Trollope. Remember, you introduced me to Trollope?"

Laverne remembered.

Dinky then read aloud, smiling, and as poetically as he could. " 'Did Lily feel the want of something heroic in a man before she could teach herself to look upon him as more worthy of her regard than other men? There had been moments when John had almost risen to the necessary point—had almost made good his footing on the top of some moderate hill, but still sufficient mountain. But there had still been a succession of little tumbles, and he had never quite stood upright on his pinnacle, visible to Lily's eyes as being really excelsior.' Story of you and me."

"Who's the Lily and who's the John?" Laverne asked, wondering if he understood Dinky even now, wondering if he'd ever understood Dinky, wondering, come to think of it, if Laverne understood Jack either. All he felt was cynical. Trollope indeed. He'd go and live with Robbie Swindon and he'd try. "What makes you think we can start all over again?"

"What makes you think we can't?"

"What would you do with Irving and Ike Bulb and Lemish and Tony and Olive and Dennis and Mr. Savannah?"

"I don't fuck with Ike Bulb, I can't find Paulie, Irv-

275

ing's a joke, Olive is boring and only into dildoes, Tony won't see me anymore, Piero ran off with some of my money, Chipper has another lover and they moved to California, Floyd I only used to make you jealous, I don't fuck with Frigger anymore, Dennis I only see when I feel the need to be a Master, and Fred Lemish is in love with me. He's a mess. Love will do it every time. You see, at least I'm honest with you. I always tell you the whole story." He then paused before adding: "Everyone is so silly. Everyone wants too much. Being gay isn't fun anymore."

"You need too much amusement." Then Laverne paused, too, to think: My, it certainly was a full six years, before adding: "Love isn't silly."

"You were the only one who wasn't silly. You were the only one who ever understood me."

"I was the only one who let you get away with you! You're too fucking handsome and too fucking clever and you always have to have your own way and I always let you and I never could believe a thing you said! Fred Lemish was right to slam you in the face. All I ever did was throw at you those mixing bowls from Crete. And miss. You ought to stay with him. He's rich and famous and you'd always eat. And he wouldn't let you get away with you. Yes, he sounds the right person for you."

"You were the right person for me."

"I was the right person for you once. No more. I'm going to go and live with Robbie Swindon."

Dinky lay back for another moment of pause. Then he rolled over and leaned down and rummaged in a drawer in the base of the bed and pulled out a long, gray two-headed dildo from days of long ago. Then he placed it, wriggling like a snake, into that space between them, where it rested ominously.

"Using this would put me on your mountain?" Laverne inquired.

"You know you were tempted." Dinky's eyes and ear were twinkling.

"I wouldn't use it then and I won't use it now."

"The poppers and the Vaseline are on your side between the mattress and the wall."

"I'm not sophisticated enough for you. You always have to try new things. You wouldn't take me as I am!" Jack picked up the dildo and lobbed it out of sight.

"And you wouldn't take me as I am!"

"No matter what I did it was never enough! You probably still want me to fist-fuck you, don't you?"

"Yes, I want you to fist-fuck me."

"I could never understand why you liked to get fist-fucked and don't like to get regular fucked. "

"Anybody can get fucked. It's entirely different. If you'd only try, you'd see."

Laverne just lay there. Robbie . . . could you come and get me now? Please! Come put your handsome silver bracelet around my neck. I mean, finger!

Dinky said: "I wish you'd get rid of your bourgeois Birmingham attitudes." He was now trying to play with Jack's cock.

"Fist-fucking would do that, would it?" Jack jumped up and started to dress. "I'm going home. Leave me alone. You crushed the flower. I gave you books. You gave me plants. Books live. Plants die. You only loved me when I said I didn't love you anymore! That's the only time you started paying any attention to me. I won't play your games. I won't! You just feed into my feeling terrible about myself! That's what my dyke shrinkette said. She said that. All you do is take mother-types like me and shit all over us. She said that, too. She said you need a smorgasbord of people. Column A and Column B. I want someone who wants me and only me! Why do I keep coming back for more? I must stop! I must like me enough! I must!

277

I won't let you sour me for someone else! I won't. I must get away from you!" Oh, it was difficult, pulling on his jeans, still wet from sweaty dancings, to love a liar, love pain and anguish and indecision, dancings in those Robbie Swindon arms, and would he, Jack Humpstone, come back to live with Dinky the Devil, and be hurt again. No! He was not going to return. He would break this bondage. He must! "Friends! Let's be buddies! We share a Capriccio card and a Y membership and a house in Southampton and let's let it go at that!"

Dinky stood up slowly, handed Laverne his shirt, and calmly escorted him out of the bedroom and down the long corridor. "Here's your shirt. Before Savannah, Ike and I, we went to Key West. You and I were going to buy a house there. Remember? It's going to be the new faggot winter Fire Island. He and I bunked with four guys I knew from somewhere. One of them fucked the second while the third shat upon the fourth. And then I pissed on all of them. Before I went to sleep. It's my shirt really. You took it. But I don't want it back."

"I'll speak to you later, I'll see you on the Island, don't talk to me of . . . shirts, this is my apartment, please get out of my life . . ." Laverne was trying to open the front door but the latch was still on.

"I forgot to tell you, Irving invited us both to his Meat Rack party tonight." Dinky unlocked the door.

Laverne was through it as fast as he could be.

That's when Dinky found Fred's letter.

Boo Boo's own communiqué to Abe's diplomatic pouch had read (as best as sweaty nighttime hieroglyphics on Hermes winged feet could be de-coded by the enemy Pop):

Sir, It has come to our attention that your Richie is an homosexual. He has therefore naturally been kidnapped.

He is quite safe but somewhat uncomfortable. He is buried under a remote piece of soil in the Meat Rack of Fire Island Pines.

The amount demanded is One Million Dollarinos in unmarked old $100 bills.

You are to bring the money to the above resting place tomorrow, Sunday, at midnight in an old suitcase.

A helpmate will greet you at boardwalk's end and lead you to your assignation with destiny.

Come Alone! To go to the Police would be callous, unlucky, untoward, and dangerous to your reputation as his Pop.

For, unless you do everything, Richie will remain buried alive and the world will know the awful truth!

Oh, did not our Abraham pace and pace, back and forth, crisscross, up and down, over and back, diagonally, wearing thinner and thinner his bedroom Oriental! So God is finally getting his revenge! For my success! For my hubris! It was like receiving a note from the President that your son was missing in action. Guilts and guilts and doubts and worries and questionings. Is this a kidnapping like is so currently popular abroad? Should I call the police? Maybe the F.B.I.? J. Edgar Hoover? No, he is dead. And the country hasn't been safe since. The President who sent me this letter? My brother, Maury, with whom I do not speak? My older son and lawyer, Stephen, who with his fine wife is away for the holidays in Aruba? Peetra, who gives me another son in Paris? Gain one son and I lose another! Ephra? How can I tell Ephra? Fire Island Pines is where faggolim go! I am meeting Fred there. Can it be true? Can my Richie . . . ? ! My Wyatt . . . ? ! Our offspring are faggolasexual queerim! What have we done?

279

Ephra! It was your fault for holding him too close! Reconciliation! I must bring about reconciliation! Is this my Mission? Come to haunt me in a Toilet Bowl? What is God trying to tell me? What is Richie trying to tell me? He is trying to tell me that he's a lazy queer who wants a lot of money. That's what he's trying to tell me. Oh, the conniving son of a bitch.

For Abe of course smelled the something fishily off kilter. His Wyatt had delivered the note himself. How could his Richie be in danger? How could dangerous kidnappers be lurking behind him in all those dancing fairies? Did he not know his own son and self? His own son was kidnapping himself! Should he call Mr. Bronfman to discuss his recent experiences with his own kidnapped son?

He walked around the apartment. Now he was thinking of Richie and now he knew why. And everything reminded him of Richie. The messy toothpaste tube. The camp pictures of the pudgy boy always on the losing Color War team. His ballet tights! Why didn't I realize then!

But why doesn't he come right out and say it? Pop, I'm a gaynick and I want more money. Because I would slam his tuchas and send him off to our branch in Australia. That's why. And make him marry that ugly Marci Tisch.

And he knows it! And so now he blackmails me. And he will tell the world his secret before he tells to me. He becomes the conniver! Oh, Abraham Bronstein, how your words come back to smack you in your ass.

Ephra, who at dawn had come in from her own adjoining suite, had queried: "You are not sleeping?"

"How do you know I am not sleeping?"

"An ex-wife knows."

And seeing him worried, and embracing him, and hoping that his crisscrossings on her rug meant Hope, she asked him: "Abraham, are we having by any stretch a reconciliation?"

But when she heard him greptz in surprise and saw him traipse her rug anew, she returned to her own bed, this time to dream of horses.

Randy Dildough had not received a letter. His came in a phone call. Myron Musselman again. The 217 holiday weekend situations for *Bronty, The Last Survivor* were definitely not biggies, they had no legs, this stinker, loser, bomb, meant twenty-three million dollars of P-P's money down the toilet, whoever's responsible for this one had better have a pretty good idea for what to do next or else he's in a spot of trouble all his own.

Randy, of course was responsible for this one.

Would the convergence of all ill auguries never cease?

Randy hung up the phone but held on to the receiver. He was momentarily sorry he'd not brought that Robbie Whatshisname back. He could now fuck the shit out of him. But he'd ditched that fawning niceness when some déjà vu from somewhere suddenly became uncomfortable. Probably just as well. Jesus Christ, I probably saved his life.

He picked up the phone again. A call to R. Allan Pooker sleepily informed him that Timothy was one of his starlets. He was on his way, to Fire Island in a Rolls.

So once again Randy felt his rise to the occasion. He would have to go to Fire Island to save his new James Dean.

But Timmy had been crowned the new Winston Man. The younger smoking market is so important. He was now sleeping in the arms of Hans, in his elaborate villa, Utopia, on the bay at Tuna, in Fire Island Pines.

And Irving, also on the Island, but alone, in his villa, Chain Male, on Doctor's Walk, overlooking the ocean, in The Grove, unpacked his Vuitton of leather, studied his yet-to-be-pedigreed-dog collar, and wondered once again if his meting out of vengeance, or more therapeutically, a lesson, or less euphemistically, scared the living shit out of him, would Get Dinky Back, particularly when the pupil had been so tardy with the teacher, much less showing up at school.

But as he unwrapped his package from the Marquis de Suede, he congratulated himself. What experienced teacher could not find a way? And it would be the Ultimate Humiliation. And it would be tonight!

And Boo Boo Bronstein, who'd zipped to Fire Island drugged out in his Porsche, and taken the ferry across, and stepped out at last and on to its hallowed famous dock and boardwalks, but walked with head down to the ocean's edge, now sat staring at that water in the glaring new day's light and wondering . . . what the living, fucking, shit have I done?

At some time or other between April and November, the 2,901,019 faggots in the New York City area come to Fire Island.

It is one of the most beautiful places on earth.

Here they attempt to play house. It is as much a home as any of them ever have.

282

And Memorial Day Weekend is its Champagne Launching!

Open House!

The crowds are pouring in. The seaplanes unload every three minutes, only twenty minutes from New York. The ferries (the *Queen,* the *Duchess,* the *Princess,* the good ships Lollipops) are overburdened and heaving back and forth from the mainland town of Sayville, only ninety minutes from New York, as fast as royal ladies can. The Firefly buses from the city have tripled their charterings to standing room only.

For, if God were to take a ribbon of land and sand and wave His Magic Wand over it, proclaiming: "You're beautiful!," the result would be Fire Island Pines.

It's a couple of miles long. It's perhaps half a mile wide. Boardwalks crisscross each other like the neat darns of socks. Lots are filled to overflowing with desirable homes that adjoin and tumble into each other among spreading pinery and evergreenery and all-pervading fun and love. The sand by the ocean is the whitest and the widest. The water is the bluest. The sun tans more evenly here. Since it appears more often. The stars, of course, shine much more brightly. Both up above and on this beach below. Dancing is more fun and eating is more fun and sex is much, much more fun, and strolling under the moon at three o'clock in the morning or watching tangerine sunrise or popsicle sunset—everything, EVERYTHING!, is more fun. And filled with hope. Which is more fun. For everything, naturally, must always have Hope.

"If the Outside World is ugly and not many laughs and doesn't want us anyway, what's wrong with making our very own special place, with our dancing and drugs and

283

jokes and clothes and music and brotherhood and fucking and our perfectly marvelous taste!"

"You are absolutely right. There is simply nothing that is ugly at Fire Island Pines. The eyes are bathed with constant delights. Uglies and uglinesses are simply not tolerated. Go Away! Shoo!"

"We have created our own aesthetic!"

"You mean our own Ghetto."

"This place is all about belonging, the love of friends, Togetherness!"

"And the Quest for Beauty."

"And the search for Mr. Right."

"Oh, I don't know about that."

"We play here too much."

"Never too much."

"I think we come here to be hurt and rejected."

"Oh, I don't know about that."

"But don't we talk about it endlessly."

"What it all *means*."

"What does it all mean?"

"Oh, stop it!"

Yes, everyone talked about its essence endlessly. Such a complicated place. While one could say: Picture any old ocean resort, full of houses side by side for which we've saved up all year long, with a few scruffy pines, lots of tracing wild foliage, intermixed with not a little poison ivy, and poof, you have Fire Island Pines . . .

. . . that would not be the case at all.

For if, as 'tis said, it takes a faggot to make something pretty, they have outdone themselves on this Island of Fire.

The faggot part of Fire Island is really two communities. The Pines is newer, classier, and more expensive

284

and amusing, and has better shops and handsomer, younger, more affluent fellows, and bigger houses, more tastefully decorated, and for all these reasons the older and less stylishly oriented go to Cherry Grove. This granddaddy community of the entire Island, dating back to 1869, more of bungalows called "Oh, Lay!," "Prison of Zenda," "House of Payne," "Last Resort," yes, older socks darned less neatly, takes its name, calmly enough, not from the loss of women's virginities o'er the seasons, but from a profusion of fruit trees that has survived time, tides, hurricanes, and man's unchanging habits.

Pines people only go to The Grove to visit, to fuck with one of those headier, less stylish types, or to dance at Billy Boner's magical Ice Palace.

The Pines once supported a large population of same, but most of them withered and died when a larger harbor was dredged to provide more room for the visiting flotillas, always in residence, known variously as the "Bagel Brigade," "Jewish Navy," or "Mama's Little Tugboats." Why rich Hadassah ladies with big hairdos and bigger husbands should wish to come and park their yachts alongside twenty-four-hour faggot discos (The Botel for Tea Dance and The Sandpiper for nights when that magical Ice Palace seems simply too far away) is an interesting sociological question not in the scope of our survey.

Before 1954, The Pines land was barren. Fat Truman Toss and his birdlike wife, Tessa, had bought up a great deal of it, via Tessa's father's New Jersey All-Inclusive (later to become part of Myron Musselman's P-P group of families), and Aorta Crawfish, a single lady, had squatted on much of the rest. There were few buyers in those pioneer days. But in 1963 all hell broke loose, when electricity was installed in The Pines before The Grove, and fellows from the latter attempted to move those scant two miles Eastward. Alas, they ran smack into a very stern

"Families Only!" and "Single Gentlemen Need Not Apply!" policy rigidly enforced by the Tosses. Yet, since nothing could deter a group of fellows desirous of decorating upward, away from kerosene heaters, ice boxes, and candles, to refrigerators, dishwashers, and candles, buy in they managed to do, via female friends, mothers, and other helpful types.

A great deal of the land is still owned by Aorta, usually away living it up in Menton, on the French Riviera, close to the Italian border town of San Remo, where she has located the world's most perfect piece of chocolate cake, and the Tosses, still unfortunately ever present, but now "so in love with all our nice young men!," plus a chiropractor's wife from the mainland, and the gas man, Bath, all owners speaking the local dialect which, as in all summer resorts, precedes each vowel with a dollar sign.

Thus, while 73% of The Pines is straight-owned, 99% of it is faggot-occupied.

There is between The Pines and The Grove an area of one and one half miles, that place of myth and story, called The Meat Rack. Suffice it for now to say that it is located where indicated, that it is a lot of trees and bushes and hills and dunes, and that in it—day or night, twenty-four hours a day, seven days a week, we never close—a lot of fellows are playing with each other.

Fred had first come to Fire Island Pines when he was thirty. He wasn't ready for such beauty, such potential, such unlimited choice. The place scared him half to death. It was a warm and sunny weekend and there were one thousand bathing-suited handsomenesses on The Botel deck at Tea Dance. They all seemed to know each other and to touch and greet and smile at each other. And there he was, alone. Though he had acquired his 150-pound body for the first time (of his so-far three: the first for himself, the second for Feffer, number three, with muscles, for Dinky), he still felt like Mrs. Shelley's monster, pale, and with a touch of leprosy thrown in. Not only had he no one to talk to, not only did the overwhelmingness of being confronted by so much Grade A male flesh, most of which seemed superior to his, which would make it difficult to talk to, even if he could utter, which he could not, floor him, but everyone else seemed so secure, not only with their bodies (all thin and no doubt well-defined since birth), tans, personalities, their smiles and chat, but also with that ability to use their eyes, much like early prospectors must have looked for gold, darting them hither and yon, seeking out the sparkling flecks, separating the valued from the less so, meaning, he automatically assumed, him. Their glances his way seemed like disposable bottles, no deposit, no return. He felt like Mr. Not Wanted On The Voyage, even though it was, so be it, his birthday.

Many years would pass before he would discover that everybody else felt exactly the same, but came out every weekend so to feel, thus over the years developing more flexible feelings in so feeling.

After that initial dose of the sun's rays, he had spent continued years of climbing executive ladders in filmdom, learning he could write screenplays, in New York, in London, in California, looking for love, adapting *Lest We Sleep Alone,* looking for love, running after Feffer, looking for love, looking for himself, joining up with Abe, how to unload fear and anxiety, looking for, what else is around?, and why are the ways of the world so complicated, the roads so long and unmarked, and all answers so elusive?

Two years ago he had tried again. He returned to

share a house with Anthony and Sprinkle, plus an acquaintance Fred had not spent time with since Kamp Kogunt kounselor days in Maine, plus his lover, who was always stoned, and a friend of theirs who spent most of his time balding his head with Nair. Anthony and Sprinkle, newly united in togetherness, were always off on romantic journeys to The Sunken Forest beyond The Grove. Fred was left to contend with what he decided, nobody's fault, was a bad mix. And as anyone at The Pines can tell you, a good mix is what's important.

So he threw himself into the daily routine of beach, nap, dance, nap, dinner (Sprinkle that year was very Into health foods and salad dressing made with honey), nap, dance, sleep, all interspersed with as many tricks as could be turned (that was his year for 170, pounds, not tricks, but probably tricks as well), and as many strolls along the strand as spirit, weather, crowd, and energies commended.

He learned to say Hello!, to walk down beach and boardwalk with his head held high and his eyes front and center and learned how to nod and smile to faces fucked with, danced with or next to or near, or just encountered though not properly introduced. He thus became known as a friendly sort, though he felt his friendliness, like Algonqua's, was only a tool to make everyone like him and keep him from sinking into the sands of complete ostracism. He really felt like the fat girl in the sorority house who knew everybody's name and secrets but had precious few of his own.

It was only last year, in welcoming Grey Gardens, that he realized how many friends he had in this, his world. Though of course how long still the road. And naturally how elusive those answers. And where else was there to go? New York was home. The Faggot Capital of the World.

Then, as now, he preferred not to consider his artistic laziness. He knew he was now expert at fashioning screen-

288

plays from other people's inspirations. Yes, adaptations he could do. But to be more original? Try something more ambitious? When asked about this inactivity, he would mumb'e about the ridiculousness of the medium, the lack of creative satisfaction it provided the writer, as well as being "full of idiots," "only good for action," "difficult to work with meaning, irony, intellectual arguments, layers of subtlely, like the great words of literature." No, he yearned for the whole hog. In art as in his life. Well, Abe now was giving him his chance.

Then, as now, the Fire Island image was the same. Always before him. Thousands and thousands of handsome men. All over the place. Wherever eye could see. All touching, holding, hands or arms upon each other, all touching, the Brotherhood! No wonder all kept coming back, again and again, in memory and in truth. Such Beauty. Such narcotic Beauty!

And here it was again another Memorial Day Weekend. How time flew. Here it was, all beginning again. Here it was, tomorrow, so be it again, ipso facto again, another birthday.

So, filled again with renewed Anticipation, Enthusiasm, Possibilities, Potential, HOPE, now that I'm over Dinky!, he shouldered his mini-duffel of summertime's wardrobe, took off his Weejuns, rolled up his painter's pants' legs, climbed down and out of the machine that brought him here, and waded from the seaplane to the shore. Then down the strip of sand, then up onto the dock, which passed some Mama Tugboats that led into a boardwalk that passed the Marketeria, and to The Botel's steps.

Oh and My God, Yet and Once Again!

For there they were, up there, yes also yet again, had they never left?, those bathing-suited hordes! But more than ever! They spilled over the railings and off the deck and down the steps like some rich soufflé gone crazy. Tea

Dance. Six O'Clock Madness! There were more here than he'd ever seen before!

Years of training suddenly went for nought. Fred wanted to run. But he couldn't move. Gorgeous bodies blocked his path. He couldn't even get a toe hold on the stairs. He stood there pinioned. A dangling perfect calf from up above behind him. A flawless rounded tush and waist in front. Get a hold on yourself, Lemish! Reglaze that smile of bonhomie upon your puss. Dinky, do I want you now!

For as certain as the second cookie always comes on the heel of the first, the rushing need returns. The memories of those first four weeks with Dinky. When he didn't have to cruise and look and seek. When he didn't have to confront all of this! When he had someone to look forward to each evening.

Lemish, you *are* in trouble.

Ladies' Home Journal, here we go again.

Tarsh, the red of his beard matching the red of his Polynesian-Prince sarong and dyed-to-match Keds, yelled at him: "Fred! Hurry! You'll be late! Where's your costume? Hans's Hot Party at Utopia! It's in honor of Timmy Purvis. Get dressed immediately. What are you going to wear? I told you to bring a costume. Did you bring a costume?"

A profusion of confusions, in the midst of Annie Hall, né Grey Gardens, Bay at Beach Hill, a very large, cozy, Cape Cod, built on the mainland in 1884 and floated over fifteen years ago, full of bedrooms, tacked on round the ancient hull like some jaunty Holiday Inn, full, too, of mismatched pillows and a yellow-based spackled mock-Pollock floor, of a hundred colors, prone to squeaks and everything leaning the wrong way, including a kitchen where nothing worked, a house beloved by all, particularly when someone was fucking, when the total foundation swayed.

Josie and Dom Dom were debating over artificial daisies or lilies, Gatsby was Jimmy Connors, Fallow was still naked, Frigger would only go so far as to add a Beverly Hills Health Club T-shirt to his jeans and peek-aboo Jockeys, Bilbo wore a parachuter's jumpsuit full of pockets for his pills, and Bo Peep tonight was truly an angel.

Mikie rushed in, wearing his simple basic twinkydom: gym shorts and hooded sweat shirt and sneakers, these would have to do, Mikie had no money for wardrobe and was forgiven for this lack, and tambourined his welcome to them all: "Good evening! I am so happy we are all now here! We are now in permanent residence at last! I know good things will come our way this summer! I shall personally build flower boxes for us all and I shall polish my moldy brass bed so that it gleams and smiles and I shall continue my experimentation into the tambourine and I shall fuck fuck fuck like a bunny!" And he looked around at all his friends, his family, with love.

Frigger, only a visitor for the weekend, and fresh from his triumphs in the city, said: "It's good to be back. Los Angeles, you know, isn't into having their cocks sucked. Just into doing it. Out there I'm just another cock sucker. A Californicator. Here I'm in demand. That's really the major difference between the two coasts."

Making the final decision for them both, Dom Dom parceled out the lilies equally for him and Josie. "Here you're an ingénue," he said to Frigger, "and there you're an ingénold."

Josie, his Bronson head freshly rebalded, accepted the lilies with queenly pride and proceeded to commence stitching them on to their matching white leather shorts.

"Yes," he said, "having had five mothers and fathers, Frigger appreciates the need for change."

Bo Peep sidled over to Fred and said, his halo already in place on a gilded coat hanger: "It's the oldest story in the world. You want him back, don't you?"

"Want him back? Me? I can't imagine to whom you are referring." And he kissed Bo Peep and rushed off to his annex off the back rear deck to change.

Everyone else stood around the red Parsons table to witness the ritual. Carefully, with a sharp razor blade, his small, muscled body tensed and hunched over as in the best safe-cracking movies, his fingers most delicately poised and ready to commence, his mind now completely given over to this important concentration, Tarsh was preparing to cut the dust.

With a precision that would give pride to any surgeon's mother, Tarsh lowered the boom on the small cake of rock, gently hacking off minute crystals, which he then further minced and pulverized as only the best salad chefs can do. The hands and eyes of only a leader were required, because if sure hand and perfect judgment were in any way second-rate, if the crystals were not reduced to near-nothingness, not only would the damn stuff blow away, but dust could be dangerous.

While Winnie's death was still remembered, no one talked about it. Nor was last month's demise talked about, of Nubie Knisel, a waiter, who mistook his thirty-ninth story Columbus Towers living room for a ground-floor flat and also walked out of his window to say hello to the world, causing one of his guests to inquire of his roommate: "Who will replace him? My unemployment's running out," and the roommate to reply: "Mine runs till fall."

Tarsh then amalgamated his handiwork with dill weed and rolled the mixture into joints. His expertise was then passed around to all. And all of them, plus an arriving

292

Anthony, in jeans and blazer, and a nervous Wyatt, dressed all in white, both happily welcomed for the weekend's final days, puffed up their lungs hugely on the precious dust. For dust was a hundred and fifty dollars a gram by the rock, if The Gnome liked you, and if he didn't, he didn't have any.

Fred rushed back in, now dressed and ready, get these parties started, get this weekend started, get this lifetime started, keep busy, keep active, involved, the mind devoted to diversions calculated to keep the heart at bay! He had thrown on his hunter-green satin Champion boxing shorts and blue sweat socks and battered old Jack Purcell tennis shoes with the extra-long laces and had inspirationally polished it all off with a topping of his maroon hooded Harvard sweat shirt.

"Is this not a hot outfit?" he inquired of them all.

"Look at you, Tante," Anthony came to kiss hello and offer up young Wyatt for the same.

"A very hot outfit, Tante Fred," a still quivering Wyatt tried to do his best.

"A very hot outfit indeed!" Mikie banged his tambourine.

Fallow arranged the sweat shirt so that it draped more effectively and Frigger, punching a soft fist in Fred's hard stomach, announced: "You win Most Improved Camper Award," before appending: "I should have slugged him seven years ago."

"Did you ever meet his parents?" Fred asked.

"No. He always made me drop him off four blocks from his house."

Fred declined a lung of dust.

Wyatt inquired: "Don't you take drugs?"

To which Anthony replied: "No, he's got a career that he likes."

So once again drugged-out states were being reached,

perhaps never left, a direct continuation from last evening's opening—or was it the night-before-that's closing? —a memorial arch, a parabola from event to event, time was as of this moment again ceasing in importance, from here till . . . , life would be one long expansive curve of . . . LIFE . . . , corseted only by the roll of events, parties, dancings, perhaps a handsome nameless number in the night, a kiss, a bump and grind of pelvic contact, a fuck, a farewell, another party, of course The Meat Rack, let's hurry and get started or we'll never get there!

After a day of further consultations with his interior, with his guilts, with his memories, with Ephra's rug, with his banker, with that infernal, eternal, internal question: What am I truly wanting?!, this is now suddenly an expensive question to answer!, but not with Ephra, the Police, the FBI, the President, his brother Maury, or his son and lawyer Stephen in Aruba, Abe took Ephra, who insisted upon accompanying, "The Divine Bella is telling me this is now the In Place," in a Carey rented Cadillac and chauffeur, toward whatever destiny awaited him on that Island 'cross the bay.

They took the *Island Queen,* on which they sat huddled in a corner amidst a throng of men, dogs, cats, groceries, stereos, barbecues, green plantings in red pot-lets, and bags and bags of Mark Cross, Fendi, Gucci, and the ubiquitous M. Vuitton. Abe kept his eyes on his own ancient Abercrombie & Fitch carpetbag, in which resided, just in case, a down payment for his son, ten thousand dollars, all in new fifties, Alvin Sorokin had not had old ones, and had said it had been enough trouble to open the bank especially for an important depositor as it was.

Abe's stomach did not cease its heavings, even after the *Queen*'s did. Upon disembarking, he tugged Ephra as

294

best he could along through further throngs—of fellows, weekend tourists, mainland gawkers, Hadassah yachtsfolk —and found and checked into The Botel on the reservation made long ago by Fred.

"This room is not de luxe by any standards," Abe said, looking around the bunker of ill-used bed and chair and concrete walls. He then lowered himself, in his old white Palm Beach, onto the sagging double mattress, after all these years to sleep with Ephra, who will sleep?!, trying not to notice the stains on spread and blankets, or on upholstery and rug. And, he thought, now on poor Abe as well. But, trying to put a good face to it, he heaved himself up again and walked out to the bunker's third-floor balcony. "However, there is a pleasant view of the harbor, though I am worried that so many men dancing down below will give us little sleep." Yes, who will sleep. How can I tell her? What should I tell her! What am I hoping for? Should I stop hoping! Mission, please to come!

Ephra was not thinking of sleep. Nor was she thinking anymore of men, whom she was learning, with the cessation of communications from and to her husband, to put out of her own interior entirely. She was, however, equally as nervous. Sunburst. Where is Sunburst? What will I find at Sunburst? How do I keep myself from Sunburst?

Was she hungry for a little bite? No; was he? Not ready. She said she wished to do some shopping at the smart boutiques below. He said he wished to locate some cigars. Both respected the other's desire for some off-shore leave alone.

Tarsh led his costumed lot from Annie Hall. He held Bo Peep's happy hand as he led his parade of fifteen or so down the few short blocks to Tuna. He chanted for them

295

all: "We are going forth to find new things in all our plumage! We're going forth and forward, our arms within the arms of friends!"

Mikie picked up the beat upon his tambourine. He blew a kiss to Fred. "I love you, Fred." And Josie and Dom Dom, now playing the Island's famous lovers, in matching lilied white, like two book ends to his queryings: What am I doing here! a Harvard man and almost forty! and still alone!, walked on either side of Fred and said: "I love you, Fred!" as well.

They marched toward Tuna, twenty of them or so, picking up bodies along the way, parades just happened in The Pines, just coalesced along the boardwalks, thirty of them or so, growing to forty as they walked along, this parade, in startling shades of lime and yellow and magenta and silvers and golds and buffs and many shades of white and pink and peach and pomegranate, let's start this night most colorfully!, and emblazoned T-shirts and Dordogna del Dongo wraparound trousers, the latest, newest, kick, with strings which, when tautly pulled and knotted, made crotches bulge with added interest, and popper holders on necklaces and pill holders on bracelets and wrist sweat-ers for ethyl and Puma high tops and Adidas low siders and bunches of flowers and key rings and toe rings and pure funk and athletic finery to rival locker rooms and since the evening was warm and young, items on the back soon became items in the hand, such a lovely, lovely beginning, just wait till you see what I'm wearing later!, yes such a lovely lovely beginning to our day.

Bilbo then fell down. The group stopped and waited. Finally, Fallow took a Drenden from his Mic-Mac shirt, which made an ensemble with his jodphurs from Tibet, and depressed it neath the fallen fellow's tongue.

"I'm tired of being the only one doing this," Fallow

said. "Why don't any of the rest of you fuckers donate your own Ups to keeping this one going."

Bilbo, revived, jumped up and uttered: "Oh, tacky, tacky world, that justice be so sere, hypocrisy so convolute, and wickedness so much the way!" He then, with thanks, reimbursed Fallow with a Drenden of his own, plus one for interest.

So then they could start up again. Tarsh, who spoke louder on dust, their Energy Force, like some head kid in camp, which they all desired him to be, who wanted to make decisions when Tarsh would make them for us?, began the creation of their calendar.

"We're going to Hans Zoroaster's!"

And everyone was happy to go to Hans Zoroaster's first.

Hans's invitations had made their way into the hands of the Hottest Men, who peopled every party, crested with the Zoroaster motto—TRUE BEAUTY MAKES MEN DUMB—in Attic Greek, in raised purple lettering to catch the fingernails of all the queens who would naturally give the Tiffany cards the scratch test. He lived in a truly wizard house on Tuna. The house, nay, estate, nay, palazzo, had been built to impress, few having spent as much as Hans to throw up three-storied rooms dabbed with chandeliers and pedigreed ornaments from famed antiqueries. What matter if the ocean's air warped them all in several seasons? This was Utopia indeed. Here Hans would, when necessary, retire. What spa in the Old World offered so much? This would be his Riviera unto death.

Timmy on Tuna was encountering his first real problems with success. "Please, Mr. Zoroaster, I don't feel like it very much at the moment."

Timmy had already let Hans suck his cock three times since he was discovered, like Lana Turner at the counter of Schwab's Drug Store, on the floor of The Toilet Bowl those many long moons ago. None of these nibblings found him hard; what was hard was how he was going to handle this apparent single-minded effort of his talent scout to shoot him starward.

Hans had tried continually to remind himself to be patient and understanding. The poor boy had been through trauma and this launching to empyrean Beautydom might be warping. Yes, best be patient, best go easy, see that he's meant to last. So he whispered, while hired Fireflies buzzed about in exterior rooms preparing for the party's on-slaught: "I am making you a star, my most handsome, most perfect," and hope that this message, in all its complexity, would somehow get across.

Timmy thought he'd better say it now. Before the throngs arrived. Crowds had recently had a way of mixing things up in his already mixed-up life. "Mr. Zoroaster, you may not fuck with me. You may never fuck with me. I must be faithful to the memory of my own beloved Winnie. You may kiss me if you must. But this is all I can allow you to do."

"Please, child, please!" Hans was thrilled to be experiencing those delicious tensions that made involvements real.

"No."

So Hans lay back on substantial sheets of Porthault and considered what to do. Nothing. Ah, was not love so wonderful and life such a pain.

Dinky, too, was lying back and playing with himself. He was in Ike Bulb's small and ugly house on Aeon in The Grove. Ike Bulb was a vasectomist who looked just like

Dinky's father and whom Dinky had met through an *Avocado* ad when Laverne became impotent. Ike had advertised for a Master to tie him up and lead him around and stand over him. Dinky liked the hassle-less sound of this and liked it more when Ike bought him his first leather and took him on trips—Italy, India, Key West, Savannah, soon there was one to Senegal for a conference on Erection Problems in the Emerging Nations, and Ike wanted to try dark meat, though Dinky didn't. Ike was also allowing Dinky a kitchen restoration on his Bucks County farmhouse and there just might be the rest of the house to do over after that.

Here, in The Grove, Ike lived in gloomy colors. As if gloomy colors and curtains and carpets and dinginess, with sagging bed and plywood wardrobe and lonely camp chair, no room in this bedroom for more, might put off burglars or appear more sadistic or wear better throughout the years. Dinky obviously hadn't yet remodeled.

Dinky was using Vaseline, a tough, unyielding lubricant, and a favorite of Ike's, who had not yet arrived. He was watching, at the same time, the Champions Program on Channel 9, a good relaxer, these, plus a Desnobarb. Two ladies from Montana were doing Synchro Swim, a competitive event new to him. They were performing to the tunes of Mahler's "Resurrection" Symphony. The two ladies had tiny lilies in their hair, which was lacquered and knotted tight, like Esther Williams, whose ghostly spirit obviously hovered over the Olympic-sized pool. It was eerie to watch the effortlessly perfect unison, every toe jut and arm arc and body twist harmoniously calculated to match the other's, that the two ladies achieved. They got points for keeping it together.

The ladies finished. They had been perfect in all ways. Judges from all over the world awarded them a composite score of 9.9, to much applause. "These ladies have shown greater synchronization than ladies in Japan and Australia and Goa and Austria and the United Kingdom!"

"I'm certainly glad I'm a faggot," Dinky said out loud, before drifting off to sleep.

Tarsh led his band back toward Annie Hall to change. Hans's Hot Party at Utopia had peaked within an hour. The entire Zoroaster stable had been there. There had been too many beauties, who stood around in the showroom like so many props for the evening, and this was too intimidating for simply everyone, even the beauties, who kept staring at Timmy, whose beauty now made them dumb, and so no fun was had by all. Gracious exits were politely made. But Hans had been seen holding the hand of Timmy, which was more or less, for Hans, the point of the party anyway—even though Timmy kept taking it away—so at least Hans could register a partial success, even though he'd now be eating shrimp for days.

"Read any good books lately?" Fred could not resist trying on a beauty. No, Fred. That's bitchy. Don't become a queen.

In Hans's Master Bedroom, Anthony had found Fred trying on a bit of leather.

"My God, Tante! What are you doing?!"

"Tante, what are we all doing?" came Fred's reply.

"What is happening to us?" Anthony agreed. "I think I'm going crazy."

"We're all going crazy. We're out of control. I think it's the end of the world."

The two best friends embraced.

"I'm sorry about your Winston Man," Fred said, taking off Hans's vest.

"Which one? What did you decide to do about Dinky?"

"Which one? Where's Wyatt?"

"I've lost him again."

The two best friends again embraced and then parted to pursue their separate careers.

Yes, Tarsh led his band from Hans's back along the boardwalk and back toward Annie Hall to change.

Drugs were perking, drugs and dreams were building, night was darkening nigh.

Bilbo screamed out loud: *"We are all drugged out of our tits!"*

Fred thought: You name it, somebody's on it.

MDA, MDM, THC, PCP, STP, DMT, LDK, WDW, Coke, Window Pane, Blotter, Orange Sunshine, Sweet Pea, Sky Blue, Christmas Tree, Mescalin, Dust, Benzedrine, Dexedrine, Dexamyl, Desoxyn, Strychnine, Ionamin, Ritalin, Desbutal, Opitol, Glue, Ethyl Chloride, Nitrous Oxide, Crystal Methedrine, Clogidal, Nesperan, Tytch, Nestex, Black Beauty, Certyn, Preludin with B-12, Zayl ... and the Downs, keep it mellow, don't get too excited, Downs make us feel so sexy!, Quaalude, Tuinal, Nembutal, Seconal, Amytal, Phenobarb, Elavil, Valium, Librium, Darvon, Mandrax, Opium, Stidyl, Halidax, Calcifyn, Optimil, Drayl, a portable pharmacy, the drug store incarnate, mustn't forget the Magic, The Gnome is here with Magic, and all of the above, plus his list of grasses, mixed, permutations, or straight versions of the grasses: Mexican, Jamaican, Colombian, Thai, Pakistani, Lower Urdu, geography, the study of, becomes such fun, Moroccan Hash, Red Lebanese, Black Afghani, Hawaiian, Kentucky Bluegrass, Bridgeport Blunder, Mantanuska Thunderfuck, Wildbush, Black African, American First.

Everyone is beyond the beyond. Except Fred Lemish. Everyone's where they want to be. Except Fred Lemish.

This is it. We've found it. This night of nights. This

summer of our lives. Can it last till Tuesday? When's Tuesday?

So Ephra Bronstein had made it to Fire Island and Ephra Bronstein had found her way to Sunburst and Ephra Bronstein had kickings in her kishkas and Ephra Bronstein wanted to go home.

She had nervously inquired directions, which had been graciously given by two older gentlemen, albeit holding hands. Then she suddenly thought: perhaps it is nice to see two older gentlemen so affectionate at such an age.

Yes, she'd found Sunburst. But there were many houses on Sunburst and none of them called out to her: "Your Nancellen lives here!"

So she walked round and round the block. Twice. Three times. Frightened. Such a nervous Nellie. Not to know that only a few years ago her own Richie had walked round and round a block, six times, twenty times, before his own kicking kishkas kicked him into entering his first gay bar at Yale.

Then she heard it. Then she heard the call.

"Your Nancellen lives here!"

And Ephra turned and there she was, the tall specter of her rose, standing amidst flood-lit geraniums and hollyhocks, not quite so tall as she.

And immediately she received another interior klunk, which sent her on her way, back toward the safety of that harbor.

She ran smack into a group of . . . were they Orientals? They certainly had slanted eyes and long dresses with slits up to their armpits. These foreigners impeded her progress and Nancellen caught her up.

"My Q. M., you've come this far. Why not come all the way?"

302

A logical question. Ephra tried to make herself illogical. If she were to be logical, she would ask for a glass of hemlock, a knife, and a slit up through her heart.

"I cannot. I cannot! Please to let me go!"

"You look radiant tonight in your Lilly Pulitzer," Nancellen smartly changed the subject to Ephra's dress of chartreuse pansies.

". . . you like it . . . ?"

"Very much."

Ephra's eyes were wet. "I bought it with Abe in Miami Beach a thousand years ago."

"If you like, I'll take you to Bendel's. I get a courtesy discount there. And we can buy some new things to make you more of the moment and display your loveliest features."

Ephra's pansies wilted. No one had ever wanted to feature her or momentize her before. And at a discount. She knew her fate had come. Out here, on this tiny island, her heart had been touched, and somebody, at last, had said: I care.

And in they went. Into that house. On Sunburst.

Adriana's house on Widgeon was British Empired for the night. Union jacks and pearlie buttons and bowler hats. Crowns, tiaras, neck ruffs, bobbie outfits, and fake crown jewels floating on a rubber raft in the pool. Coins minted in honor of the Queen's Coronation were tossed by blackamoors in guardsmen's toppers and little else from the roof. Forsyte Saga and Upstairs Downstairs and everyone Edithed out of their Heads.

And on her deck, the safety guarantee for which advised three hundred, welcoming her four hundred guests, stood Adriana. In sashes and stars and British blue and red, a dress of awful stiffness and terrible dimensions, and on her head she wore a crown and in her hand she waved a wand and all her true proportions were so swollen as to create more awe than admiration. Yes, Adriana understood how much louder a cock can crow in its own henhouse.

She greeted all with: "I am La Grande Dame de l'Île de Feu!"

Her Dordognian guest beside her was all in rugger whites, or were they cricket whites?, looking, whichever game it was, just like a young man. She had looked across the crowded deck and located her mark. She said of Randy Dildough: "I shall accept him for what he is and understand and give him air."

"Nonsense," her regal hostess ruled. "Don't falter now, my sweet. You've come this far. Now you must go all the way!"

Randy had not seen Dordogna among the squeeze of the Four Hundred. He had just arrived, in his own J. Press suit of light canary yellow, plus dark glasses, and he was fully uninformed of the plot that had filled the guest bedroom adjoining his with the Captain of the Rugger-Cricket Team. Yes, Randy had just arrived and the tensions of his minglings midst so many men, more than ever!, were tingling more than ever in his crotch. Yes, everything was proceeding normally. He was looking for his Timothy Purvis Dean. He was casting his eyes around this deck, darting them from face to face and crotch to crotch, just like everyone else's were darting around, too.

"It's like being in the Court of France," Adriana continued, surveying her kingdom with pride. "We must know every innuendo, when to step forward and when to step back and when to disappear. And, of course, when to pounce."

Fred looked around and thought he might know three fourths of the four quarters. Tarsh, in his British-Prince

304

sarong, found, with his own eyes, a big and beefy, dark young hairy Jewish man, his favorite type. And this young man turned out to be a Rabbi. Even better. And Bo Peep religiously noted the attraction. And Fallow and Frigger eyed a slim young cutie simultaneously. And Fallow got there first. And Laverne looked around while plucking his old daisy: I love you, Robbie, I don't love you, Robbie, all I want is peace of mind. And Maxine, in Taylored sequined tights, looked around for Patty, where was Patty, the absence now too long, am I now officially a grassy widow, and what to do re: Billy Boner, who had called and asked to purchase Balalaika? And Garfield Toye, the famous orgy giver, modestly received the many compliments for outdoing himself, was it just last Friday eve? And Fred introduced himself officially to Jack Humpstone: "I'm still in love with Dinky Adams and I don't know what to do." To which Laverne, no help at all, replied: "Now why'd you go and do a silly thing like that?" And Jacente supervised his fabulous tape, booming out to all his favorite numbers. "Now Is the Hour For Us." "Paint My Diddy Every Color of the Rainbow." "A Him To My Mother's Favorite Anthem." "What a Difference Not Having You's Made In My Life." And Bella and Blaze jotted down the names of all the famous guests for their respective publications. And Mikie banged his tambourine to the chant of "I love you all, I love you all, I love you, love you, love you, All!" And Tarsh kissed his new Rabbi and asked him: "Do you have any religious guilt?" "I don't think so? Which religion? But then I was just ordained." And Gatsby announced to Fred: "I'm stuck on Chapter Three. I'm giving it up. I want to have some fun." And Fred tried to hug his friend back into writerdom. But Gatsby had caught sight of another Robert Redford, just his type. And this Robert Redford was that punishing beauty, Lance Heather. Who had seen at last

305

his Randy Dildough, after all these years, vengeance for desertion still unachieved, I'll bet I'll get him later in The Meat Rack, leave him here for now. And off ran Lance from Gatsby's sight. And Anthony returned with punch for Wyatt. A Wyatt once again not here. And Fred saw Anthony holding cups for two. And young Timothy Purvis saw Randy Dildough. And Randy Dildough did not see Dordogna del Dongo. But Hans Zoroaster saw Timmy Purvis and Randy Dildough looking at each other for much too long a moment. And Dordogna del Dongo saw the same. And at this moment, Fred found Dinky's roommate, Dodger the Lodger, who told him: "He's staying in The Grove, at Ike Bulb's, last house on Aeon Walk, on the left, this would be a good time, Ike's not due till late, though why you still persist, Dinky wants rockets, you're not sending up rockets, yes, why do you persist?"

Then Bilbo climbed up on a table and officially proclaimed: "I pronounce this party and this summer as of this moment Launched!"

And Bilbo and the table both fell down.

And at this moment, Fred thought he knew why he persisted.

A further melee was occurring around Tarsh and Mikie.

"You borrowed my douche and didn't clean it out," Tarsh had teasingly said to Mikie.

And Mikie, whose drugs were not yet working, which made him very cranky, could not believe his ears. "I number one didn't borrow it, and number two if I had, which I wouldn't have because I have a douche of my own, I would have cleaned it out, because everyone knows I'm very clean, and anyway how could I have used it when I haven't been fucked in weeks!" And then he started to cry. For how could his beloved Tarsh, who always led them with such good advice, be so threatening to him now?

Yes, at this moment, Fred thought he knew why he persisted.

As faces turned to watch both Bilbo righted and Mikie slighted, Randy Dildough slipped quickly up and pulled Timothy Purvis softly away and into a cranny off the kitchen and there he took him in his arms and kissed him with all the passion and need and longing and commitment he was now prepared to make. And Timothy Purvis, desiring to be free of Hans, whose perennial tongue and hands were now and again and still approaching near, just over Randy's shoulder right, allowed himself to be kissed by Randy and responded with all the passion and need and longing and commitment he was now prepared to make.

"You silly child!" Hans Zoroaster, with his best heroic gesture of Do or Die, tried to pull the boy away from this unknown scavenger.

Wondering if he should slug an older gentleman, Randy was about to do so when impeding hands meant just for him slipped round his neck as well. Dordogna, a Do-or-Die-er, too, had approached this gathering of the hands.

Hans continued: "How can you throw me all away! People will kneel at your face! People will say 'He reminds me of Winnie Heinz!' For I am giving you the place in my stable of your true beloved Winnie Heinz!"

So Dordogna, her arm now safely through her Randy's, commenced an incantation all her own. "Do you know, Rancé, I was talking this very afternoon to your Chairman, Mr. Musselman, Mr. Pip Musselman, who is an old and valued, cherished, very personal friend. And do you know, Rancé, we said such nice things about you! He was so happy to hear we, too, were friendly. Although I gather you have a troublesome film about a dinosaur. Such a cute idea, a film about a dinosaur. Perhaps it will catch fire in the suburbs. Would you like to see the rest of the house?"

Randy nodded dumbly, because he could see in the vista, the horizon, the mirage in the crystal ball just three feet before him, one old man kneeling in front of one youngster and said youngster now holding said older man's hand. Randy, for this moment, personally felt extinct.

Yes, would the convergence of all ill auguries never cease!

Fred leaves for his journey. Rockets, eh? Well, I've got rockets, Dinky's got sparklers, and that will have to do.

Richard Bronstein didn't have rockets. But he wanted some. Rockets for courage, apotheosis, metamorphosis, anything at all that would help him move along. He felt awful.

When he'd finally summoned the courage to pick himself up and off the beach and have a look around this Forbidden Island, he'd found all his worst fears transmogrified into flesh. Oh, so much flesh! Everywhere! Everyone was Mr. America. And he hadn't been able to be even a Mr. Soho Loft. His workouts hadn't worked out at all. He wished he'd brought his tape measure so he could check to see if his muscles had deflated. He couldn't look anybody in the eye. They can see I'm a loser. They can see I've got the smallest cock in captivity. They can just see it! He tried taking off his shirt, with the hope that his upper torso might induce a customer into pulling his package down from the shelf. I guess it's because I don't have a sun tan. They all have healthy sun tans. I've been staying indoors much too much. I'll bet they're all rushing off to candlelit dinners for eight or ten. I don't have any place to eat dinner. With friends. Can I learn to eat spaghetti? No, Richie, that would be running away.

308

If his body wasn't in the pristine condition he'd desired for this revelatory ordeal of a weekend, his mind wasn't so hot either. He obviously had not been thinking too clearly these past few days. Or else he had been thinking much too clearly. He couldn't decide which. The clearheadedness of his decision to undertake his undertaking in the first place had been made under drugs and now he wasn't so certain he could be so clearheaded without some more. For his clearheadedness might be running down. But he'd taken more than he had ever taken. Certyn and Orange Fluff made it easier to believe. But he wasn't so believing at present. And another hit of Certyn hadn't helped. Maybe another hit of Magic. Maybe he'd run into The Gnome. Like he'd run into Garfield Toye.

Boo had slipped into The Marketeria with his shirt back on and his head down again to purchase the necessary sustenance for underground living. They had been sold out of Drake's Yodels so he'd had to settle for two dozen Devil Dogs instead. If Pop comes at midnight like he was told to and I'm buried and Wyatt stands on top of my grave until Abe agrees to fork over the one million, that shouldn't take more than one hour of haggling, Pop is so stubborn, which means one Devil Dog every two and one half minutes. I hope Wyatt is a good negotiator. He seemed to know so much in The Toilet Bowl. Everything seemed so logical in The Toilet Bowl. I wonder if they have free shrinks in Australia. Oh, God!

For there at the check-out counter was Garfield Toye. That gay activist and member of his brother's law firm. Who had always given him the knowing eye in Stephen's office. But to whom he'd always given the bum's rush. "Don't shit where you eat, Richie," had always been his motto in Stephen's office, where he signed papers for his various trusts.

"Richie Bronstein, as I live and breathe!" Garfield had positively exuded, his suspicions now confirmed.

"Unh, hi, Garfield."

"I'm certainly glad you and yours are finally getting it together. I'm really proud of you!"

"That so. Any particular reason?"

"I just ran into your Dad and I think it's wonderful that you're all out here *en famille!* A family that plays together stays together. Truth and honesty are best! I invited him over for a drink to my house on Sunburst. Why don't you come, too? I've simply got to rush now or Nancellen will be furious! It's the last house on the right."

So Abe was here and the die was cast and the cast wanted to die.

And where the fuck was Wyatt? Who was meant to meet me on the beach at ten. It's ten. Have I lost my helpmate? We were meant to have a dress rehearsal. So I could try on a hole for size.

So Boo Boo was beginning to feel like he did when he was a kid running around the apartment, was it Fifth Avenue or Park Avenue then?, in his ballet tights with a paper bag at midnight on December 31st to catch the New Year and bring it in. But he'd never caught that fucking New Year and did anything this weekend look like he was going to improve his record?

But then he bent to pick up the shovel and watering hose and poncho. And there in the sand was a penny. A penny alone was a lucky penny. In those New Year paper-bag-catching days, he also loved to pretend when he found a lucky penny that just by picking it up he'd find another one under that. And so on. Until he had all the pennies in the world. And then he'd be rich. Which he was about to become tonight. At midnight! A lucky omen!

"Hello, Uncle Richie." Wyatt approached his crazy uncle from out of the darkness.

310

"Where the fuck have you been!"

"I had to throw up a couple of times."

Well, thought Boo, don't lousy dress rehearsals always mean an opening-night hit?

So, grabbing Nephew and load of implements, he allowed the former to guide him and his latter, recollecting from somewhere "and a little child shall lead them," hoping he'd soon be leading himself, toward that more propitious spot in The Meat Rack where he was going to dig his grave.

Fred was walking the same ocean's ledge, but further along, near The Grove, toward Dinky. He was now Chinese Water Torturing himself with why he was walking there. Why can't I stop? Why do I still want him? All my years of therapy, why can't I fit all the pieces of this puzzlement together? Why can't two intelligent men rationally discuss the matter? Why am I refusing to look at his . . . peccadilloes for what they are? Perhaps that Dennis was an old friend with whom he had a pre-existing engagement, which he had overlooked in the heat of the banana. Oh, come on. What about all that in-and-out-and-over-and-above The Scene shit and all those items in the Wicker Exhibition that I'm choosing to overlook in the same tumidity? Inter-Chain. Leather. Dennis. Letters To and From the World. "Neurotic anxiety comes from a libido that has not found full employment." Most helpful. We'll both get jobs. We both *have* jobs. Me to be a dogcatcher and him to run away from the pound. Two cocks jet-propelled by fear. I think I should go on unemployment. Stop analyzing so much! I can't. That's like asking me to give up chocolate. But I have given up chocolate. More or less.

And then he was lapped by the overbearing vision of

Algonqua, which stopped him in his sands. He saw her in the black and whiteness of his Washington Square; she had paid him a recent visit; she had been sitting in her bathrobe, her legs spread wide apart, unconsciously, of course, providing a view of Mommy's interior regions to son's shocked and embarrassed eyes.

And she had been talking about Lester.

"He loved me, dear, I know that, and he needed me, I know that. Yes, he was dependent on me and I know, deep down, he loved me and I helped him. I might have thought of leaving him, but we didn't do things like that in those days and, anyway, I had made my commitment. He was the man I had picked. He had so many wonderful qualities. So I said to myself I will try and make him strong and successful, because I am strong enough for both of us. Everything would be all right."

And Fred, whose most persistent childhood fantasy had been that he might be relieved of the two of them in an auto accident, and have brother Ben for a father, had wondered who this Pollyanna was talking about. Wonderful qualities? Lester?! He had wanted to yell at her: You manufactured a marriage that wasn't there! an "us" that never existed!

He hadn't so proclaimed and now here he stood, on the sands of Fire Island, deep in waterfront coverage, on his way to Dinky Adams, wondering why, and realizing that she might have been him, Fred Lemish, talking about the Dinky Adams he was on his way to.

At this cross-sands of insight, knowledge, and, dare we hope, Growth!, Fred was accosted by a short young man with a sweet face and a nice body and a kindly way. He had come straight up to Fred under the rising moon and said: "I've been looking for someone like you all of my life."

Fred thought: Another druggie, though he's cute.

312

"I mean it. My name is Leon. I can tell about these things. I can sense them. I'm never wrong."

While he proceeded to put his arm around Fred, draw him into embrasure, then down to the sand, he also managed to relate that he was, truly, a Canadian multi-millionaire, from one of the oldest families in that country, and that if Fred would come live with him and be his love, Fred would never want or need. "You're wonderful. You're just my type. I need a lover just like you. Let's go back to my place. I really like to get fucked. Do you like to fuck? I just know you're the one. I just know it. I'm never wrong."

"Are you on drugs?" Fred asked.

"Heavens, no! You don't do any of that either I hope. But you know, years ago everyone drank too much. Now it's drugs. Drinking was much more messy. I drink. Although not now of course. Now I'm stone cold sober. Let's go to my place."

Fred tried to be polite and kind. "I'm already in love. I'm sorry." And he attempted to pull himself up and away and on to Dinky.

But Leon was persistent. Many millions obviously gave him courage. "I'll wait for you. Just tell me where. I'm very patient."

"I said I was already in love."

"I know you did. I don't care. It has to be over sometime. I'll bet it's not working out. You've tried the shit. I dare you to try the real thing! I'm only here till tomorrow."

"Please excuse me." Fred was up, but Leon was holding on to a leg from below.

"Toronto's really very close. And I just love New York."

"Come on, let go!"

"I don't want to."

"Good-bye, Leon." Fred finally managed his freedom and was starting to head Groveward.

"I'll find you!" Leon called. "When I find someone like you, I don't let go just like that!"

Fred stopped and said to him: "You don't know anything about me."

"I don't have to. I can tell."

Fred started walking again. Jesus. He sounds just like me. And what did I know about Dinky?

Yootha Truth, who had a partial share in a house on Shady, and who would be making a guest appearance tomorrow night at The Ice Palace, was sensing a need for change.

"I think Dolly Parton sings for America and I would therefore like to sing like Dolly."

Rolla did not agree. He skated nervously back and forth across the worn linoleum floor. He thought the status quo should remain status. Things were going very well. There was already money for the bank. "How can you sing like Dolly Parton? Dolly Parton is soft and white and bouffant blond and biggest tits. She is southern white voluptuous. You are black dinge trash, gruesome and guttersnipey. Your growing legion of fans identifies you with the sewers and toilets from whence you came. You cannot disappoint them, Yootha. It is a good image and not one to tamper with."

"It's time to change all that."

"People will talk. They'll say Yootha Truth is turning her back on her own kind."

Yootha Truth turned oceanward as he carefully chose his next words. The ocean cannot actually be seen from Shady, but it is not all that far away.

"I'm proud of all the things we've done, Rolla. But

314

I'm just so proud of the new things I'm going to do. I don't ever want to leave faggots. But I don't think it's fair for anybody to put limitations on a person. You put limitations on yourself, and I don't feel I have any limitations. I feel I can do anything I believe I can and I'm going to give it a good shot, with I don't care who's in my way as my attitude. Yes, I am Yootha Truth of the Faggots, and that's what I'll remain. But people outside must hear my music, my true, real music, and I must do my very best to find it and let them hear it and the new real me. If they ask me if I'm a turncoat, I can only say I'm Yootha Truth."

Adriana's empire had emptied, "my goodness, don't they run off quickly!," she said running off quickly, after them, to the next party, was it the Oriental one?, in her ball gown, she hadn't time to change, leaving Randy with Dordogna, Jacente's tape still playing endlessly, now seductively, Dordogna thanked the God of Music, and she took Randy's hand, he seemed to take it willingly, what else could he do at this moment in time?, a friendless arsonist facing a disastrous dinosaur, Timothy-less on an island of Timothys, and she led him into the tent-draped sanctuary that was Adriana's Moroccan boudoir, scene of her ancient triumphs, where they lay back on large Casbah pillows thrown not casually here and there across the floor. Then, like Paul Henreid, she lit them both joints and they huffed and puffed and held the relaxing smoke deeply inside of them.

"Peace at last," she said.

"Peace at last," he shivered.

Randy looked up at the ceiling of gauze, softly puffing its own self in and out with the ocean's entering breezes. One of these breezes brought with it The Smell

315

of His Mother's Lap. He had not had this sensation since he was a child, when he would fall asleep with his face in her crotch, rather pungent it was, like marigolds that were twelve days old. He had queried Dr. Lure why The Smell of His Father's Lap did not wrinkle his nose in the same way. Dr. Lure had added this all to his article on "An Unusual Case." No, he must not succumb to memories. He must fight against the past.

"Do you know," he started, "I wonder if it would really be profitable to find a new James Dean? Perhaps interest in him has peaked and subsided. And didn't he grow old unattractively? He was handsome in *East of Eden,* but by *Giant* he was a wreck."

"You know, I think you are absolutely right. I didn't know you were looking for him, but I entirely agree."

"And I read somewhere recently that he had false teeth."

"Completely unattractive. I agree."

She was pleased with herself. Already they were in agreement. Such a distinguished houseguest corralled so quickly. She must contain her excitement. Act One of her new drama, perhaps even Act Two, was here upon them. Could she somehow bring it off . . . a happy ending . . . red hair in the sunset . . . Act Three . . . ?

He was trying to conceal his stage fright. Deep down he hoped she would show some concern for his rocky (in one way, not the other) condition, did he require a re-call to Dr. Lure?, well this *was* a re-call to Dr. Lure, though how she was to know he was butterflies inside if he said nothing, if he remained the inscrutable stone face beside her, if he never gave of himself even a teeny bit, he couldn't answer, nor could he answer if asked what he would specifically like her to do, expect her to do, should he be in the position of making the request, which, if he only knew it, he was, there was nothing this woman would not at this moment in time do, to please him, to put him at his ease, which he was not.

Well, it was difficult to relax when he still had that stone mountain ahead of him, that mountain with a surface of glass, so that he could grab no purchase, how to purchase?, he'd always been able to buy anything his heart desired, now, how, could he fuck her?!, be Sir Edmund Hillary, properly, without visions of Purvises dancing in his head?

Not that she pushed. Or was in the least insistent. Not at all. Dordogna *was* patience. Had she not had much experience with faggots? The one thing she knew was not to push.

"I am going to be on the cover of *Gentlemen's Quarterly*," she said demurely.

"That's wonderful," Randy said, appreciating the importance of the press. He then made himself do it. He bent to kiss her nose. She remained demure. He appreciated the gesture. Her lips tasted faintly of strawberries. Was it strawberries or raspberries that gave him a rash?

"They want to photograph me with a man," she then said, holding his hands and playing with his fingers. "Would you like that?"

"Yes, I would like that," he answered. Yes, I would like that fine. Good publicity for the Musselman cause. He removed his fingers. He did not like it when she played with his fingers.

Dordogna pretended not to notice the rejection. Calm, patience, they were like little children who must be led unobtrusively but deftly to the pond.

"You like Dordy's outfit?"

"Yes." He did not like her nickname.

"Did you know I made it myself?"

"Where do you find the time?"

"I have time."

Randy caught the implication. Dordy bit her lower strawberry. Oh, sometimes it was so difficult, one had to watch every word and syllable, lest innuendo slip in. Everything could go awry with unpropitious meaning. It was all so . . . so subterfugitive. One could not even say "how are you today?" without worrying. Oh, why was there no front door? Why was one always forced to use the back one, to tread like hired help?

"Dordogna . . . ?"

"Yes, Rancé?" She had decided she liked his full name better. He was trying to tell her something. Good! He was attempting to communicate.

"Please call me Randy."

"Yes, of course, Randy . . . ?" She was back to demureness again. Demureness was safe. "Tell Dordy . . ."

"Dordogna . . ."

"Yes . . . ?"

"I . . ."

"Yes . . . ?"

"I've had a simply terrible weekend." There. He had said it. It had not been difficult.

"Tell Dordogna." He seemed to prefer Dordogna. What is this telling me?

Now he realized it would become more difficult. He wished to confide in her, but how could he talk about those things with . . . with the woman he would sooner or later have to fuck? How could he tell her about intimate inner voices (I'm afraid, I'm afraid) she would be able to use against him, like ammunition stolen by the enemy and bombarded volte-face?

"Oh, Randy-ran, you are such a closed book. I am not your enemy."

How was she reading his mind so?

"However are we to know each other, from deep

318

within me to deep within you?" She wondered if this might not be too pungent.

It was. He perceptively cringed.

Oh, well, I have started. "How are we to *share?* We must share, or we shall become selfish old people, crotchety and spiteful." I am only speaking the truth. How hard it is to make them see the truth.

"My goodness." He was aware of the inadequacy of his response.

"So tell me about your weekend and why it was so terrible."

He couldn't do it. Not this weekend anyway. Perhaps another weekend.

Dordogna, with her impeccable timing, she had not built up her international men's wear consortium without impeccable timing, sensed the time was Now. In the darkness, though there was a lambent, blessedly complimentary glow of just visible light from . . . somewhere where the God who looks after moments like these was so looking after . . . , she slipped out of her soft white knickers and soft white tank-top and soft white knee-length stockings and soft white sneakers, revealing *Lo!,* a body more akin to a soft white little boy's than to the female Randy has so feared.

Though there is that patch to which he is accustomed to seeing a handle, now no handle, how to handle?!

She stood up over him, stretched out over him, upward, sinuously, running her hands over her body and trying her best to act as little-boy-like as she knew how, and she knew how, trying to transmit to him vibrations and fantasies of boys' camps or school dorms or swimming holes or army barracks or wherever the fuck and whatever the fuck he would get off on fantasizing, she didn't care what he dreamed of so long as he got it up and in and she would take over from there, wherever it was, she'd ride him to the moon and stars, oh if only she could do it, bring it off, add another faggot to her bracelet of charm, she wanted this one badly, he was so famous, and powerful, an association of equals, we could rule the world!, she wanted Cunard Rancé Evin Dildough, she wanted the world to know that she had turned this man on, had turned on the man whom no other woman had turned on (little realizing that no one would believe it when and if she did, it not being in the nature of people to believe that which they do not wish to believe, and they wish to believe "Once a Faggot Always a Faggot," an old saw of a song with certain truthful teeth) . . .

"You like what you see, Randy?"

She had bent back down to see-level and put her finger in his mouth, so that he could not answer, and another finger in her cunt, so that he certainly could not answer, circling this latter round and around so that, with the tricks imagination and lighting could play in such dimly lit environs, all of them being invoked by her and prayed for by him, he, he really did, now, once and for all, want to fuck a lady, get it over with, be able to boast I HAVE FUCKED COOZE, be able to join the ranks of MEN, all his films' producers with their broads, and with these tricks of imagination, it was just possible in this dim light to conjure, also dimly, that what was sticking out of her privates was not her gyrating finger and fist but a prick and balls, that's it fella, think Fella, think prick and balls and dong and schlong and willy and rodney and unit and snake and joint and Mr. Wigglestick and Willy the one-armed trouser worm, think every name from every stage of your educational development!, think banana and bird and bone and ding-dong, dingus, dink, dork, flute, front porch, gadget, hammer, hang-down, honker, hose, hot dog, joy stick, kidney wiper, knitting needle, lance!, lollipop, longfellow, muscle, nightcrawler, pecker, pee pee,

320

peter, piccolo, piston, poker, pole, pork, prong, pud, roger, rupert, sausage, scepter, schmuck!, think schnitzel, schwantz, sewing machine, slug, spout, sword, tom-tom, wand, wang, water pistol, weener, wienie!, wheezer!, wishbone!, worm!, Ying-Yang!, and yes, Yes, *YES,* her upper torso certainly looks like a lithe young boy, think Purvis!, *Think Timothy!,* think that beautiful young boy who is here, now, in your arms, at last, forever, *She is turning him on!,* her secret, she thinks (she's not aware of his vocabulary), is obviously her patience and persistence (Adriana had told her of her own younger days: I would come to Fire Island and when the little fairies came home from their flittings and they had not been successful, then I would act like a little boy, and become subtly aggressive and then quickly suck their little cockies and tell them how strong they were and how attractive and masculine and soon I had them hard and ever so quickly so that they knew not what was happening I would pop them into me and they are fucking me and they are so excited and together we are so excited . . . ah memories . . .), yes her patience and her persistence, and his vocabulary, and her young boy's body, that helps, too, of course, and now Dordogna has Randy in her mouth, yes, it is growing, is Randy in Dordogna's mouth, yes, he is leaning back and growing and keeping his eyes closed and thinking of Timothy and he is all right as long as he thinks of Timothy and keeps away from those breastlets, thinking this is not half so bad, this is feeling good, *Please God let my cock stay hard,* yes, it is hard, it is harder, it is hard enough, yes, it's certainly hard enough, thank you God, prayers offered up by both communicants . . . and Dordogna is slurping away, she is smelling good, perhaps a bit too good, Randy only knows from sweat and armpits, butch, masculine smells, Dordogna might consider this, leave a used jockstrap around, perhaps wear it herself, now she's got him hard, she is ready to legerdemainize the moment, make history, effect her switcheroo, now in the darkness she does it! *He does it!,* an exchange of orifices has been made, one for another, he is placed inside her, once more returned unto woman, she is managing to sit on his still hard, *Still Hard,* cock, and feel him in her, yes, Hooray!, she has managed Another!, she has succeeded in seducing another faggot, another faggot has entered her, she is riding her cock horse to Banbury Cross, except that Randy is not President of Marathon Leisure Time for nothing, he knows something is afoot, or is it amouth, one mouth does not feel like another, there's been a double cross, he opens his eyes a slit, fearing the worst, then seeing it, *He is fucking a Woman,* his prick is in her slit, oh Randy Ran, such revolting words, such a turn-off, words like slit and cunt and cooze and pussy and muff, she is riding high but you are beginning to slowly sink in the West, dead sails in her red sunset, until she sails that mite too high and out you flop and dribble, Apollo splashdown, soft and slippery and desiring liberty, and you fear that there is one thing a woman frowns upon and this is a slippery flopdown, but no!, Dordogna is a gentleman: "Ah, that was nice, Randy, so nice, you make love so nicely . . . ," who is this woman kidding?, it's time to take my pickle and get out of this pickle, she, sensing that Act Three is yet to come, speaks softly, very softly: "We must dine tomorrow, I am having your conglomerated President, Mr. Musselman, my good friend, Pip Musselman, you will come about nine . . . ," and how can he turn down such an offer?, how can he turn down this woman who tells him he fucks her so nicely?, oh confusion, oh tempora, oh mores, no, lesses, again, at this moment, definitely lesses, and he helps her back into her sporting attire, and he re-enters his canary yellow, and they stand up, and retrace their pathway back to the empty living room, the Island's noises, rumblings,

322

becks-and-calls, just out there, I'm coming, I'm coming, and Randy knows that, like one of his many movies, he wishes to, in the tradition of the Great Western Heros, Get Outta Town.

Mikie's drugs were heading him the wrong way. He couldn't even bang his tambourine. Even the hood on his sweat shirt seemed to be pulling him down. Finally he wailed out loud: "How can I throb in full communion to this Island's beat! How can I transcend my unsuccessful identity!"

For his beloved friend, Tarsh, and he were still not talking. But Tarsh's Rabbi had disappeared.

"My drug salad with dust is not taking me toward passionate abandonment and why am I the only one who has such paranoia with my chemicals!"

They were on the beach. The moon was beautiful. The sand was white and soft. Distant music wafted from both The Pines and Grove. Yes, they were on the beach. Thirty or so. From Adriana's they'd dressed as Orientals. The Oriental Party had been nice, the opium most mellow, though such a chore to smoke, paper hangers and glass plates required an adeptness not readily available, and all that clink chink music grated on the nerves.

Then they'd changed for Tad's Brazilian Party. Lots of Carmen Mirandas. Beer imported from Rio. Parrots, too. And, well, who needed parrots Tad's had failed to hold. Where next? Whose party next? Yes, they were on the beach. Forty of them or so.

"I want to demonstrate and receive all joys!" Mikie continued to wail. "I wish to be a beautiful living organism and have shattering disco and dancing experiences and travel into places beyond time and be triumphant over the flat emptiness of modern life!" And I love Tarsh more than life itself and now I want to die.

Tarsh rummaged in his Brazilian-Prince sarong and pulled out some further invitations. "There is a party where we must wear high heels. Is anyone interested in a party where we must wear high heels?" He read from the graven invitation to them all: " 'Sling backs, open toes, mules, stilettoes, T-straps, wedgies, spring-a-lators, enna jetticks, but *no* flats.' They seem to be rather emphatic re: no flats."

No one wanted to go to this party.

"I can't even thump my tambourine!" Mikie wailed yet once again.

"Somebody shut her up," said Fallow.

Tarsh finally went to Mikie and held him in his arms. "Mikie, let go! Lose control! Let your paranoia drip away!"

Mikie felt better in Tarsh's arms. But still he begged for information from their leader. "How! How do I let go? I'm not the Master of my Life! I promised me the Summer of My Life!"

Tarsh just held Mikie and mumbled: "Let go, Mikie. Let it all go."

Bilbo said: "I believe there's a party in honor of the blueberry. Evidently they do interesting things with blueberries. I hear they're quite good with blueberries."

No one wanted to go to this party.

So Tarsh momentarily placed Mikie to one side and rummaged again in his folds for yet another card. And he smiled. Of course. How could he have forgotten!

"The Feather Party!"

And they all cheered, fifty of them or so, now running from the beach, taking shortcuts back to houses and to change. Yes, how could they have forgotten! The Party of Parties!

And had not Tarsh officially now proclaimed: "We're ready for The Feather Party!"

Feathers were about to fly on Sunburst.

Nancellen, ever resourceful, had brought matters to a head. She had carefully dabbed Ephra's lap, stained with nervously spilled scotch, with a washcloth one-two-three-four. And Ephra had cried out "oh-oh-oh-oh!" with each punch of Martex. Yes, Nancellen had gauged her every shot. She could have been in acupuncture.

She lived in a Bath-owned house, furnished by Wife of Bath in summer-rent shades of warring colors. But Nancellen had chotchkied it up in Early American, with round hooked rugs and several rocking chairs and innumerable hurricane lamps. She had been summering in The Pines for many years. She was one of those dykes who do not like the company of other dykes. And since she certainly wasn't keen on straight men either, all they wore was old suits, this left only faggots or solitude or . . . the possibility that someday her Queen would come.

Ephra's stain did not depart. It restained itself like some contantly blossoming ranunculus, some long-sequestered perennial determined under the most obtuse of growth conditions to sprout and spread. *I shall love at last!* I shall have my first clitoral orgasm! Yes, Ephra had of late been dipping into *Cosmopolitan* and wished to be a Cosmo Girl.

Nancellen at last threw in the washcloth. She could hold it no longer and finally took the armful that was Ephra still in her Lilly Pulitzer into an embrace and, from on high, bent down slowly slowly slowly to kneel, kiss, nibble, blow, and whisper: "Oh, my Mama, oh, my Queen." It was a touching moment.

Ephra, heretofore not a caster of soft nothings, our Ephra, mumbled back, as best she could midst all that tower's tonguings: ". . . daughter . . . at last I have a daughter . . . ," and then the two sets of lips met, in vibrant co-mingling hues of Tangerine Temptress and Autumn Rose, meeting and touching and feeling soft and warm, on Sunburst, with the moon so bright outside. Yes, a touching moment.

Nancellen now floated on a wave of Mission Accomplished, clear sailing from here on, was there nothing so perfect as a trick sighted, wooed, captured, won, was this the love she had sought so many years and never found? Thank God Garfield probably got waylaid along the way.

And Ephra, poor Ephra, what-am-I-doing-here-Ephra, was trying hard to loose her moorings, still caught on those confusing thoughts sloshing around her Park Avenue brain. Where was Abe? Who wants Abe? Abe will only find another poopsie. And make another pisher. To add to the two he's already made who never call and say hello. So, Abe, I am with a poopsie, too. So, Abe, you are not the only one to have a poopsie and a hotsie totsie. And guess what, Abe? My poopsie totsie is taller and bigger and prettier than any of yours! And also guess what, Abe? I think I am becoming a fegalette or whatever is the feminine for fegalim, just like I read about in your bottom drawer.

So logical and illogical thoughts now vanished for them both as they surrendered. Ephra, that something warm now running down the inside of her legs, striking out on its own, forming its own tributary, this way to freedom, this way!, this way to new discoveries, she had never been an explorer in her entire life, was beginning to cry softly, the tears now mingling into tangerine roses and autumn temptresses and Nancellen was tasting the

326

wonderful salt that, when mixed with love, becomes non-fattening sugar, yes, Nancellen now has tears of her own, do you see me, Mama?, do you see me all you men and faggots?, dykes are not the same as faggots, we can love!, we can make commitments!, pulls and clutches her new Mama and they fall on the wide expanse of Early American quilted living-room daybed, tearing off items of imprisonment, outer garments, rolling over and over and round and down and about, making up for all those years of menly incarceration, menly games, menly demands, menly men, and Ephra found herself feeling Free, and found herself sucking those lovely fingers, "You could have played the piano," and found herself enjoying kissing and being kissed and nurtured, her breasts caressed and loved for what they were, not for what they gave or stood for.

"My dearest Nancellen, can you hear me . . .?" she now spoke in a voice modulated with a never-before-heard tone of love and affection and caring, not even her own children had heard this tone, ". . . is this please love?"

Abraham Bronstein, was it not ever thus?, stood on that outside deck on Sunburst plotzing to keep his philosophic stance. He had walked around and around this Island and now he had to walk around and into this! He had seen men kissing on the ocean as they watched the moonrise. He had seen male bodies holding, coupling, even making love. Two-men fuckings for the world to see! He had seen and he had thought: Here is The Toilet Bowl outdoors! This is worse than Berlin both before and after the troubles! Worse than Nazis! Are my Richie and my Wyatt doing this!?

And now he had seen Ephra Bronstein doing this too.

Yes, Abe was plotzing hard to keep his philosophic stance. What is she doing? I know what she is doing, but what is she doing! How do I feel about hearing such inner sounds as: "Oh, my Mama Ephra, my Q.M., you are so good, you feel so good!," and watch the ex-wife of years and years go crazy, letting herself go unto mashugadom, not knowing that she's thinking: Abe, you pisher, you were a lousy lay, you never made me feel this good, good-bye, Abe, good-bye plastic covers on furniture and blue poison in bowls, you may now, Abe, piss wherever you want to piss, as long as it's not on me, I am now Living!, and he watches her go bonkers before his very eyes, throwing up stockings and garter belt and panties, undergarments, years of impedimenta to the path of pleasure.

Yes, Abe was plotzing hardest to keep his philosophic stance. On the one hand, here was a long drink of poopsie who might once and for all take an ex-wife off his hands. On the other hand, what did I do to make this ex-wife stick her hands in that! One wife, two *kinder*, no, three *kinder*, no, three ex-wives, almost four, and three *kinder*, how many suits of guilt can one man wear! Richie blackmails me, Wyatt helps him, Peetra kidmales me, and now even Ephra, too! On the one hand, what kind of Abraham gave birth to all of this? On the other hand, what kind of Abraham must put up with any of that! If I throw away all old suits, can't I then be Free?

He didn't know which hand to hold. Where were his answers? God, you are not giving me my answers. God, you are only giving me more problems. Is this my Mission? Please to give me a remission. Missions are for goyim. Priests and monks and men who went into the jungle.

Exhausted, he looked at his watch. He bent over to pick up his old suitcase. Soon it would be time to go into the jungle.

●　●　●

Tarsh stood on the roof of the Feather Party, an enormous compound at Bay Walk's end, from which he could view the world. He laughed and laughed. Laughing gas made him laugh. It was another Hollywood premiere! Dueling searchlights once again were stabbing the sky. And down below, 456 simply gorgeous men were all in feathers! Completely, partially, symbolically, elaborately, tastefully, gaudily, repulsively, humorously, expensively, all in feathers! MGM in its hey-day could not have improved on this!

The host, Montoya, a Venezuelan painter of horse canvasses, had done it again. Last year he'd decreed they come in Red. The year before that was Roaring Twenties. The year before was Pink. The year before . . . oh who could remember, but it had been Fun!

Bilbo yelled up at him: "Do you know how fucking expensive fucking feathers are on the open market and how fucking expensive it is to be a fucking Philippino fairy bluebird!" Then he just as quickly flew away, crowing: "Cock-a-doodle-do! Any cock will do!"

Frigger, in a huge pumpkin, which covered him from shoulder to crotch, orange-feathered, waved up and yelled: "I'm Pumpkin, Pumpkin, Peter Eater!"

And Fallow, who had outdone himself, in St. Laurent blazer, navy with maroon piping, from which the sleeves had been removed and replaced with ostrich feathers of a length suitable for Sally Rand, yelled up as well: "If you snooze you lose!"

And both he and Frigger, arm in arm, as best they could, walked off for cruising closer to shore.

There were balloons and streamers and miles of carnation leis and twenty huge coconut palms flown in from Hawaii and a group of feathered yodelers from the Bernese Oberland and lanterns by the yard and mountains of fruit and cauldrons of pure and impure

329

punch and the loudest of Esquino's music and much kissing and holding and smiling and happiness and cares begone! We are here at Fire Island Pines to start the summer of our lives and the city and the world and our jobs and our hassles are far away, far, far away, again, again, again we reach for fun, who needs that world?, over the harbor and far away, we're here, we're here, and let them, over there, say about us what they will, who cares, who fucking cares!

A tired Anthony yelled up: "Have you seen Fred? Have you seen Wyatt?" Anthony carried only a token chicken feather, not being one for costumes.

"I haven't seen them!" Tarsh yelled down. "Isn't this wonderful!" Then he wondered where his humpy Rabbi had disappeared to. He'd been nice. No religion wants us. We're going to have to invent our own.

In great excitement, Bella rushed up to Anthony. "Can you believe it! Bruce Sex-toys is rumored to have spent twenty-three hundred dollars of his very·own money on his Roman centurion outfit with its flowing cape of cascading tiny tuftings falling down six heavenly feet plus two inches to his gorgeous booted garnished toes!"

"Who are you supposed to be?" Anthony studied Bella's vaguely cowboy outfit.

"I'm Roy Rogers!"

"You look more Dale Evans to me." *Oi*, Anthony, even your jokes are old and tired. Forget that child and go get some sleep.

They were joined by a young man with a snake in a feather boa coiled round his naked body, its head peeking over his own shaved dome.

"Hello, Sanford," Bella said, stepping back a bit. "How are you tonight? How's . . . Abner?"

"I'm a work of art," Sanford said.

330

"We can see that," Bella agreed, stepping just another step away, for safety's sake.

"Everyone is worshipping me. They are watching me and worshipping me. I am beautiful and desirable and completely unobtainable."

Anthony agreed. "The snake gets in the way."

Up on the roof, Tarsh decided 'twas time now to descend.

Fred found Ike Bulb's on Aeon. The television was still on in the bedroom as Fred slipped in, the Home Team now playing the Padres, and he turned it off and smiled down upon the resplendent naked figure of his awakening Dinky, or his ex-Dinky, or his soon-to-be-again Dinky, I must be stronger now than ever before, this is our last act, kid, I have to have some answers Now, yes, his Dinky resplendently displayed upon the knobby bumps of Ike's ancient chenille spread. "Hi, there, sport's fan. Let's talk. Where shall we begin?"

As the recipient of both a nasty letter and a right to the jaw, Dinky did not smile back. "You've said it all," he said. And since his nakedness was now rather obvious and now obviously rather appealing to Fred, who was looking at him with those 17-page-Ode-to Potential-and-Possibility eyes, Dinky reached over speedily to the camp chair on his left and extracted a black leather g-string from the pile of his coming evening's more formal attire. "I framed your letter and hung it on my wall. I've never been called a loser before." He quickly slipped into the g-string and zinged it into place.

Ah, yes, Fred noted the stack of After Six, Wardrobe from the Wicker Collection. Let's talk about that. He had noted, too, the Vaselined cock's glinting. I won-

331

der who the lucky recipient was. Let's talk about that.
And who's he leathering up for? Let's talk about that,
too. So talk, Freddie, Fred-chen, talk. You're here. God
damn it, talk! That g-string is very sexy. It carries his
cock and balls nicely. It fits around his waist nicely. It
fits into the crack in his ass nicely. I am shivering nicely.
I think I am getting off my course. "Where'd you buy
that? The g-string."

"I had it made in Florence."

"I never knew you'd been to Florence." I always
wanted to go to Florence. I was saving Florence and
Venice. For me and Mr. Right. Fred felt his tongue go
dry, in need of some Vaseline itself perhaps, and desire
a life of its own perhaps, and commence a circumnavi-
gation up that crack perhaps, yep, I am definitely getting
off my course . . . just as my arms want to throw a quick
tackle and just as my mind fears that all any of this would
accomplish beyond a scrimmage would be yet another
incomplete forward pass. And all of me again penalized
for being off sides. Please note that at this stage of "our
romance" and "our relationship" you are so intimidated
and off-balance that you are afraid to touch him. Another
Dennis might jump out from under the bed. "Listen . . ."
Fred tried again.

"I'm listening." Dinky was looking at Fred while
now entering his epauletted leather shirt, slipping into
it sinuously and snapping it closed slowly, first all the
snaps up the front, and then the cuffs. He fit inside it
snugly and handsomely, like Yul Brynner in a sinister
Western. More shivers from Fred.

"Shirt from Florence, too? I never knew the Italians
were so into leather."

"Ike bought it for me in Hong Kong."

"It fits you very nicely."

"He knows my measurements."

"I guess I didn't want to know about Dennis or Irving or Savannah George who doesn't mean anything to you, or Ike. Unh, who exactly is Ike?"

"I was just being honest. I always like to tell everyone the whole story. I know someone who'll make you a shirt in New York. You'd look good in leather."

Hmmm. The whole story. Stories from the Wicker Library. That I read without a library card. Talk about a Pandora's Box. How do we talk about those? "You made some incredible promises this weekend."

"You shouldn't have run away. You didn't have to slug me. You could have come back with us. We could have hidden you in the closet and you could have watched." Dinky had now reached for two cock rings, black leather bands, one inch wide, studded with silver knobs, with snaps. One by one, he applied these to his wrists. "Think you could have got off on that?"

Fred watched the application. Fred listened to the missed opportunity. Fred fantasized the missed opportunity. Fred's crotch was sorry it had missed opportunity. Fred saw Dinky, in shirt and g-string and cock-ringed wrists only, tilt his head to one side and smile up at Fred.

But Fred said: "OK, buddy. You're very beautiful to me. If you can't handle that, if you can only do it with strangers and everybody else but me, I'm sorry."

Dinky suddenly reached for his pants. He stood up and he started pulling them on. He did it sensuously, with punctuated looks at Fred, first one leg inserted in the supple, clinging cowhide, then the other, then bending to smooth and form the surface to the contours of his thighs and calves, like a lady with her nylons, then standing tall for a squeeze-in of and a pull-up over that perfect palazzo of a tush Fred had tasted how many aeons ago, then a front tug-up, until his g-stringed balls and cock bulged out, Hello!, before he pushed them down and in, good-bye, then a suck-in of his stomach and a zip-up of the fly and a snap-closed to the package very firmly at the top.

Fred had watched it all. Fred was going crazy. Dinky relaxed. He sat down on the bed and he said: "Sex doesn't mean a fucking thing. You just don't understand that. It's just a sensation. Stick a popper up your nose and you might just as well have a dildo up your ass as me."

Yes, Fred had watched it all. His case of the Shivering Nicelies might just be on the brink of No Control. Oh, what fucking Holy Grail resided in those leather pants?

Don't you know, Fred? Can't you see?

He fervently attempted to return his argument to its course. "I'm going nuts seeing you with everyone else! Sex and love are different and any faggot given half a choice will take the former. And probably fucked with Adolf Hitler if he'd been cute!" Oops, he's pulled on some atheletic socks and here comes the first boot. "And after all those incredible promises, I'm wondering just when you're scheduling us in for a serious try at the latter."

Yes, on-going was boot one. Dinky was tugging it on. It was a most handsome black boot, military-style and polished to a mirror, and he placed his pant's leg inside of it and began a meticulous lacing up the front. Fred had admired them before and Fred was admiring them now. Fred's crotch was deep in admiration. "You know, I really want to be friends with you," Dinky said. "Friendship is better. I like being friends with you."

Holy shit. That's what Feffer said, too. Feffer who also made me feel so wonderful. Feffer who also wasn't so keen on talk of love. Feffer who so recently made his

334

debut into the Big Top. I certainly do pick them. Why, Fred? Why! "I don't want a friendship with you! That's something else entirely. You don't fuck with your friends. And every faggot couple I know is deep into friendship and deep into fucking with everyone else but each other and any minute any bump appears in their commitment to infinitesimally obstruct their view, out they zip like petulant kids to suck someone else's lollipop instead of trying to work things out, instead of trying not to hide, and . . . unh . . . why do faggots have to fuck so fucking much?! . . . it's as if we don't have anything else to do . . . all we do is live in our Ghetto and dance and drug and fuck . . . there's a whole world out there! . . . as much ours as theirs . . . I'm tired of being a New York City–Fire Island faggot, I'm tired of using my body as a faceless thing to lure another faceless thing, I want to love a Person!, I want to go out and live in that world with that Person, a Person who loves me, we shouldn't *have* to be faithful, we should *want* to be faithful!, love grows, sex gets better, if you don't drain all your fucking energy off somewhere else, no I don't want you to neutralize us into a friendship!, for all of the above!"

Dinky had reached over for boot two. On-going was boot two. Very quickly!

"Unh, Dinky . . . do you think you could stop dressing for a moment and . . . unh, stop running away from me and yourself and answer me . . . and . . . unh . . . where did you say you bought the boots?" Fred, forget about the fucking boots! He may not be answering you, he may not be hearing a thing you're saying, you may be firing dying shots at the Alamo, but listen to yourself! You're getting back some of your old zip! Now what about your proposal? Not that there's room to kneel down. But you still haven't asked him. Do you love me, Dinky, at least enough to try?

335

"Paris. I bought them in Paris. But I know a place where we can get you a Hot pair in New York."

"I never knew you'd been to Paris." Which Rolex did I take on that trip to Paris?

Up-lacing was boot two. Dinky suddenly yelled out: "What you want is a heterosexual marriage! But the straights don't have it any better!"

"Funny you should bring that up . . ." Fred now looked at the ceiling, out into the dim living room of Salvation Army overstuffeds, at the plywood wardrobe. Anywhere but at Dinky. Now's your moment, Fred. Afraid of the rejection? No! Want to be fucked by him in all that leather? Yes. I also want a marriage. A commitment to play house. So what? What's wrong with that? Why am I letting him intimidate me out of my fantasy. No, it doesn't have to be a fantasy. I'm beginning to think that the only fantasy is Dinky. Has been Dinky. He's beginning to look less and less like a housewife. Or a husband. But carry on, Fred. You've come this far. It's sales-pitch time again. The coach pep-talking the team in the locker room at half time, no I guess this is the third quarter and I'm behind 103 to Nothing, no it's probably five minutes till the final pistol, no it's probably all over already and I don't know it. Sure wish I could sit down on the bench. But with all of Dinky's dressings and all of Ike Bulb's ancient items, there's precious little room to sit down . . . "Oh, that's a tiresome subject! Heterosexual comparison! Why do all faggots dredge that one up? Straights don't compare themselves to us! We're all the same anyway. We've just got an added dose of the clap." Fred tried to pace in mini-steps. Too bad Ike doesn't have a bigger bedroom. Maybe one of these days Dinky will break down the walls. "I've lived all over the world and I haven't seen more than half a dozen couples who have what I want."

Dinky's voice chirped up in relief: "Then that should tell you something!" Then he broke the lace and cursed and set to work reknotting it with speed. "That's why my friendship is better. For all of the above."

"Yeah. It tells me something. It tells me no relationship in the world could survive the shit we lay on it. It tells me we're not looking at the reasons why we're doing the things we're doing. It tells me we've got a lot of work to do. A lot of looking to do. It tells me that, if those happy couples are there, they better come out of the woodwork fast and show themselves pronto so we can have a few examples for unbelieving heathens like you that it's possible. Before you fuck yourself to death." That should do it. Send him right out into the arms of the world. "Hey, Dinky . . . , sooner or later you're going to have to make a commitment to someone. Which means making a commitment to yourself. And a commitment to the notion that our shitty beginnings don't have to cripple us for life." Ouch. Fred felt a growl of reproach from his stomach. "You know something? I'm beginning to think that that's all we allow ourselves to feel. Shitty." Another retort from the interior. And still no room to sit down. Or kneel.

And still not much help from Dinky.

But then Dinky looked up from his successful knotting with a very big smile. "I like myself fine."

"I'm beginning to wonder if you do. And I'm having a tough time with myself. And you're not helping me any." So why are you here, Fred? It's got to be more than Algonqua's Commitment. Algonqua's Red Crossing.

Dinky finally finished with the boots. They looked good. He looked at Fred. Fred wasn't looking so good. "You know, you analyze too much. You want to know too much. I don't want to know."

OK, Lemish. You hear that? You want somebody

who doesn't want to know? All your life has been a journey to find an identity. Why are you letting this loser help you lose one? He sure is a vision, standing up in all that leather. Your crotch, please note, has not ceased its admiration. He thought you were a vision once, too. For a couple of weeks. Your crotch, please note, wants a return engagement of that admiration. "You don't want to know why you do the things you do?"

"No. Why should I?"

"So you might stop doing them."

"I like doing them. If I knew why I did them, I might not like doing them anymore. Come on," Dinky was now trying to get past Fred in the narrow space, "let's go to Irving's party."

"Irving's? What kind of party?"

"Who knows? If it's in The Meat Rack, it's probably the whole lot. Leather. Piss. Shit. Your outfit isn't right, but no one will notice. We'll start work on improving your wardrobe next week." He clapped Fred on the shoulder with his hand, like an officer encouraging the enlisted man out into battle.

"You into piss?" Fred asked.

"Sometimes. There's a guy in Brooklyn. I told you about him. I like his piss." He started rummaging through his civilian clothes hanging in the plywood wardrobe.

"Oh, shit," Fred finally sank down on the now vacated mattress, realizing that once again nothing was being resolved. And trying not to ask himself why he still wanted for a lover/husband-wife someone who liked a guy-in-Brooklyn's piss. "You can't give me what I want. And I'm still fucking hooked on you. Why can't I let go? Why am I still holding on to somebody who can't give me what I want?" Fred! He's heard you utter these blasphemous words!

But the fucker still doesn't say anything. Where's

338

your proposal now? Your knees still ready? You still want him? Yes. Then ask him.

"Why can't we get it together?" Fred asked softly. "What better trinity for a love affair and a good relationship than two guys who share mutual affection and attraction, mutual interests, and terrific sex? You always said on paper we make so much sense. The fucking with you was always wonderful."

"Yes, it was."

"Can't we do it again?" You're back to begging, Fred. You shouldn't have to do that, Fred.

"Sure. We'll do it again." Dinky was still rummaging, but now down on his knees, in his little canvas carry-all on the floor.

No. There couldn't be. Fred restrained himself from looking for Dennis under the bed. "How about right now?"

"No, not right now. I told you I've been feeling very nonsexual lately. I also told you we're going to Irving's party."

"What's Ike Bulb to you?"

Dinky found his plastic bag of pills and stood up. "He gets off on watching me do it with other guys."

OK, Lemish. Another Dennis isn't under this bed. He's in it. How many fucking roles can this Dinky play fucking? All things to all people. Save me. Save himself. And it's that self I say I want. Is it there? Do I still want it? Do I want to do it with Dinky and have Ike Bulb, whoever he is, get off on watching the two of us doing it? I hate to admit it, but I wouldn't say No. Oh, Fred. When are you going to say No?

"Want some drugs?" Dinky offered, selecting several for himself.

"No."

"You never would trip with me." Dinky swallowed two Desnobarbs. "You and I, we'll do it together for Ike. We'll do a scene of our own. Would you like that?"

"Where's Cosmo?" Fred asked, looking around suddenly for the cute little white Bedlington terrier who looked just like a lamb and who seemed to Fred at this moment to probably be the only recipient of Dinky's completely unwavering affection. On their first date, a thousand years ago, was it only last March?, Dinky had come toward Fred (come to think of it, wearing these same leather pants, I didn't even notice . . .), holding Cosmo's leash, Cosmo straining, strutting forth, forward, in front of Dinky, so excited, in anticipation. Such a good omen, Fred had thought.

"He's run away out here. But he'll come back."

Fred jumped up and took Dinky in his arms and tried to embrace him and kiss him. But March was a long way away and the room was still too stuffed up and so the bodies and the lips, for both, had trouble connecting.

"You've already fucked half of New York," Fred said. "I've fucked the other half. You told me you were in the bars since you were seventeen, you had your muscles at twenty-three. There isn't a scene you haven't seen or done. And you're only thirty. Why can't you imagine something better? I dare you to change! And try for something better!"

"My bulldog Fred," Dinky managed to mumble as Fred managed to connect with an earlobe. "I told you we'd work on our relationship." He rubbed his hands up Fred's new washboard stomach. "You feel good." He poked his hands in Fred's crotch to see if it still was deep in admiration. It was. "You still turn me on. We're not finished yet. I still want to keep seeing you. Let's go and grab some donuts before Irving's. I know how you like your donuts."

Then Dinky took Fred's hand and pulled him from Ike Bulb's, out the front door, down a length of Aeon. "Did I tell you," he asked Fred half-way to the donuts in the harbor, "I've bought myself a motorcycle!"

● ● ●

340

A putt-putt was heard in the distance. Everybody at the Feather Party at Bay Walk's end rushed to the water's edge. In the distance an enormous barge was heaving into view, floating downbay, all lanterns and banners and pennants and actual trumpet voluntaries blown by a corps of six.

As the barge came closer, figures could be seen waving. Then, from the barge itself, an enormous noise clapped the air and a zooming rocket was set off, accelerating itself up into the sky, its trail of tail all patterned dots of gold and silver. It reached a height, then hovered for that magic moment of graceful Nureyev stop-frame in space, then zoom-zoomed some more, then exploded and went up yet higher and farther and faster and out into a million different Technicolored hues and prisms and palettes and primary colors in speedy space and time, until these exploded yet further up, its exhaust then reforming, regrouping, reuniting, into one gigantic FEATHER! The Crowd on shore went wild!

And then at the same moment, the very same moment!, as if from out of nowhere, feathers and feathers and feathers, ten thousand million zillion trillion *feathers!* were released into the air, up into the atmosphere, out into the world, up and over and cascading gently down . . .

Yes, The Crowd on shore went wild!

Then the barge pulled up to dock. Now its occupants could be seen. Visions. Beauties. Silvers and golds. Royalty. Gods. Reigned on by feathers. Oh, what a Night of Nights!

Then the shoulders of four of the most perfect golden men, all from Laguna, bore, like some potentate of old, or new, a throne. And on this throne, all in gold himself, lacquered and gilded and shiny and beaming, was the King of Beauty himself, Hans Zoroaster.

And on a second throne, borne also by Lagunans, a tinier crown upon his head, himself in gleaming skin of silver, was that new face of our era in time, the Prince Regent, Timothy Peter Purvis.

Oh, it was a long way from Essen and a long way from Mt. Rainier for them both!

And Timmy waved to his new Kingdom, as they waved back to him.

And grabbing Bo Peep's hand, a hand happy to be held, a hand happy that Rabbi had disappeared, that had been too close a brush with religion, now there was some hopeful breathing space, Tarsh yelled to him and all: "It's like living in a movie! Only better! This is our religion!"

We now come to our Penultimate Climax. It happens in that place of myth and story. The Meat Rack!

And here the convergence of all ill auguries . . . never ceases.

"What do you think of a Nazi party?"

"Nazi but nice."

"Do you think Hitler was gay?"

"No. His lampshades would have been pleated."

"Do we go too far?"

"Does a nigger carry a radio?"

There are now 53,492 faggots on the Fire Island Pines-Cherry Grove axis. Contact with the mainland has ceased till dawn. 12,720 are dancing at The Sandpiper, The Botel, or Billy Boner's premier palais de dance, The Ice Palace. 7,904 are prowling boardwalks and beaches looking for action. 17,904 are already in action. 9,989 inside. 9,989 outside. 57 are sleeping as best they can with such loud music playing all around. Most of the above and any of the rest will, at some time between now and when said dawn will spread its rosy cheeks, hit The Meat Rack.

Dr. Irving Slough has been holding his annual party for years, and on this weekend, which also brought the perennial Cycle and Leather Convention to The Grove. Mixed with our local brothers are all those handsome visitors from far across the sea and nation. Fifteen hundred members representing fifty states and forty international delegations adding another fifteen hundred plus two hundred from The Homeland alone. The S.S. *Berlin* had brought in quite a load. And all in leather, too.

And since Irving generously held his party in The Meat Rack, receiving the kind permission of the U.S. Parks Department to so do, said party was hardly an exclusively catered affair. Yes, Irving welcomed all. Here he could wear his finery with no fear.

"Welcome, Hans!" Irving greeted his best friend, still all in gold but burnished with a coat of leather, giving the right tit he'd so recently repierced a tug. "Tonight I pull you into pleasure, no?"

"Yes!" Hans Zoroaster giggled in anticipation. "A tug into our own special world!"

So, picture if you will, a particularly scenic nook, slightly off the beaten path, just to one side of the main highway through these woods, in this veil of myth and story, equidistant from The Pines and Grove, an open patch, trod down by years of Indian braves, deer, then men, surrounded by tall evergreens and ringed with low ones. The moon was just able to klieg it into atmospheric confraternal welcomeness. And since 'twas the beginning of the new day, Everyone was or shortly will be here!

And was there not much finery everywhere! Iron crosses and swastikas and military marching boots with soles like heavy slabs of darkest bread. Visors and helmets and caps and hoods and bayonets and swords and rifles and holsters and bullet belts plugged full with poppers. And on Irving's belt, the smart executioner's mask he'd borrowed from Hans to later case his head. Very smart. Very sinister. As Irving wished for it to be.

Other guests, of course, were down to basics. Not everyone was into leather. Jeans and work boots. T-shirts tucked into jeans' back pockets. Skin. Flesh. Cocks out naked or encased in mini-leather cases all their own. Ready. Everyone and everything ready. To be put to use. Ready for the sounds and acts of slurpings in the night. No music. No music for this Meat Rack party. Puerto Rican d.j.'s were not welcome here.

And off to vale right was a coffin. Billy Boner certainly knew how to set the scene to receive R. Allan's present of beyond-the-pale Paulie. With candles!

"Hi, there, Irving!"

"Hello, Ike!" The two men in their heavy outfits of hides and metals embraced as best they could without emitting static. Dr. Ike Bulb was a short and compact, middle-aged man, with a black goatee and a bald head, tonight looking like a small cowboy in spiked Eulailia boots and waving black chaps branded with the sign of the Double X Ranch.

"I notice some of our boys over there are contemplating playing with their feces," Ike happily observed. "Nice to see it. Think I'll go and join them. Nice to see the boys dealing with ambivalent areas of experience. Nothing to fear but fear itself. Dinky here yet? I just got off the last boat."

"Not yet, not yet," said Irving, rubbing his palms together in anticipation. "You know Dinky, too?"

"Of course. I thought he told you. He told me all about you."

Irving's palms ceased their happy rubbing and commenced a not so happy rubbing. Fred Lemish *and* Ike Bulb *and* me?!

And near that coffin swung a swing.

Oh, not your common, ordinary, everyday garden-variety swing. This swing looked like the soft saddle for a horse, but stretched out by four tight ropes of chain that

344

wrapped around four sturdy pines for strength. Yes, Irving had thoughtfully, very thoughtfully, bought this swing and swung this swing, and upon this horseless saddle Dinky would be taught his riding lesson!

Boo Boo Bronstein had just finished digging an enormous hole the size of him, beneath some trees in what he hoped would be a secluded-enough glade, Wyatt hadn't told him there'd be so many nightcrawlers in the distance, with the shovel he'd borrowed from somebody's garden, and dangled into it the long watering hose necessary for breathing from the Underworld that he'd derived from somebody else's, and lined it with the poncho he'd adopted from yet a third's. Wyatt also hadn't told him there'd be a real coffin here already up the path a piece. Was that a good omen, like his lucky penny, or just one of those dramatic scenes he'd been told by Wyatt to expect? All of his exertions had left him more than tired and he looked down into his excavation, he preferred not to think of it as his grave, imagine digging your own grave, no, don't imagine it, I'm not crazy, I'm courageous and confident, about to become the conniver Pop always wanted me to be, a Cake-and-Cookie Heiress With a Straw To the Outside World. I wish I had more Certyn and some Drayl.

The famous kidnapping case to which his own paid homage was perpetrated by two crazies who had whisked a rich young heiress from a Georgia motel away to Florida, where she was then buried deep beneath some palms. She was given the nourishment of both food and drugs. She remained underground until her Pop had forked over the cash to the two crazies. Which he did. An assignation in the mootlight. In an old suitcase. And then her Pop dug and dug and dug until he found her. And then her Pop held her in his arms and told her how much he loved her. And had missed her. And had worried about her. And prayed for her. And promised that if she were safely in his arms ever again, then everything, anything, she wanted would be hers. The dummy only asked for a new wrist watch. Her own had gone on the fritz under all that dirt. But they lived happily ever after.

Was it too naïve to think that such a simple plan could work a second time? Of course the two crazies were caught and punished, sent to jail. But since, in his case, the two crazies were mishbocha, this knobby problem was solved in advance.

Yes, Richie, Boo Boo said to himself, I know you're scared. I am, too. But you've come this far. Why not go all the way? Play your thing out, Richie. Don't think that Dr. Rivtov would hardly approve of any of this. Even if it is your Rites of Manhood. I'm going to lie down now, Richie, in my hole, and rest. All those Ups and all I feel is down. When Wyatt comes back from getting his sweater and finding me more drugs, he'll wake you up and slip you your hose and I'll wrap myself up in my poncho, just like overnights at Kamp Kedgeree, and he'll shovel the dirt carefully over me and my Drake's Devil Dogs and then he'll go and get Abe, or does he get Abe before he shovels?, no that doesn't make sense, I'm just so fucking tired I can't think.

I'll pretend I'm Boris Karloff in *The Mummy's Tomb*, Boo Boo Bronstein thought before he drifted off to the first real sleep he'd had in several days. Well, maybe it's more Buñuel than Boris Karloff . . .

And Randy Dildough, too, was idly drifting underneath these trees. He had excused himself from Dordogna with "I'm going to catch a nice whiff of the night air before we hit the sack," and had strolled down that boardwalk and into The Rack instead, following, naturally, the crowd.

Now he stood in front of a group of Nazis. They were having a circle jerk. Just like boys' camp, school dorm, or army barracks.

"Won't you stain your leather?" he heard one of them ask.

"I Scotchgarded."

Randy walked on.

Jack Humpstone walked beneath these trees as well. Our Laverne. Shirtless. He still was looking for his answers. He didn't know how or why, but his feet had pulled him once again to Dinky's directions. He'd find that Dinky and somehow excise him from a system still begging to be purged. He realized that he was watching the two rival journalists who were Bella and Blaze engaging in a chug-a-lug contest. They drank from pitchers replenished by the kindness of relieving strangers. Leather Louie was the judge. The Leather Louie who had given Patty that tour of the Dakota territory a hundred years ago. "Pushed to a greater connection to the ultimate to find out who and what we truly are." Patty. Word had just leaked out about Patty. Now dead Patty. Our triumvirate now destroyed by fire. How to tell Maxine? How to cope with all myself? How to answer Robbie? Where is Dinky? Yes, so many problems for our Laverne.

Bella finished first. And Blaze gagged midway through his fifteenth pitcher and thus was ruled a "Tilt." Fifteen pitchers! A new record!? Hardly. But the evening was still young.

Blaze modestly, if less charitably than he could, embraced his competition. *"Women's Wear über alles again!"*

"Well, my dear," Bella said, "like the late, great Duchess of Windsor, the heart has its reasons." Then, flicking a few drops from Dale Evans now not so Oxydol white, he politely inquired of his rival Fourth Estater: "What are you working on now, dear? I so enjoyed your last *Avocado* piece on all our famous brothers."

"Thank you, Bella. Coming from you, that's praise. 'New Frontiers,' I call it. I'm including force-feeding, baby

347

talk, nipple teasing, black-sock fetishes, smoke, enforced dress codes, enemas, catheters, foreskin stretching, boot licking, rubber wear, diapers, dungeon discipline, entertaining the handicapped, and how to build your very own indoor ranch for Western activities. I think it's so important that we more and more get in touch with our inner and formerly so repressed selves. And my publication is backing me to the hindmost."

"Gorgeous. You must tell it all."

Leather Louie agreed. With his hand on the rubied swastika so smartly medallioned over his black leather chest, he intoned in the original Italian: *"Non ha l'abito interno, prima alcun, c'ha l'estremo dell' arte e della vita!"*

And both Bella and Blaze begged for a translation: "What does it all mean?"

Leather Louis kindly obliged: " 'One doesn't achieve inner discipline until one reaches the extremes of art and life.' It's Michelangelo."

Jack Humpstone nodded, and set forth again to find his own extremes in art and life and Dinky Adams. And to find out who and what Jack Humpstone truly was.

On the outskirts of Irving's multifaceted party, Fred was just behind Dinky, who was running interference and pushing through and into the heavy leathered throngs. Fred felt rather silly in his Harvard sweat shirt. He'd been to Meat Rack parties before. But he'd not been to them when he'd been in love with one of the guests. He saw Dinky nodding to familiar faces, shaking a hand or two, exchanging looks of secret pastimes shared with others, occasionally a disdainful rejection to an inquirer's eyes, plus not a few nods of Maybe, You Look Interesting, Let's See What Happens Later. Yes, Fred noted all the variations. Dinky certainly knew his audience and how to handle his crowd.

"Inter-Chain 207." Someone stopped to introduce himself to Dinky.

"Inter-Chain 101," came Dinky's pleasant reply.

207 was bearded, swarthy, burly, tall, and scary. Dinky stared him down. 207 looked down. "My code is C-1, D-3, I-27, B-4," 207 mumbled.

"I thought so," Dinky slapped him on the back. "Nice meeting you, though."

And then Fred heard Dinky converse with another Inter-Chainer.

"Maybe," Dinky said. "I have been feeling a great need to order somebody about."

"And I've been feeling a great need to serve someone as Master." Possible Slave was medium and dark and not bad-looking, with resemblances to Fred. "Can I call you?"

"Maybe," Dinky answered.

"When can I call you?"

"This week is bad. Try me the week after."

"But would it be fruitful?"

"It could be."

"Is that a Yes?"

"We'll see."

"That sounds like a No."

"Maybe."

"So it is a No!"

And having happily received his rejection, said Slave unhappily walked away.

New Things! New Things!, Fred tried to calm himself. It's a weekend of *New Things*! For my script or for my life? Christ, where's Abe? I forgot about Abe!

"Hello, Laverne," Fred heard Dinky say.

"I'm Jack again. Just plain Jack. No more Laverne. Patty's dead."

"Oh. I'm really sorry to hear that."

"He got burned up in the fire. I don't know what to do."

Dinky pulled out his little sack of pills. "I'm on Desno-barbs. They help a lot."

"How many did you take?"

"By now, I think five."

"Give me four. No. Six."

"Laverne wants four Desnobarbs. Laverne shall have four Desnobarbs."

Dinky pulled out four tablets and depressed them under Jack's tongue. "Maybe we could find Robbie Swindon and give him four Desnobarbs, too. No, twelve." Then he took Jack by the hand, saying "Come along, Laverne," and he led him through the layers of crowd and toward some trees where he was noting that someone had so thoughtfully erected such a handsome swing.

"Isn't it nice to travel again, Laverne?" Fred heard Dinky say. "We took some nice trips together. Isn't this a nice trip?" He looked over his shoulder and waved to Fred. "Come along, Fred."

Under a bower not so far away, Gatsby, still in tennis whites, was also walking under this moon and sky. A little nighttime walk. If I'm not going to write, then I'm entitled to a little nighttime walk. Then he once again saw the face that had intrigued him earlier. Belonging to Lance Heather. But Lance Heather now was all in leather. Ooops, Gatsby, you don't want any of that! Why are you following him? You're curious? Stop being curious. He sees me and he's giving me a smile. OK. I'll go along just for the smile. Wait a minute! Why is he running? He's disappeared.

Randy was now deeper in the forest. He was not in the mood for watching chug-a-lug contests. Or Nazis. Or old farts jerking off over bodies in coffins. Or to find out who the lucky swinger was or who was making mud pies or in the various pairings and groupings of various bend-overs and lean-tos and reach-ups and hold-heres and suck-theres. All scenes that just yesterday might have turned him on. But now

350

seemed rather . . . nonapplicable, impertinent to his current problems. Decisions, decisions, he had to make decisions! What to do, what to do, and who to do it with? A crossroads!

At a crossroads, between pines and pines, could it be?, did his eyes deceive him?!

Young Timothy looked, as always, perfectly perfect. He was still all plumaged up from crown to sneaker. In his little silver nappy, all of him continued to glisten irresistibly. He'd left the Feather Party when too many people tried to touch.

Randy happily offered his hand once more. "You're still the handsomest man I've ever seen."

"Oh, it's you again. Mister See-Saw. Mister This Time Nasty, Next Time Nice. Mister Now You Want Me, Now You Don't. Please don't tell me you're going to make me a star. I already am a star. Please make up your mind and go away."

"This time I'm not going to go away."

"I'm the Winston Man now."

Randy thought the kid might be losing his marbles. Too much too soon. He sure is pretty tough. "I'll make you even more famous than James Dean."

"I'm not certain I remember him. Did I meet him this weekend? It doesn't make any difference because I couldn't do it anyway."

"Why not?"

"Because if I've told you once, I've told you a hundred times, I must be true to the memory of my beloved Winnie. And I can only do that by being the Winston Man myself."

The kid is going round the bend. I've got to help him. I'll take him in my arms and comfort him. "It will be all right. Your Randy will make it all right. We'll go away from all the Musselmans and all the Dordognas and all the dinosaurs in this world."

351

"Are you losing your marbles?" Timmy asked, nervously evading Randy's embrace. Though not before Randy's clothes became all tinged with silver.

Randy's arms felt the emptiness. His new James Dean was slipping away. "Give him some sign that you love him! Or else he'll never be a man!," those famous lines from *East of Eden* came visiting his brain. "I . . . I . . . I . . . love you . . . ," Randy said, with hope that that fine movie's fine advice would help him now.

"You don't understand," Timmy regally said, as he adjusted his new princely crown back into kilter. "Hans told me I'm going to be the most heavenly advertised man of all time. Fifty million dollars will be spent launching me by men who will be tossed into shredders if they fail. Do you have any drugs? My energy is running away."

"I said I love you!" Randy's anger briefly spurted out. He hadn't said that before.

"Oh, I know you said it. But doesn't everybody just! It's too boring. I know I'm very handsome. And I know I'm lucky to see what's in the crystal ball at the beginning of my life instead of at the end of it. And I know I want to be looked at by everybody and to pass around my beauty so the world can appreciate my handsomeness. But I don't want to have to talk. You would make me talk. I just want to be seen. And to be worshipped for my beauty." Now that he'd said it, he felt calm, as if he'd delivered, successfully, his commencement-night address. Which, in fact, he has.

Randy, still in *East of Eden,* further memorable lines, "Father, I did an awful thing. . . Father, I'm sorry . . . Father, it's awful not to be loved . . . ," was down now on his knees, gazing up at Timmy's distant, still withheld, still elusive, still so precious beauty. "I worship your beauty," Randy said. I haven't said that before either. But everything was different before.

Lance Heather had been watching this most unusual scene from behind the protection of those always helpful pines. There, just a few steps in front of him, ready for the catch, was his unrequited vengeance. He could hurt that Dildough! He could pummel him in punishment for all the long years and months of longing and hoping and wishing he were back. But Lance stayed put. It looked like that little beauty was giving that Dildough all the lancing that he needs.

Timmy decided to put his new convictions to the test. "How much do you worship my beauty?" he tentatively inquired.

"Tell me anything you want," his new servant humbly mumbled.

"You'll do anything I want?"

"I want you." Save me from Dordogna!

Timmy said naturally the first time that came into his head. Which naturally was: "Kiss my dirty sneakers."

And Randy did so.

And Lance Heather watched in disgust as his ex-Brother in Zeus turned to mud and dust.

Timmy started to giggle. "You look silly down there, Crud Man! Now please go away and never let me see your face again!" And he took his giggles and his silver crown and nappy and he ran off through the woods.

Yep, Lance Heather thought, running in another direction, he's already broken down. No fun in doing to him what's already been done to him. Probably just as well, I probably saved his life.

After a few long and tired and unfamiliar moments on his knees, Randy pulled himself up before the count of ten and started walking back to his corner in The Pines. Perhaps I can sneak into my own bed at Adriana's. I need some rest. Dordogna, please give me some rest. Tomorrow night is that important dinner with Musselman. No, it's

353

tonight. I wonder if I'll be any good in the men's clothing business.

And in the trees beyond these trees, Gatsby again caught sight of that Lance Heather. And Lance smiled again. So Gatsby ran after him again. Why is he playing hide and seek? I don't want to play hide and seek. I think I am just about to play hide and seek. I hope a smile means a smile.

Smiles were not on the faces of Fred Lemish and Irving Slough. Not that you could see Irving's face behind his smart executioner's mask. But if you could, you would not see a smile. All my plans for vengeance are awry! I wanted to grab you, Dinky, from behind, get you in my bondage, slap a gag around your mouth of lies, pinion behind you your arms that will not hold me, then pick you up like a sack of your manure and sling you in my swing! Then rip off all your leather, peel and tear it off piece by piece by piece. Until I have you naked, in my power!, then bind you hand and feet with all these belts, and then, slowly, slowly . . . do to you what this other young fellow is doing to you already! And you are loving it!

Yes, Dinky was dis-splayed upon that swing, that horse-less saddle now gently rocking neath these sturdy pines, his naked body Desnobarbed and glistening in the moonlight's spotlight, no necessity for bound hands or feet, all was proceeding willingly apace, with such an approving audience admiring the dexterity with which our late lovers now approached their heroic, macho, feet-of-Manhood deed!

Laverne stood poised before that asshole, his own arm Criscoed up for entry. He had himself been torn. He knew he still loved Dinky, as he loved God, but that he was, through this heroic act of catharsis, about to become no longer *in* love with him. Yes, that worked out correctly. He also knew he was having a gigantic erection for the first time in years, much harder than the semi-flopper he'd managed the other evening with Robbie Swindon, with whom he'd soon be living, yes I will!, and I'll be hard again for Robbie, yes I will! Yes, this fist-fucking of a cock-teasing son of a bitch of an almost ex-lover will break the hex and fulfill some sort of personal retribution for all those years of Everything! While his Southern Baptist God was a vengeful God, He hadn't spoken on such subjects as a vendetta via a fist-fucking. Well, maybe it was time, if He didn't approve, to leave Him aside, as He had certainly left him. Yes, through all these portals approaches our Laverne.

Fred had returned to his state of glaze. Glued to the spot. Completely inoperative and supremely nonheroic. Though, all previous versions of heroism now seemed rather out of place. And he did feel at last the need to be heroic. Yes, some sort of heroism was certainly called for. For he knew he was about to witness an extreme masochistic act. But then he wondered who was the extreme masochist? Dinky or Laverne? Or Fred? Come to think of it, that is if anyone was thinking, who was the sadist? Dinky or Laverne? Or Fred? What to do? He knew what to do. But how to do it?

The crowd was growing larger. Such a show! Such a contest! Better than Miss America! Our own Miss America! Both of them so pretty! Irving really throws a party! Irving really lays it on! Irving really finds the beauties! Irving knows our favorite fantasies! And wasn't this what Fire Island's really all about? Wasn't this what we've traveled from far and near to so enjoy! The Titillating! The Turn-On! The Permutations of yet another ringing change on Sex!

Fred looked at everyone looking. It might be some cocked-up version of a movie about doctors with Dinky on the operating table in the amphitheater's spotlight. Did Laverne really want to be playing Dr. Strangelove? Not from what I imagined for Laverne.

Jack blinked away some tears and pushed his hand in

355

a little. The fingers went in easily. Dinky, despite his claims to the contrary, must have been practicing with others. Yes, the fingers squidged in easily. A good thing I clipped my nails just this afternoon. Then the palm, bent in two as much as Jack could bend and squeeze it. Then, once inside the early walls, he clenched, ever so tightly, into the fist that gave this sport its name.

So I am finally fist-fucking Dinky. Fist-fucking is quite popular with some of the boys. I never so wanted to fist-fuck anyone before. I heard they had twenty deaths last year from holes in the stomach at St. Vincent's in the Village alone. I could punch a hole in your stomach. Just like you punched me in the face. Maybe I'll get stuck in here. I also heard about some guy's sphincter muscle tensing up and the other guy's arm turning blue and the two of them rushed to St. Vincent's stuck together like two dogs. Yes, I could punch a hole in your stomach just like you punched a hole in the last six years of my life.

But then Laverne realized that Dinky inside was so different from Dinky outside. Even with gobs of Crisco greasing the path, Jack could still feel the difference between Proctor & Gamble and Dinky. Dinky's insides were lined with lovely ribbons! Laverne's tears returned for the softness that could be Dinky. The Dinky he'd wanted. The Dinky with whom he'd cuddled a hundred years ago by that fire in Southampton after days and nights of wonderful love, and tenderness, and listening to Nina singing "There's a new day coming and a new world, too, here comes the sun, it's all right, going to be all right." Yes, Laverne had a few tears.

But he inched inward. He was sweating and he was still torn, but Dinky was smiling. Fucking Dinky was smiling. So Jack's fist started a few smiles of its own. Take that for Frigger, take that for Piero, one for Chipper, and one for Tony, take that for Olive and Irving and Mr. Mystery

Guest from Savannah, take that for Winnie and that for Floyd and that for Sprinkle and that for Harold and that for Derry and Tex and Wyatt and here's a good one for Dennis and a couple of good ones for Ike Bulb, your free medical advice, he'll look after your asshole, my God, Ike Bulb is jerking off!, here's a couple more for Ike Bulb, and are you watching, Fred Lemish, take a good look, if you want him, this is what you'll get, I wish you'd take him, I wish he'd go to you, I wish . . .

And Dinky smiled even more.

Laverne, trying so hard to be Jack, now said: "Dinky, do you know that I now have absolute control of your life? Do you know that? Do you realize that with a squidge of my fingers I could rip out your insides? I could kill you. It would look like an accident. I'd go free. I'd be free?"

Dinky opened his eyes and continued smiling up at Jack. He spoke very softly, no doubt having trouble with the words. "I'm . . . tall . . . and . . . strong . . ." And then he closed his eyes again as Jack mini-punched some more.

Tall and strong?, Fred thought he heard those words. Is that what it takes to be tall and strong? Isn't he wondering what it feels like to be dead? Isn't he thinking about all his failures, one after the other, with the persons, one after the other, to make him whole? While Laverne at last is making him hole?

Jack made a final desperate punch for freedom into farthest interior regions! Dinky only jerked yet higher into pleasure! Jack thought: only millimeters more would do it! Can I do it! Dinky only moaned out: "Jack! Oh, Jack! I feel! I can feel! It feels really good! Don't stop! I can finally feel!"

Gasps of admiration from the crowd! Look at those doors open! That guy can really take it! Yes, gasps of admiration from the crowd! Except from Cary Lemish. Everyone

357

is thrilled to be witnessing this major sporting event. Except our correspondent on the spot, our Mr. Lemish. So who's making you stay here, Fred Lemish? When are you going to say at last: I don't want . . . that? When are you going to ask at last: Where here is pleasure? Or joy?

Jack? Laverne? said: "Will you leave me alone, Dinky? Will you give me back my apartment? Will you grow up and go your own way and get out of my life and let me go on with mine?" He punched in a little more.

And Dinky jerked up higher, higher, burbling, murbling higher: "I can feel!"

And Jack suddenly wondered just what he was accomplishing. He'll always have me in his power after this. And I can't kill him and maybe it's too bad for all of us that I can't.

But Humpstone tried again. "You now have all of me, Dinky. You have all my arm up to your elbow. Will you throw away your leather and your dildoes and your cast of thousands and your lies? Will you? Will you!" And he clenched his fist against the farthest region's wall.

Dinky just continued to jerk up in pleasure and smile at heaven. That elusive heaven. Now so close. Now almost here. He tried to say a few more words to Jack. "I . . . I . . . I . . . want . . .your . . . other . . . arm!"

There. He had said it. Did Lemish and Laverne realize that in these words lay Dinky's answer?

The crowd at least was most impressed. Gasps of empathy and admiration and hero-worship and the manifestation of same as fists shot up and clenched and reclenched like applause. Oh, heroes of old, ancient Greece and Rome, Thrace and Asia Minor, Crete and all points East and West, make way, make way, make way for Dinky Adams! Yes, gasps of pride for one of their own went up from all around.

Except of course from you-know-who.

You-know-who is still in his aisle seat, first row of the

orchestra, Mr. First Nighter, a bit hysterical, looking at his leading lady and wondering, hoping, praying that this might just be their most cathartic, final, truly final, curtain. He waits for a few tears of his own. They're not coming. My face and eyes and feet are numb. I can't take it all in. You're in heaven, Dinky. You are now evidently up in heaven at last, completely fulfilled, smiling magnificently, you don't even know I'm here, yes, up in some heaven where two partial arms of your ex-lover who is still your lover because of course he can't kill you, of course he's still in your system, he can't get out of your system, that I understand, yes, up in some heaven where all of this takes you. Thank you, God.

Around them, pairings and groupings and bend-overs and lean-tos and reach-ups and suck-anywheres and hand-me-downs and Nazis and international fellows and local boys are going crazy. Fist-fucking's such a turn-on! Under this moon and stars. Under these sheltering trees. In these shadowy shadows. Our own special world. Cocks and mouths and lips and tongues and assholes all are meeting, greeting each other, joining the fun of this party, making one of their own, our very first mixer of the season, having ourselves a ball! Or two.

And down on his knees, Hans is having two as well. At last he has his Irving, plus an Ike, two cocks with big heads in his very own mouth, which is known as Giving a Remington, immissio penis in os, in os.

"Terrific party, Irving!" Ike happily thanks his host.

"That Dinky, he is all yours, Ike?" asks back Irving, still laced up like a Kislav phantom.

"What's that you're saying?" Ike begs for a translation.

"Dinky! Yours?!" Irving spits the words most clearly through his mask of slits.

"As much as he's anybody's. I don't expect anything from him and I never tell him I love him, though of course

359

I do, but he knows I don't expect him to love me back . . ."

Hey, Lemish! Do you hear that, buddy?

". . . oh that feels good! . . ." Ike is pleased with Hans.

Irving unbuckles his belt. His leather gear now sags down to his ankles. His sagging tits now showing, his crossover bucklings unbuckled, yes, his gear now down on the ground and showing all. It's never going to happen, it's never going to happen, my Faustian bargain comes now to haunt me when it's too late for anyone to come . . .

"I'm coming! I'm coming!" The sounds of Dinky's feeling coming to fruit.

Irving grabs that Hans away from shaving two, and sticks that Hans in front of his own crotch. And tugs him now toward pleasure. "I tie *you* up and gag you up and stick my filthy jockstrap in your mouth and fuck your asshole while I fuck your head, and force my cock into your mouth while shoving dildoes up your ass, and then sit on your face, while I work your tits, tug your tits and stuff my big balls in your mouth, and jack off on your tits, and fuck you like a dog, with my jockstrap in your mouth, yes I fuck you Well!, both mouth and ass and head! . . ."

Hans is now in heaven, too. At last he has his Irving all alone. He's been tugged into his pleasure. His connection to the ultimate. To find out who and what he truly is. I love it!

And lean-tos and hold-ons and I'm comings and groupings and pairings and boots off and boots licked and Nazis kneeled before and under and Fred wonders what would happen if all their toys and all their costumes were taken away? They might be forced . . . to love.

He looks at Dinky and Laverne. One Revenge Fuck pummeling One Punishment Gratefully Received. Jack, are ʼhat will happen to me?

ʼhen he looks at the Three-Ring Circus ringling all ʼim. Thinks of Feffer on his cross. Looks at Dinky in his swing. What else is there . . . ? Is this my competition? Is this my Age that's rapidly approaching? Yes, Fred looks at all and thinks immortal thoughts, not of Adams, Dinky, for a change, but of Miller, Henry: "We are no longer animals but we are certainly not yet men." Which happily at last gives him a tidge of courage to think heroic thoughts of Lemish, Fred: "The fucking we're getting's not worth the fucking we're getting," and it's time to go . . .

So, feeling that the now discovered smithy of his sex appears no longer worth the foraging, he bends to kiss his Dinky " 'Bye" and he turns to leave.

He couldn't go very far. He walks into the trees and bumps into a group of fellows all relieving themselves in a hole. Holes are quite popular this evening with some of the boys.

And said baptismal by golden showers has awakened our sleeping prince, our Boo Boo Bronstein, from his nap. He thinks some coffin thoughts. Am I buried? Am I dead? Is this Heaven? It's raining in Heaven. What's happening? It's happening! All those gorgeous handsome men up there are looking at *me!* I like it. I like it! I'm a Number! It feels so warm and good. It feels like Candlewood Lake. It doesn't hurt at all! He stretches. He opens his mouth to taste. Am I dreaming? No . . . I'm tripping! My mouth tastes bitter. Wyatt's . . . somebody's come and put some drugs into my mouth! I'm tripping. I feel wonderful. I'm in the Pits of Sexuality at last!

And he jumps up and rips off his clothes. And stands tall neath the showers. And holds up his arms like a winning player after the winning game. And his fellow players, fellow teammates, fellow helpmates, help him from his whole. Fanny Brice in the single spot about to become a star. Twenty stage-door Johnnies here to claim all starring parts of him! He's pulled up and out and into these many many many arms of many many men and many mouths. Much

361

love. He lies back into arms. Many arms. Much love. He's passed around like the football in a secret and intricate play. He yells out to all as he's shouldered and hipped and handled. He yells out to all as he displays his hardly earned perfections, one by one. "Take my big delts! Take my big lats! Take my obliques! Take my rippling stomach! Take my fatless calves! Suck my tits! Suck my medium-sized cock! Take my medium-sized cock! Take all of me! My name is Richie Bronstein! At last I'm a Fire Island Star!"

And again crowds cheer! Irving's party runneth over into this! And Boo Boo's cheering, too. He's a crazy kid in a candy store with unlimited choice. All fantasies are here to suck, and suck and suck and suck. He throws himself further and farther in and among, letting arms cradle him, letting arms hold him, letting arms love him, and he feels their stomachs, their big round stomachs, so full of much experience and life. And thanking God that he likes older men. There's lots and lots and lots of older men. And he loves these older hands on his young cock. And loves them feeling his fine hard youthful body, all over, all over, yes definitely all over, as he rushes now into another fat man's arms. A fat man standing by his graveside's edge. With an old suitcase. Oh, this one feels good, too. This one feels so good. "Hey, Mister, I'm yours, I'm all yours, you feel good, hey, Mister, can I come and live with you?, would you please get down and suck my cock!"

"Oh, my Richie!"

"Oh, my God!"

Was it not ever thus? Well, not quite ever *thus*. Yes, watching on the one hand and dropping his son's cock with the other, Abe Bronstein now wonders if this is finally his last plotz. What more is there to take? My kleine Wyatt leads me into this! My kleine Richie in a pit of piss! The only thing that's missing is Wyatt's kleine cockalah as well! Oh, God, you are being naughty to your Abe tonight! *Please*

362

tell me what to do! Or else these Nazi natives in the jungle kill! These Nazis come too close!

Richie's trying to run but Abe is holding him tight.

And Richie, the son, the heir, what thinks he of this moment in time and space? Do I: wish I were dead? or . . .

"Pop, just give me a wrist watch and we'll call it even-Stephen!"

"Oh, my Richie, you make for yourself a world more awful than the one you try so hard to escape!"

Richie is bawling, heaving heavy tears. I'm tripping, yes, I'm tripping, this isn't really real!

"No, Pop, it's your world! I'm just living in it. In the suburbs."

Ah, the age-old conflict.

As the Nazis move in closer for a better view . . .

"Richie! Please to come home with your Pop! Look, I bring you money!" Maybe I don't show him. These Nazis will steal it away!

"One million bucks!?" Richie knows now that he's really tripping.

"Only now ten thousand," Abe tries his best to whisper. "A holiday weekend. The bank was undercashed."

"What do you mean only ten thousand! I didn't go through all this shit for only ten thousand! I want my one million dollars! I want my one million dollars!" Richie's still trying to run, but Abe's still holding him tight.

"That's it, Cutie, hold out for the one million!"

The simply riveted audience roars and cheers! What an act! Irving, can you throw a party! Importing live actors for such a scene as this! Though why didn't he hire two pretties? That old one's pretty ugly. But the young one! . . . The crowd moves closer in to get a better look.

"I want my one million smackarolas!"

"I give you smackarolas on your tush!"

363

"Mary, you better be rich because you ain't pretty enough to go home to on your own!"

"Richie . . . ," Abe tries to whisper softly again, "we are perhaps in some concentration camp? . . ."

"It sure as hell ain't Australia! Let me go! Let me go!"

"I promise you to make me like you better!"

"You promise! You promise! Who can believe your promise!"

"Sweetie, that's telling her exactly how it is!"

Richie's still trying to run and Abe's still trying to hold. Storm Troopers, S. S., Gestapo, Himmler, Goering, Ilse Koch are all just over there!

"You will believe me! You must believe me!" Forgive me God my Father for I have sinned!

And God gives now his answer to his Abe, who takes his younger son and hurls him to the ground. And pins him under his girth of years of living and food and knowledge. And the son knees back in protest and suffocation and not quite so experienced heft. And together they toss and they turn, like some biblical nightmare brought up to date. Over and over and side to side and up and down and round and about. "Richie, come back!" "Pop, let me go!" "Richie, listen to your Father!" "Pop, you don't understand!" And now the Pop starts swatting pop flies at the fence. Finding the tuchas and hitting to right field, hitting to left, splaying his mitts. Splat and splat and *Splat*! Take that and that and *That*! And oh the crowd is cheering! Spanking's such a turn-on! Such a pretty ass is showing! "Pop, you hurt!" "Richie, you hurt!" And Richie and Abe are intertwined as ne'er before. Or as e'er before. Hitting and elbowing and kneeing and scratching and off sides and on sides and slugging it out and who's got the penis, who's got the testicles, where is the rectum, where is the scrotum, who is the Master, who is the Slave, which one the Top Man, which one the

Bottom, who the Dominant, who the Submissive, who the S and who the M, and which one's got the BALLS!?

Abe is spanking his Richie and Fred is watching his Abe.

Echoings. . . . of Lester . . .

"Pop, you're too heavy! Get off of me! I'm shitting in my pants!" Yes, where now were Sidney Greenstreet, Coburn, Laughton, and Eugene Pallette? On top of him. "You hurt!"

" I hurt! *I* hurt! What do you know of hurt!"

"My million, Pop! Mine!"

Ah, the age-old conflict. Splat. Splat. *Splat*.

"You get what I give you! You get when I die or you reach fifty! Whichever event comes first!" Oh, they come closer and closer to punish me! They come closer and closer to kill! "Or you marry that *mies*keit Marci Tisch!"

"But she's so ugly!"

"Millions of my dollars are not so ugly!" Splat!

"But that's blackmail!"

"I teach you how the world is run!" Splat. "I teach you how to blackmail properly!" Splat! Oi, *more* Nazis?!

"First I'll tell the world."

"First I give you this!" *Splat!* Oh, this one comes closer! In black boots and with rifle and swastika and whip and . . .

Abe lets go of his son. Richie slips away. The Nazis and the piss have saved his Richie. Abe falls back in the end zone. His penalty kick has lost.

Richie yells back at his Pop: "Hey, Pop! You never really loved me at all!"

"Do you think that ugly really is his father? . . ."

The crowd immediately grows nervous. Starts to back away. "This is pretty heavy."

"Yes, I love you, yes, I love you, but it is now too late."

But who has heard him say these famous words? The pop has said I love you to the son. The scene and dream of every son who's backed away beneath these sheltering trees. He's said he loves me. He's said he loves me. The sheltering veil now shelters. God has forbidden a fantasy might come true! That would be too scary!

Boo Boo zips away, past a few departing theater-lovers.

"Who *was* that?"

"I don't know."

"Some silly queen."

"I'm sorry, Abe." Fred bends to kneel, then sit, beside his Abe. Then rock him back and forth within his arms. Such a weekend, such a Mission, such an old suit caked with mud and piss and Richie.

"I'm sorry, Abe-chen."

Abe refocuses. Looks at Fred. No words. No smile. No return of affection to his movie helpmate. He plucks Fred's arms from his dirtied suit like poopsies from his past. He heaves his white-haired bulk from mud to standing tall. As he's done many times before, he now does once again. Then, with anger, hate, and vengeance, the Big Three, he utters these ringing words: "It's your fault! It's all because of you! The Fall of the House of Bronstein! And all because of you!"

Then stomps and chomps away our Abe. And lights up a cigar. And then sees Wyatt's kleine not so kleine. Being tended to by a lady dressed like an English Queen. Well, at least my Wyatt's found a lady. No, it's probably a man. Wyatt! Where did you get *that*! Freaks! Everyone in this place is freaks! I must go back into the world! I'm free. I'm free! I find another poopsie! And take her to Florida. For what is a Palm Beach doing in these pines!

He turns to Fred to yell his final curtain speech. His final fadeout Ode. His epilogue. And truly bringing down the house.

"No movie!"

For what world wants to know of this!

Fred sits in the mud alone. His empty arms still feel the warmth where Abe had briefly rested. I loved you, Abe. I loved you . . . Lester . . .

Yootha Truth is crying. He's been watching his Guardian Angel, his Handsome Stranger, His Doubleday Deliverance, the hovering presence who is the shadow that is Billy Boner, sitting in love and admiration, satisfaction and completion, of dead Paulie in his coffin.

"He doesn't love *me*, Rolla!"

"We must go on, dear," Rolla answers, trying his best to skate off in the mud. "We must not let ourselves sink into soap opera."

And Gatsby has finally tackled Lance Heather under some farthest, furthest pines. And peeled away the layers and layers of leather. And how they tossed and turned and clutched each other dearly in the poison ivy. And kissed and cuddled and touched and kissed and embraced and kissed . . . until . . . until . . . *until!* . . . *my God!*

Gatsby looked down at the cock that once had been Lance Heather's. He didn't have any. Just a piece of skin. "I . . . I . . . had an accident . . . a party . . . we played a stupid game . . . Russian Guillotine . . . I lost . . . I'm lucky I've got this much left . . . would you fuck me please?"

Yes, such a night of nights. In our Meat Rack. That place of myth and story. Yes, such a night of nights.

Fred now succumbed at last to his case of the shivering crazies. He ran and ran. Back to The Pines, back past costumed cruisers, men with TV camera heads and glowing penises lit up inside lamé pants and much regal tribute to the British Empire, feathered Orientals, high-heeled Brazilian blueberries, twinkling twinkies. The Grove might be all

367

in basic leather, but The Pines continued on its froufroued
way. Yes, he ran and ran. My fault? This weekend I have
lost a Dinky, lost a Feffer, lost an Abe. My fault? *My fault?!*
But have I found myself?

He was right back where he started from. He rushed
into a house in which he dimly recollected dining well once,
many years ago. It was empty and he hit the refrigerator and
some Royal chocolate pudding. In the cupboard he found
a box of Kensington Gardens chocolate-covered oatmeal
cookies from our northern neighbors in Canada. Canadian
cookies were evidently as bad as American. When he died,
he used to fondly quip, his autopsy would reveal one part
Nabisco, one part Keebler, one part Horowitz Margareten,
one part Bronstein, no, no more Bronstein, and all the rest
chocolate. He departed this way station of sustenance and
went next door, also presently uninhabited, and there, there!
—God was finally giving him something good this night, this
weekend, this Memorial Day weekend—was a box from the
most perfectly perfect Dumas Pâtisserie. One cheese Danish
and one raisin Danish and one brioche. A threesome. He
would splurge lightly. And it was Heaven! Did no one know
what they were missing to eat any other Danish but a
Dumas Danish! He recognized the distinct familiar co-
mingling tastes of butter and sugar and cheese and soft
raisins, actually plump, which he would soon again be if
he did not this instant cease. And the brioche was all his
trips to Paris with Mikie II and others. He ran out of this
kind stranger's residence and down some blocks on a sugar
high. At another obviously emptied house on Coast Guard,
on the uncleared dining-room table—cleaning up is left till
morning—was one box of Bloomingdale's Corné de la
Toison d'Or. These he would not buy in Bloomingdale's because the rude salesladies refused to sell them by the piece.
Only the half-pound. Unfair! These chocolates are sold by

the piece in their native Belgium. And wasn't buying a half-pound . . . well, poor Gamesmanship? He bit into one, two, three, four, five, six, no wonder he preferred not to buy a whole half-pound, eating only half of each. They were not his favorites. Though better than Godiva's, once also Belgian, now American-made by Campbell's Soup, and robbed of their once distinctive flair, particularly when their saleslady on Fifth Avenue transfers them from ugly New Jersey cartons of brown to low, enticing trays of gilt at the same time as she passes her crimson nails through her greasy hair. No, he was not a Godiva fan. He preferred above all others the miraculous Teuscher's, from Zurich, here perfection had been achieved, the perfect chocolate, it was possible!, now returned to New York, which he had written Mimi Sheraton about and she had written in the *Times*: "these mellow milk chocolates that many connoisseurs consider to be the world's finest . . ." Oh, Dinky. I'm a connoisseur. Out of Coast Guard. To another dark house, on Driftwood. A further fix. On the icebox he found half a bar of that new chocolate from Cadbury's, from his beloved England. Milk Chocolate Filled With Fudge. The perfect combination. On paper it made so much sense. He'd been wanting to try it for quite some time, always avoiding the temptation. Now here it was in some strange house on Driftwood. So he finally bit into it. This most anticipated sensible combination from Mother England, Filled With Fudge. Oh sadness of sadnesses. Grotesquerie. It was revolting. Watery fudge obliterating their distinctive milk chocolate's taste. Was everything passing into second-ratedness? The goodies now baddies? In chocolate as in life? Including self? *My fault?!* He wondered if someday, should he ever write anything else again, some graduate student somewhere would do a dissertation on the sweet symbolism in the life of Fred Lemish.

A moment on the lips. A lifetime on the hips.

• • •

Fred's first fuck of the New Era, A.D., After Dinky, appeared miraculously, under the new moon, same stars, as Fred emerged, phoenix from the ashes, from the ocean, after a dip following the three-mile jog he'd had to take to work off all those calories so recently consumed. Ah, yes, the patterns continue. And there stood the lean and youthful gorgeousness who was—Fred didn't know his name but knew his face from . . . somewhere—and under these stars and moon, right now, they just threw themselves at each other, instant attraction, instant moon and romance, instant high, just like the movies, on the beach, from here to eternity, "let's go to my place," "let's do it right here," and down they fall, Fred already naked, Mr. Quite Possibly Great Love Number III shortly so, "I knew you'd be sensuous," this handsome stranger saying, "You're such a handsome man, I've seen you around and hoped we'd fuck, you're such a handsome man," yes, here is this handsome man calling Fred a handsome man, when will you start believing it, Fred?, you want Mikie to believe he's got a brain and Tarsh that he could accomplish great things and Gatsby that he could be a fine writer and Josie and Dom Dom that they could be faithful lovers and Anthony that he could write Academy Award-winning scripts and . . . Dinky that he could love you, could have loved you, so why can't you believe that you're a handsome man? Particularly when such a handsome man is naming you a handsome man. And now the sensuousness of this moment, this night, these two bodies under those heavenly bodies, feeling each other all over, all over, each of you tasting the other, each of you bending to kiss the other hello down there, oh it is so fucking sensuous and wonderful and you are both into that abandonment to pleasure that only fucks like this, could this be love?!, can so inspire, and kiss kiss kiss, it's so good to be kissed again, Dinky wouldn't kiss, can this be the last of

Dinky?, certainly is one hell of a body this guy's got, wonder what he does for a living, and oh! what lovely armpits, almost as good as Dinky's, *No!*, No More Dinky!, oh, it's all too much, and we kiss and cuddle and suck and tongue and fuck and rim . . . Dinky! Get out of my fucking head! I'm fucking!, and kiss and cuddle and tongue and fuck and rim . . . It's going to be harder getting rid of you than I thought! . . . and kiss and cuddle and tongue and suck and fuck each other, using spit and careful to keep the sand away, and back again and suck some more and kiss some more and taste the sweat and glue yourself together at last, together, together, you cling and clamp yourselves together and reach for those stars and for that moon and for those heavenly bodies, I'm coming! Me, too! The two of you together from just the excitement of holding each other each to each come and come and come and yes it was wonderful and is wonderful and this is someone I must see again and again, the Beginning of Love, *Wait a minute!!!*, I'm falling again, falling into fantasy again, falling for a body again, just like I fell for Dinky's body, turning a Hot Number into love, I'm making sex into love!, just as Handsome Stranger jumps up, pulls on his jeans, adjusts his silver bracelet, pecks a quick kiss, and says: "I've got to rush, I'm meeting my new lover, we're going to live together, starting tomorrow, so you mustn't breathe a word of this, but my name is Robbie Swindon, I'm listed, and you sure have a Hot body and I hope that we can do it again."

Fred lay back naked, all alone again, looking up at all those stars and moon. Then out across the ocean and toward old England. Nothing's changed. It's all exactly the same. Noogie & Nagasaki . . . what did they say? Oh, who gives a fuck. What do I say? I say I know what I want and I ain't gettin' it. I say I'm settling for too fucking little. I say the whole set-up I've set up is out to sabotage me. I say I'm not going to find love here. And even if I could, how could it survive and grow? I say it's time to move on. I say I think it has been . . . is my . . . fault. But why?

Fred headed for his last dance in The Grove.

He approached The Ice Palace. There it was, the premier Island dance hall, a huge clapboard, turreted, magical, old-fashioned, twinkling, indeed palace of a place, just there, coming toward him, in the full moon's spotlight, coming closer as Fred started running closer, the music growing louder, enticingly louder, as he ran up The Palace steps and paid his entrance fee and pushed his way through and among the many thousands of sweaty, half-naked bodies on the outside deck and into the hot arms of its insides, its chamber of chambers, high inside fingers jutting up to heaven, that elusive heaven. Again wonderful lights that twinkled everywhere. Miles and miles, a million miles of Mylar and mirrors, to reflect and deflect and gleam and smile and wrap them all in such a pretty package of Life. Again the necessary heat that music and energy and dancing and brothers generate so emphatically. Fists pounding up and down to the beat of one of their own disco anthems. Release. So much release. So many dear ones touching. Here to be touched. So close. But not too close. No hassles. No problems. No involvements. Please no hassles and involvements! Just let's dance. Which Fred proceeded to yet again but for the last time do.

This is one massive cake of solid body, thousands, Hot Men, radiating enough heat to defrost Arctic wastes and I am being pulled into it and I am dancing and dancing, oh we are so many bodies, plowing my way through bodies, bashing and twisting and poppers passed like party favors and seven men now hold me and we swing and sway and sweat becoming One!, and I am dancing with strangers and dancing with friends and we are plucking each other from this vastness and I am a madman and here is Renny Collage Maker and William Distinguished Professor of Literature who keeps him, asks no questions, and looks the other way, and here is Kristos Rosenkavalier who gave his lover a silver rose, only to be left same night by same, and Dick and Dora Dull who've been together twelve years and own three houses together and never seem to talk to each other and Matt Desk Clerk who's so shy and to whom I once said "I want to open you like a can of peas," but decided not to and Tidgy Schmidge who just likes hairy asses and Terry TWA who flies in dope from Kansas City and sweetness Alex who, with me, is the only D.F.B. on the entire Island, Drug-Free Bodies, our own exclusive club, Alex sure looks lost tonight, and Harvey Pharmaceutical Researcher and Ron Would-Be Artist who's our clap doctor's lab boy and B.L.T., for Beautiful Legs and Thighs, who fucked with the entire cast of Grey Gardens one rainy night and Lovely Lee, we dance so lightly, we're The Old Smoothies, he crying: "Not bad for two old Jews!," I jumping up in the air to yell: "Call me Mikhail!," and there is Washington Department of Agriculture Jack, last summer's notorious cock teaser (though he could take lessons from Dinky) who left me after tongue-kissing me for two hours while Bobby B. showed us slides of the highlights of the summer-before-that, and Kenny Textile Designer who lost seventy-five pounds and is finding them and John Book-Jacket Illustrator who wants to do mine if and when I ever write one, maybe now I'll write one, and Martin Set Designer who lets us use his set of weights for working out out here and Mark Costumier whose lover left him "for a drag queen! the ultimate insult!," and dear architect Charlie, we were lovers how many years ago when we were young?, and Milton Hustler who's writing his memoirs, he's done it with many of the world's most famous and finest, and Ronny whose father wouldn't give him the money to buy the house he wanted so he cried, and Olive, my God, I'll bet he's the Olive who was my Dinkied competition, he's still wearing a costume, some schmata of polyestered silver, it looks like he stole it from his mother, and here's Gatsby: "I'm moving, Fred, I'm getting the hell out of here, I'm going to Santa Fe, I'll get a job as a waiter . . ." No, Gatsby!, you mustn't give up . . . I'll miss you . . . and there's that crazy Elizabeth Taylor dancing all in black, he sure is sweating—no, I think they're tears . . . and here's Bella: "Fred, I have momentous news! Billy Boner has just announced that he will open a brand new baths, with three hundred rooms, just like a Grand Hotel, with wall-to-wall carpeting and a Jacuzzi with sitdown service for fifty and a master steam room and five little saunas and home-baked pies and cakes and donuts," and here is Frigger: "This place tonight is hot as a mother's love," and here is Fallow: "I've danced so much my legs feel amputated," and here is Bilbo: "You'll look good shorter," and here's tiny Pinky clinking finger cymbalettes: "My cymbalettes! I was invited to seven houses tonight! I feel like I've been picked to pledge the best fraternity!" and Mikie, my beloved Mikie . . .

"Oh, Fred, I was going to go home. But I'm crazed. I can't go home. I'm just being pulled along. This is my home."

Fred holds Mikie close, then Mikie breaks away and twirls and throws up his arms to wave at bodies swinging, yes actually swinging, out and back, over and out, like monkeys, from the rafters, those old beams, out and over the crowd, the dancing hordes reaching up to grab their feet.

"Oh, Fred, is it not a transcendent evening!" Mikie yells. "The quintessential Fire Island experience! Everything is in balance! My dancing has at last found a new center of gravity! I am dancing with my own true self! At last! I have never danced like this in my life! I have turned myself on at last! I love you, Fred!"

"I love you, Mikie."

"God must be trying to tell us something, Fred. There are too many of us. We must not be bugs. And Fred, look! I have a new crystal for our Rolex. I can see the time again!"

"That's nice, Mikie."

And Mikie rushes off to dance. Please Fred, don't let me love another Mikie. Or another Dinky. "Josie!"

Fred rushes to Josie's side. He is standing on the cavern's mirrored edge. He wears a New York Yankee's uniform. His balded head now shows a shadow. Is it five o'clock already? He's crying.

"Oh, Fred! So much energy! So much!"

Fred now holds this dear friend close, too.

"Oh, Fred. Summer after summer. Another repetition of a repetition. Weekends without number. All the same thing. Starting up all over again. Do I have the courage to leave it? Go somewhere? Go to where? To do what? So much energy. So much. Why leave it? Why stay? So much. Toward what end?"

But then he suddenly smiles at Fred, mumbles: "I'm sorry. Excuse me. Don't know what came over me. I'm fine," and extricates himself from Fred's concern, and rushes back into the pack to pull his Dom Dom, who's a New York Giant, away from another body, reclaim him for his own, at least for now, at least for now, and start to dance.

Fred watches Anthony standing on the dance floor's edge alone. Anthony is unhappy. Anthony has seen his lover, Sprinkle, his kissless lover, Sprinkle, whom Fred has found so wanting, home from Mom in North Dakota, dancing in a tight circle of handsome young men, his own age, he hadn't even called to say "hello, I'm back," what kind of lover is that?, all these young men now kissing each other and feeling each other, naked bodies and hands into crotches and what kind of lover is that? Anthony then sees his best friend, Fred, standing on the other side alone. Over heads and bodies and years, the two friends smile at each other and walk to meet by the door.

"You OK, Tante?"

"As well as can be expected," Fred replies. "How about you?"

"The same."

"That good?" they both joke simultaneously, as they smile and hug.

"Where's Dinky?" Anthony asks.

"I think he's lost out here. Where's Wyatt?" Fred asks.

"I think the same."

Anthony looks out at the crowd. He looks at Sprinkle. He looks around for Wyatt. "One of these days I'll find somebody. And I'll teach him to sing all Dick Powell's songs. And all about Ruby and Fred and Ginger and days of long ago. I'm tired. I'll see you tomorrow. And come Tuesday, Tante Fred, your Anthony launches another Winston Man unto this world."

Fred watches Anthony plow his way through bodies on his way out. Then he feels a tap on his shoulder. Dinky stands there beside him, adjusting Fred's Harvard sweat shirt. Fred blinks. How can Dinky be standing? In one piece? Not cleft unto twain? As was Fred.

"You OK?" Fred asks.

"Sure. Why shouldn't I be?" Dinky answers, still adjusting. "Your outfit still isn't right."

"No, it isn't right," Fred agrees.

Dinky follows Fred's eyes after Anthony. "He's a

nice man, a Hot Man," Dinky says. "But he's given up. He's admitted defeat. Why do you always get so upset and run away? What I did doesn't mean anything."

Why don't you say it, Fred? Yes, it does. To me. It's the deeds that talk and count. Action is character, old F. Scott said. Yes, it does. To me. But what's the point, Dinky? What's the point?

Dinky takes Fred's hand and pulls him out of The Palace and across its deck and down its stairs, like crossing the moat and back to life, and they start running, Fred wondering how Dinky can run, Fred wondering how Fred can run, down a boardwalk, past little bungalows, "Love's New Sweet Song," "Love Is Here On Bay," "Over the Rainbow," then down another boardwalk, and back to Aeon and Ike Bulb's.

But they don't go inside. They go around to the back. A back that Fred hadn't seen. He blinks his eyes. He's in the most beautiful garden, Fairyland. Here, among some sand and scrub pines, nestles, is growing, a huge symphony of flowers and planters and weeping tubs of willows and man-made stars of light and cupolas and gazebos and cozy swings for two and tiny benches for intimate picnics and breezy lanterns swinging out to say Hello.

"It's the most beautiful garden I've ever seen."

"Ike let me make it for him."

There is even a big soft Indian blanket all laid out. Has Dinky come to get him? Or was he looking for just a someone, anyone, else? Is Dinky now back in reality, or was he still Desnobarbed out there where Fred, anyone, could not reach him or touch him? Has he got Laverne and All Others out of his system and is he now ready for my dare of Love?

What am I doing?

For Dinky has pulled Fred down to blanket level and now once more is commencing a playing with the

Lemish cock. In and under the hunter-green-satin Champion boxer shorts goes that Adams hand. And up and under the hunger-green Champion boxer shorts goes that Lemish cock.

What am I doing?

I'm falling for the bait again. My fantasies are overdriving into No Control again. Put on the brakes, Lemish. Screech this tin dinky to a halt.

Fred removes Dinky's hand. Echoing's of Lester's "You are Unwanted, I reject you through and through."

Dinky lies back on the blanket, then to sleep. Echoings of Lester's "You are Unwanted, I reject you through and through."

Fred leans back, too, and lies down beside that Dinky, and closes his eyes, and sees that Dinky standing over him. Dangling his long black leather belt upon Fred's stomach. What's a little dangling long black leather belt? Fred sees Feffer. Fred sees Abe. Fred sees Lester. He waits for it to happen. Whomp. Whomp. Whomp. No, it doesn't turn me on. Whomp. Whomp. Whomp. Yes, it hurts. The whomps turn into thumps. The thump-whomps turn into splats and the splats turn into slashes and the slashes turn into beatings and the beatings turn into . . . tears. Yes, Fred Lemish is finally crying. As the last piece of his puzzle falls finally in his face . . .

His arms still feel the empty warmth of Abe and Lester. He takes the sleeping Dinky in his arms. They're still empty.

. . . I've been looking, seeking, demanding, the love of Lester all my life. As if . . . as if . . . as if a dinky Lester's love would make me whole and everything all right. As if wrestling Lester's love from Dinky's stone would make everything all right. Lester would have loved me. I chose another Lester and tried to make him love me. So I could be lovable.

378

But Algonqua's "Love" would send a strong man under. Her "Love" would bury any man alive.

What a double-edged fence.

No wonder it's been so hard for me to have just the one thing I've wanted the most. Love.

And no wonder I've never had it.

I wanted a fantasy and that's what I got. If I'd chosen a real person, I would have had to face up to a real relationship. Too scary. Too full of Mom and Pop.

But that's exactly what I chose.

What a double-edged fence.

The smoke screens now are clearing.

A guy who wanted to love too much chose to fall in love with someone who didn't want to love at all.

Yes, that says something about The Wanter—and His World.

OK, Lemish. Your journey now begins. Your work is now cut out for you. Your hard work. From this moment not one other opinion matters but your own. There will always be enemies. Time to stop being your own.

So long, Dinky. Good-bye. You're just not right for me. I want some pleasure and joy from my feeling. I must have the strength and courage not to let you or this scene dictate my emotions. It's hard to say good-bye to you. But I must have the strength and courage to say No.

At this point tears turn to anger. Anger finally arrives. How dare we have treated ourselves and each other so badly? Anger. For love unrealized. For settling for so little. For humiliation and its pleasure. For foolishness revealed. For having loved half a person. And therefore having hoped only half fully. For being putty. For cowardice and being Lester's sissy. For selfishness. For playing the petty game of dangler and danglee. For life still undefined. For lies. To self and others. For the lack of courage to be faithful. To self and love. You and Me,

Dinky. We've been both the same. I fell in love with a role player, not a role model, and I've been just the same. It was my fault.

And anger for having to give you up. For being forced to do just what I blame every faggot for so doing. But loving you is just a bad example. My fantasies run wild, just like yours.

Fred lets his Dinky go.

He stands up, feeling tall and strong beneath these stars and moon. And the anger and the tears now join to strike his stomach. They bloat him so that the skin around his waist, his once "love handles," which Y exercises had taken away, now appear once more.

He's ready to explode!

On Dinky?

Well, perhaps that would be too cruel. Symbolically, perhaps. So let's send Fred Lemish to void in the bushes. For these are Dinky's, too. His garden of delights. His weeping tub of willows. His vines. His annuals still bulbing. In this his special world. On these bushes Fred now shits.

Good-bye old shit. I don't know who's shitting on whom. But I do know we've got to stop and change. One of these days we must stop shitting on each other. And go out into the world and try to live with a bit of pride. Whether they want us or not. But thanks. I've learned a lot from you. You had to go through me before I could come out the other end. You taught me things I needed to know: Try to stop being naïve. Try to grow up. Try to make a commitment to adulthood. Yes, you were my dress rehearsal for the real thing.

So thanks, Dinky. And thank you, Feffer. Thank you, Abe and Lester. Thank you, two clairvoyants, four astrologers, one palmist, and a couple of crystal balls. And thank you, Messrs. Cult, Nerdley, Fallinger & Dridge.

And thank you, Algonqua, for the courage to go out and try yet once again.

And thank you, Fred.

Yes, it's time to get angry, not at The World and Them, but with Fred Lemish.

Yes, we were the quintessential faggots, Dinky. One cock teaser and one doormat. Afraid of love. Using our bodies as barter instead of our brains as heart.

Dinky stirred and opened his eyes. He asked: "What time is it? George is coming. Have to meet George." And then he slept again. Back to sleep again.

Yes, so long, Dinky. What did that fine old gentleman, Eric Hoffer, say? Anger's a prelude to courage? It takes courage not to be a faggot just like all the others. And as that other fine old gentleman, Sam Johnson, said: Courage is the greatest virtue, because without it there can be no others.

Hey, I'm starting to be a great virtue.

All those disparaging, pejorative Reasons! Well, I've worked them through. The unexamined life is unlivable, old Socrates said. Well, I've examined. Now I must fight hard not to let them bring me down and back to thingdom. And what if none of them is the right one? Or there might be others. Yes, I've examined. Now it's time to just *be*. Just like I have brown eyes. I'm here. I'm not gay. I'm not a fairy. I'm not a fruit. I'm not queer. A little crazy maybe. And I'm not a faggot. I'm a Homosexual Man. I'm Me. Pretty Classy.

A cleaner and wiser Fred Lemish now re-enters his Champion boxer shorts and leaves his Dinky Adams. In his garden. His beautiful magical garden.

He walks down the length of Aeon. And out of The Grove. And back along the ocean's edge. The sun is coming up. Blessing the new day. Fellows are everywhere. Still. Once again. Arm in arm. Arms around shoulders

and waists. Everyone smiling. The dancing's over for this
night. Haven't we shared a night of nights! A night of fellowship. We have danced and partied and drugged and
Meat Racked and we have survived no sleep. Together.
Together. Yes, we have braved and passaged all these rites
together. Though we may not know each other's names
nor will we necessarily speak when next we meet.

The beach is filled with all my friends. All dressed in
white. A huge white billowing tent awaits us. Someone is
giving a Dawn Party. A Welcome the New Day Party.
Strawberries and white wine and chocolate-chip cookies.
All my friends. All sitting on the sand. Arms around each
other. Touching. Holding. But not too close. Please no
hassles or involvements. Sharing this moment. No one
speaking.

Yes, all my friends are here. It's hard to leave you.
All this beauty. Such narcotic beauty. Yes, it's hard to
leave.

What I want is better though!

No. Just different. I'm going to have enough trouble
changing myself. Can't change everyone else too. Can't
change those who don't want to change. I want to change.
I must change myself. Be my own Mom and Pop. Allow
myself the something better Lester never did. Be strong
enough for Me. I feel better . . .

They all sit around in circles, on the white sand, the
ocean at low tide, the laps thus gentle and far away.

"I love you."

"I love you."

"I love you."

"I love you."

"I love you."

There are hundreds, thousands, passing the message
of love from body to body, touching neighbor's hand, then
lips gently kissing, softly as those distant lapping waves,

382

under disappearing stars and moon, and the rising sun, thousands, hundreds of thousands, millions of handsome men, sitting cross-legged on the sands, celebrating this morning and this summer's love.

Fred is here, and so is Mikie and Tarsh and Bo Peep and Josie and Dom Dom and Frigger and Fallow and Gatsby and Bella and Blaze and Sanford and his snake and Laguna beauties and Dick and Dora Dull and Bruce Sex-toys and B.L.T. and Irving and Hans and Timmy and Charlie and Ike Bulb and Alex and Tidgy Schmidge and Tony and Olive and Dennis and Laverne and Robbie Swindon and Morry and Hubie and Jefferson and Montoya and Lork and Carlty and Yo-Yo and Dawsie and Pusher and Tom-Tom and Maxine again Maxine and Feffer and Yootha Truth and Miss Rolla and Vladek and Cully and Midnight Cowboy and Lovely Lee and Garfield and Wilder and Harold and Anthony and Wyatt and Boo Boo and an Older Gent and R. Allan and Billy Boner, and the ghosts of palest Paulie and Patty and his Juanito and remember Winnie Heinz?, and Leather Louie, Lance Heather, Adriana, s.s. BERLINERS all, The Gnome, Derry, Floyd, Sprinkle, Tad, Kristos Rosenkavalier, Canadian Leon, Pinky and his cymbalettes . . . and and and the group keeps growing, friends, and new friends, joining every moment . . .

Fred stands and watches them. Yes, it's hard to leave.

Then his eyes turn toward land.

There goes Dinky. Handsome Dinky. Such potential Dinky. That elusive Dinky. There goes Dinky, along the boardwalk, striding forth to meet the ferry, to meet his Georgia Peach, arriving on the Red Eye Special, there goes Dinky, striding forth, Cosmo on the leash before him, little lamb, to welcome George, good luck George, good luck all of us . . .

... yes it still hurts ...

. . . there goes Rolex Submariner Number IV . . .

... yes I'm still scared ...

. . . the group keeps growing, so many for our growing group, many many many millions who wish to welcome The Summer of Our Lives.

Two other discos opened last night. ContreTemps closed. Heavenly Garage looks to be a winner.

I'm 40.

Happy Birthday Me.